C000066540

ARES

JAYSON ADAMS

ARES

Copyright © 2023 by Jayson Adams

All Rights Reserved

First Edition

Book and cover design by Jayson Adams

ISBN: 978-1-7379376-2-3

Published by Fiction Factory Books

www.fictionfactorybooks.com

This is a work of fiction. All characters and events portrayed in this novel are fictitious, and any resemblance to real people or events is purely coincidental.

To Rachel, Gage, Eden, and Liam

"Before we begin our descent, Commander, I have a message to play for the crew."

Commander Kate Holman managed a near-perfect poker face despite the unwelcome voice in her helmet. Only her clenched jaw betrayed her anger. It wasn't just the outrageously poor timing of Julian's ask that drew her ire, moments before the seven most critical minutes of their journey. His pattern of almost daily callous acts and slights had numbed her to his antics. What really riled her was his use of the main comm line instead of a private channel. Julian's lack of discretion meant they would discuss the matter in front of the entire crew.

What could the message possibly be? Had Julian not irritated the shit out of her for the past five months, she might have asked. Regardless of its content, there was only one answer Kate could give him, but she'd take her time delivering it—she was the mission commander, not a lackey waiting on his every word. She dragged her gloved finger along her station's screen, swiping the next page of the pre-landing checklist into view, and set it scrolling with a casual flick. Guiding their craft from atmospheric insertion to touchdown was the real business of the moment. A Mars landing was a tricky affair where even the most minor misstep could mean skittering across the thin atmosphere to carom off into space, burning up in a meteoric streak of pyrotechnics, or forming the newest impact crater on the dusty red plains. They needed to devote all their attention to landfall.

The commander dispatched two checklist items with leisurely taps. Julian stared at her from four stations away, the shine of the overhead lights repeating along his helmet and the portion of his smooth, shaved head that peeked from his communications skullcap. Surely, he understood now was not the time for distractions, that she'd have no choice but to deny his request. So why invite a public rebuff? He was up to something; she couldn't see what. "Julian," she said, hiding her annoyance behind her taut tone, "we're a few minutes from entering the atmosphere, the point where all the you-know-what really will hit the fan. We need to focus on one thing, which is getting to the ground safely. Let's hold off on your message until after we touch down."

Kate quickly dismissed three more items on the checklist. Commander Glenn Wiles, her second-in-command, would oversee their descent, though she'd closely monitor their progress. Women had made great strides during NASA's eighty-four-year history, but she still felt the weight of being judged as a *woman* commander. The mission needed to be perfect, every execution flawless.

"That will be too late, I'm afraid."

This time Commander Holman swiveled fully from her station and faced Julian, all remnants of her former poker face melted away. For any of the other astronauts under her command, her answer would have been the end of the discussion, eliciting silence, a sheepish nod, or at most a meek "yes, ma'am." Julian seemed to operate from a different mindset, one where her decisions were never the final word.

"I have orders to play a message for the crew *before* we enter the atmosphere," said Julian.

Orders that she didn't know about? Bullshit. "Orders from whom?"

"Assistant Director Pearson."

Kate's cheeks flushed, all eyes landing on her. As the number two person at NASA and the champion of their trip to Mars, Assistant Director Pearson was certainly within his rights to communicate directly with any of her astronauts. But why would the AD, himself an Air Force veteran, disregard the chain of command? She fumed, in part at the delivery of secret instructions to a subordinate, but mostly at being forced to give Julian his way. "Well, let's have it," she grumbled.

The capsule's main viewscreen came alive with the black glow of an empty data feed, then snapped to the NASA logo suspended against a bright white background. The image switched to Assistant Director Pearson seated behind his desk, looking thin and squirrelly as ever. His dark, narrow-set eyes hovered under his bald crown, and when he smiled, the left side of his mouth rose higher than the right. "Crew of the *Ares*, I want to congratulate you on your impending achievement, the first humans to land on the surface of Mars. For the next year, you will perform research and explore the Martian surface, an amazing accomplishment we should all be proud of." The assistant director slid a cigar—a Macanudo by the band—from a desktop humidor as he spoke. He clipped the end and held his torch aloft, puffing the cigar to life. He seemed about to speak but paused, turning the cigar sideways and studying it, apparently impressed by its flavor. "Now the other day in the Capitol, a senator approached me, almost chased me down through the halls, in fact. I'd sparred with him many times in the Appropriations Committee. Never considered him particularly bright. In any case, he'd somehow gotten a look at the off-budget figures for your mission and asked me point blank how the hell in these fiscally challenged times I could justify spending over nine hundred billion dollars on ten roundtrip tickets to Mars."

The assistant director paused for another puff of his cigar, the end glowing red behind the nub of ash. "The good senator had a point. And the answer to his question begins with our first visit to Mars, the Viking landers in '75. Twenty years went by before we would return, with two orbiters, a lander, and a rover in the '90s. We sent another orbiter in 2001, two more rovers in 2003, an orbiter in 2005, a lander in 2007, and twenty-one more missions in the thirty-five years after that. And those figures only cover American interest in the red planet. There were also the ESA and Chinese missions. And I won't even bother to mention the Russians—those poor devils couldn't touch a craft down on that planet to save their life." He puffed again. "My point is that an astute observer would guess there must have been some development on Mars to have triggered such intense interest. That brings us to your mission, ladies and gentlemen. There's only so much you can do with rovers and landers and satellite imagery. The next phase of our interest in Mars involves boots on the ground, your boots, in search of a payout for a wager that began five decades ago. And while I'm sure a year's worth of abrading rocks and drinking your own wastewater will prove scientifically enlightening, it's this other interest, this *classified* interest, that's the real reason for your trip to the red planet."

Stunned silence filled the cabin as the assistant director relit his cigar.

"Everything we've trained for, all our preparation, that was a front for some classified mission?" All attention shifted to Mission Specialist Casey Morgan, the expedition's astrobiologist. Several of the other astronauts nodded in agitated agreement.

"Some of you might find this news upsetting," continued the assistant director. "Let me assure you, as a practical matter, nothing has changed.

You'll still carry out all the studies and experiments you've prepared for. They're all still very important, because they serve as a smokescreen for the true goal of the mission. Security Chief Julian Grimes and Mission Specialist Joseph Cheney have been briefed on those particulars. While the rest of you go about your assignments, Grimes and Cheney will handle all details and execution related to the classified task. You are to give them your full cooperation."

Kate stole a glance at Julian. He watched the video message with a dispassionate expression, hands folded in his lap. How long had he and Cheney been preparing for this secret aspect of their mission? From the start, if the AD was serious about it being the true reason for their trip to the red planet.

"Commander Holman." Kate jumped at the unexpected mention of her name. "I apologize in advance for delivering this next part in a pre-recorded video stream rather than face-to-face. To drive home the importance of your mission's primary objective, I am placing Grimes in charge as the acting mission commander, effective upon your landing."

The news elicited a self-satisfied smirk from Julian. For Kate, the assistant director's declaration knocked the wind out of her, a sucker punch straight in the gut. The years of toil, the wrecked marriage, the sacrifices she'd endured to secure the command of a lifetime all whisked aside like so much rubbish. Her heart ached, the memories of her late mother beaming in awe of her daughter's achievement forever footnoted. The commander's shoulders slumped forward, and her chin quivered beneath her bowed head. A tear fell, then a second, splattering inside her helmet.

Someone was watching.

Kate discovered Glenn looking on from across the capsule. Flustered, she reached for her damp cheeks, but her hand smashed into her helmet. She buried herself in her station.

"Your mission is a momentous endeavor," said the assistant director, "one which will likely change the course of human history, and if we're lucky, the bottom line." Kate looked up at the video, catching Pearson's final puff and his crooked smile. "Best of luck, *Ares* crew." The screen went dark. No one stirred, the flashing lights of their terminals the only movement within the capsule.

"Do the geniuses back home think we're all idiots? That is a crock of bull … *shit!*"

The words came from Allison Voss, shocking even for the normally testy Mars station engineer. "Hold on, Allison," said Kate.

"The mission of the century turns out to be a front for a classified operation?" asked Mars station chief Miriam Sato.

"Wait, wait," said Kate. The rising emotions risked overshadowing the important job that still remained. She needed everyone to keep it together until their spacecraft reached the ground.

"While the rest of you go about your assignments," said Dr. Clayton Fisk in a mocking voice, his index finger in front of his mouth and curled around an imaginary cigar, "Grimes and Cheney will manage the classified task, which is the true reason for your mission. Please give my two toadies your full support as they search for the lost pleasure dome of Xanadu."

Julian's face reddened. "Disrespect towards a superior officer is a court-martial offense," he said.

Fisk laughed. "My official designation is 'Spaceflight Participant.' Are you saying you intend to make me an officer?"

A loud whistle squelched the commotion and gathered everyone's attention.

"Thank you, Glenn," said Kate. She reviewed the upset faces staring back at her around the cabin. "I'm as shocked as the rest of you about the message we just received. But right now, we're about a heartbeat away from a crash landing. We need to make sure this spacecraft touches down safely. So please, put everything you saw out of your minds and—"

"Commander Holman's right," said Julian. "There's no time for grumbling. We all have a job to do."

"I'll thank you not to talk over me." Kate had lost count of how many times Julian had interrupted her during their flight to Mars. An unconscious habit or deliberately malicious, either way, it was damn irritating. "And if you don't mind, Julian, I'll give the directives on this ship. Your reign begins the moment we touch down. Until then, I'm still the mission commander."

Julian threw Kate a spiteful glance but said nothing more. He turned back to his station.

Kate chided herself for her outburst. She'd normally never have hurled such sharp words, but they'd taken a lot from her that day. She wanted to scream at Julian, scream at the assistant director. And maybe she would, but not then. None of it would make one damn difference if they didn't reach the ground in one piece.

"All stations report with pre-landing status," said Glenn.

Kate dispatched the remaining items on her checklists and swiped back to the main screen. Her display filled with an image of Mars's western hemisphere, a mottled orange disc floating against a starry backdrop. A gray dot, the *Ares* capsule, slid along a dashed white arc that traced the spaceship's trajectory. A halo of annotations reported the craft's speed, altitude, and other vitals.

Sweat beaded on Commander Holman's palms, growing to a torrent that emerged faster than her gloves could wick away. Her pulse accelerated and she lapsed into a series of shallow, rapid breaths. Her suit peppered her with chimes, warning that she teetered on the edge of unconsciousness.

She was panicking. But why?

You know why.

It couldn't be that. She'd conquered the past. And in any case, an atmospheric landing was nothing like a touchdown on the airless Moon.

Then why'd you ask Glenn to handle the descent?

Glenn was her rock, her steadfast lieutenant. During the two years of training for the Mars mission, her reliance on him had steadily grown. In spite of several annoying habits, he had a good heart. She trusted him as much as she trusted herself, maybe more.

You didn't answer the question.

Ignoring the nagging voice in her head, Kate focused instead on her breath. She returned to the relaxation techniques from the long-ago therapy sessions. Her pulse and respiration dropped to more normal levels. She'd pulled herself back from the edge, but she wasn't out of jeopardy. If the mere thought of the touchdown had so easily chipped away at her hard-fought recovery, what would happen during the actual landing? Each descent stage carried its own unique perils. Each would become a dangerous stressor. If she didn't manage her mental state all the way to the ground, she risked a full relapse into debilitation.

"*Ares* at nominal orientation for atmospheric entry."

Kate girded herself for their hazardous entrance into Mars's exosphere. In less than two minutes, atmospheric friction would bleed off the bulk of the

12,500 miles per hour they'd marshaled to hurl their capsule between the planets. On visits to the *Ares* vehicle assembly building, she'd fixated on the craft's slim heat shield, their only protection against the 3,500 degrees Fahrenheit that easily surpassed the melting point of their stainless-steel hull.

"Speed decreasing ... 10,000 ... 8,000 ... 6,000. Exterior temperature readings nominal."

Kate licked her lips. Even catastrophic descents appeared normal at first. The flames that lapped the craft's underside probed the heat shield for weak spots in its bonded ceramic, the slightest imperfection in its metal alloy, hunting for any pathway to the delicate spacecraft. Kate's vital signs crept back up. She shook her head to rid herself of the morbid thoughts and focused again on her breath.

"Ten seconds to chute deployment."

Commander Holman breathed easier. They'd survived the brunt of atmospheric entry, though they still raced to the ground at 900 miles per hour. She gripped her restraints where they crossed in an "X" at her chest, the action ingrained from the simulator sessions on Earth.

"Three ... two ... one."

Multiple g-forces pinned Kate in her seat as the craft rocked and shimmied. She gritted her teeth through the violent movement. An exterior camera relayed video of the chute soaring above the capsule, a great white jellyfish scooping the rarefied Martian air beneath its bell, its tentacles tugging at their hull. They decelerated, but their speed bottomed out at 235 miles per hour. Mars had enough atmosphere to burn up a craft on entry but not enough to slow it for a landing.

"Preparing to jettison heat shield."

Kate fixated on her terminal screen, desperate for the landing target acquisition icon to appear. Once the ship discarded the heat shield and exposed the downward facing cameras, the computer would have milliseconds to locate landmarks and make course adjustments. Any hiccup could result in them touching down far from the HAAB. As it stood, even a perfect landing meant a two-kilometer hike to the Mars base.

Pop!

Ten explosive bolts propelled the shield away from the capsule. Turbulence besieged the small craft with the exposure of its less aerodynamic underside. The commander squeezed her restraints tighter.

Seconds ticked away, but no target acquisition lock came. Had something damaged the cameras? Or worse? Kate extended a nervous hand to query the computer when green symbols cascaded across her terminal. The *Ares* had located its touchdown target and fired its thrusters in short bursts to position itself within the correct descent window. Another green icon emerged, signaling landing gear deployment. The system of struts, trusses, and shocks deployed from its stowed configuration was necessary but not sufficient for landfall—the *Ares* still fell far too fast to touch down.

A deafening whoosh flooded the cabin. Kate closed her eyes as the *Ares* entered the final and riskiest landing stage. Air rushed through exposed intakes to the atmospheric braking system, an experimental series of manifolds that compressed the meager Martian air prior to releasing it as a roiling pocket of high pressure above the capsule. The ram brake in essence thickened the air under the parachute enough to float the spacecraft to the ground. That was the theory at least. Even with all the simulations and prototype trials on Earth, Kate couldn't shake her concern that their landing would be the first test of the system on the red planet.

"Speed dropping. Ninety seconds to touchdown … eighty … seventy."

Kate followed their steady deceleration on her terminal. She forced herself to relax, her fears unfounded. The ram brake worked, and in less than a minute they would touch down, becoming the first humans to set foot on an alien planet. The culmination of two decades of planning. The dream of—

"We've got a problem," said Glenn. His deep, usually firm bassoon voice contained the slightest tremolo of fear.

"What is it?" asked Kate.

"We're coming in hot."

Indeed, Kate's terminal still showed a steady decrease in their downward velocity, but the computer projected they'd hit the ground at roughly four times the nominal landing speed. At that rate their craft, the *Ares* capsule and everything in it, would crumple on impact. "Can we get more deceleration out of the brake?"

"Negative," said Glenn. "We've got maximum airflow through the intakes. We're just not getting enough pressure out the topside."

Two stations away, spacecraft engineer Laura Engles, a red bandana wrapping her skullcap, unleashed flurries of taps on her terminal screen. "The air's quite cold ... much colder than it should be," she said with a hint of southern twang. Her accent, usually well hidden, always surfaced in agitated times.

"There's a storm front building," said Miriam. "NASA's been tracking it for the past few days."

Engles grunted. She was a caring, sensitive person except when she slipped into "engineer" mode, as she called it. At that point, she was all numbers and logic.

Schematics and reams of text scrolled on Engles's screen. Her finger settled on a graph and its accompanying table of numbers. "The designs assume a higher minimum atmospheric temperature. The lower temp throws off all those calculations. The system's scooping air, but with the cold, it can't produce high enough pressure beneath the chute."

Kate had pushed for sending a scaled down version of the *Ares* to Mars, outfitted with the experimental brake. She'd worried anything less than an actual atmospheric test on the red planet would leave their whole touchdown to chance. The mission planners cited budget constraints that made such a test impractical. They instead showcased all the data they collected from their slew of earthbound trials and simulations, insisting they'd accounted for every contingency. Apparently, they'd missed one.

Klaxons blared and revolving emergency lights bathed the cabin in red chaos, the machinations of an AI co-pilot that had thrown up its hands. It could do little more than signal to its human wards their pending demise.

"Forty-five seconds to impact," said Glenn.

Kate scooted closer to her terminal and called up the main control screen. Her hand trembled as she swiped through the displays for each of the spacecraft's subsystems, desperate for any recourse that could help them survive the landing.

Shouts and turmoil erupted to her rear. Kate swiveled in her chair—she found Fisk, the mission's interplanetary geologist, standing free of his restraints. Terror gripped his face. "Are we there yet?" he roared, like a child on a road trip.

"Sit down and remain strapped in!" Kate yelled.

The professor landed back in his chair with wild eyes, the ferocity of her order driving him to near hysterics.

She shouldn't have snapped at Fisk—as a civilian, he lacked the extensive survival training that was a hallmark of the Astronaut Corps. She just needed them all in their seats. Whether she figured out a way to ease their impact or not, an unrestrained body would become a dangerous projectile inside the cabin.

"Thirty seconds."

Returning her attention to her station, Kate's eyes landed on the photograph taped to the bottom edge of her terminal. Her children's faces stared back: Amelia, calm and collected; and Ben Jr., with his toothy grin ....

Kate resumed swiping. She stopped and backtracked to the thruster control screen. The attitude thrusters changed the spacecraft's orientation using bursts of compressed gas, but even if they all pointed to the ground, they wouldn't generate enough force to put a dent in their downward velocity. She scrolled instead to the controls for the third stage separation thrusters, powerful mini-rockets designed to push the capsule away from the booster during liftoff, at the end of the third stage burn. Ordinarily, those thrusters would have completely exhausted their fuel supply, but Kate had shut the system down early, holding some propellant back.

"Twenty seconds."

Kate checked the fuel levels. The tanks contained more than she hoped, but would it be enough? She'd also have to guess when to fire them. The thrusters burned at full force—there was no adjusting their output like a retro rocket. Starting them too soon would only delay the capsule's fatal impact, too late and the thrusters wouldn't have enough time to slow the craft. Either way, the *Ares* would slam into the ground.

"Ten seconds. Brace for impact. Seven ... six ..."

Mouthing a prayer, Kate tapped the ignition button. The third stage separation thrusters roared beneath the craft at full burn, slowing the capsule's descent enough to calm their computer co-pilot. In a blink, the AI cancelled the crash klaxon and secured them from red alert. Kate's station showed the *Ares* hovering a meter above the ground.

The thrusters cut out.

The *Ares* lingered in the thin air for an instant until gravity restarted the capsule's downward fall.

Klaxons wailed for three quarters of a second, ceasing when the *Ares* slammed into the ground. The ship shuddered and the cabin filled with the sounds of wrenching metal. Shocks squealed beyond their tolerances as they strained to dissipate the spacecraft's momentum.

The impact mashed Kate into her seat. She waited for the capsule's underside to hit the ground and impart the full force of the crash to the fragile hull. The *Ares* would burst at its seams. When they'd first announced the Mars mission, Kate had imagined standing on the planet's surface and taking in the Martian sky. In her final moments, the ruptures would at least allow her a fleeting glimpse of the ruddy canopy.

The contact with the ground never came.

Kate's terminal, a patchwork of flashing red indicators, screamed about failures in multiple trusses and the complete collapse of a landing strut, but reported the capsule's velocity at zero. The landing gear held. She sat dazed for several seconds as reality sank in. They had survived the touchdown.

Screams of delight and relief echoed within the cabin.

"Ladies and gentlemen," said Glenn, beaming with sweat beaded on his brow, "welcome to Mars."

2

"Give me a live view outside," said Julian, still strapped in his seat. He wasted no time in asserting his authority as the acting mission commander.

"Yes, sir," said Engles. After a handful of taps on the spacecraft engineer's terminal, a thin strip of the *Ares*'s hull slid up and away, exposing sections of thick glass that ringed the capsule above their monitors. The *Ares* astronauts, still recovering from their brush with death, sat riveted by the panoramic view of the Martian landscape. Dunes of smooth, red dust continued for kilometers, peppered with black basalt rocks and outcroppings. Small hills rolled in the distance, and beyond them, a jagged mountain range unfolded beneath the red planet's butterscotch sky.

Commander Holman, rendered breathless by the sight, forced an inhale. In a few minutes, Mars would be crunching under their boots. Goosebumps stippled her skin.

"I don't know about the rest of you, but I'm ready to get out of this can," said Fisk. He released his restraints, rose from his chair, and stretched his arms. "While you're all collecting your things, I'm gonna use the litter box." He streaked toward the entrance to the lower crew compartment. "Don't leave without me."

"Negative," snapped Julian. "You should have attended to that business before our descent. For now, rely on the facilities in your suit."

"You mean my personal hotbox?" asked Fisk, holding fast a few steps from his station. He frowned. "How can they build a space suit for twenty-five million dollars but forget to include an air freshener?"

Kate undid her restraints and stood. She grabbed the top of her chair, steadying herself on unsure, wobbling legs.

"Easy does it, everyone. It'll take some getting used to being in gravity."

The gentle admonition came from Dr. Nathan Palmer, the mission's medical specialist. The planet's pull, a third of Earth's, was stronger than Kate expected. The conditioning to lessen the effects of their months in zero gravity hadn't prepared her as well as she'd expected.

The capsule teemed with the sounds of excited chatter and shuffling bodies. The *Ares* astronauts fell into a line that snaked from the hatch, circling around the cabin. They leaned into bulkheads and stations as they countered the deck's eight-degree tilt, the wounded spacecraft listing from the collapsed landing gear strut.

Kate scooted in front of Glenn, taking her place at the head of the line. Her heart raced, though not to the rate driven by her anxiety before their landing. She was about to make history as the first human to set foot on Mars.

"You're in my spot."

Engrossed in the moment, Kate hadn't noticed Julian sidle up to her. Dazed and not understanding his comment, she could only blink back at him.

"The mission commander is always the first to exit the spacecraft," said Julian.

Kate looked on, stunned, as Julian muscled his way between her and the hatch. The other astronauts tottered in their bulky suits, making room as best they could while fighting to avoid falling backwards. When the line again settled, all the bustle and excitement that previously filled the cabin had dissipated, leaving a leaden silence.

Julian's white, boxy breather pack blocked Kate's entire field of view and knocked against the outward bulge of her helmet when he moved. From the days of the Apollo Eleven Moon landing, the mission commander always exited the vehicle first, but how could Julian's last-minute elevation upend an event NASA spent a year preparing just for her? "Julian, the mission planners choreographed my descent down the ladder," she croaked, "wrote a speech for me to give … for the cameras, I mean … they're filming right this minute, outside the capsule."

Julian tapped a code into the keypad embedded in the bulkhead, then turned to Commander Holman. "They instructed you on how to climb down a goddamn ladder?" He smirked and turned back to the hatch. Kate wobbled in her place in line, gobsmacked.

A thin stripe of red light pulsed around the hatch, and a klaxon sounded. The wail waned with the cabin's evacuating atmosphere. Silence returned, and with it, the bleating stripe encircling the exit calmed to a steady red. Julian yanked the handle, freeing the latches that secured the door in place.

He pushed the hatch out and open to a flood of bright Martian daylight. Standing in the doorsill, he beheld Mars. Kate shifted left and right, angling without success for a view beyond his bulk.

Julian thrust his arm to the right, outside the spacecraft. A leg followed. In a blink, he'd disappeared.

Kate stepped up to the hatch. Poking her head through the opening, she spotted Julian clinging to the capsule's exterior, gripping a ladder whose shallow rungs jutted from the fuselage. Julian scrambled six meters to the end where, balanced on the final rung, he wheeled about and faced the Martian surface. He remained there, unmoving for several seconds. Apparently overcome, he was likely gathering his thoughts, struggling for the words to match a flood of emotions. "If you want—"

Kate had resolved to offer the short speech NASA penned for her, but the instant she spoke, the security chief simply hopped to the ground. He ambled a few paces from the capsule before rotating back to face the *Ares*. Peering at the hatch, he met Kate's gaze. "What the hell are you all waiting for?"

Springing into action, Kate swung out onto the ladder and descended, pausing on the last rung like Julian. No one had spoken to mark the occasion of humanity's arrival on Mars, the momentous achievement of setting foot on an alien planet. Should she still recite her prepared remarks? The sight of bootprints in the loose soil killed the thought. What was the point? He'd taken the first steps on Mars. Julian's grand indifference had defiled both the moment and the land.

"Say the words."

Commander Holman peered upward, squinting with the glare of the Martian sky. She found Glenn looking intently at her from the hatch. "It doesn't matter if his boots landed first," he continued, guessing her thoughts. He grinned, an annoying, unconscious reaction that struck whenever the weight of his sincerity overwhelmed him. "Say the words anyway. They're important."

Kate's eyes met Julian's. He scowled and violently thumbed at her to get down.

"Armstrong would've been a footnote if Aldrin had spoken in his stead."

Glenn was right. The history books would have forever quoted Buzz Aldrin, the second man on the Moon, if Neil Armstrong had skipped his historic remarks. Kate spotted an exterior camera filming the event, its red "recording" light active. The video, after a fifteen-minute delay, would be seen by billions.

Kate surveyed once more the Martian landscape, their home for the next year. She took a deep breath. "On Earth, Ares is the Greek god of war. Though we arrived in a craft called *Ares,* let the first steps we take on this alien world be ones of peace and goodwill, steps that forsake our ignoble spirits—violence, strife, greed, deceit. Let us walk upon this new land as Adam and Eve first walked in the Garden of Eden, absent the sins of man."

Hopping from the ladder, Kate floated to the ground in the slow-motion Martian gravity. Cheers and claps rang out from the astronauts in the capsule. She stepped away, creating space for the others to descend.

Glenn landed next. He strode to Kate and patted her shoulder as he shook her hand. "Congratulations, Commander Holman," he said, smiling. Kate smiled back.

The rest of the *Ares* crew exited the ship, with Engles the last to step onto the ground. She joined the others where they had assembled in a broad circle a few meters from the spacecraft.

"Let's head out," said Julian.

"We have to perform the final suit checks first," said Kate.

"I already did that," said Julian.

Kate erupted. "*You* may have done it, but as mission commander, it's your job to make sure that *everyone's* checked their suits."

"Uh … OK …," said Julian, visibly flustered and irritated, "then let's do that."

Let's do that? The suit checks hadn't been a glimmer in his mind. If Julian received advance notice of his elevation to mission commander, he'd failed to review the duties that came with the position. The Manual dictated suit checks after every landing, better to discover a problem while still near the vehicle than halfway to their destination. The responsibility to ensure all such checks had been performed fell to the mission commander. He was derelict in his duty, and that dereliction could endanger lives. Despite them wrenching her command from her, she wouldn't stand by and allow one of her astronauts to get hurt, or die, because of his negligence. She vowed to keep them all safe, even if he would not.

"Everyone please, thumbs up on green suit check," said Kate. Thumbs rose around the circle. Her own suit indicators—containment, pressure, oxygen reserves, temperature, navigation, reclamation—all rested safely in the green, per the soft, sheer graphics of her heads-up display.

Suit checks complete, Kate returned to the *Ares* and tapped a ground-level keypad. The capsule's door swung gently back into place, latching flush with the rest of the hull.

Julian scanned the Martian horizon. "Where's the HAAB?" he asked, a hint of concern in his voice. Was it really the first time he'd thought about where they were headed?

"It's that way," said Miriam, pointing to the west. "We're in a slight depression, which is why we can't see it from here."

Julian started forward, then froze. He turned to Kate. "If we're all done with the babysitting tasks?"

Kate chafed. Ensuring no one died on the way to the HAAB was hardly babysitting.

"Then let's head out."

The astronauts followed Julian's lead across the virgin Martian terrain. They marched over friable dirt, stamping vibrant red bootprints where they crunched through the crusty, darker top layer. Their shuffling left a gentle cloud of red dust hovering at the ground in their wake.

The *Ares* crew spread into a line that spanned twenty-five meters, single file save for one pair of astronauts. From their suits, Engles and Casey: the former a beanpole, the latter all curves. Everything she'd seen of Casey Morgan suggested a strict preference for men, but the chatty astrobiologist was never one to turn down attention. Kate brought up the rear, Julian's prescribed spot by custom. Not once did the security chief look back to check on the others. Most thrust into the role of mission commander would rise to the occasion. Only twenty minutes in, all signs suggested the opposite for Julian.

Kate trudged along, the expanse of Martian landscape interrupted mainly by Glenn, with his signature straight back, directly ahead. His perpetual perfect posture had clued her to the fact that most men walked with a slouch, especially those more than six feet tall like him.

Glenn cast a backward glance—had he sensed her thoughts about him? He stopped, allowing Kate to catch up, resuming his march once she reached his side.

"May I have the honor of walking in the presence of Commander Kate Holman, hero of the Ares mission?" asked Glenn.

What did he mean? She could ask him to elaborate, but sometimes with Glenn, moving on as if he hadn't said a word was the least irritating option.

"You know, at the time I didn't fully understand what happened with our landing. Only since we've been walking have I put it all together. *You* were the one who fired those thrusters, not the computer."

Kate said nothing.

"The thing is, those thrusters should've exhausted their fuel supply during our liftoff from Earth. They were set to burn to completion, to give us an extra boost."

A boost that would've gotten them to Mars all of three minutes sooner. "An inconsequential amount of extra thrust," said Kate.

Glenn thought for a second. "You shut down the thrusters, during liftoff, before they finished their burn," he said. "Did the computer flag a problem?"

Kate hesitated. "No." And could they please leave it at that? "Can we maybe switch to a different—"

"No sign of a problem during what was, by all estimates, a perfect takeoff, but you altered the pre-programmed launch sequence anyway?" Glenn's voice, full of dismay, shrank to a whisper, though they spoke on a private comm line. "That's a big deal, Kate. They've tossed people right out of the Corps for less. If something had gone wrong, that would've been the first thing they checked. Whatever possessed you to end the burn early?"

The answer seemed plain, but Glenn's expression suggested he was genuinely baffled. Kate struggled to maintain her composure.

"Oh," he said, mortified. "I ... never mind ... I see." If Glenn could have avoided dredging up the incident on the Moon, he would have—of that, she was certain. His penchant for sometimes saying the wrong thing had reared its head. "Well, your instincts five months ago saved the mission. Saved us all in fact. They should give you a medal."

"I don't want a medal," spat Kate. "I want my command back."

Glenn went quiet—a relief. Maybe they could walk in peace, not talking about the mission but taking in the first few pristine moments on Mars.

"How much do you know about this new objective?" Glenn asked.

"Nada," said Kate, irritated with the continued conversation and the topic. "That video was the first I heard of it. I learned about it at the same time as everyone else."

"So, with Grimes as mission commander—"

"*Acting* mission commander," corrected Kate.

"OK," said Glenn. "But my question is, does this mean you'll be taking over my duties?"

"I'm not assuming this is permanent," said Kate. "Or will even last very long. So no, proceed as if nothing's changed. I'm counting on you to keep tabs on the crew's well-being. With this disruption, it's more important than ever that you help with morale."

They managed several paces before Glenn's thoughts spilled out again: "It doesn't set a good precedent, whisking your command away from you like that."

"Evidently, there's some shift in priorities from up high," she grumbled.

"Yeah, but why the secrecy, and the awkward transfer of command? The only thing I could think was it had to be straight from the OPP."

The Office of Planetary Protection. "You think they found something?" asked Kate. "A sign of alien life?"

"They'd want to move quickly to contain it," said Glenn.

Kate kept quiet, her reserve that time inviting him to keep talking. With the AD shutting her out, any short-term explanation would have to come from piecing together whatever tidbits of information she could gather.

"Don't get me wrong, I don't know anything more than you," added Glenn. "What I said is pure speculation. It's all I could think for such a drastic action." He stopped and navigated an exposed basalt ledge that protruded from the soft earth. After a high step, he offered his hand to the commander and whisked her up to join him. "Whatever it is, I can't believe no one briefed you on it. It's not like you're a security risk. You have the highest clearance within NASA." His head tilted as his attention drifted to a wispy white cloud far above. "Maybe they deemed it need-to-know."

"This is my mission, Glenn." Kate's chin quivered and her eyes brimmed with tears. "*My* mission. There's no one who has a greater need to know than me."

They walked the following minutes in a hush. The *Ares* had landed in a wide, shallow basin, the remnants of an ancient impact crater. The terrain climbed gradually towards the basin's edge, rising steeper in the final hundred meters before the rim. After a spate of focused and determined paces through powdery, ankle-deep silt, they arrived at the lip and paused, surveying the land to the west. In the distance, a white-skinned structure gleamed among its dull red surroundings.

"HAAB sweet HAAB," said Glenn, lifting his sun visor for an unfiltered look. "If there *are* aliens here, they're gonna think we're giant hamsters."

HAAB stood for "Habitat At Ares Base," but with its maze of tube corridors and off-shooting cell compartments for living and storage, the astronauts declared it short for "habitrail." The structure's windows and solar arrays winked weak sunlight back at them.

"And there's the *Gaia*," said Glenn.

Kate studied the spaceship that stood half a kilometer from the HAAB, the silvery rocket that would ferry them home. "We'll need to check the propellant levels, first thing," she said. The *Gaia's* fueling station, a thin nuclear reactor that silently split subsurface ice into the hydrogen and oxygen that would power their return trip, sat a couple hundred meters from the Mars base. "I expect its tanks are topped off after a year."

"We haven't even made it to the HAAB, and you're already thinking about heading home?" asked Glenn.

"The *Gaia* is our fallback if there's an emergency," said Kate. "It needs to be ready to go at a moment's notice."

"Commander Holman."

The voice was Miriam's. "This is Holman."

"Do you think we could take a break?"

Probably more than prudent. They'd been hiking for thirty minutes through unfamiliar terrain in bulky suits designed for outer space after a half year of limited movement. Kate had become a bit winded herself but had chalked it up to walking and talking.

"I asked Commander Grimes, but he told me we need to keep moving. The thing is, I'm out of breath."

Kate's blood boiled. Julian's apparent desire for a fast start didn't justify a death march. She cut to the broadcast channel. "Hey, everyone, this is Commander Holman. Let's take a ten-minute break." The jagged line of astronauts that extended thirty-five meters immediately halted, except for the figure at the front.

"Belay that order," said Julian. "We're gonna keep going until we reach the HAAB." No one responded to his decree. Several astronauts hunched over, placing their hands on their knees.

"I'm beat," said Fisk. "I could use a rest."

"Me too," chimed in Casey.

"We're not that far. Only another klick or so. Anyone who's tired can rest when we reach the HAAB."

"I agree with Commander Holman," said Dr. Palmer. "We should stop for a ten-minute break. This is the most exertion any of us have had in the past five months."

A tense stillness filled the comm. Julian faced the rest of the *Ares* astronauts from the front of the line. Sunlight glinted off his helmet, its white surface aflame under the red sky. Hands on hips, disgust oozed through his pose. "Ten minutes, starting thirty seconds ago," he said. "Not a moment more."

Three astronauts ahead, a helmet swiveled back towards Kate. The reflective, golden visor hid the face, but the suit's short stature revealed its occupant's identity without a doubt. Miriam's sheepish hand rose, and a whispered, "Thank you," filled their private channel.

"No problem."

Glenn lowered onto a rock, barely high enough to keep him off the dirt. His long legs splayed like a grasshopper's—he could almost kiss his knees. He lifted his visor, the hue from the reddish soil setting his brown skin aglow. "Tell me again why we're lugging these space suits across the Martian countryside and not our Mars suits designed for the job."

"It's no mystery," said Kate. The Manual dictated that astronauts wear EVA suits on all vehicle excursions.

"A holdover from the sixties, when all they did was spacewalk. Or land on the Moon, which is like a spacewalk, 'cept you kick up a bunch of dust. But here on Mars? It's not like we need all this internal cooling to keep from overheating in the sun."

Yes, a dumb rule, but like all dumb rules, it had the same justification. "It's policy, Glenn." The Apollo-era mission planners left no notes about why they felt the need to codify the plainly obvious requirement of exiting a vehicle in a spacesuit. The Ares mission planners considered Mars suits for their landing but worried there might be some issue they'd miss if they did anything other than follow the directive to the letter.

"You're right, standard protocol: CYA," said Glenn. "Meanwhile, *we're* the ones left managing all this bulk. With our Mars suits, we'd probably be there already."

Of course they would. Kate had flagged the problems with using EVA suits on Mars. Glenn's complaining was a pointless return to old battles lost. "Not much to be done about it now," she said.

Glenn squirmed on his rock, working to get comfortable. He steadied for an instant before shifting again. "I don't think Julian's going to like you ordering a break like that."

"Let him not like it," said Kate, fishing with her lips for the tube from her suit's water reclamation system. She sipped. "Why the hell are we driving so hard when we've got folks about to expire?" She took another sip. "We astronauts take care of our own."

"'We take care of our own'—that was the number one thing they drilled into us in astronaut school," said Glenn. "Why do I get the feeling Julian skipped those first two weeks?"

"Commander Holman." Julian's voice in her ear gave her a chill. "Can I have a word with you?"

"Go ahead," said Kate. She made a face at Glenn that mirrored her dread, though he couldn't see it through her sun visor.

"Come to my forward position."

Forward position? Sometimes Julian talked more like a military man than a member of the Astronaut Corps. "On my way." She flipped back to her private channel with Glenn. "Julian wants me to come see him." Scanning ahead, she spotted the security chief pacing, a ball of anger and frustration waiting to loose itself on her. "If I'm not back before we start moving out, can I task you with bringing up the rear?"

"Sure thing, Commander." He saluted from his tenuous roost, gangly legs still splayed near his cheeks.

Kate plodded to the front of the line, weary like the others and in no hurry for her audience with Julian. She offered a limp wave, a quick raise of her hand at the wrist, to each *Ares* astronaut as she strolled past. They all sat on rocks or the ground, but not Julian. No longer pacing, he stood facing her as she approached. Sun visor lifted, his dark eyes glared from their deep sockets beneath his tall forehead.

"This is how things are going to work here on Mars," said Julian, Commander Holman still four meters away as he spoke. "I give the orders, and the rest of you follow them. Is that clear?"

"They needed a rest, Julian," she said, her hands pleading. "Five months in a capsule—"

"*I* will decide if we do or don't need a break."

Kate perched herself on a knee-high boulder a meter from Julian, black basalt like the others and with a rounded top. Her legs and feet roared in relief—she'd apparently needed a break too. "Except Doctor Palmer's medical authority supersedes yours," she said.

"Palmer didn't have the idea of stopping until you placed it in his head."

"As mission commander, you're responsible for the well-being of your crew," said Kate. "It's your job to find out if anyone needs a break, to make sure we don't have astronauts passing out before we reach our destination."

"Miriam asked for one," said Julian. "So did Engles. I decided to push them rather than waste time sitting. They can sit all they want in the HAAB. The most important thing is getting there."

"But what's the big rush?" asked Kate. "It's not like the HAAB's going anywhere. And neither are we. We're here for an entire year."

"I want us to get settled ASAP," said Julian. "Or have you forgotten about our primary objective."

Visions of the AD's video came flooding back, as did her emotions. "What's all this B.S. about a classified op?"

"It's not B.S.," said Julian.

"Oh no?" Kate's hands balled to fists. "What about leaving me in the dark about the whole thing ... taking my command at the last minute?" She hadn't intended to get into it with Julian out in the Martian wilderness. She'd planned to confront him once they'd acclimated to their new home. His comment set her off.

"All of that came from the AD," said Julian. "If you want an official explanation, you'll need to take it up with him." He placed his hands on his hips and struck a condescending pose. "If you're wanting my personal opinion on why you were kept in the dark, why you lost your command, I would think it has to do with your past. To be honest, I'm not sure how you remained in the running to lead this mission." His tone dripped venom, a black mamba striking with poisonous words. "When they gave you the *Ares,* I guessed it was all for show, a nice PR opportunity for NASA. I don't know that they ever intended for you to actually lead. Sometimes events seem mysterious, like they're the product of complicated machinations. Generally, the answer is much simpler. It's usually just what you think it is."

Julian eyeballed the line of seated astronauts. "Break time's over," he announced. "I promised ten minutes, but you'll have to live with six. The HAAB's not that far. If you're exhausted, you can rest when we get there. Gather yourselves and move out." Without waiting for anyone to follow, he marched off in the direction of the gleaming station.

The *Ares* astronauts, Cheney, Voss, Engles, and the rest, slogged past Commander Holman. Still perched on her rock, she stared off at the angry red hills that rippled along the morose, ruddy horizon.

An open hand appeared before her. Kate ignored it at first but eventually looked up. Glenn towered above her, his white helmet and its golden visor framed by pink sky. He offered his hand again.

Commander Holman reached up and locked her glove in his. Glenn helped her to her feet. The two set off after the others, trekking across the Martian plains.

3

"Love you, Mom!"

Kate reached for her daughter's cheek. She had to settle for a caress of her cold computer screen.

"Oh, and don't forget the warmer packs I gave you so your feet don't get cold in your boots. You don't want to get frostbite on Mars."

Kate smiled. Amelia was an old soul: wise and practical, strong and inquisitive. So much like herself at nine years old.

"I'll get Ben. BEN!" Amelia disappeared, replaced by several fading shouts. Kate cherished the daily messages from her two children, even if the extreme distance made real-time communication impossible. She'd never finished one without tearing up, at least until then, the first message she'd received on Mars.

A small, round face with large brown eyes appeared on the screen. "Hi, Mommy."

Ben Jr. looked upset, on the verge of crying. Maybe Amelia had been rough in collecting him.

"When are you coming home?"

Kate fought back tears. Her four-year-old went in and out of grasping the concept of her protracted journey.

Amelia reappeared in the frame. "Not for a long time," she said.

Tears trickled down pudgy cheeks. "I want Mommy," wailed Ben Jr.

Amelia grabbed her brother and caressed his head. "Don't worry, Ben, I'll take good care of you until Mom comes home. I promised her I would."

The floodgates opened, sending rivers down Kate's cheeks.

"We've gotta go—Dad's calling us for dinner," said Amelia. "We love you. Byeeeeee." The two children spoke the final words in unison, the trademark ending to their check-ins.

The video message lingered on the last frame. Kate wiped her face. She'd been away from her children for five months and wouldn't touch or hold them for another year and a half. The thought was unbearable. As excited as she was about the Mars mission, her children's absence tinged every day with sadness.

Commander Holman closed the playback window and stood from her desk. She'd record a message to Ben Jr. and Amelia later. Time to start their first full day on Mars. Already showered and dressed in a blue station jumpsuit, she scooped up a light jacket and exited her cell. Her reflection followed her down the tubeway, quavering within each pitch-black, oblong window. Rising before the sun meant a lead on the others. She'd grab breakfast, and with it, a few precious moments of quiet to herself.

Kate emerged from the tubeway into the Spine, the HAAB's wide, cylindrical central corridor. The gleaming white elasticine walls echoed her footsteps as she moved through the sleeping station. She passed three more tubeway entrances, their lights low from inactivity, and arrived at the DFAC. She stopped cold at the entrance.

"Good morning, Commander."

Kate could do little more than blink back in momentary shock at the sight of Fisk, the mission's interplanetary geologist, beaming at her as he chomped on a granola bar. He stood in the center of the HAAB's spacious dining facility, a meal preparation space that included a twelve-burner stove, dual ovens, a restaurant fridge, dishwasher and compost station, and an island with a sink.

"How was your night?" asked Fisk.

Hopes of quiet alone time dashed, Kate plodded into the DFAC. "I've had better," she said, rubbing her neck. Her first night sleeping in gravity in half a year left her stiff and exhausted.

"Me too," said Fisk. "I couldn't get comfortable on that thing NASA calls a bed. Back home, I have a king size with a pillow-top mattress—like heaven. Some days, I almost don't want to get up."

Small talk in the morning: a fate worse than death. Her introvert brain needed time to ease into a new day of human interaction. Ignoring Fisk, Kate set about assembling her breakfast. She picked through the galley's cabinets, loaded by NASA with an assortment of dishes, cooking utensils, and prepackaged food. Kate found the bowls, cornflakes, and a spoon; boxed milk chilled in the fridge. Her favorite protein bars, however, weren't apparent anywhere. She quickened her search, beating back a mild panic.

"Usually, people ask why I have a king-sized bed," continued Fisk, taking the initiative to float the question himself. "It's because of all the 'traveling' I do when I'm asleep. I move around, flop around, all night. Sometimes, I'll wake up, and I'm lying straight sideways across the bed." He took another bite. "But all things considered," he said through a mouth of granola, "I was grateful not to have to listen to Julian's snoring."

Bundles of shrink-wrapped, dried pasta and coffee greeted Kate as she opened one of the last unexplored cabinets. On a hunch, she pushed the packages aside and peered to the far back of the space. Through the tunnel of foodstuffs, she spied a stack of purple wrappers with a red stripe. Relieved, she withdrew a bar from the pile and clutched it to her chest.

"Saaaay... what's that?" asked Fisk, eyeing Kate's bar. He pinched off a piece of granola and extended it to the commander. "Trade you for a taste."

Kate studied Fisk's offering, the leading edge still moist from his last bite. "I'm not a big fan of granola," she said, marshaling a quick excuse.

"No problem," said Fisk. He popped the morsel into his mouth. "I was thinking it'd be better to try a piece of your bar instead of grabbing a fresh one for myself. I'd hate to waste the whole thing if I find out I don't like it after a bite."

"If you make the slightest move for one of my raspberry bars, your arm will come back without a hand," said Kate with no hint of humor. "These are my favorite protein bars from home, which I made sure the mission planners stocked for the trip. They're here because of me, so don't even think about taking one." She closed the cabinet door and positioned herself in front of it with folded arms.

"My apologies," said Fisk. "I like trying new things. But I get why you wouldn't want to share if all you've got is what's in that cabinet."

"NASA stocked bars here so I wouldn't have to dig through a year's worth of food on my first day. There's plenty more in the Pantry, but they're for me alone." Spending her early morning with Fisk was bad enough. Having to ward him off her special protein bars was an additional annoyance.

"Got it, Commander," said Fisk. He smiled and offered a sorry salute, his thumb outstretched and the bend in his wrist creating the image of a man shielding his eyes from the sun. Astronauts didn't even observe the military custom. As a civilian, he had doubly no business saluting her at all.

Kate collected her bowl and headed to the long, communal table and its matching benches in the center of the DFAC. She sat in the middle, facing the room's large bay window. The remnants of night painted the panoramic view in dark, colorless tones, the nearby rolling hills barely visible. The glow above the distant skyline's modest peaks heralded the rising sun.

Fisk had trailed Kate to the table, but rather than grabbing a seat, he remained standing. An unexpected bit of good fortune—she'd take it. The commander hunched over her bowl and dug into her cornflakes. Hopefully he'd clue in that she cared more about her breakfast than conversation.

"Say, any more info on the secret op?"

Kate had almost forgotten the last day's events, which included Julian's ascension to mission commander. She shook her head, responding to his question as much as attempting to rid her mind of the unpleasant memory.

"You know what I think?" asked Fisk. "I think they've found some kind of alien technology."

"Seems like a leap," said Kate, speaking through a mouthful of cereal without looking up. His claim sounded nuts, in fact, but she didn't want to engage.

"That's what it's always been about," said Fisk. "Starting at Roswell, which was a genuine close encounter, by the way, the government's always been trying to learn as much as it can about the aliens' advanced technology. It means building more lethal weapons, designing faster planes and rockets to deliver those weapons, flattening enemy cities, turning tanks and ships to slag, teleporting behind enemy lines, hitting the enemy with overwhelming lethal force."

Kate stifled a groan as Fisk lowered himself onto the bench across from her.

"It's all about gaining a military advantage over the enemy."

She studied Fisk from a meter away. How had she never noticed the smattering of hairs sprouting from his nostrils? He was generally unkempt, a university professor too wrapped up in his work to care about personal hygiene. His dark hair curled in wisps where it grew on the sides of his head, hinting gray at the temples. His eyes sparkled with an excitement fueled by rocks and conspiracy theories. Neither topic appealed to Kate.

"All the various governments know aliens are real," said Fisk. "People think the United States doesn't want to confirm it because they're worried

Americans will lose their minds. That's not it at all. The issue is none of these governments knows what the others know. If we confirm an alien sighting, if we say, 'yes, aliens can turn on a dime and accelerate at Mach twenty,' that draws the attention of the other governments. They'd all be interested in having that kind of technology for themselves. If we say it's real, they set their scientists on figuring out how it's done."

"What about the UFO encounters the United States military *did* confirm in the early twenties?" asked Kate. "All the film they released of unexplained aerial phenomena. And what about all the classified UFO files made public soon after by the Canadians and the French?"

"Subterfuge," said Fisk. "Diversions to get other governments to waste their time and resources on a wild goose chase."

"Uh-huh," said Kate, her mind struggling with the contradictions. She wracked her brain for an alternate topic. Fisk wore sweats and a headband. "What's up with the exercise gear?"

Fisk munched his granola bar. "I wanna hit the gym before everyone gets up," he said. "A little stationary biking will get the blood pumping."

Kate amended her previous observation: his excitement stemmed from rocks, conspiracy theories, and mountain biking. He professed on Earth and during the trip to Mars that he'd be the first man to mountain bike on the red planet. She'd repeatedly insisted it would be too dangerous. "You still think you're going out there?" she asked, nodding at the bay window.

"Absolutely," said Fisk, grinning. "My bike was waiting for me in my cell, just like I packed it. I've already oiled the chain and inflated the tires." His eyes became dreamy, the geologist losing himself in his imaginings. "I can see the headlines now: 'First MAMIL sighting proves there's life on Mars.' I can't go out riding in my biking shorts ... but maybe I can stretch them *over* my suit."

Kate asked NASA to disallow Fisk's bike on their expedition, hoping they'd agree with her on the foolishness of riding. They'd declined to nix it outright, but she still had the final say. "We've been over this—"

"I know, I know, you're not keen on the idea," said Fisk. "I'm gonna convince you it's safe. But first, I need to regain the strength in my arms and legs."

"Be careful not to overdo it," said Kate. The weightless five-month flight to Mars had weakened their bones and muscles, even with their prescribed exercise regimen. "We're all adjusting to the tug of gravity."

"Don't worry, it'll be a short workout." Fisk pushed himself up from the table. "Gotta save some energy for the sauna." With a wink, he turned and left the DFAC.

Kate ate another scoop of cornflakes, savoring the cold milk flowing over the rough texture. Each bite unleashed a sensory explosion after months of sucking meals out of pouches. On ski trips with her children and now-ex-husband, they'd spend the first mornings in their rented cabin reaching for any familiar comfort—a bowl of cornflakes, a cup of coffee—in a completely foreign space. As the days progressed, that space would become a second home. Their arrival at the HAAB mirrored those first few days in a new cabin. They'd all settle in before too long.

Kate hoisted her spoon again, but her arm stopped mid-travel with the sight of a new astronaut entering the DFAC. *Miriam?* The waifish station chief marched to the galley. *Why's she up so early?* A classic computer nerd, Miriam gravitated to a later schedule. Whatever the reason, Kate's alone time would be short-lived: Miriam poured a cup of coffee, sauntered over to the communal table, and planted herself on the bench across from the commander.

"Good morning, Miriam." Though nearly Kate's age, Miriam seemed far too young for her position. Her delicate features, a product of the Asian side of her Japanese-Jewish heritage, heightened her youthful appearance.

"Morning, Commander." Unlike Fisk, Miriam said little, at least early on. Half asleep, she squinted through her glasses and took a tentative sip of her hot coffee.

"Surprised to see you awake this early," said Kate.

"Not my idea," said Miriam. She attempted a second sip. Her thin fingers cradled the mug, an oven-fired ceramic cup with thick walls and her name scratched on the side. The hand-crafted going away present came from her niece. The station chief had allocated part of her personal weight budget to bringing it along. "With the HAAB's exterior qualifications happening today, NASA woke me early to coordinate with them on the storm."

"The one we saw yesterday on the way down?" asked Kate.

"Yeah," said Miriam. "It's enormous. The latest satellite readout shows it's headed our way."

"Is the HAAB in danger?" asked Kate.

"They don't think so," said Miriam. "They just don't want any of us out in all the wind and dust."

The inspections wouldn't take them far from the HAAB, but standing even a meter apart, they'd risk becoming disoriented and lost if the storm brought whiteout conditions. "How long before it arrives?" asked Kate.

"Fourteen hours, give or take," said Miriam.

"More than enough time for what we need to get done outside."

Miriam nodded and said nothing more. She took a sip of her coffee, then brought her legs onto the bench, crossed them, and closed her eyes. The station chief often lapsed into moments of meditation no matter where she was.

Kate ate several more spoonfuls of her cereal. After emptying the bowl, she unwrapped one end of her protein bar and took a bite. Waves of ecstasy flowed from her tongue. She savored the tartness of the real raspberries, the sweetness of the shredded coconut, the subtle nuttiness of the almond milk, and the creaminess of the chocolate coating. The indulgence, vegan no less, contained the right balance of carbs and protein that would sustain her energy levels. She'd need it for the long day ahead. Kate delighted in a second bite of her bar. She took a third as a new figure entered the DFAC.

Julian?

The acting mission commander wore his tan Mars suit, his helmet in the crook of his arm and filled with a cache of small tools and equipment. The black hood from his suit's thermal layer covered his ears and shaved head. Julian paused, apparently not expecting to find others awake. He proceeded to the communal table and stopped at the far end, the one nearest the entrance. He emptied his helmet onto its surface.

"Where are you off to?" asked Kate.

Julian rummaged through the pile of equipment, sliding items into the loops and pouches of his suit's utility belt. "Getting ready to head out," he said, while continuing to sort his tools.

None of the tasks they needed to complete that day had been handed out to any of the *Ares* astronauts. Julian had poor leadership skills, but would he really take an exterior assignment for himself, one of the coveted, few opportunities to walk on the planet's surface? "I thought we'd have a sign-up sheet for day-one duties, draw straws or something for the people who wanted—"

"Getting ready to head out with Cheney for our primary objective," said Julian, halting his packing to level a steady gaze at Kate. He resumed stuffing equipment into his belt.

The comment rendered Kate speechless. Regardless of the importance of Julian's "primary objective," whatever that was, they'd all be in trouble if they neglected day-one work items. "Our number one job right now is to get settled in—"

"We got settled in last night," said Julian, still engrossed in his packing.

"But we need to perform a visual inspection of the HAAB, both inside and out. We're not really able to settle in until we've completed all the steps of the cert—"

"You don't need me or Cheney here to do that," said Julian, looking up. "You might be scrambling until sundown, but the eight of you can definitely manage."

"There's a storm coming, Julian," said Miriam, the station chief jarred from her meditation. "The one NASA was tracking before we arrived. It's a monster. The computer predicts it'll be here later this evening."

"Yes, I'm aware of the weather report," said Julian. "That's part of why we're going out there now." He slid the last item, a compact, telescoping pickaxe, into a loop on his belt.

"Will you be close by?" asked Kate. "It's not wise to venture too far from the HAAB, not with the storm bearing down."

"All details of the objective, including our destination, are classified," said Julian. "There's nothing I can share with you about it."

"You can't tell us anything, even now that we're all here on the planet?" asked Miriam, incredulous. "You really think what you're working on will stay secret for an entire year?"

"It better," said Julian, "unless one of you has a Top Secret/SCI security clearance and a need to know."

"That's a military clearance," said Miriam.

Julian froze for an instant. He'd apparently revealed more than he intended. The secret assignment wasn't a NASA-driven shift in priorities after all. Julian and Cheney were tasked with a *military* objective.

"I didn't sign up to support some secret military op," she added. "I'm a pacifist."

"The only reason you're here on Mars, pacifist Miriam, is *because* of this op," said Julian, regaining his composure. "Or did you think the military and all those black-budget agencies chipped in six hundred billion dollars because they were feeling generous?"

"But why head out there now?" asked Kate. "We only just arrived. We're going to be here for a year—"

"The AD stressed to me the importance of our primary objective, and how I'm not to let anything stand in the way of completing it. In my judgement, that means setting out right now. If that storm turns out to be one of those freak year-long events, I can't return to Earth saying I missed my one opportunity."

Julian was correct about Mars's unpredictable weather, dust storms that would engulf the planet. But those storms typically lasted a month, two tops, not a full year. The notion they'd be pinned down in the HAAB for their whole time there seemed excessive.

"Me and Cheney leaving now doesn't make a difference," said Julian. "You'll be focused on getting the station operational. You'll all be so busy you won't even notice we're gone."

"But if you get into trouble, *we're* the ones who'll have to risk our lives to come to your rescue," said Kate. "Like Miriam said, none of us signed up to support a secret military op. We're scientists and explorers, not soldiers."

"Glenn used to be a Marine," said Julian, hoisting his helmet to the light. He rubbed a smudge inside the clear ovoid. "You, Kate, you're an ex-Air Force pilot. I know for a fact you've been on missions, combat missions, where the objective changed right out from under you. That's how things go sometimes. It's why I know that what I'm saying isn't all that hard to understand." Julian lifted his helmet and rubbed the smudge again. "You need to stop worrying about what might happen to me and Cheney. I want you to focus on getting the HAAB into operational readiness—those are my orders for you, Kate Holman."

In that instant, Kate understood what had irked her so much about Julian during their trip to Mars. He'd carried himself as if *he* were the leader of the mission, not her. He'd merely paid lip service to her being in charge. In retrospect, his ascension to acting mission commander was no surprise. He'd simply bided his time until the announcement.

"Cheney and I will be back before the storm hits." His helmet cradled under his arm, Julian spun about and walked out of the DFAC.

Miriam and Kate sat a few moments in silence until the station chief rose. "I'll be in the control room." She grabbed her coffee mug and left.

Kate stared out the broad window, catching the first orange rays as they spilled over the far-off mountain ridge. The sun floated into the sky, smaller than on Earth, a white disc ascending against a red wash. She took another bite of her raspberry bar and tucked the rest in her jumpsuit pocket. The remainder would be her reward for making it through the day.

4

"Commander Holman."

"Go ahead."

"You asked me to keep you apprised of the storm."

"What's the latest."

"It's not good."

Kate stood in her Mars suit on a graded section of red soil in the shadow of the station's Greenhouse. Her eyes flew to the eastern sky. The mountain peaks visible in the early morning had disappeared, shrouded by a towering dark wall of ruddy dust.

"The storm's moving a lot faster than projected," said Miriam. "It'll arrive sooner than we thought."

Lightning flashed, its neon tendrils striking from the turbulent cloud tops. The static electricity signaled highly agitated dust particles in the atmosphere. The storm would pack a punch, but hopefully spare their electrical systems. "We're almost done out here," said Kate. "One more cell to inspect." She'd pushed Fisk and Voss to work quickly. Completing the HAAB's exterior qualification ahead of schedule would give them more time to help the others with the tasks inside.

"It's not you I'm worried about," said Miriam. "It's Julian and Cheney. When they left this morning, they thought they'd have 'til sunset to return. If they're shooting to be back by then, they'll be trapped in it for sure."

"Have you informed Commander Grimes?"

"That's just it—I can't raise either of them on their suit comms."

Commander Holman cursed softly. If they couldn't reach Julian over the comms, they'd need to find him on foot. She pulled a set of compact scopes from a pouch at her hip and trained them on the western horizon. Kate hunted for any sign of movement along the crest where the two men had dipped from view earlier that day. They'd been fools to venture out before the onset of a major storm, the hard stop of its arrival leaving no margin for error.

"Did they say where they were going?" asked Kate.

"No, ma'am, and they didn't file an excursion plan either," said Miriam.

No excursion plan, even under seal? At a minimum, his carelessness would draw a mandatory reprimand in his service record, though Julian seemed unconcerned with the rules in the Manual, or the repercussions from not following them.

"However, Cheney's suit pinged the basin relay tower for about an hour after they left," continued Miriam. "Probably an oversight, considering how secretive they've been."

The coordinates from those pings would reveal the route the two men took, at least up until the signal cut out. They'd likely discovered their mistake and silenced Cheney's suit. Kate swore a second time, her worst-case scenario beginning to play out. Julian's rash decision would put additional lives at risk. "Upload the data to my suit."

"Yes, ma'am," said Miriam. "But before you go off trying to find him, I'll point out that Julian's the mission commander. That makes him responsible for his own skin, and for Cheney's because he dragged him along."

"*Acting* mission commander," said Kate. "This is still my mission, Miriam. The AD might've given it to Julian, but I'm gonna get it back, and when I do, I don't want it to come with a list of dead astronauts."

"Roger that," said Miriam, sheepish in her reply. Kate's response to the usually spirited station chief had more bite than she intended. "Data's coming your way."

Kate needed to wrap up her work outside. "Fisk, Voss." Their helmeted heads peeked from behind the Greenhouse. She waved them over.

The two astronauts showed up with expectant faces. Their suits were dusty orange, with pristine, tan rivulets where creases had kept the dirt at bay. Brick-red earth soiled their palms and knees. They'd spent a good portion of their time on the ground, inspecting the connection points between compartments.

"We calling it a day, Commander?" asked Fisk.

"No," said Kate. "I called you over because of the storm. It's coming in a lot faster than we thought. Julian and Cheney are still out there. I need to warn them so they can head back in time."

"That's no problem," said Fisk. "Voss and I are old hands at this now. We can close it out on our own."

Kate addressed Voss. "I want you to finish qualifying the Greenhouse, and then head in to coordinate completion of the interior integrity checks."

"Should go quicker, at least," said Voss. She'd spoken under her breath, but the suit comms had amplified the comment.

"I didn't catch that," said Kate. Irritation had prompted Voss's remark. The question was why.

Voss brought herself to attention, apparently not expecting her comment to have gone beyond her helmet. "I guess I haven't understood why you've been out here, directing me. And Fisk."

Wasn't the reason obvious? "This part of the HAAB's qualifications needs to go right; otherwise, we're all living and sleeping in a structure that could fail. We could all die. That would end this mission pretty quick."

"We both know I'm fully capable of supervising the external qualifications on my own," said Voss. "I don't need someone watching over me. It feels a little like you don't trust me to do my own job."

The commander wasn't normally one to micromanage, but everything needed to go perfectly with the HAAB's qualifications, especially as she was now angling to reclaim the title of mission commander. In her zeal to regain her position, she'd stepped on the mercurial station engineer's toes.

Voss took Kate's silence as her cue that the conversation was over. She made a motion to go but stopped herself. "Oh, and regarding the genius professor here," she said with a nod towards Fisk, "please don't leave him with me. I've never met a grown man who could complain so much about so little. Frankly, I prefer wine with my dinner, not while I'm working." She whirled about and set off for the far side of the Greenhouse. Fisk, confused for a moment, started to follow.

"Mission Specialist Fisk." The professor froze mid-stride. He looked sheepishly back at the commander. "You're with me," said Kate.

Fisk crinkled his nose, incredulous. "I'm with you *where?*"

"I can't go searching for Julian and Cheney alone," said Kate. "I need someone to come with me."

"And you're saying that someone is me?" asked Fisk. Kate nodded. "What about Voss? You didn't even check if she wants to go."

"I need Voss to oversee the work inside," said Kate.

"I can do that," said Fisk. "I have a whole lab of grad students back home. I'm very good at telling people what to do."

"Voss is also the HAAB's engineer," said Kate. "We can't risk losing her searching for Julian and Cheney."

"But we can afford to lose me?" asked Fisk.

Kate shook her head and walked away. Every moment she wasted arguing with Fisk was a moment longer they risked getting caught up in the storm themselves.

Fisk's bootsteps crunched over her suit audio as he scrambled to catch up. He pulled alongside her. "What about Glenn? Or Engles?" he asked.

"They would be excellent, *dependable*, choices," said Kate. "Problem is, it'll take too long for them to drop what they're doing and get suited up. By the time they come out, we could be halfway there already."

"Where's 'there'?" asked Fisk.

"Wherever Julian and Cheney are," said Kate. "Miriam sent me a trail for us to follow—"

The crunch of Fisk's boots ceased. "I respectfully request to remain here at the HAAB," he said.

"Request denied," said Kate, without looking back. She activated her suit nav and fed the coordinates from Cheney's tower pings. A green trail materialized across her faceplate, stretching to the horizon on a due west heading. She set off on the glowing path, with Fisk again scrambling to catch up.

The terrain turned rough beyond the manicured earth around the HAAB, featuring rocky outcrops that resembled a mad artist's attack on sculpting clay. Red silt, some coarse, some fine-grained, covered the flatter surfaces and lined the crevasses.

"Is that…?" asked Fisk ten minutes into their trek. He stooped and examined something near his boot. "It is!"

"It is what?" asked Kate, maneuvering for a sight of whatever the fuss was about.

"Mudstone!" said Fisk. He crouched, brushing his gloved hand over large, flat blocks of dark stone. "This means standing water existed here for quite a while. You don't get this kind of sedimentary layering without an extremely long time period for the silt deposits to solidify."

Kate studied the rocks. They appeared to be nothing out of the ordinary. "Let's keep going." She began walking. The professor eventually followed, leaving his find.

"Look at this!" said Fisk minutes later. "Shale!" He crouched and grabbed a section of thin, flat rock that jutted from an outcropping. A fragment broke off in his hand. "It's incredibly fissile." Fisk offered the shard for the commander's inspection. "This forms when minerals settle out of an aqueous suspension." He set a knee down—

"Fisk!"

The scientist jumped to his feet and stood rigid, like a child caught being naughty.

"We don't have time for a geologic tour," said Kate. "There will be plenty of opportunities for that *after* we find Julian and Cheney."

"Aye, aye, Captain," said Fisk. He banged his hand against his helmet with an awkward salute.

"You're not an officer, so don't try to salute me," said Kate.

"Aye, aye, Captain," said Fisk.

"And this isn't the Space Force, so don't 'aye, aye, Captain' me."

"Aye, aye… I mean yessir."

"It's ma'am."

"Yes, ma'am," said Fisk. "And I'm sorry. My whole life is rocks. I hope you can understand the excitement of walking on a planet's worth of stone that no one has ever explored."

"I get it, Fisk," said Kate. "We just don't have time right now."

Kate continued plotting a careful path along the jagged landscape. The rugged terrain soon quieted, opening onto a broad section of rolling land littered with rocks that ranged from pebbles to small boulders. Farther west, the ground sloped gently downward, forming a shallow bowl-like depression. At the bottom, they shuffled through a stretch of fine red silt so deep it covered their boots. Perhaps the remnants of a long-dead lake.

"By the way, Commander, where exactly are we going?" asked Fisk. Flashes of light played on his face as his nav received the route from Kate's suit and rendered it on his heads-up display. "Oh, you have *got* to be kidding me," he said.

"What?" asked Kate.

Fisk laughed. "OK," he said, "of course. Of course!"

"What are you talking about?" asked Kate, growing annoyed.

"This trail we're following, where it's leading us—it ends not five hundred meters from the Face."

"The face of what?" asked Kate.

"The Face on Mars," said Fisk. "I *told* you this secret black op is about retrieving alien technology."

"You don't really believe that, do you?" asked Kate. "In aliens, I mean, carving a giant stone face on Mars, pointed up to the sky?"

"Photos don't lie," said Fisk. "The photos in question came straight from the Viking 1 flyover in 1976."

"Did you attend the briefing on those images, the ones of the Face and the nearby 'pyramids' and all the other supposed structures in Mars's so-called city of Cydonia?"

"I didn't want my mind polluted with disinformation," said Fisk.

"You mean you didn't want to sit there for two hours while they methodically debunked all those claims of aliens on Mars."

"It's case closed, then," said Fisk. "Like I told you, all these governments, including ours, are in the business of claiming aliens don't exist so they can keep their discoveries to themselves."

"You really think there's something to the original Viking lander images?" asked Kate. "Those lo-res images certainly show what looks eerily similar to a human face, but NASA analyzed the heck out of them. In the end, they proved the Face is just a rock formation."

"They didn't *prove* anything," said Fisk. "That 'analysis' was a snow job, and a pretty bad one at that. Someone ran the original image through a bunch of filters 'til they got a photo with all the detail washed out."

"Subsequent images taken with higher resolution cameras showed the Face to be a completely natural rock outcrop," said Kate.

"The camera that took those photos was built under contract by a company whose owner is an avowed Face skeptic," said Fisk. "Somehow, he was also the lone person NASA assigned to process all the camera data *before* revealing it to the world. So no, I don't trust the higher-res data either."

"You're telling me the Face is real," said Kate.

"I think it hasn't been proven otherwise," said Fisk. "And the problems with the official explanation don't help. I also found it very interesting how they had a meeting to debunk all the theories, but not two weeks later, they revealed they were placing the HAAB three kilometers from the Face."

"I don't remember them telling us we'd be that close."

"That's 'cause they never uttered those words," said Fisk. "In fact, they were very careful not to let on about the Face being nearby. Do you remember the satellite photo where the HAAB's location was marked with one of those upside-down teardrops? When you have a point of interest like that, you center it in your photo. Do you recall how the teardrop was down in the lower-left corner? That's because if they had centered it, we would've seen Cydonia off to the left."

"Yeah, I do recall that," said Kate. "The teardrop being off-center struck me as strange. I figured they wanted to show the major land formations to the east."

"Did you know that wasn't even where NASA wanted to put the HAAB?" asked Fisk.

"What do you mean?"

"I have a buddy, a friend from my undergrad days at Princeton. He used to work … let's just say somewhere within the military industrial complex. He's a little bit paranoid, but his information is always spot-on. When I told him where they were setting us down, he said there had been a whole back-and-forth between the military and NASA over where to place the HAAB. Did you know NASA wanted us near the equator? There's more sunlight, the temperatures are not as extreme, and the planet spins faster there, which makes rocket liftoffs easier. The military nixed that plan—they threatened to pull the funding. So here we are, above the fortieth parallel."

The deep dive into Fisk's conspiracy theories strained the limits of Kate's patience. "All this talk is hurting my brain," she said. "Can we focus on following the trail for now?"

"Of course, Commander. We don't need to discuss everything today." He grinned. "We have an entire year."

Kate stifled a groan as they trudged forward. They traveled through more rugged land that gradually shifted to a smooth plain of long-dried mudflats. Red dust filled the arterial network of cracks between the clods. After twenty-five minutes, they stopped for a break, sipping water from their suits' reclamation systems. The Face loomed ahead, though too far to discern any significant details in the hazy distance. The commander fixed her scopes on the formation. She couldn't say much about the top, but from the side it appeared to be a flat-topped mound of striated rock. "For all the claims of intelligent design, it doesn't look like anything special to me," she said. "It's just a mesa."

Fisk snatched the binoculars and studied the Face. He remained quiet for once. Apparently, the scientist *could* be silenced; it just took facts he couldn't dispute, ones that came from his own eyes.

Kate glanced back at the HAAB, its gleaming white cells and tubeways silhouetted against the advancing storm. "Let's move," she said.

The two resumed their march. On their left, a small sandstone mesa, river-carved according to Fisk, rose from the flat plains. Cheney's path paralleled the gentle curve of the formation's pitted rock face, steering them progressively southwest. After twenty more minutes of walking, they reached the dot at the end of the green nav line.

"This is where the trail cuts out," said Kate.

Fisk didn't respond. He stared at the Face, agape. What had been a mythical alien carving in a grainy photo was now in full view, a massive assemblage of sedimentary rock whose natural origins were clear and indisputable.

Kate switched her suit comm to the broadcast channel. "Julian, Cheney, this is Commander Holman. Do you read?"

A low hiss fed back over the comms.

"Julian, Cheney, do you read me?"

More gentle hissing.

"Now what?" asked Fisk.

"I'm not sure," said Kate. She'd figured they'd have a good chance of contacting the men once they arrived at the end of the trail. The commander eyed the lightly rising terrain between them and the Face. "Maybe if we're on higher ground."

Kate led Fisk up the shallow slope, a stretch of smooth rock with a network of hairline cracks. They paused at a ridge line where the land dived for thirty meters, then flattened out in the final run to the base of the Face. The immense sandstone structure towered in front of them, nearly a kilometer high.

A roughly round, black patch, situated at surface level, interrupted the red and orange striations that marked the side of the Face. Kate removed her scopes and scanned the feature. "Looks like there's an opening in the rock."

"You mean a cave?" asked Fisk.

"Something like that." By her scopes, the opening measured two meters wide and three meters high at its tallest point. She couldn't make out any details within the deep black—the cavity had to extend a good ways into the rock.

"That's where they are," said Fisk.

"You don't know that," snapped Kate. Fisk talked as if relaying a well-known fact, but his claim was based on nothing at all. "You have no idea where they are. You're only guessing they even came this way. They could have easily headed off in any other direction at the end of Cheney's trail."

"Oh, they're definitely in there," said Fisk. His eyes widened, the geologist entranced by his imaginings. "The Face *is* an alien edifice. And we just found the way in. NASA must've discovered artifacts, weapons or technology, spoils so compelling they sent a live astronaut extraction team."

Contacting the men would end the debate and get them started back home. "Julian, Cheney, you copy?" Their vantage point on the ridge provided kilometers of visibility in almost all directions. The Face was the exception, though with luck, reflections would bounce the signal around it. If the two *Ares* astronauts were nearby, they should've picked up her transmission. Nothing but the faint hum of a silent connection filled the channel.

"You can't reach them from here," said Fisk. "All that red in the rocks is rust, iron oxide. The ferromagnetism creates an electromagnetic shield the comms can't penetrate." His jaw went slack with more imaginings. "Besides, they're probably in a vault room—no telling what exotic material it's made of."

Kate muted Fisk's channel, giving herself space to think. Even if the two men ignored her hails, the comms would still show a connection lock. Julian and Cheney weren't anywhere on the open plains or were too far away to worry about trying to help.

The clock on her heads-up display nagged. Kate looked back to the HAAB, its network of cells hidden behind the smaller sandstone mesa. Clouds at the storm's leading edge floated high in the eastern sky, spitting lightning against a roiling dark gray backdrop of dust. "We'll go down and take a look inside that opening. If we don't make contact, we'll start back." She didn't want Julian and Cheney to die, but she could only do so much to counter stupidity. They'd spent enough time trying to save their asses. "C'mon," she said, stowing her scopes and starting for the Face.

5

Kate moved at a methodical, cautious pace down the incline, towards the Face. "Careful," she said, looking back at Fisk, "the surface is pretty slick." With the smooth ground underfoot and its steep angle, they were both one misstep from catastrophe.

Fisk nodded, head down as he concentrated on the placement of each step. He snuck a split-second glance at the Face, perhaps to get his bearings. The moment his eyes left the ground, his front boot skated half a meter downslope. Fisk yelped as he fought to stop sliding, bending his knees and extending his arms as if balancing on a surfboard. He came to a halt in a low crouch.

Kate had watched the near disaster unfold. Helping him would be tricky —she'd have to move up and across the slick berm without slipping herself.

"I'm OK," said Fisk, answering Kate's worried look with a raised thumb and an uncertain smile. He shifted his weight enough to lift his back boot. The footing under his front boot gave out. In a panic, Fisk stood tall, bringing his feet together and thrusting his arms up like a ballerina. He jutted his hips first left, then right, as he shimmied, attempting to regain his balance. His maneuver arrested his slide but left the bulk of his body weight out over the fronts of his boots. He fell forward, tumbling past Kate the remaining seven meters down the embankment.

"Fisk!" Kate skittered down the slope while fighting to avoid taking a tumble herself. "Are you all right?" she asked as she arrived at his side.

Fisk, in a heap at the base of the embankment, pushed himself to sit. "I think so," he said, staring upslope in a daze. He noticed Kate's outstretched hand and, after accepting her help to his feet, brushed red dust from his Mars suit. "Guess it was slipperier than I thought." His eyes took on a distant look as he scanned his suit's self-diagnostic scrolling up his heads-up display. "Everything seems to be OK—no containment breach, at least."

While Fisk reviewed the report, Kate ventured to the opening. It was a cave, with a mouth wide enough to accommodate two people standing abreast. She activated her suit's flashlight embedded at her wrist and aimed it inside. Rugged rock walls continued for fifteen meters before fading into the darkness.

"Any sign of them?" asked Fisk, arriving at the commander's side.

"None," said Kate. The ground was too hard for bootprints, but if the two men were inside, she might have transmission line of sight to reach them. "Julian, Cheney, do you read?" Still nothing on the comms. She'd only committed to checking out the entrance. Without a sign of the two men, the risk of entering the cave outweighed the odds of finding them. They would do no more. The search was over.

"They could be incapacitated," said Fisk. He stared into the cave, his cupped hands shielding the sun's glare from his faceplate. He chuckled. "It would be kinda funny to turn around now, only to find out later they were both facedown a few meters from the entrance."

Damn Fisk and his ramblings! The odds of both men being unable to respond were close to zero, but if they headed back and Fisk turned out to be right, she would never forgive herself. She waved her light down the tunnel again—no telling how far it stretched. They needed to start back for the HAAB, but Kate couldn't shake the vision of Julian and Cheney in distress, trapped in the dark beneath a pile of rubble, praying for rescue. "We'll go in," she said, reluctance in her voice, "but let's be quick about it."

Kate and Fisk proceeded into the opening. The gentle patter of their bootsteps echoed from the rough walls in the thin Martian air as they followed the commander's flashlight beam. The cave shot ahead another twenty-three meters, disappearing in a sharp bend to the right.

The rock walls mesmerized Fisk as they walked. "This cave likely formed as an outlet for snowmelt," he said, "back when Mars had free-flowing water. It probably leads all the way to the top." He raked a portion of the chamber with the bright beam of his suit flashlight. "These strata tell the entire story of this structure's formation." A section at chest height caught his attention. He trained his light on the spot and poked it with his finger. Several small chunks of reddish-brown stone tumbled to the tunnel floor.

"Let's go, Fisk," said Kate, exasperated with the research scientist's latest distraction.

Fisk grabbed a piece of fallen rock the size of his fist. He squeezed, pulverizing the stone in his glove. "This rock's fairly soft," he said, rivers of soil trailing between his fingers. "I wonder how solid this cavern actually is."

Kate's face went pale. She hadn't given much thought to the cave's stability. Marsquakes were real. They could wind up trapped themselves.

Fisk responded to the commander's panicked look. "I'm sure it's perfectly safe," he said. He clapped his gloves, batting away the dust. "It would have to be pretty stable to have remained intact for so long."

Should they turn around? Kate dismissed the thought and instead moved faster into the cave. They'd come this far—it made little sense to end their search just yet. They'd explore a bit more before starting back.

"Barreling down this tunnel doesn't exactly make it easy for us to find them without being discovered," said Fisk. "I guess you're not too concerned about bumping into Julian?"

"I *am* concerned," said Kate. Julian seemed almost crazed that morning when he talked about the mission remaining a secret. "Right now, I'm focused on saving their lives. There's a good chance if they get caught out in that storm, they won't survive."

"What do you know about him?" asked Fisk. "Julian, I mean."

"Not much," said Kate. "He's an Air Force veteran. Has degrees in chemistry and materials science. I tried talking to him a few times when he first joined the team. I couldn't get him to open up." Translation: even then, he'd been a condescending asshole. She gave up trying to connect with him soon after that.

"Psychopaths are never keen on idle chitchat," muttered Fisk.

"Why do you say that?" asked Kate.

"That's serial killer one oh one," said Fisk, "though to be fair, Jeffrey Dahmer might've chatted you up a bit before he excised your liver."

"No, I mean why do you say Julian's a psychopath?" asked Kate.

"A feeling I have," said Fisk. "He gives me the willies. His lapdog Cheney, too. I wouldn't want to be alone with either of them … in a dark cave, for instance."

Julian could be intense, but he wasn't a psychopath. Not a true one, anyway. NASA's rigorous psychological fitness protocol would have weeded him out early on.

Activating his flashlight again, Fisk broadened the beam and shined it on the tunnel roof. "You know who would have a field day in here is Dr.

Morgan. Sedimentary rock is ideal hunting ground for micro fossils." He shut off his light. "Maybe she and I should take a trip out here sometime."

"So sort of a date, then," said Kate with a slight grin.

Fisk blushed. "Of sorts," he said. "A scientific date, you could call it. An interplanetary geologist and an astrobiologist ... I bet we'd make some amazing finds."

This wasn't the first time Fisk had mentioned astrobiologist Casey Morgan. A brunette beauty with ample curves and large brown eyes, she'd turned heads all during their training on Earth, as well as their journey to Mars. Every man on the mission likely had some interest in her; Engles too. "I'm not sure about coming to the Face, but I'm sure she'd be interested in working with you. You should ask her."

Fisk blushed again. "Perhaps when you see her next, you could suggest it …."

"You don't need my help," said Kate. "She's very approachable. You should try talking to her."

"What's that ahead?" asked Fisk.

The question at first seemed like a feeble attempt at changing the subject, but Kate's flashlight beam had landed on something in the distance. The object came into view as they drew closer.

"A dead end," said Fisk. A solid mass of boulders and rocks blocked their path.

"Or a cave-in," said Kate. It wasn't clear if the tunnel simply ended, or if fallen rock had closed off the path. "Either way, we can't continue forward. Let's—God, Fisk, what is it now?"

Fisk was frozen, peering down. He crouched, snatched at the ground, and returned to standing with something lying flat in his palm. The object was shiny—metallic—and cylindrical, a rod about twenty centimeters long and two centimeters in diameter. "Well, what are *you* doing here?" he said. He brushed away dirt, revealing more of the object. Strange triangular symbols covered its surface.

Kate returned her attention to the pile of rubble. This was madness. Between Fisk's preoccupation with his discoveries and the foolishness of entering an apparently unstable tunnel, she'd had enough. Julian and Cheney should never have left before the onset of the storm. At a minimum, they should've arranged to keep in contact with the HAAB. If they died because of all their bullshit secrecy, that was on them. She'd gone above and beyond to look for the two men. "Julian, Cheney, this is Commander Holman, over." Silence. She hadn't expected a response, not so deep within the rock. Her final call served as an end cap to their efforts. "And with that," she said, spinning on her heels, "we are finished with this adventure." She started back towards the cave entrance.

"Julian here."

Kate froze. She exchanged a shocked look with Fisk. It took her a moment to respond. "Uh, Julian, this is Kate. We've been trying to reach you. The storm's picked up. It's going to arrive much sooner than we thought. Fisk and I came looking for you."

"Where are you?"

"We're—"

Fisk frowned and shook his head. He slashed his finger across his throat, then pointed up. His eyes were wide, insistent.

Kate heeded what she assumed was a warning not to reveal their true location. "We're about a kilometer east of ..."—no, best not to mention the Face at all—"... two kilometers west of the HAAB. Where are you and Cheney?"

A pause, then Julian again. "Close to your location. Cheney and I are wrapping up. Don't advance any farther west—stay where you are. We'll come to you. ETA twenty minutes."

"Roger that, staying put." Kate killed the comm.

"Twenty minutes?" said Fisk, suddenly terrified. "It took us half that long to walk this far into the cave."

Fisk was right: ten minutes to exit the cave and another ten to make it back to where Cheney's suit issued its last ping. They needed to be at the rendezvous point before Julian; otherwise, he'd see her and Fisk coming *from* the Face. "Run!" she whispered.

6

Kate rushed with Fisk back through the cave towards the entrance, the beam from her suit light bouncing along the passageway's rough, striated walls. Their boots kicked up dust that lingered in the thin Martian air, leaving a fog behind them.

"What I don't understand is how we were able to talk to them at all," said Fisk between pants. "We have no luck reaching them 'til we're standing under a kilometer of solid rock?"

Their contact with Julian didn't make sense, but Kate offered no guesses. She wanted to focus on getting out of the cave and back to the meeting point. There'd be plenty of time for speculation later.

Fisk said nothing else as they continued ahead. She almost wished for more of his prattle to mask the sound of her huffing within her helmet. Although moving at a faster pace, the snaking path seemed much longer than she remembered, each bend revealing only another stretch of tunnel.

At last, a dim patch of light appeared in the distance—they barreled to the exit. Kate stopped just inside the outlet and held Fisk back with an arm. She peeked her head out: no sign of Julian or Cheney. Commander Holman stepped from the entrance, followed by Fisk. Both astronauts squinted in the Martian daylight. Though much brighter than the cave, the world outside had darkened since they'd left it. Black-gray storm clouds filled the entire eastern sky, advancing on a retreating sun.

Kate studied the rise they'd descended to reach the Face. Scaling the hill would be a challenge, but they had no other choice, nor any time to waste. "Let's get to the top of the berm as quick as we can," she said.

Commander Holman started for the rise but soon halted—Fisk wasn't following. He'd walked farther along the base of the Face, stopping seven meters to the right of the cave opening. He examined the solid rock wall. "Fisk, we don't have time!"

Fisk didn't move to join her. Instead, he reached for a section of the cliff face. As he pulled his arm back, a sliver of black emerged, like the sliced edge of a large, ragged circle. The sliver grew ....

Another cave! A massive sheet of material with a print matching the cliff's rock pattern hung from the top of the opening. The fabric hid the entrance, at least to a casual observer.

Were Julian and Cheney inside? Kate's mind raced. The second cave likely zigzagged beneath the Face, like the one they'd left. The two shafts may have jogged close in spots, with the rock separating them thin enough to pass her comm signal. If Julian and Cheney *were* in that cave, they might be rushing for the exit, possibly seeing the silhouette of an astronaut holding back the fabric. "Drop it!" Kate shouted, the best summation of her thoughts she could rally.

Fisk complied for once—perhaps he'd thought the same. The two Mars astronauts sprinted for the berm. Kate arrived first and let her momentum carry her up the incline. Her boots slipped as she clambered on the slick slope. For every few meters forward, she skidded one or two back. Fisk had a tougher time. On each attempt at scaling the rise, he never made it more than a couple meters up the bank before sliding all the way down to its base.

Perched a few meters above the base of the berm, Kate took a moment to think. Their boots had decent treads—she'd noted as much during their practice hikes in the Nevada desert—they just weren't getting enough traction. Mars's lower gravity was to blame …. On a hunch, Kate crouched, then sprang forward, leaping ahead while jumping as high as she could. She floated into the air and, with the arc of her flight, landed several meters upslope. Before her boots lost their purchase, she repeated her angled hop, touching down farther up the embankment. Fisk caught on to her technique. He managed to jump-skip up the slope behind her.

What would they find upon reaching the top? Even if Julian and Cheney had been in the second cave, the two could be at the rendezvous point already, boiling with rage at their absence.

Kate's final jump-skip delivered her over the top, and with it a view of the wide-open Martian plain. No one else was in sight. Relieved they hadn't been beaten back, she waited for Fisk. Once the research scientist reached her location, the two scrambled for the end of Cheney's trail.

Arriving at the rendezvous point, Kate and Fisk caught their breaths. They hunched over with their hands on their knees, taking in great gulps of oxygen. The commander scanned the ridge. Twenty-five minutes had elapsed since she'd spoken to Julian, but the other two astronauts had still not come into view. She reopened her comm line. "Hey, Julian, just checking on you guys. Are you almost here?"

No response. Julian and Cheney were evidently still far enough inside the Face that her comm signal couldn't reach them.

Kate monitored the ridge for any sign of the two astronauts, the task growing harder with the waning sunlight. During their scramble from the cave, she'd prayed Julian and Cheney would take their time getting back. Standing idle as the storm approached, she grew more and more annoyed by their delay.

At thirty-four minutes after her last contact with Julian, fifteen more than he'd promised, a shadowy figure floated up and over the embankment. A second followed. The two headed towards her and Fisk, starting the near-kilometer trek to their location. One silhouette moved with a labored, awkward gait and carried their right arm across the front of their suit. Kate sighed—a broken arm, or worse, would explain their delay, but a wounded astronaut was the last thing they needed in their race back to the HAAB.

As the two drew closer, the reason for the hobbled figure's shambling became apparent: a tan sack, slung over his shoulder, swung side to side behind him. Far from injured, the arm across his chest held in its hand the bag's drawstrings.

"Whaddya think's in the bag?" asked Fisk, who also watched the approaching astronauts. "Doesn't look light, that's for sure." He gaped, glassy-eyed with wild imaginings. "Maybe a golden statue of the Martian king."

"That kind of talk stops now," scolded Kate. "I don't want you accidentally tipping Julian off to our time out here."

Fisk's right hand jerked up from his side but quickly fell back, a salute apparently held in check. "You have nothing to worry about, Commander. I won't say anything that could raise suspicion."

Kate frowned. "I'd rather you didn't say anything at all."

Minutes dragged for an eternity before Julian and Cheney arrived. Both astronauts were out of breath, with beads of sweat trickling down their faces despite the temperature-controlled confines of their Mars suits. Red earth caked their gloves and knees. They'd kneeled and used their hands for whatever task they'd performed.

"We've been waiting," said Kate, unable to stifle her irritation. She last spoke with Julian forty-five minutes prior, more than double the promised arrival time. She eyed the acting mission commander as he adjusted the sack on his shoulder. "And that extra weight's going to slow us down."

"Everything's under control," said Julian.

"What's in the bag?" asked Fisk. "Spoils, er ... soils?" He blanched. "I'm an expert on dirt and rocks."

"The bag's contents, even the fact I'm carrying it, are both classified," said Julian. "As far as you two are concerned, it doesn't exist."

Kate shot Fisk a glare that could have melted lead. The geologist sheepishly looked away.

"Commander Holman, you and Fisk need to get back here. Now."

Miriam sounded odd, and not because of the mangled acoustics in the Mars suit helmet. Stress charged the station chief's voice, a level of concern she hadn't heard before. "Julian and Cheney are here."

"Well, while you were waiting, that storm really shifted into high gear," said Miriam. "You *needed* to start back fifteen minutes ago. As it stands, you'll catch the leading edge. But even that'll be better than what's coming after."

"Roger that," said Kate. "Everyone activate your suit navs." The system's green path dashed into the distance inside her helmet's faceplate. The other astronauts' faces lit up in glowing green. She eyed Julian's sack again.

"Let's head out," said Julian before Kate could say anything. He set off marching across the darkening plains, with Cheney in tow.

"After you," said Kate, motioning Fisk to proceed. She would again bring up the rear.

The four astronauts traveled single file over ancient mud flats and basalt flows, the rising winds flinging aloft the loose dirt. Dust devils danced, some with columns ascending a hundred meters into the air. The towering storm front loomed a kilometer ahead, its ruddy color washing to grays in the dwindling sunlight. The glowing green path that overlaid Kate's view of the Martian wilderness appeared to scale the wall of dust, climbing from its base halfway to the sky.

Kate swallowed hard. She'd soon find herself enveloped by the storm's dusty fog; they all would. She fought off flashbacks of the incident on the Moon. *The mind takes cues from the breath. Panicked breaths suggest a panic situation. Keep the breath smooth and steady, and the mind will follow.* Kate heeded her old therapist's words, brought her breathing under control. Her mind settled down.

Traumatic events haunt us when they take on their own meaning in our minds. They spin their own stories if you let them. The key to sapping their power over you is taking your own meaning from them. The crash on the Lunar surface had opened Kate's eyes to what could go wrong during a routine landing. She'd declared the event a lesson in preparedness. That lesson had saved them yesterday, the propellent she'd held back at liftoff averting a fatal disaster while touching down.

Kate looked up. The storm front was nearly upon them. While lost in her thoughts, they'd quickly closed the gap, or the storm had. Julian seemed close enough to touch it. Even weighed down by his haul, he'd run up a good ten meters between himself and Cheney. They'd all spread far from each other. The incident on the Moon had also taught her the importance of sticking together in a zero-visibility situation. Her friend might be alive today but for lack of that insight. "Hey, guys," she said, "I'd like to suggest we tighten up before we enter the dust cloud."

"There's no need," said Julian.

Julian replied in a flash, without an ounce of consideration. Sometimes it felt like he nixed her ideas just because they came from her. If she suggested they continue breathing, he'd probably order the opposite. "I was realizing that with our current spacing, we're going to lose sight of each other inside the—"

"Everyone's on their suit navs, Kate," said Julian in his usual patronizing tone. "Getting back to the HAAB is as simple as following the green line. Or what, you're thinking we hold hands? Like we're in kindergarten?"

Kate didn't press it. She wanted to avoid appearing weak in front of Julian. And they *were* all on their suit navs, though the same had been true on the Moon.

Julian encountered the gray wall first. His body faded, each step making it harder to distinguish him from the fuzzy background, until in a blink he disappeared. Cheney dissolved next, followed by Fisk.

Kate continued on. She expected to hit a mass of swirling dust, but the hard transition never came. One instant she was approaching the wall, the next, a ghostly reddish-gray fog surrounded her.

Visibility rapidly deteriorated. Fisk had a lead of only eight meters, but it may as well have been eighty. Julian was right that following the green line would get them back to the HAAB, but walking within view of one another afforded a modicum of safety. They were lone hikers in a harsh, foreign wilderness, going against at least the spirit of the Manual's guidelines on solitary excursions. Julian probably hadn't reconsidered her request to march in a tighter group, but they needed to maintain contact with each other, visual or otherwise. "This is Kate, checking in," she said on the broadcast channel. "Is everyone doing OK? Please sound off."

"Fisk."

"Cheney."

"We're all OK, Kate," said Julian, exasperated. "If anyone runs into trouble, call out over your comm. If not, there's no need for the chatter."

Radio silence it is. She resumed her lonely march to the HAAB, quiet but for the wailing wind and the nav's dispassionate call-outs of direction and distance.

After fifteen minutes of moderate calm, occasional wind gusts buffeted Commander Holman. A major blast lasting several seconds pushed her backwards. She held fast, digging in her boots. The storm was worsening. Luckily, the HAAB lay close—according to her nav, only ten minutes away.

The halo of visible ground steadily shrank as she walked, contracting to less than a meter. Lightning flashed the world in electric white. Kate listened for a boom that never arrived. Did lightning work on Mars as it did on Earth? Or had it been too far to hear the thunder?

Lightning flashed again. The green path faltered, flickered, then snapped to orange.

"GPS connection lost."

Kate halted. The storm's electrical interference was scrambling the signals from above. Her suit had the most recent directions to the HAAB but could only estimate her position relative to them. "Julian? Fisk?" No answer. "Cheney?" She switched comm channels. "Miriam?" Nothing from the control room.

Fighting the fear her nav was completely confused, Commander Holman trudged on. What else could she do but put her faith in the glowing path? She leaned into strengthening gusts that threatened to topple her and crouched during squalls, making herself smaller against the wind. With each step, the orange dot at the trail's end increased in size.

"One hundred meters."

She was nearly back. A couple more minutes of walking would bring her home. She quickened her pace.

The orange dot expanded to a meter in diameter and slid beneath her feet, or appeared to in her helmet's augmented reality display. "You have reached your destination."

Kate looked around. *You have got to be frickin' kidding me!* Contrary to her suit nav's cheerful declaration, the HAAB wasn't visible anywhere. She staggered on, but with each stride, the scene remained unchanged. Dread welled in her core. She'd have to shelter in place, or risk becoming hopelessly lost in the Martian wild.

She took a few more paces. The red-gray expanse of dust before her seemed to brighten a bit, growing lighter, somehow whiter. A proximity sensor chirped. Arms outstretched, Kate took one more careful step, then another. A large white plasticine panel materialized from the fog, flat with a slight curvature at the top. She'd found the HAAB!

Hands pressing the station, Kate pantomimed her way along the panels until she felt the main airlock and the controls to open it. She tapped the entry sequence on the keypad. Locks disengaged, and the door slid aside. She stepped into the chamber and quickly commanded it shut. Quiet engulfed her, deafening after thirty minutes of the storm's constant roar. She launched the pressurization cycle. Ten seconds later, the red light above the inner hatch cycled green. Kate grabbed the handle and pushed.

Commander Holman stumbled through the open door into the Spine. Exhausted, she lowered herself onto a bench in the makeshift excursion prep area. She released the seal on her helmet and removed the ovoid bubble, setting it next to her. Kate exhaled in relief. She'd made it back to the station.

"Where's Cheney?"

The question came from Fisk. The geologist curled forward on a bench facing the airlock, helmet off and forearms on thighs. His hair flailed in mad wisps. He regarded her with weary eyes.

"He's not back?" asked Kate.

"He's not," said Fisk with a shake of his head. "He should have been back before me."

Cheney wasn't the only one missing. "Where's Julian?" asked Kate.

"He took off down the Spine right when I arrived, carrying his bag of ... he took off down the Spine. I asked him about Cheney as he left. He said there was nothing to worry about, that Cheney would be the next person inside."

Kate's face went pale. "Cheney, this is Commander Holman. Do you copy?" Static answered back. "Cheney, this is Kate. Do you copy?"

"I don't think suit-to-suit transmissions travel very well beyond the HAAB's panels," said Glenn, arriving at the airlock.

"Miriam, you there?" asked Kate, her voice shaky, each breath a chore under increasing anxiety.

"Yes, Commander, I'm here."

"Cheney hasn't made it back to the HAAB. The rest of us are in. Can you try contacting him?"

"Roger that," said Miriam. The line went silent for thirty seconds. "I've hailed him several times, but no response, Commander."

Kate's chin quivered. Her hands balled into fists. Snatching her helmet, she stood and raised the ovoid above her head.

Glenn hooked Kate's arm. "Hey, you can't go back out."

"I *have* to!" said Kate, her eyes wild. "Cheney's still out there."

"Glenn's right," said Miriam on the open comm channel. "It's zero visibility. Winds are picking up beyond what you just came through. Comms are down with all the electrical interference from the storm, and navs are probably useless too. Anyone who goes out there now, the odds of them making it back to the HAAB are close to zero."

"But we can't *leave* him out there," pleaded Kate. Her voice dropped to a whisper. "He'll die."

"No, he won't," said Glenn. "We've all trained for this kind of situation. He'll hunker down. His suit will protect him from all the grit and keep him warm and hydrated. His breather pack can produce almost ten days of oxygen. We can go out looking for him when it's safer."

Hands still balled, Kate walked to an oblong window on the opposite side of the corridor. Red grit, illuminated by light from the Spine, swirled against the clear panel. Beyond it lay the backdrop of the black Martian night. Violent gusts pressed into the HAAB's plasticine walls.

"Let's get you changed out of this gear," said Glenn gently with a hand on her shoulder. "Some warm tea will raise your spirits."

Enjoy a cup of warm tea while Cheney remained out in the storm? Kate glanced back at the airlock door.

"There's nothing more to be done right now," he said. "All we can do is wait for a break in the weather."

7

Commander Holman walked in a daze the entire way to her cell. Physically and mentally exhausted, she peeled off her Mars suit, and stepped into the shower. She stood amidst the steam, the water slightly too hot, with her palms flat against the panels and head hung forward. Back on Earth, where conservation was the order of the day, she would never have indulged in such a long shower. At the Mars station, each drop of water, whether flushed down toilets or scrubbed from the air, was fully reclaimed and reused. Warmed by the excess heat from the HAAB's fusion power plant, every shower had an infinite supply of hot water. She'd need that much to wash away her sins.

Wash away my sins? There's not enough water in the Universe to do that. She'd exited the Lunar tribunal with a clean service record, but nothing could reach into her mind and erase the second guessing.

The spray from the shower head went limp, then spurted in a bubble-fueled burst. It gurgled twice before resuming its steady flow. Apparently, there was still air in the lines. She took the interruption as her signal to finish up.

Kate emerged from the shower, toweled off, and threw on a station jumpsuit. Like her Mars suit, "K. HOLMAN" appeared on a neat label stitched over her heart. The label hadn't ever struck her as odd but suddenly seemed strange—was it there to declare ownership of the item or to specify who was inside? Standing naked in the shower where she had no name tag at all, was she still K. HOLMAN?

The commander shook off the existential questions, the ones that surfaced only when she was agitated. After rubbing her short hair dry, she combed it with her fingers, pulled on a pair of boots, and headed out of her cell. She'd been singularly focused on Glenn's suggestion of a warm cup of tea, the motivation she'd used to get herself cleaned up. She strolled to the end of the tubeway where it adjoined the much larger Spine and turned right for the DFAC.

Kate's eyes darted as she entered the communal space. Palmer and Engles played a game of chess. Voss lounged on a couch, curled up with a book. She didn't bother to check who else was present, concentrating instead on reaching the drink machine. The commander grabbed a hot chamomile tea, then took a seat at an empty, two-person table. Beyond the bay window, dust swirled in the warmth cast by the room's lights.

"Mind if I join you?"

She hadn't noticed Glenn in the DFAC, or his approach. She didn't want company, just wanted to be alone with her thoughts. "I don't—"

Before she could deter him, Glenn took the seat across from her. He set his own drink down, a mug of steaming tea with the aroma of jasmine, cradling it in his hands. Kate sighed and settled in again to watching the storm.

"Did you get a chance to review the operational readiness report?" asked Glenn.

Kate's mind had drifted. His question jolted her back. "The what?"

"The operational readiness report," said Glenn. "I was wondering if you'd seen it yet."

"Oh," she said, "no, not yet. It was waiting for me on my terminal … I didn't stop to open it." She sipped her tea—too hot.

"The door to one of the storage cells won't close all the way," said Glenn. "Do you remember any problems with that section of the HAAB during your exterior inspection? I'm thinking a support strut might need some adjustment."

"Strut what?" Kate's mind had drifted anew.

Glenn smiled. "It's not important," he said. "How're you doing?"

The commander stared off through the window at the howling storm. "Me? I'm OK."

"You don't seem OK," said Glenn. Commander Holman didn't respond, consumed by her thoughts. "Don't worry, Kate, we'll find him."

"We shouldn't have lost him," said Kate. "That's why I brought up the rear, to make sure no one got left behind." Tears flowed. She wiped them away. "It just feels like the Moon all over again."

"This is nothing like what happened on the Moon," said Glenn.

"Really? Visibility zero, an astronaut missing?" Kate wiped away more tears. "We should have stayed put the moment we hit the storm, should've hunkered down out there. Or I don't know, a million things we could have done differently."

"But your suit navs were working," said Glenn. "At least they were at the start. If you're all just following the green line, there's no need to stay put." He sipped his tea. "I think you did the best anyone could have."

"Tell that to Cheney's family," said Kate. "After the incident on the Moon, I made a personal visit to Grace's ... Mission Specialist Phong's husband. I owed him that much. I'll never forget the vacant look on his face. Before that, losing it out here was just a hazy possibility. Her death made all that real. Losing her drove home the high stakes of our rush to lay claim to the solar system." More tears welled. "I never want to lose another teammate, never want to deliver that kind of news again."

"Well, our acting mission commander was the one officially responsible for getting you all back safely." Glenn nodded towards Julian, sitting across the way at a table with Casey. "You're here beating yourself up, but if there's any blame to be assigned, or condolences that need to be delivered, it should be on him."

Julian and Casey were having an animated, jovial discussion, all smiles and laughter. "Does he seem like a man who gives a shit that one of our own is lost out in this mess?" asked Kate.

Glenn regarded Julian, her second-in-command's pursed lips hinting at the disgust he felt for the spectacle. "The acting mission commander certainly has his own priorities," he said, disapproval in his voice. His eyes wandered back to Kate. "Once the weather clears, we'll go out and search for him."

"What if it doesn't?" asked Kate. "These storms can last a month. The one back in 2032 went for almost six. His air'll run out in ten days."

"Hey," said Glenn, his voice steady and reassuring, "what is it you tell me? One step at a time. Odds are this storm will end soon, in which case all your worrying will have been for nothing."

Maybe Glenn was right. Maybe the weather would clear soon. Perhaps it was clearing as they spoke. Kate activated her wrist comm. "Hey, Miriam, any updates on the storm?"

Clacks and taps came through the open channel. "It's still dangerous outside, but there is one new development," said Miriam. "Latest satellite imagery shows an opening in the storm, sort of like the eye of a hurricane.

The official forecast says it'll skirt by us, but there's a forty-one percent chance it'll sweep over our location."

"What's the timeframe?" asked Kate.

More taps. "Roughly this time tomorrow. I'll have a better idea of what we're looking at in eighteen hours."

"Keep me apprised." Kate's attention returned to Glenn. "Even if that opening doesn't pass directly overhead, it may calm things enough for us to start a search."

"If it's still whiteout conditions, I'm going to recommend against it," said Glenn.

"If it seems like our only opportunity, I may have to take it under advisement," said Kate.

"Excuse me?"

The shout came from the center of the room, where Julian and Casey sat at their table. Casey shot to her feet, her face a ball of anger.

Julian blinked at the astrobiologist with a bewildered look. He rose, spewing an unintelligible stream of words.

Casey slapped Julian, a loud thwack on the cheek. It silenced him. "And just so there's no confusion in the future, I find you disgusting. I wouldn't sleep with you if you were the last man on Mars." She snatched her jacket from the chair back and stormed out of the hall.

Julian remained frozen for several moments before landing back in his seat. He drained the last few drops of his drink, his eyes lingering on his empty glass.

"It's gonna be a long year," said Glenn.

8

Kate huddled with Miriam in the HAAB's cramped, windowless control room, studying the latest photo from the Mars weather satellite. The image, an expanse of curdled cloud tops, filled the three-meter-wide central monitor, bathing the darkened space in orange light.

"That area to the southwest is the Cydonia region," said Miriam, pointing at the left side of the photo. "The marker is us," she added, aiming her finger at the inverted red teardrop in the center of the clouds, "and that's the break in the storm." She referred to a small section of the Martian landscape visible through a ragged hole in the swirling dust southeast of the marker.

Peering at the image, Kate strained for a sense of the opening's relative size. "You say the break will pass over the HAAB?"

"Or close to it, according to computer projections," said Miriam. "It's almost here and moving rather quickly. Once it arrives, we're looking at maybe twenty minutes of calm."

Kate studied every feature within the roughly circular window through the storm, praying for a miraculous sighting of Cheney's tan Mars suit among the smattering of rocks. They'd received neither sign of nor signal from the lost astronaut since returning to the HAAB the day before. What would they discover when the weather lifted? A grateful Joseph Cheney, safe where he'd sheltered in place? Or possibly nothing at all, the man disappeared without a trace. *Even that wouldn't be the worst outcome*, thought Kate. Until they found Cheney, he could still be alive. The worst result lay between the two extremes: a Mars suit facedown in the dirt, its occupant motionless, like the images that continued to haunt her dreams.

"It's thirty-five minutes to sundown," said Miriam. "It'll be dark when the storm whips up again."

Commander Holman ignored the station chief, continuing to study the hole in the storm. The Manual frowned on nighttime excursions, concerned that disoriented astronauts would get lost in the black. But breaking that rule offered a chance at closure, the opportunity to end her distress over Cheney's fate. "We don't have much choice."

"Now you're sounding like Julian," said Miriam.

Kate didn't disagree. "This might be the only chance we get before the storm subsides," she said. Hearing the words helped build her resolve.

"You can't go out there alone."

"I know," she said, after a wan smile. The Manual was more insistent about solo excursions: it explicitly forbade them, day or night. But entering the storm, no matter the time of day, would be extremely dangerous for a two-person team. She couldn't order another astronaut to accompany her on a high-risk trip. She wouldn't compound their problems by endangering an additional life.

"And even if you could go, I doubt Julian will allow it," said Miriam.

"He doesn't have to know?" Kate's eyes begged for understanding.

"You know that's—"

"What if it were you out there?" asked Kate. "What if you were hurt, or your suit was on the fritz, and we had a chance to bring you in?"

"I wouldn't want you to die trying to save me," said Miriam.

"And I won't die trying to save Cheney," said Kate. "Between the break in the storm and my suit nav, I'll be OK." Her assurances seemed not to satisfy Miriam. "I'll start a twenty-minute timer once I'm outside. If I don't find anything, I come right back in."

Miriam blinked at Kate but didn't launch a fresh protest.

"Promise me you won't tell anyone," said Kate.

"Promise me you'll turn around when the timer hits ten."

"I promise," said Kate, raising her hand as if swearing an oath. She would definitely turn around at the halfway point, if the situation warranted it. If her gut told her another five minutes of searching might be best, or perhaps ten … she'd have to assess that in real time. "Thank you, Miriam." The commander bolted out of the control room.

Back in her cell, Kate slipped into her Mars suit's black inner thermal skin and pulled on the bulkier tan outer layer. She worked fast, skeptical Miriam would keep quiet about her plans. She couldn't have Julian stopping her.

Kate snatched her helmet and darted out of her cell. At tube's end, she poked her head into the Spine—empty. She dashed for the airlock, moving quick as she could, encumbered by her suit. She avoided glancing down adjoining tubeways as she passed, worried her eyes might meet another astronaut's.

Reaching the Spine's end, Kate praised her luck at not being caught. She opened the heavy inner airlock door and jumped at the sight of the figure standing inside the chamber, their arms crossed in disapproval. Her instincts had been right—Miriam couldn't keep quiet.

"You can't go out there by yourself." Glenn faced her in the center of the airlock, fully outfitted in his Mars suit with his helmet attached.

"You can't go," said Kate. She donned her own helmet and secured the clasps. "I can't risk anyone else's life by asking them to come with me."

"You're not," said Glenn. "I'm coming without you asking."

"Glenn—"

"Rescuing Cheney is one thing, but doing it while breaking all the rules is no way to go about it," said Glenn. "We need you to come back alive. The odds of that are pretty shitty if you try this alone." He strode to the inner airlock door and closed it. "Now c'mon, let's get out there. Miriam said we won't have a lot of time."

"Curse you, Miriam," said Kate over a private channel to the control room.

"Good luck, Commander," said Miriam. "And remember, ten minutes, then you turn right back around. Not a second more, or I alert Julian."

Irritated, Kate muted the channel. Her whole plan was getting worse by the minute. Being saddled with Glenn was bad enough. Would Miriam actually tell Julian if she didn't start back in time? Hopefully she wouldn't have to find out. Kate stepped to the airlock's exit and punched the large red egress button. The chamber evacuated its air and slid aside its heavy door.

The two astronauts stepped from the airlock into a swirling world of twilight and dust, the bright beams of their wrist-mounted flashlights sparkling off the mineral-infused grit in the air. The reddish, compacted earth outside the HAAB fanned out for three meters before disappearing beneath the storm's fog.

Kate reopened her comm line to Miriam. "When does the break arrive?"

"You're standing in it," said Miriam. Kate stared in confusion at the roiling mess, what she'd imagined would be a clear patch of calm. "Move fast, Commander—it's only going to get worse."

Commander Holman switched to the broadcast channel. "Let's go."

"One sec," said Glenn. "Set a twenty-minute timer," he commanded his suit. He looked over at Kate. "Miriam told me about your promise."

Frowning at the remark, Kate hoisted the emergency locater from its strap at her waist and flipped on the power. The device's soft amber screen came alive. She tapped the rubbery buttons on its keypad, adjusting its sensitivity settings.

"With Cheney's transponder, it shouldn't take long for us to locate his body," said Glenn. Mortification flashed across his face. "I mean, to find him, wherever he is."

So Glenn believed Cheney was dead. All his affirmations about the missing astronaut being alive had been so much idle talk. Kate fought back a fresh rush of despair as she concentrated on her task, holding the tracker at arm's length and swinging it in a broad arc from south to west. The device flashed red. She swept the scanner a second time—no change.

"Of course, that's assuming this thing can pierce the storm's electrical interference," said Glenn.

Anxious to find Cheney, Kate's previous sweeps had been quick. She scanned again, moving slower, taking more time. Halfway along the scanner's arc, the light above its screen turned solid green. She held it steady. "Got him," she said. "He's five hundred meters that way."

They headed off at a brisk pace in the direction of the transponder beacon, sticking close to each other as the remnants of twilight gave way to night. Their helmets, infused with a warm yellow, bobbed like fireflies in the darkness. Kate, in no mood for small talk, appreciated Glenn's silence. He was probably focused on keeping up.

After nineteen minutes of slogging through the storm-churned Martian wilderness, the countdown timer chimed. Kate disregarded it, barreling into the growing wind.

Glenn held up. "We have to start back, Commander. We'll be overdue as it is."

"We're close," said Kate. Too close to start back right then. "Another ten or twenty meters." She proceeded, unsure if Glenn followed and hesitant to find out. She stole a glance by swinging her flashlight wide to the left and turning her head, pretending to track the beam while in fact peeking to her rear. Glenn hadn't said a word but had resumed the search. He stumbled along a little over a meter behind.

Kate's heart thumped in her chest. They'd soon locate Cheney, soon resolve the mystery of what happened to their colleague. She staggered forward in the wind and dust, her flashlight beam nearly doused by the gale.

A rise emerged a few meters ahead, not black like the basalt rock that dotted the landscape but reddish, a solitary pile of Martian dirt the wind should have long ago swept away. She drew closer, the lump lightening in color to a mix of tan and red. The top of the mound took on a rounded shape, the contour of a shoulder.

Glenn and Kate scrambled to the mound, Cheney's crumpled form. They crouched beside their lost crew mate who lay on his side, entombed in windswept rusted soil. The two Mars astronauts dug into the dirt, scooping it with their gloves.

"His comm module's busted," said Glenn, nodding at a white, palm-sized dome of thin mesh at the top left of Cheney's breather pack. A large dent consumed most of the unit, and its antenna dangled from a wire that ran to the slender coil's original attachment point. "Explains why we couldn't reach him from the HAAB."

She glanced at the damaged module but didn't reply, more concerned with assessing Cheney's state. Working together, they removed most of the surrounding dirt, enough to roll the limp astronaut onto his back. Within the churning wind and dust, Kate aimed her light beam at the man's helmet. A layer of red earth covered the ovoid. Glenn swiped the faceplate. They both froze as Cheney stared at them with an air of astonishment, thick lips gently parted, his open eyes unmoving.

Kate wanted to look away but couldn't, felt she shouldn't. Her mind flowed like molasses as her body stiffened with shock.

"Miriam, we found Cheney," Glenn mustered into his comm. "He's dead."

"I …eed you …o to get …ack here, pronto," said Miriam. Her voice was choppy, the transmission having difficulty piercing the storm. "Kate broke her …omise to …e, and … you're … amount of danger."

Kate's fingers started for Cheney's face. She sent them a short distance before catching herself—the dead man's eyes couldn't be closed, inaccessible behind a shield of glass.

Glenn placed his hand on Kate's arm—she shuddered at his touch. "We need to go," he said.

"Help me move him," said Kate.

"He's dead, Kate," said Glenn. "Taking him back with us isn't going to change that."

"Help me move him anyway," she said.

"You heard Miriam," said Glenn. "We needed to start back a while ago. Carrying him will only slow us down."

"I'm not leaving him," said Kate. "Not a second time."

"We can come back for him when the storm's over," said Glenn.

Kate ignored him. She crawled to Cheney's head, his face upside down as she gazed upon him from above. Burrowing her hands beneath his shoulders, she grabbed at his armpits and stood. She managed to lift the astronaut's torso and drag the lifeless body a meter before she had to stop. She adjusted her grip and dragged anew. Her heart filled with grief as she struggled to move her dead colleague's remains.

The body flew out of her hands.

Glenn threw Cheney over his shoulder. "I've got him," he said. Kate began to push back, but he cut her off with a shake of his head. Even allowing for his slight build, Cheney and his suit had to weigh sixty pounds in Mars's lighter gravity. Glenn seemed to handle the weight well enough on his muscular frame. "Lead us back."

Kate looked off in the direction she'd thought they'd come. She was greeted by a black wall of Martian night. The wind had grown stronger over the past five minutes, punctuated by powerful gusts that peppered them with sand. The break in the weather had moved on, giving way to the storm's full brunt. She activated her suit nav.

"Calculating route," her suit replied in its faintly artificial lilt. Seconds ticked by, many more than usual. "Unable to determine route," the system reported finally, relaying the error in red letters on her heads-up display.

"Glenn," said Kate, her voice quavering, "my suit nav can't determine the way back."

Glenn blinked at her, stunned by the news. "Lemme check mine," he said. Seconds passed. His suit's response bathed his face in red light. "No luck." He looked skyward, as if attempting to peer through the storm's blanket. "Damn planet's basically a giant ball of rusted iron." He batted at the whorls of dust dancing nearby. "All this ferromagnetic material is blocking the signals from the GPS satellites."

Without their suit navs, they couldn't get back to the HAAB. They'd be stranded in the storm, lost like Cheney. "Miriam, our suit navs aren't working," said Kate. "Miriam?" A minute ago, their connection with the station chief had been spotty. Now, there was no answer at all. Kate's stomach dropped. "Let me try my nav again."

"Go ahead if you like," said Glenn as he lowered Cheney to the ground, "but I don't think it'll come back online until the storm dies down." He dropped to one knee and settled next to the body. "Did Miriam have an estimate on how long it'll last?"

A day. A week. A month. The models hadn't existed long enough to accurately predict weather on the red planet. "Unable to determine route," the computer replied in Kate's ear. "Dammit," she said.

"You may as well have a seat," said Glenn. "I think we're gonna be here awhile."

Kate resisted the idea, but eventually joined her second-in-command on the ground, amid the wailing dust and wind. Her head hung, weighed down by their predicament. Because of her, both she and Glenn were lost out in the storm, a storm which had already taken a life in less than a day. Would that be their fate as well?

"I'm sure Miriam's trying everything she can to reach us," said Glenn.

"She's probably crapping a brick," muttered Kate, sinking further into sadness as she envisioned the panic she'd likely inflicted on the station chief.

"I wonder if she's informed our mission commander yet," said Glenn.

"*Acting* mission commander," Kate huffed. The reminder that Julian had been handed her command was the last thing she wanted to hear.

"Do you really think we'll be calling him 'acting' mission commander a year from now?" asked Glenn.

Kate's head shot up, her icy glare lancing Glenn's innocent expression. He was so clueless sometimes about the right and wrong things to say in the moment. He'd meant no harm, but she couldn't restrain her erupting anger. "No, we won't be calling him 'acting' mission commander a year from now," she seethed. "I'm gonna get my command back long before then. *I* was the one who trained two years for the position, not him. Julian's barely qualified to pick his nose, much less lead this mission." She grabbed a handful of Martian soil and flung it into the storm. "I've already messaged the AD about it. I refuse to stand by and let thirty years of my life spiral down the drain."

Glenn raised an eyebrow. "You've been on the Mars mission since you were nine?"

"What do you think?" snapped Kate. The commander regretted her sarcasm. She took a second to bring her anger under control. "Ever since I was little, I felt I was destined for something big. When I was eight years old, my grandma and I watched the Chinese launch the first of their Kuàng mining spacecraft to the asteroid belt."

"I remember that launch," said Glenn. "The director of NASA was in a little box on the screen as the cameras followed the rocket into the sky. He was downplaying the whole thing, said there was little interesting science left to pursue with asteroids." Glenn shook his head. "They canned him the next day."

Kate nodded. "Even my grandma saw how that launch would spur all space-capable countries to stake claims across the solar system, how it would set off the second space race. She said to me then, 'For the US, there's nothing bigger now than space.' That's how I latched on to the idea."

"Of going to Mars?" asked Glenn.

"No," said Kate, exasperated, "of becoming an astronaut. Only later, when they announced the Ares mission, did I jump at the chance to lead the first team of people here."

Glenn leaned back, his arms angled straight behind him, palms flat on the ground. "So what comes next?" he asked.

"What do you mean?"

"After this mission's over," said Glenn. "You said you felt destined for something big—I'd say this certainly counts. What will you do with your life once you achieve your dream of thirty years, when you're back home?"

She'd considered the question at times over the years, more frequently as the crowning achievement of her career had approached. "I plan to spend time with my children."

Glenn laughed, a guffaw that rattled Kate's ears as it reverberated within her helmet. His reaction dissipated quickly. "I'm sorry," he said to the commander's scowl. "I really thought you were joking." His expression shifted from jovial to contrite. "It's just that it'll be such a big change: Kate Holman, former Mars mission commander, the newest stay-at-home mom."

"Ben would tell you that being a mom is the most important job in the world." One of the many arguments she and her ex-husband used to have.

"Sarah and I decided not to even think about children while I'm on active duty," said Glenn. "We're going to start a family when I get back from this mission."

"Kids were never part of the plan for us either," said Kate. "Amelia was an accident. Ben didn't want his daughter to be an only child, so we had Ben Jr. four years later." Her children's faces came rushing back from the day's video update. Ben Jr. looked miserable, asking again when she'd be home. And Amelia had calculated the seconds until the *Gaia* capsule's splashdown. She declared it the largest number she'd ever seen. "Having children really changes your perspective. I needed this mission for me, but after it's over, I owe it to them to be around, to be a mom." Kate thought a bit and laughed.

"What's funny?" asked Glenn.

"Nothing," said Kate, shaking her head. "I realized as dangerous as this job is, the only real fear I have is my children growing up without a mother. I'm sure they worry about it too, well, at least Amelia. Ben Jr.'s too young to really understand." Their faces appeared in her mind's eye. "Such a burden for a child to carry. And with all the risks we take, such a huge chance that it might come true."

Dust eddies danced around Glenn, the storm's intensity increasing. "At least the riskiest part of this mission is over," he said. "We landed safely on Mars. Now we sit back and relax for a year … that is, if we don't die out here in this storm."

If they didn't die? Kate grew silent, pondering the prospect she'd managed to push out of her mind, the real possibility the storm could take their lives. They *had* survived the riskiest part of the mission. What irony to die a few days later, not half a kilometer from the station.

"We'll make it back to the HAAB," said Glenn, likely noticing the consternation his words had triggered. "And for what it's worth, you deserve to be mission commander." He grinned, his annoying sign of sincerity bursting forth. "If there's anything I can do to help you get your job back from Julian, just ask."

Despite Glenn's penchant for saying the wrong thing, he did have a good heart. Kate had learned that much during the years training together for the mission. "You're a good friend," she said.

"Thanks," said Glenn, "but mostly I don't want to take orders from that prick for a whole—" A fuzzy smudge appeared on his heads-up display. He fell quiet, studying the image.

Kate scrutinized the smudge, trying to make sense of what his suit could be showing him. The sight was strange, too faint and delicate for an image rendered on an LED screen. It was also off-center, one side stretching past his faceplate, beyond the bounds of his helmet's display ....

The fuzzy smudge wasn't inside Glenn's helmet; it was a reflection. Kate turned: a dim, luminous white cloud hovered in the distance.

"You see it, too," said Glenn. "I thought it was a mirage."

"Definitely not a mirage," she said as she stood, angling for a better view. No natural light sources existed on Mars. The glow had to be manmade. "I think it's the HAAB's exterior floods."

Glenn rose to his feet. "You're right," he said, grinning. "Miriam just saved our asses."

"And I'm sure we'll never hear the end of it," said Kate. She offered a silent thanks to the resourceful station chief. "Let's go, before something happens to the flood lamps, too."

"Roger that," said Glenn, hoisting Cheney's limp body over his shoulders. The two set off across the Martian black, dashing for the far-off glimmer of home.

9

Doctor Palmer offered no words as Kate and Glenn arrived at the medbay with Cheney's body. Palmer's vibrant blue eyes greeted them through thick-rimmed glasses perched above his reassuring physician's smile. With his six-foot frame and chiseled jaw, he'd been called "Clark Kent" more than once. "Man of Steel" was also apropos, given his unflinchingly calm demeanor.

The two astronauts, still clad in their Mars suits, lumbered to the center of the modest space. Glenn hoisted Cheney onto the examination table. Dr. Palmer donned a pair of medical gloves and moved to the far side. Red soil covered Cheney's suit from torso to legs, and condensation fogged the inside of his helmet's faceplate. He lay in an awkward backbend that thrust his chest so far into the air his head dangled. The doctor unclasped straps that ran around each shoulder, rolled the dead man on his side, and removed his breather pack. He let Cheney settle again onto the table, this time resting flat on his back.

Palmer loosened the connector at Cheney's right glove and tugged. A pale hand emerged from the suit sleeve, the nail beds a cadaverous blue. The doctor clipped a medical scanner to the index finger, prompting the examination table to speak in a tinny, artificial voice: "Patient Joseph Cheney, Mission Specialist. Condition: deceased. Body temperature four degrees centigrade."

"Huh," said Palmer, "I'd expected frozen solid."

"The suit's still functional," said Glenn. "As long as there's power in the cells, it's designed to keep its occupant at a comfortable temperature."

"Four degrees isn't exactly balmy," said Palmer. He traveled to the head of the table and slid his hands to Cheney's neck. His fingers manipulated the clasps that secured the helmet to the suit. "I understand our acting mission commander won't be paying a visit," continued the doctor without looking up from his task. "Wonder if he'd do *me* the courtesy, if this were *me* lying on the table."

Kate didn't disagree with the sentiment. She'd implored Julian to meet them at the airlock, warning his apparent lack of interest would send the wrong message to the crew. Julian insisted he was indisposed. How could he not see his duty to at least spend a moment with the man who died carrying out his orders? Maybe if she'd been more blunt, he would've reconsidered—probably not. Their acting mission commander seemed strangely indifferent to the well-being and concerns of the *Ares* astronauts.

Applying slow twists, Palmer worked the helmet back and forth. In an instant, it jerked free of the suit, causing the doctor to stumble backwards. Head liberated from its protective shell, Cheney stared unblinking into the bright lamps above the table. Fleshy lips, a muted shade of blue, parted slightly. Palmer examined the dead man's eyes, opened his mouth, and checked inside his nose.

"Whaddya think happened, Doctor?" asked Glenn. "I mean, that led to his death?"

Palmer turned Cheney's head to either side, inspecting his ears. "The suit should have kept his body at room temperature but only managed a few degrees above zero. That suggests a containment problem." He raised Cheney's right arm and ran his gloved hand over the Mars suit's tan fabric, stroking it smooth. He repeated with the left arm and continued along the rib cage and abdomen. Working his way to the foot of the table, he flattened the material covering the fronts of Cheney's legs. "Here," he said to Glenn, "help me turn him over."

The two men inserted their hands carefully under Cheney and lifted, rolling him up and over. They gently resettled the body on its front.

"What's that?" asked Glenn, pointing to a line of caked red dirt at the back of Cheney's left leg, mid-thigh.

Dr. Palmer brushed the dirt away, revealing an opening in Cheney's suit, a slit about ten centimeters wide.

"Is it a tear?" asked Glenn.

"The edges are too smooth," said Palmer. "It's more like a cut." The doctor pried the hole open with his fingers. A metallic weave showed through several additional sliced layers. "Was he carrying any kind of tool that could've done this by accident?"

Glenn pursed his lips at the suggestion. "You're poking your fingers through two layers of Kevlar, Doctor. It would have to have been pretty sharp to do something like that, in one go anyway."

"Could he have cut his leg on a rock?" asked Palmer.

"He could've fallen backwards, I guess," said Glenn. "But it would have been an incredibly sharp rock to cut through all those layers of suit."

Palmer's brow furled. "This breach wouldn't have incapacitated him, at least not immediately," he said. "Why didn't he radio his situation?"

"His comm was also damaged," said Glenn. "That must've happened before his suit lost containment; otherwise, I imagine he would've called out for help."

The doctor dug through a pouch on the side of Cheney's leg, fishing out a clear plastic bag with several tan swatches of material and a slender tube of adhesive. "His emergency kit's intact," said Palmer. "Why didn't he attempt a patch?"

"Maybe he couldn't reach the tear," said Glenn. "Or maybe during all this he was knocked unconscious."

Palmer studied the dead astronaut's skull. "I didn't notice any sign of head trauma. That—"

The table interrupted: "Patient Joseph Cheney, cause of death: inconclusive."

"Damn," said Palmer, "I was hoping I'd get lucky with the scanner. Now I'll have to perform a full autopsy."

"Why do you need an autopsy?" asked Glenn. "Seems like the cause of death was asphyxiation due to containment breach."

"That's what I assumed too, but the scanner doesn't think so," said Palmer. "It thinks there's a different cause but doesn't have a clue what." He removed Cheney's other glove and examined his hand and fingers.

"You OK, Commander?"

Glenn's question jarred Kate. She hadn't spoken since their arrival at the medbay, entranced by the lifeless body as she pictured the astronaut's last moments. Based on where they'd found him, Cheney wouldn't have been more than ten minutes from the HAAB. He hadn't wandered off or gotten lost in the storm. He'd gone down just off the green line back to the station. "I walked right past him," she said, her voice quiet and quavering. "Walked right past him while he was gasping for air."

"It was whiteout conditions," said Glenn. "There's no way you could've seen him even a meter off the trail."

"What were we doing out there in the first place?" Kate asked, tearing up. "If we had stayed here at the HAAB, Cheney's suit would never have been cut. He would still be alive."

"Cheney was out there on Julian's orders," said Dr. Palmer. "Julian knew the risks."

"So did I," Kate muttered.

"But Julian was in charge," said Glenn. "In the end, it was his call."

"I should've insisted they stay."

"It wouldn't have stopped him from leaving," said Glenn. "He was hellbent on getting out there. The way that S.O.B. runs this show, if you had done any more to try to stop him, all you would've seen for your troubles is a written reprimand and confinement to quarters."

Glenn was probably right, though his reassurances provided little solace. An astronaut from her mission, *her* mission, had died. She'd failed in her vow to keep them all safe. "Thank you, Doctor. Please inform me of developments." She glanced a final time at Cheney and drifted from the medbay.

10

Commander Holman meandered down the Spine, head hung and spirits low. Once at her cell, she changed out of her Mars suit and settled onto her couch. The storm raged outside, flinging dust against her compartment's bay window.

Kate let her head fall back. She couldn't just sit there, alone with her thoughts. She needed to get out of her cell. The DFAC was out of the question—she'd either be consoled or feel the room's eyes on her.

Maybe she would pay Fisk a visit. For all his annoying chatter, sitting with him was better than the other options. She'd also deliver the update on Cheney herself.

Kate left her quarters, head lowered and with a determined gait, hoping to avoid engaging anyone along the way. She dashed down the Spine and into the tubeway that hosted Fisk's cell, stopping at the first door on the right. She stood outside in the low light, reconsidering her plan. Getting out of her cell felt good, but was she really up for conversation? Before Kate could start back, some part of her willed her hand up and mashed her finger to the button. A muffled chime sounded through the station's thin panels.

No response.

She pressed the button again.

Soft shuffling carried from the other side of the door. "Who is it?"

"It's Commander Holman."

A pause. "Yes?"

He didn't sound interested in visitors. She barreled ahead anyway. "I have some news about Cheney. I was wondering if I could come in."

Another pause, then a sliding bolt. The door opened a sliver. Fisk's eyes appeared in the dark crack. "Who else is with you?" he asked.

"No one," said Kate to the odd question.

Fisk pulled the door open far enough to stick his head out into the tube. He scanned the corridor, apparently unsatisfied with the commander's assurance. Returning to the shadows of the foyer, Fisk opened the door wider and motioned her inside. She'd barely cleared the threshold when the door slammed closed behind her, followed by the "chunk" of the deadbolt's slide.

Fisk's cell was a cave, the glow from a computer monitor and a nightlight near the apartment's small galley providing the only illumination. Kate picked her way through boxes and equipment strewn along the entry, eyes adjusting as she made her way to the couch. She dodged a stack of clothing on the floor and nudged a pile of undergarments, condition unknown, that straddled the cushions. She sat with her knees angled in and arms drawn tight to her body, minimizing her chances of brushing against the muddle.

"Would you like some tea?" asked Fisk.

A silhouetted skyline of plates, bowls, and open food containers extended across the galley's countertop in the dim light, a mess that had bloomed after only two days on Mars. Kate shuddered to think what Fisk's apartment looked like on Earth. "Sure," she said, gambling he'd have a clean coffee cup. "Earl Grey."

Fisk grabbed a mug from a cabinet, filled it with water, and loaded it into his galley's small microwave. While the water heated, he fished a tea bag from an open drawer beneath the countertop.

At the microwave's chime, Fisk removed the mug and dropped the tea bag inside. He handed the drink to Kate, then settled into the rolling chair at his desk and swiveled around to face her. "What's the news about Cheney?" he asked, scooting closer.

Kate bobbed the tea bag. Steam buffeted her face as she peered into the mug, fighting to maintain her composure. "The storm let up enough for us to go back outside," she said. She struggled for the next words. "We found Cheney." Kate forced herself to look up from her tea. "He was dead."

"Oh," said Fisk. His expression shifted from surprise to confusion. "I thought he had a decent chance of survival."

"He did," said Kate. "Seems there was a containment issue with his suit." Fisk stared listlessly at her, lips parted. He was taking the news hard. "Are you OK?" she asked.

"I'm fine," he muttered through a daze. "I just wish I knew what it's all about …."

What it's all about … the meaning of life?

"Those damn triangles," he said, answering her inquiring look.

"Triangles ...?" asked Kate. Had she missed something about Cheney when they brought him in? No, that couldn't be it—Fisk hadn't seen any images of the deceased astronaut.

"Yes, the triangles," he said absently. "They're all I see when I close my eyes."

He wasn't talking about Cheney, hadn't fallen into despair at the news of his death—Fisk meant the rod, the strange silver artifact they'd discovered in the cave. His mind had returned to solving the riddle of the bar's origin and purpose. Kate scanned the room for the item. It wasn't visible anywhere, at least not amid the clutter and dim light. "Have you made any progress figuring out what it is?"

Fisk emerged from his trance. "Nothing I'm ready to discuss, but I'm optimistic I'll have news soon." The professor looked crazed in the backlight of the computer monitor, a fevered expression and hair erupting in tufts above his ears. "You haven't mentioned it to Julian?"

"I haven't seen him since we've been back."

"Good. Let's make sure it stays between you and me." He sat forward in his chair and dropped his voice to a whisper. "Julian might try to kill us if he discovers what we found. The fewer people who know, the better."

Kate cocked her head. "You don't literally mean 'kill.'"

"I do," said Fisk. "After our trip to the Face, I did some digging on our acting mission commander. It wasn't easy, by the way. I had to get help from my friend back home to dodge the search filters."

"Search filters?" asked Kate.

"You think no one's monitoring our searches?" asked Fisk.

Kate had never considered the possibility. They'd been advised to use the network judiciously, and to refrain from movie streaming and porn. Did anyone really care if she searched for the latest Phoenix Suns basketball score?

"The thirty-minute round-trip latency between here and home, they take advantage of that," said Fisk. "They stick a literal man in the middle. If they don't like what we're looking for, they cancel the search. To us, it silently fails, and there isn't a damn thing we can do about it. If you think debugging a glitch with the IT department was bad on Earth, it's next to impossible way out here."

"You have any proof they're monitoring us?" asked Kate.

Fisk dismissed her question with a wave of his hand. "I don't need evidence," he said. "We're on a secret mission. Surveillance is standard operating procedure." He relaxed back into his chair. "I could tell Julian was a bad seed the minute I met him. I tried digging up info on him then, but the searches came back empty. Knowing that Cheney was in on the conspiracy allowed the Snow Owl to make some cross-references." The geologist extended his arm behind him, fishing blindly for something on his desk.

Snow Owl?

"My friend back home," said Fisk, reading the question from Kate's face. "The person I mentioned on our way to look for Julian. 'Snow Owl' is what he calls himself. And now that you know, I need you to forget I ever said his code name. It's supposed to be a secret." He thrust his hand out to her with a self-congratulatory grin. "Take a look at this."

Kate took the item he'd retrieved, a slip of paper with the letters "SF" in its center. "What's this?"

"That's the message from my friend."

"This is the message—the *entire* message?"

"Yup," said Fisk, with a smile and a nod. "We have a very low-bandwidth communication channel. It allows us to bypass the watchers but makes long messages tedious. We aim to keep our exchanges short." He wagged his finger at the slip. "Guess what it means."

Kate wracked her brain, searching for how the two letters could possibly relate to some significant aspect of Julian's past. "San Francisco?" she finally ventured.

"No," scoffed Fisk. "Turns out the whole bit about Julian being an Air Force pilot is a bunch of bullshit. He's actually an active-duty member of the Space Force."

Kate massaged her temples as she contended with Fisk's wild ravings. "You deduced all that from those two letters. That Julian is a member of the Space Force, an active member, which means he's been lying all this time about being in the Air Force?"

Fisk beamed. "Yep."

"Seems like a stretch," she said.

"What else could it mean?" asked Fisk. "My friend is very thorough and has lots of connections. He certainly wouldn't bother sending an inconsequential message about Frisco."

Fisk was talking nonsense. His paranoid streak had surfaced during training, but she hadn't paid it much mind. Their trip to the Face seemed to have fanned his delusions. "Let's pretend those two letters mean exactly what you say they do, that Julian's not an Air Force pilot, that he's a soldier in the Space Force. How does that change anything?"

"It changes *everything!*" said Fisk, spittle flying. "Members of Space Force are ruthless killers, almost mercenaries. The only conflict they ever fought in had accusations of death squads and hooded executions. They don't give a whig about anyone tangential to their mission." He wiped saliva from his mouth with the back of his hand. "We're being led by a man who likely considers us expendable." Fisk's eyes darted around the room, as if confirming they were still alone. "If he's lying about his past, what else is he lying about? And what would he do if someone came close to blowing his cover? I have to believe killing is on the short list. Look at what happened to Cheney."

"Cheney's death was an accident," said Kate.

"Was it?"

Kate never imagined otherwise. The notion of Julian killing Cheney was borderline insanity, an unhinged suggestion based on no facts at all. "Whatever this secret op is," she said, "the two of them were working on it together. It's not like Cheney would've stumbled on to some information he didn't already have."

Fisk's eyes twitched. He was struggling to reconcile his ravings with her logic, like a computer on the verge of crashing under an enormous load. He was a lot less stable than she'd realized. She regretted dragging him to the Face. Being cooped up in his cell was probably worsening his condition. She needed to get him out among the living. "Why don't we go hang for a bit in the DFAC? Let me beat you at cards."

"Can't you see we're flying blind?" pleaded Fisk. "Without understanding what this op's all about, we don't know what the stakes are. Our only clue right now is the rod—it has to be connected somehow." The geologist brought his palms flat to his face and rubbed his eyes. "I can't join you out there because I don't have time for anything else."

Fisk had grown agitated during her visit. She wouldn't fan it further. She sipped from her mug, stood, and placed her hand on his shoulder. "I should be getting back to my duties."

"Of course, Commander," said Fisk. He escorted her to the door.

Was it a good idea to leave him in his current mental state? What else could she do, short of reporting him to Dr. Palmer? If Fisk was right about having answers soon, perhaps the situation would work itself out. Perhaps his disposition would improve once they got past the whole mystery of the rod. "Fisk," she said, pausing in the foyer, "please let me know if I can do anything."

"Just be ready to come back here when I crack it," said Fisk. He laid his finger aside his nose. "Watch for my signal."

11

Kate surveyed the freshly plowed rows of processed Martian earth, her face full of frustration.

Day three of the raging dust storm filtered the noonday sun, leaving only weak red light to drift in through the Greenhouse's glass panels. The paltry rays weren't concerning—even on a clear day, Mars lacked the solar radiation to keep most food crops alive. They could raise their vegetables and greens with farm lamps if they needed. What they couldn't do was grow plants without water.

"I've got a million other places to be, Commander," said Allison Voss as she marched into the Greenhouse, hands buried in her jumpsuit pockets. "What's up?"

"I was hoping you can tell me," said Kate. She gestured at the parcel of reddish dirt. "We've got seeds in the ground, ready to grow. All we need is some water."

"You have to activate the irrigation system," said Voss in a patronizing, impatient tone as she started for the control station.

"I did," said Kate. Did she really think she didn't understand how the Greenhouse worked? More likely, it was Voss being her usual, less-than-personable self. The child of two psychiatry professors, Voss and her siblings had grown up in a household of psych experiments and mind games. She'd once described how her mother and father would hold contests to see how long they all could go without speaking to each other. Allison was a brilliant engineer, but not always pleasant to be around. "I've also run the diagnostics twice," added Kate. "System keeps saying the valves are open, only there's no water coming out."

"Probably something simple you overlooked," said Voss.

Kate didn't appreciate the condescension but preferred not to get into it. Hopefully the station engineer would just fix the problem, and she could be on her way.

Voss tapped the control panel, a computer touchscreen mounted on the Greenhouse wall. She navigated to manual irrigation and pushed a set of three sliders. After a fruitless wait for water despite wide-open valves, she ran and reran the diagnostics—no change.

"See what I mean," said Kate, vindicated with Voss reaching the same dead end as she had, and unable to resist making that point, if subtly.

Voss groped under the touchscreen for the power cable and pulled. "Sometimes these systems need to know who's boss." She waited a few seconds and reconnected the cable. When the unit booted into the main screen, she swiped to the manual override pane and pushed the flow control sliders again. "Check it now."

"Still nothing," said Kate, hoisting the end of the dry irrigation tube she'd earlier fished from the dirt.

"All my life is dealing with systems designed by idiots," grumbled Voss as she crouched beneath the touchscreen. She inserted her thumbs in two tabs embedded in the wall and removed an access panel, exposing a cavity filled with red pipes. "I was right," she said. "It *was* something simple you overlooked."

Behind a panel Kate didn't know existed?

"The Greenhouse is shut off from the mains," continued Voss.

"Why would it be shut off?" asked Kate. "I thought water's been circulating through the HAAB for the past twelve months."

"Everywhere but here," said Voss. "The Greenhouse is like an open faucet. With no one around, any kind of problem could have flooded the entire station." She grabbed the handle of a large ball valve and tugged.

"That's doing it," shouted Kate as water gushed from the irrigation tube onto her jumpsuit sleeve and front. She dropped the line before the onrush could soak her more.

"Guess one of the genius mission managers missed adding this step to the operational readiness checklist." Voss pressed the panel back into position and joined Kate at the furrows. "Shouldn't be doing *that*, though." Water exited in ragged spurts from the irrigation tube's fretwork of holes.

"Same thing happened in the shower the other day," said Kate. "It's air in the lines."

"Can't be that," said Voss. "It's a closed system."

Kate frowned. "You said yourself the Greenhouse lines haven't had water circulating through them."

"They haven't," said Voss, "but all the air in the Greenhouse lines has already been expelled. The air causing these spurts is coming from farther upstream, but they bled that out at the start of the qualifying trials."

"Seems to be settling down," said Kate. The water flowed from the irrigation tube in steady streams. "Looks like we're in business."

"See how smoothly things go when you don't try to do my job?" said Voss.

"If it ever seems like I'm trying to do your job, it's only 'cause I want to take a crack at solving the problem before roping you in. I know your time is precious." Voss had been irritated at being summoned to the Greenhouse. She didn't warm with Kate's pronouncement. "In any case, you've earned your pay for the day."

"If that's so, I'm taking the rest of the day off." The station engineer didn't seem to be joking.

"I'd give you the month off, if I could," said Kate. "Unfortunately, there are too many other problems that require your attention."

Voss seemed genuinely shocked by the declaration. "For the record, you've admitted I'm underpaid," she grunted. "Don't be surprised if I call you as a witness at my grievance hearing." She thrust her hands into her pockets and headed for the door.

"Hey, Allison," said Kate, stopping the grumpy engineer before she left. "We're all working like crazy to settle in, but try not to let it get you down. Don't forget, this is the trip of a lifetime. There are so many other engineers who would've killed for your spot on this mission."

"That's 'cause the brochure didn't mention traveling fifty-five million kilometers to spend time inside dark crawlspaces sorting through mixed-up tubeway wiring." She resumed her departure, grumbling all the way to the exit. "And to top it all off, there's not an ounce of gin in this rat maze. Probably never occurred to the genius who provisioned this place to send any alcohol 'cause they're still living at home with their parents ...."

Kate watched Voss exit the Greenhouse. She was a pain in the ass at times, but NASA chose her because she was the very best at debugging complex systems. The *Ares* crew was lucky to have her on the mission, even if sometimes it didn't feel that way.

Commander Holman walked to the touchscreen station and switched the system to automated control. With the computer in charge of tilling, planting, watering, light exposure, and soil health, they'd have little to do but harvest the bounty. They could survive without the Greenhouse, but Kate welcomed the addition of fresh vegetables to their diet of freeze-dried and prepackaged food. She tapped her comm on her wrist, opening a channel. "Miriam, this is Kate. You can let Mission Command know the Greenhouse is up and running."

"Roger that, Commander," said Miriam. "I'll also inform Julian."

You do that. Julian had sequestered himself in his cell since returning from the Face, with seemingly little concern for the HAAB's operational readiness. Kate had worked with Voss and the others to complete the final structural checks, and to bring the remaining systems online ... like she was the mission commander. She bristled at the thought of shouldering Julian's responsibilities while he lounged with *her* title in his quarters. "Anything from the AD?"

"Still nothing, ma'am."

No reply to the video message she'd sent two days ago. The lack of real-time communication with Earth unnerved her, but there was nothing to be done. The extreme distance left no other option.

"Maybe he's busy," added Miriam.

So busy he couldn't respond with a timeframe for regaining her command? Unlikely. Short of some other explanation, that meant the AD was ignoring her message. "Or maybe the transmission was lost."

"Everything shows green on our end," said Miriam.

It didn't rule out a problem at Mission Control. Fisk was right, at least, about the challenges of debugging long-distance communication issues. "I'll give it another day," said Kate. "If I don't hear back, I'll resend."

"Very good," said Miriam. "I do have an update on the storm. Latest computer projections show it clearing out in the next twelve to eighteen hours."

"Acknowledged," said Kate. They were waiting for the storm to end to put Cheney in the ground, to say goodbye to their fallen colleague with a proper burial. They could attend to that task tomorrow, a last bit of morbid business before settling in for their stay on the red planet.

12

Fisk and Palmer held Cheney's body aloft while Kate tended to the outer airlock door. Sparkling sunlight greeted them as they filed out onto the manicured, ruddy ground.

Kate stood for a moment outside the airlock, taking in the spectacular view. The mountains and hills to the east sparkled against a vibrant pink sky, the air freshly scrubbed of dust and dirt. *Not unlike Phoenix after a storm,* she thought. She loved the crisp days in her hometown when the rains washed away the smog and grime. If only such a pristine, perfect day didn't have to begin with somber proceedings.

The three marched to a stretch of ground twenty meters from the HAAB's southeast corner, where the other *Ares* astronauts waited. Glenn and Engles stood apart from the rest, at the head of the one-by-two-meter hole they'd hollowed out of the hard earth earlier in the day.

"Need some help?" asked Glenn, greeting Fisk and Palmer as they approached. The two men had handled the chore of carrying Cheney's body with no apparent struggle. Maybe he worried about the tricky task of lowering their departed colleague into the grave without dropping him. He joined in, not waiting for a reply.

Kate replaced Glenn in the spot next to Engles. As long as she'd known the spacecraft engineer, she'd always worn a bandana that matched her mood. She claimed to own thousands but brought "only" a couple hundred with her to Mars. They'd been heavy enough to count against her personal weight allocation for the trip. The day's color was black; she wore the pitch square tied to her skullcap.

"Why here?" asked Engles. Even with the additional bulk of her Mars suit, the slender astronaut appeared as if a strong wind could whisk her away.

"What do you mean?"

"For the grave," said Engles. "Why this spot?"

Kate had chosen the plot, at the back of the HAAB and far from most windows, to avoid a constant reminder of their fallen crew mate. The cool logic of her decision was too dissonant for the moment, a handful of minutes before they'd put a fellow astronaut in the ground. "Julian declined to choose a spot, so the task fell to me." Hopefully she could escape elaborating. "Is there a problem with this location?"

She responded with a tightening of her lips. "No, Commander, just making small talk." Engles hunched forward, managing the weight of her suit ... and something else.

"You OK?" asked Kate.

Engles considered the question. "I don't know," she said with a trace of southern twang. "It's ... it's just ...." Tears raced down her high cheekbones. A quick shake of her head set them flying. "My brother-in-law—my sister's husband—passed away two years ago. He died during a training accident. We were there, my mother and I, at my sister's new house ... there to help her pick wallpaper for the back room. I remember the black car pulling up, the men in their uniforms filing out, hats in their hands ...." Engles's lips tightened again. "My sister, when she saw them come up the drive, she started trembling."

Kate had performed the dreadful driveway walk herself: after her recovery from the incident on the Moon, during her first trip back to Earth. She hadn't been the original bearer of the news, but the moment was no less raw. "I'm sorry," she said, all she could offer in a search for words.

"It's ... it's OK," said Engles, shaking off more tears. "Time heals .... I just ... I know what this kind of loss is like. I wasn't close with Cheney, but I feel for his family." She swallowed—it caught in her throat. "It will be difficult for them ... when they get that call."

Calling on Cheney's family would be difficult too, though officially it wasn't Kate's responsibility. The task fell to Julian, perhaps the worst person for the assignment. When asked about his progress on the eulogy, he declared he'd made none and wouldn't be attending the ceremony. "The living have no time for the dead," he'd said flatly. His statement had been in character, but the words still left her speechless. Kate wasn't close with Cheney either, but she'd find time to reach out to his family after Julian delivered the news.

Palmer, Fisk, and Glenn, still holding their fallen comrade, positioned themselves around the grave. They adjusted their grip on Cheney and carefully lowered him, wrapped in a sheet from the medical center, into the ground. The body settled onto the exposed layer of subsurface ice that covered the planet a meter below the topsoil.

Engles sniffled and picked up a shovel. "I have to help Glenn," she said, and walked to the nearby heap of excavated red soil. The two heaved earth onto the makeshift mummy, fashioning a compact mound. Rather than a tombstone, Glenn erected a small American flag on a short pole. The fifty-two stars and thirteen stripes hung limp in the tranquil air.

Kate set the eulogy scrolling on her heads-up display. With Julian's abdication, she assumed the duty of composing the short speech. She'd originally scoffed at the idea of using one of the Manual's sample tributes, boilerplate sprinkled with "insert name here" fields that reduced the task to filling out a form. She relented in the end—she was no poet, and the moment demanded more than her clumsy prose could provide. "Today, we pay our respects to Mission Specialist Joseph Cheney." The words came out weak and quiet. The commander boosted her voice. "We streak across the heavens like the gods of old, even walk upon alien worlds, but in the end, we are all still mortal. Cheney's death was not in vain, for he died in the pursuit of knowledge and the furtherance of America's expansion to the stars. We honor his sacrifice and his memory, our fallen friend, colleague, countryman, and the first human to perish on Mars." She quickly crossed herself and bowed her head.

Half a minute later, Kate looked up. The others still stood around the burial mound, all with hung heads except for Fisk. The interplanetary geologist stared at her from across the grave, his eyes afire and his wispy hair flailing within his helmet. He pressed his index finger against his faceplate, the end pointing at the sky. Kate followed his finger but found nothing in the clear expanse of Martian butterscotch above.

She glanced at Fisk, who again pointed skyward with his index finger pressed against his faceplate. After a second fruitless scan of the area above him, Kate scowled at the professor. She couldn't decipher his cryptic message and was fed up with trying. "Thank you, everyone," she said.

Heads rose. The *Ares* crew fell into a cheerless, single-file line leading to the airlock. Kate brought up the rear, her boots landing in slow, heavy thuds. There wasn't a more tragic event than putting a fellow astronaut in the ground.

Back in her cell, her terminal chirped—a comm request from Fisk. She tapped open the connection. "Yes?"

"Are you coming?" asked Fisk. His monitor-brightened face hovered before the backdrop of a dark room.

"Coming where?" asked Kate.

"To my quarters," said Fisk. "You got my signal, right?"

"What signal?" asked Kate, her mind still weighed down from Cheney's burial. "I don't know what you're talking about, and I don't feel like—"

"I told you to watch for it," said Fisk as he placed his index finger alongside his nose. "My helmet got in the way, but I thought you understood."

Fisk was babbling nonsense, wearing her patience thin. "Look, today has already started out—"

"I've cracked it," said Fisk, beaming. "Figured it out. Solved it."

"Solved what?"

"The puzzle," he said. "The mystery of the you-know-what that we found you-know-where."

The metal rod from the Face? "You mean the r—"

"No, not over the comm," said Fisk, his eyes ballooning as he headed off the commander. "It's not a secure channel." Not secure? Each comm line featured end-to-end encryption. She started to ask another question, but he cut her off again. "Just come to my cell," he announced, and closed the connection.

He had to have meant the rod, the most likely explanation for his cloak-and-dagger silliness. Kate had arrived at her own opinion on its origin not long after meeting with Fisk in his cell. His obsession with the item had been concerning. The mystery resolved to his satisfaction, he could finally end his time cloistered in his quarters and resume his regular duties. The day was becoming one of closure: they'd said their goodbyes to Cheney, and soon the mania sparked by the rod would end as well.

Upon arriving at Fisk's cell, the geologist silently ushered Kate inside and closed the door. The disarray was an order of magnitude worse than on her previous visit. Articles of clothing lay strewn about the space, like an explosion from a hamper that left fabric shrapnel everywhere. Dirty plates littered most flat surfaces. Scientific equipment sat along the floor, next to the containers that had held it. A monumental mess, but not the biggest shock.

"Hello, Commander." Mission Specialist Casey Morgan waved from her perch on Fisk's couch as Kate entered the cell.

Commander Holman beheld the scene in disbelief, barely able to speak. "Can I have a word with you?" she asked Fisk.

"Sure thing. Let's talk in my office." He smiled towards Casey. "We'll be right back," he said while motioning the commander to the rear of his cell.

By "office," he meant the bathroom. A towel lay across the threshold, a harbinger of the mess likely waiting within. No way would she set foot inside. Fisk stepped into the small room but she held fast at the entrance, sliding the door as far closed as she could. "I thought you wanted to minimize the number of people who know about what we found," she whispered.

"Yes," said Fisk.

"But you invited Casey?"

Fisk blushed. "You said I should try talking to her. I got kind of lonely while I was holed up in here, so I took your advice. Turns out she and I have a lot in common." Kate stole a glance at Casey—the astrobiologist replied with a shrug, a playful roll of her eyes, and an enticing smile. "I can't help if it that's the effect I have on women," added Fisk, thumbing out the door towards Casey. "It's why I no longer teach undergrads. It got to be I was spending more time fighting them off than lecturing."

"I see," said Kate, trying not to let too much skepticism come through her voice. "To be clear, I don't have anything against Casey; it's just I thought we agreed to keep a low profile on this so word wouldn't get back to Julian that you and I had been at the Face."

"Casey understands the importance of keeping this a secret," said Fisk as he pulled a granola bar from a jumpsuit pouch. He unwrapped the end and took a bite. "She won't tell anyone else—she's given me her word."

"You can count on me to keep a secret." Surprised, Kate's eyes flew to Casey, who'd apparently been listening in on their exchange. "As God is my witness," she continued, raising her hand as if taking an oath, unfettered breasts pressing into her tight blue v-neck. She blinked at the commander with her large brown eyes and dark hair that ended in bouncy curls at her shoulders. Kate understood why Fisk hadn't been able to resist inviting her, but as for keeping their trip to the Face a secret, she didn't trust for a minute in the astrobiologist's professed discretion. Casey was a brilliant scientist, by far the smartest member of the *Ares* crew, but she was also a social creature with a penchant for conversation and somewhat self-absorbed. The ones who couldn't stop talking inevitably tripped over their own tongues, stumbling into topics they shouldn't broach.

"Regardless, you've got nothing to worry about with Julian," added Casey.

"No?" asked Kate as she stepped from the doorway. She made her way to the couch, trailed by Fisk.

Casey smiled again and shook her head. "Julian may seem scary sometimes, but it's really more of an act. Underneath, he's actually very nice."

Underneath what, exactly? What did she see that no one else did? Wasn't he the creep she'd fended off in the DFAC?

Fisk made his way to his desk. Commander Holman and Casey joined him, positioning themselves on either side of the geologist. The surface was a cluttered mess but for a mostly clear patch in the center harboring a folded bundle of cloth. "And without further ado ...." Fisk peeled back the corners of the fabric, laying each one flat, unveiling the item recovered from the Face. The artifact looked as Kate remembered: a thin, gunmetal gray cylinder that would easily fit in the hand, riddled with black triangular etchings. The rod, polished perhaps, glinted under the stark white light of the desk lamp.

"So this is it," said Casey. Fisk nodded. "Clayton mentioned the two of you found something," she added, responding to the disapproval in Kate's knotted brow, "but that's all. He didn't give me many other details."

Fisk gaped at the item, enraptured as if beholding a talisman. "As far as physical characteristics, it's about twenty centimeters long. Its length is ten times its diameter, a nod to our base ten counting system. Not only that, the ratio of the rod's circumference to its diameter turns out to be *exactly* Pi."

Wasn't that the definition of Pi?

"Its surface is perfectly smooth, except for the markings," continued Fisk. "I haven't determined the exact composition of the metal, but it's an alloy so durable it hasn't tarnished in all the eons it's been here on Mars."

"Eons?" asked Casey. "As in thousands of years?"

"That's right," said Fisk.

"Wait a second," said Kate. "Why isn't it just a pushrod or something fallen off a Martian rover exploring the cave?" That was the conclusion she'd reached. Fisk hadn't even launched into his theory of the rod's origin, but it already seemed absurd, veering towards aliens and fringe science. His outlandish claim raised her hackles, her visit now an annoying waste of time. "You're a scientist, right?" she spat. "Ever heard of Occam's Razor? The simplest explanation is always the best."

"A piece of metal from a rover was my first guess," said Fisk. "The problem is these symbols." He pushed the rod with his finger, rolling the thin cylinder across the cloth and showing more of the triangular marks that covered its surface. "They're not random scratches. It's writing, but not alien scribbles, if you think that's my theory. It's cuneiform, ancient Sumerian. That dates this rod to ten thousand BCD."

The declaration left both women flabbergasted. Kate could hardly get the words out. "You're suggesting this metal rod we found sitting in the cave, kilometers beneath the Face, has some connection to Earth over ten thousand years ago?"

"I'm not suggesting anything," said Fisk, still gaping at the item. "It's what's written here on the rod. Have you heard of the Anunnaki?" Neither woman had. "It's a familiar name to those of us who believe aliens visited us in the past. The story goes that the Anunnaki, beings from another world, created the human race as slave labor to mine gold on Earth."

Kate laughed before she could catch herself. She drew Fisk's ire. "You ever wonder why humans care so much about gold?" he asked. "Why we find value in it? The element itself has no intrinsic worth, only what we ascribe to it. The legend of the Anunnaki explains why we're so obsessed with it."

"How does any of this relate to the rod?" asked Casey.

"The writing on this rod mentions the Anunnaki. It says they brought humans to Mars to mine gold here as well. They lived in the Cydonia region. All the structures—walls and buildings and even pyramids—hinted at by the overhead photographs really do exist. They're not just shadows, or the mind seeing what it wants to see."

Casey scratched her jaw. "Lemme get this straight—human slaves, bronze age people, shuttled to Mars," she said. "And what, living under a dome? Working in space suits? What did they do for water and food?"

Fisk's mouth opened and closed, like a fish out of water. He rubbed the back of his neck as he searched for an answer, words evading him.

"Now you're an ancient cuneiform scholar," said Kate. Despite her best effort, her words came out laced with sarcasm.

"Sumerian," Fisk said, voice cracking on his first word since his fumbled response to Casey. He straightened and fell back to his cocksure persona. "Cuneiform was a script used to write several ancient languages. In this case, it's Sumerian. But I'm no scholar. After all my time researching, I understand short spans of it here on the rod, but I couldn't interpret any old passage you gave me."

"Cuneiform, Sumerian, whatever," said Kate with a dismissive wave of her hand. "My point is you're not an authority on ancient languages. If these symbols *are* writing, you don't have the expertise to translate them."

"The computer did all the work," said Fisk. "It's standard software, the same as used by the academics back home. When I first fed in the markings, I didn't believe it myself. Most of my time working on this has been cross-referencing stretches with well-known Sumerian texts and their authoritative translations."

Kate lifted the rod. The thin cylinder was cool in her hand, and much heavier than expected. Its smooth, machined surface couldn't have been crafted by humans even a few hundred years ago. Could it be an alien artifact? Fisk's explanation bordered on the insane, but if the translation came from the computer, either the software got it all wrong, or the markings really did convey the story he was describing.

"Now here's where it gets nuts," said Fisk, without a hint of irony. "The rod describes a treasure vault beneath the great pyramid in Cydonia. That's where they stored everything they mined. It says there's an immense cache of gold ingots." His eyes twinkled, and his face blossomed into a wide grin. "We're all going to be fucking rich!"

"You mean when we drop everything we're doing and march over to Cydonia to start digging up the treasure?" asked Kate.

"Of course not, that would make no sense," deadpanned Fisk. "We should continue on with our original mission as if there isn't a fortune buried next door." The geologist huffed. "Are you telling me that back on Earth, if you discovered a king's ransom stashed in your neighbor's backyard, you'd show up for work the next day? You're *damn right* we're going to start digging up that treasure! Or at least I am, and I'm sure I won't be the only one out there. But before we kick off the solar system's latest gold rush, there's one thing we have to attend to."

"And what's that?" asked Casey.

"The writing on the rod goes on to mention the Face. It says the structure was carved to resemble a ceremonial burial mask. It's an enormous homage to Nergal, the Sumerian death god. The rod says the entire site is cursed and states several times that the area must be left alone. It warns against exploration and specifically against removing anything from it."

"Julian brought that large bag of … *something* back from the Face," said Kate.

"Yes," said Fisk. "The rod declares that anyone who ignores the warning will bring the Curse down on their head and all those with them." His expression grew dour, all the previous excitement drained away. "We have to talk to Julian, somehow convince him to take that bag back to the Face. The rod says to expect death and destruction until every last mote is returned. Unless we do, there's no point in even daydreaming about retrieving the gold 'cause none of us will be around to spend it."

Kate set the rod on the cloth and moved from the desk. She'd come to Fisk's cell expecting a rational explanation for the item and an end to the mystery, believing the geologist could focus again on his scientific investigation of Mars. Instead, she'd been forced to sit through a crazy story that had Fisk frothing at the mouth. The expectation that she'd swallow such a wild tale incensed her. Did he really think her so gullible? "You claim to be a scientist, Fisk, but too often you straddle the line between the real and the fantastical. Well, *I'm* on the side of science, and over here, we don't accept ancient aliens and curses as viable explanations for anything." She headed for the door.

"The men who desecrated the Egyptian tombs were also scientists," said Fisk. "But that didn't save them from the wrath of the mummy's curse."

Kate didn't respond.

"The rod says what it says—I'm not making it up. You can ask the computer yourself."

The commander maintained her silent march to the exit.

"You can ignore me, but you can't as easily ignore what happened to Cheney. We lost him before Julian's damned haul even entered the station."

Kate stopped in the foyer and turned back to Fisk. "Cheney's suit lost containment," she said. "The man died from exposure. He didn't die from a curse."

"Are you sure?" asked Fisk.

"Are you?" asked Kate, jabbing her finger at the geologist. "Two days ago, you told me *Julian* killed Cheney. Now you say it's some curse. Tomorrow, it'll be the flipping Easter bunny." She opened the door and exited into the tubeway.

"A good scientist can admit they don't know everything," Fisk shouted at the closing door. "The scientific method demands it."

13

Specialist Casey Morgan's raised arm froze mid-stroke, holding off on another downward blow. She'd been chipping away at a sloped expanse of sedimentary bedding, material that held great promise for chemical markers of life. Her gaze softened, losing focus, as her mind raced. *My entire time here is ruined.*

Standing from a low crouch, Dr. Morgan stared for a moment at the material she'd collected. If Fisk's crazy claim was true, that humans had been on Mars in the past, it would throw into question the source of any chemical markers she might find. The entire planet would be compromised.

Dr. Morgan kicked the specimen bucket, sending it and its contents cartwheeling across the ancient lakebed. She slammed her pickaxe into the ground and stormed towards the HAAB. Her blood boiled. The special op had something to do with the rod Fisk found. The secrecy, the shift in mission objective, it all added up: humans, improbably, incredibly, *had* been on Mars before. Julian and the powers that be likely suspected, if not knew outright, of the previous activity on the planet. Withholding that information caused her to request the wrong equipment, equipment unable to discriminate between Earth and alien life. Four years, plus the one that lay ahead and the five-month return trip, flushed down the toilet.

Back at her cell, she stripped off her Mars suit and took a long, hot shower. She dressed in a light blue terrycloth robe, lit a stick of soothing incense, and sat at her desk. She typed out a message to Julian: "Something important to discuss. Please stop by."

Her door chimed seven minutes later.

"Hi," said Julian. He raked her with his eyes where she stood in the foyer. "I came as soon as I got your message."

Dr. Morgan motioned him inside and closed the door.

Julian made himself comfortable on her couch, resting one leg atop the other as he sank into the cushions. Casey remained on her feet. She looked down on him, hands perched on hips and face in a death stare.

"Your message mentioned something important you wanted to discuss," said Julian, smiling at the astrobiologist. He leaned forward, pinched a corner of her robe, and gently tugged.

Dr. Morgan smacked his hand away. "That's right," she said, stepping closer, glaring. "I want to talk about how you and your sonuvabitch buddies have ruined my career."

- - -

Having reviewed the day's final station reports, Glenn climbed into his bed and switched on his e-book reader. He picked up where he left off in a novel on the first summiting of Mount Everest. Desolation, extreme cold, inadequate air—the challenges those mountaineers encountered mirrored their own adventure.

Ping. Ping.

The sounds came from his terminal. Glenn had retired in the early evening, likely before most of his fellow astronauts, but that was his prerogative. Settled in his bed, he preferred not to leave it. Perhaps if he ignored the chimes, they'd stop.

Ping. Ping.

Glenn sighed, threw off the covers, and headed to his desk. A notification bubble on his terminal showed an incoming comm from Engles. He opened the channel. "This is Wiles."

"Hey, it's Engles. Casey and I made a plan to play cards this evening. I've been out here in front of her cell for a couple minutes pressing the chime and knocking, but I've gotten no response. According to Miriam, the station logs don't show she's anywhere else."

The spacecraft engineer's southern accent had ebbed and flowed during her explanation. She was upset, but not responding to a door chime wasn't against the law. Heck, he'd nearly brushed aside Engles's pings. "Maybe she's asleep," said Glenn. "She did some of her first excavations today."

"Maybe ... but I can tell the lights are on," said Engles. "She also missed dinner, and she didn't make it to the station happy hour."

Skipping dinner wasn't a crime either, but Casey missing happy hour was odd, the astrobiologist always a central figure at social events. Regardless, why had Engles come to him for help? "If you're concerned, you should get in touch with Julian. He doesn't do a whole lot, but he *is* the mission commander, after all."

"I've tried," said Engles. "He won't answer my pings."

"What about Commander Holman?" asked Glenn.

"She's got a bad headache. She told me to talk to you."

Glenn sighed again. "Be right over." He pulled on his mission jumpsuit and grabbed his station jacket from the hook behind the door—in the few days they'd been on Mars, he'd learned that despite the HAAB's insulation against the harsh environment, the tubeways grew chilly at night. He threw it on as he exited his cell.

When he arrived at Casey's, he found Engles standing outside. She wore a blue paisley bandana around her neck, a favorite for more festive occasions. The spacecraft engineer looked agitated. "Still no contact?" he asked.

Engles shook her head. "None."

Glenn triggered the chime several times and rapped on her door. "Casey, this is Glenn and Engles, are you in there?" No response to any of his efforts.

"What about the override code?" asked Engles.

"That's only for emergencies," said Glenn. He didn't last long under Engles's ferocious glare, quickly tapping the eight-digit sequence into the entry keypad. The deadbolt retracted with a "chunk." He opened the door a crack. "Casey, it's Glenn and Engles." Silence. He pushed it farther and entered.

Engles had been right about the lights—Casey's cell was ablaze. The astrobiologist wasn't at her desk or on her couch, but a large lump stretched beneath the bedsheets. Glenn drew closer, spotting a mass of brown hair and an exposed arm. "Looks like she's asleep after all," he whispered. "We should let her rest."

Engles pushed past Glenn, disregarding the suggestion as she made her way to the head of the bed. The astrobiologist lay on her side, her back to them. Engles reached for Casey's bare shoulder. She gasped and quickly withdrew her hand, placing it over her gaping mouth.

Glenn stepped closer and touched Casey's arm—cool flesh. He checked her neck for a pulse. "My God," he said, looking on in disbelief. "She's dead."

14

The world moved in surreal slow motion for Commander Holman as she shuffled down the Spine, squinting through her fingers. A headache that had plagued her since the previous night continued unabated, compounded by the series of overhead lamps that lined the long corridor. She winced with each new bank, the artificial light driving needles into the backs of her eyes.

I should be in bed. Instead, she was dressed, and on her way to the medbay. Ten minutes ago, she'd been asleep in her darkened cell, seeking relief on the other side of consciousness. Dr. Palmer upended that plan, forcing her from her nap. He wanted to discuss Casey. "Julian's the person to contact," she told him. "As acting mission commander, he's responsible for all crew issues." She lectured, argued, and finally jabbed the connection closed. The persistent and stubborn Dr. Palmer would have none of it. He insisted she come see him about the matter, alone.

When Kate stumbled into the medbay, she found Dr. Palmer sitting behind his desk, cleaning his glasses. He greeted her with a grim expression that didn't lighten when he returned the thick, black frames to his face. In all Kate's prior interactions with Palmer, including when they brought Cheney in from the Martian cold, he'd always offered a friendly physician's smile. On this visit, the normally affable doctor seemed burdened by a great weight.

"Are you all right, Commander?"

"I'm fine." *The good doctor's way of saying I look like shit.* She'd caught a glimpse of herself before leaving her cell, a haggard visage with deep, dark circles under the eyes, drawn cheeks, blanched skin, and unruly strands of hair reaching out from the sides of the baseball cap she'd tugged low on her head. "I'm fine," she repeated, reassuring herself as much as Palmer. "What's so urgent you had to drag me down here? Do you have an update on the cause of death?"

"Still no idea," said Palmer, getting up from his desk. "All the test results say she's perfectly healthy. I'm hoping the toxicology report will provide some answers."

Palmer and Kate walked to the center of the medbay where Casey's body lay splayed across the examination table, covered by a white sheet from the torso down. Casey's beauty shone even in death, with her pouty lips, wide hips, and pert breasts. The bright overhead lamp set the pale, translucent skin of her face and exposed shoulders aglow. The entire scene was otherworldly, the table and everything on it a radiant white except for the astrobiologist's dark brown, shoulder-length hair.

Kate shivered, suddenly cold with the chill of the room. *Kept cold for the body.* "So you've made progress on the tox report, then?" she asked.

"The toxicology report isn't complete," said Palmer. "I'm not a medical examiner, so it was hard for me to interpret the raw data. I sent it all to Earth. It'll be a few days 'til I hear anything." The doctor froze for a moment, apparently lost in thought. He sprang back to life, grabbing a pair of gloves from a nearby dispenser and snapping them on. Palmer lifted Casey's right arm, freeing it from the sheet, and brought her hand into the light. He examined her nails, checking each finger in turn.

The cold in the room, the dearth of new details, and being forced to sit through Palmer's impromptu examination tested Kate's patience. The pounding in her skull didn't help. If only she could escape the station lights —return to her cell, crawl into bed, and wait out the headache. "If you don't have the tox report, and you don't know the cause of death, then why the hell did you call me down here?" She instantly regretted swearing. She'd let her discomfort get the best of her.

The doctor didn't seem to notice. "Because there are some other findings I need to bring to your attention," he said without looking up. Finished with the right hand, Palmer moved on to the left. After a quick scan of Casey's nails, he laid her arm alongside her body and pulled off his gloves. He swiped an electronic pad hanging from the examination table and gave it to the commander.

Kate frowned at the pad, its display a dense wall of medical jargon and tables crammed with figures.

"As part of the autopsy, I performed a routine examination of Casey's body," said Palmer. "That included her vaginal cavity." The doctor's voice softened. "Those results appear near the bottom of the first page."

Kate located the section. Her mouth fell open in shock. "Semen?" Dr. Palmer's silence confirmed she'd read correctly. They'd barely been a week on the planet, and Casey was already sleeping with someone. Evidently, some man besides Julian had a romantic interest in the astrobiologist. There was Fisk, of course, though Kate had trouble imagining him with Casey, or any woman. That left Palmer, who would be calling out his own sexual encounter, and Glenn, who was married.

"Based on the timeline, she had sex right before she died," said Palmer, "or was forced to."

"Forced to?" *As in rape?* "You found evidence of non-consensual sex? Bruises? Scrapes?"

"No, nothing like that," said Dr. Palmer. "Just now, I thought to check her nails in case she tried to fight off her attacker—they're clean."

Getting information out of the doctor was sometimes like pulling teeth. Why couldn't he cut to the chase so she could lie down? "If you don't have any evidence, what makes you suspect foul play?"

"Keep reading," said Palmer.

Kate skimmed to the bottom of the page. She gasped. "The semen is Julian's?"

Palmer nodded.

"You're sure?"

"I am," said Palmer. "Everyone's genetic profile's in the computer. Finding a match was trivial."

The incident with Casey and Julian in the DFAC—his pursuit had been so intense, it pushed her to make everyone aware of his unwelcome advances. "If he forced himself on her …"—Kate paused, searching for the best words for a delicate matter—"… that could be motive for murder." The doctor's raised eyebrows signaled the same conclusion. She hoisted her comm, arm shaking. "Miriam, you there in the control room?" Her voice quavered.

"I'm here. What can I do for you, Commander?"

Kate's mouth was dry—she licked her lips. "Are you … by yourself?" The fewer people involved, the better, at least until she got to the bottom of it.

"Affirmative."

"Can you tell me where Julian is?"

"Just a sec'." Moments passed. "He's in his cell."

"Is anyone with him?"

"Seems to be alone," said Miriam.

"Contact Glenn and Voss. Have them meet me in the DFAC, immediately. And keep an eye on Julian. Tell me if he leaves his cell."

"Ok-aaay ...," said Miriam. "Can you tell me what's up?"

"Something bad," said Kate. "Details forthcoming. For now, just get me Glenn and Voss."

"Roger that, ma'am."

Kate closed the comm channel and handed the pad to the doctor.

"How do Glenn and Voss fit in?" asked Palmer.

"They don't, not directly, anyway," said Kate. "I need to talk to Julian, but I'm concerned about approaching him by myself. Glenn's big, bigger than Julian. And Voss was a wrestling champ in college. A little insurance in case things go south." Not that she needed it. Her father had stipulated she learn Krav Maga as a precondition to dating. She could take care of herself, though she probably didn't look it. The extra muscle would ensure Julian thought twice before trying anything, if it came to that. She headed for the exit.

"It's times like these I'm thankful not to be mission commander," said Palmer.

"It's times like these I'm not so keen on it either," said Kate, without breaking her stride. She dashed out of the medbay.

15

Kate jabbed the chime outside Julian's cell.

"Just a sec." The words sailed through the walls, along with the shuffle of feet. *Even his breathing,* Kate thought, partially joking. Elasticine's superior strength-to-weight ratio made it the obvious choice for constructing the Mars station. Only after the HAAB's sections were in transit to the red planet did she learn of the material's penchant for sound transmission. She shook her head at the shortsightedness. The mission planners and their subcontractors were so busy pinching pennies, they didn't consider the problems such a lack of privacy might create for a year-long habitation in close quarters.

The cell door swung inward. In the foyer stood Julian, draped in a robe of shiny, thin material. Water beaded across his smooth scalp and dotted the floor beneath him. He'd apparently rushed from the shower to answer the buzzer. "Commander Holman!" he said, grinning with an odd enthusiasm. "What can I do for you?" She took from his smile a prurient delight in the silky material of his robe being all that separated his dripping, naked body from her.

Kate still suffered under her headache. The onslaught of light from the open door drove the needles deeper into her eyes. She stifled a groan. "Julian, I need to talk to you," she said, blinking through the pain. "Can I come in?"

Julian's smile widened but in an instant changed to a scowl. He'd likely spotted Glenn and Voss in the shadows behind. Kate was even more grateful for the foresight to ask the two astronauts to accompany her.

"Does 'I' mean you alone, or does it include your entourage?" asked Julian.

Kate sighed. "This is important."

"Well, you've come at a bad time." He spread his arms, as if offering himself for inspection. "As you can see, I'm in no condition to entertain guests."

How to avoid a full-on confrontation? Best to keep the situation light. "It wasn't so long ago the ten of us were cooped up inside the *Ares*," she said. "You didn't seem to have a problem entertaining us all in your robe back then."

Julian inched closer to the commander, his body filling the doorframe and eclipsing the light from his cell. "Now's really not a good time, Kate," he said in a quiet, firm voice as he broadened his chest and shoulders and locked his eyes on to hers. He wasn't tall like Glenn, but he had a muscular build and stood a menacing extra fifteen centimeters above her. He smelled of his cheap cologne, the fragrance that prompted the women astronauts to snicker whenever he "freshened up" in the capsule. The scent set her head throbbing.

Kate didn't budge, which seemed to goad Julian into redoubling his efforts at intimidation. "We're not back on the *Ares*, Kate," he said, the crease between his eyebrows deepening. "*I'm* in charge here on Mars, not you or anyone else. I don't know what this is all about, but I'm telling you again, now's not a good time. If you have something to ask me, stick it in an e-mail. But as far as your request to enter my cell, to meet with me here and now, I decline."

"You can't," said Kate.

Julian's eyes remained locked with hers. Her body went rigid, bracing for a physical altercation. *So this is how it's going down.*

Julian moved, but not towards the commander. He stepped back and turned sideways. "OK, mutineers," he said, "have it your way." He bowed slightly in mock deference. "Do come in."

Kate filed in with Glenn and Voss close behind. The three fanned out within the small room. The dimmed, recessed ceiling lamps illuminated the space, while the bathroom spewed stark white LED light through its partly closed door. The cell's single, wide window had its shades drawn, an apparent act of modesty. *Who the hell is he worried will see him prancing around?*

Commander Holman's eyes darted from bed to desk to couch. *Where's Julian's pellet gun?* They didn't have to secure it immediately, but they did need to be aware of its location. Was she being paranoid? Perhaps, except Julian didn't like being pushed around—as the security chief, and now as the acting mission commander, he enjoyed doing all the pushing. Who knew what could happen if he responded poorly to their visit.

Julian closed the door and came into the room. "I see you've all brought weapons," he said as he settled in an open area along the far wall between his desk and dresser, a spot that allowed him to face them all. A meter away, on top of the dresser, sat his pellet gun in its holster. *Did he position himself there to grab it? Why did they even have guns in the first place?* The Space Force developed the weapon for the moonbase, a substitute for revolvers and their errant slugs that could easily damage vital equipment or tear a hole in the base's thin skin. But that was the Moon, with nearly seventy people, a good number of them civilian support staff. The Mars mission featured a handful of professionals who had trained together for two years. They should all trust each other. To Kate, the presence of weapons seemed more a sign of man's predilection for violence than a prudent precaution.

"An insurrection, then," said Julian, setting his hands on his hips. He looked directly at Commander Holman. "You're still upset the AD put me in command of this mission, and you've convinced the others to help you impart a little frontier justice."

"I need to ask you a couple questions about Casey—"

"Casey's dead," blurted Julian.

"If you'll stop with your *flipping* interruptions, we can maybe get through this!" shouted Kate, startling herself with her outburst. She massaged her temples. After two years on Earth and five months of space travel filled with his contemptuous behavior, she'd reached her limit, especially with her headache and the seriousness of the matter that brought her to his quarters.

Julian shot her a scorching look but shut himself up, allowing her to proceed. Kate had rehearsed what she'd planned to say half a dozen times between the medbay and his cell, but her carefully prepared words slipped away, lost in the burst of adrenaline and anger. She could do little more than come out with it. "During Doctor Palmer's autopsy, he found semen. Your semen."

Julian's expression shifted to mortification. "Oh," he said.

"Yes, oh," said Kate. "That, of course, is not a crime. The thing is, Casey made that big scene in the DFAC. From what she said, everyone got the picture she wasn't interested in you ... romantically."

"That was all her crazy idea," he said, rubbing his forehead in exasperation. "The two of us have been involved since before we left Earth. Nothing serious, just foolin' around. With the restrictions on relationships, she didn't want word to get out about us. Casey figured she could throw everyone off by publicly rejecting my claimed advances. Only she didn't let me in on her plan beforehand. She said she kept me in the dark to make sure my reaction was convincing. I was as surprised as all of you when she got up and slapped me."

Kate expected a denial, just not one so elaborate. "Your story is she was kidding when she stood up in front of everyone and told you to keep your hands off her." The summarized claim sounded even more absurd than the words that had tumbled from Julian's mouth. "You're saying she slept with you willingly, and that her death afterwards was pure coincidence."

"That's *exactly* what I'm saying." Julian surveyed the room of blank stares. "It's the truth. She and I were an item. We couldn't do much of anything in the five months out here. We had a lot of lost time to make up for, and she was worried one of you would catch on. I didn't rape her, and I certainly didn't kill her, if that's what you think. You've got to believe me."

Glenn slid forward a step, moving from under the glare of a recessed light. "When Casey said those things in the DFAC, everyone thought she was serious," he said. "Problem is, with her dead, we can't know if what you're saying is true."

"But it *is* true," pleaded Julian.

Despite her dislike of Julian, Kate felt she owed the security chief at least a modicum of fairness. "Doctor Palmer didn't find any signs of a struggle," she said. "That much is true."

"'Cause there wasn't any," said Julian.

"It could have been unwanted intercourse even still," said Glenn. "You could have threatened her. As mission commander, it would be easy enough to make her life a living hell if she didn't do what you wanted. Or maybe you were holding something else over her."

"Now you're just making shit up," said Julian. "It's bad enough you want to pin rape and murder on me based on circumstantial evidence."

"You have to admit, the circumstances are pretty bad," said Kate.

Julian started to speak, but no words came from his open mouth. He closed it.

"Maybe the tube cameras can help," said Voss.

"Those were only active during the HAAB's qualification period and our trip out," said Kate. NASA used the video feeds to remotely check for problems. "They shut them off shortly before we landed."

"The only thing they shut off was the real-time feed to Earth," said Voss. "And only after I pointed out to those geniuses that keeping it going would turn our time here into a reality TV show. But I'm pretty sure the cameras themselves are still dumping their files to the station's main computer."

"With timestamps?" asked Kate. Voss's affirmative grunt brought the commander back to her conversation with Dr. Palmer the first time she visited the deceased astrobiologist in the medbay. "Palmer said the time-of-death determination is based on metabolic processes and rates that are accurate down to the minute."

"If so, the video should show if Casanova's visit to Casey overlaps with her death," said Voss.

Julian's face took on a shade of red. "You will refer to me as Commander Grimes," he roared. "Or Julian, since the decision to permit the use of first names was made before I was promoted to mission commander."

"Or, I guess, 'suspect' is also an option—"

"The recordings will tell us if Commander Grimes is involved in the matter," interrupted Kate, aiming to prevent the spat between the two astronauts from escalating.

Julian glared at Voss but stopped sparring with the station engineer. "Yes, fine," he said, "let's look at the video." He started for his dresser. "Just let me throw on some clothes."

Kate's heart raced—was he making a move for his gun? "No need, Julian." In her sudden concern, she'd shouted the words. Julian held fast, jarred by her raised voice. "I'll manage checking the clips myself," she added.

"But I want to be there when you examine them," said Julian. "They could be the hard evidence that exonerates me."

"They could be, but they may not answer every question," said Kate. She couldn't have Julian standing over her shoulder as she examined the video, arguing over the interpretation of events. She also couldn't have him, as the station's commanding officer, potentially ordering her to ignore certain lines of investigation or even destroy evidence. She needed him out of the way until she resolved the situation. "I want you to stay put while we figure this out." Kate hesitated, anticipating the response to her next statement. "Until we do, I need to relieve you of command—"

"I *knew* it!" said Julian. "This whole thing is a power play. That's all it is. A way for you to soothe your ego and regain control of this mission."

"Like hell," hissed Kate. "I'll remind you, we wouldn't be having this conversation if Doctor Palmer hadn't found your semen inside a dead woman, who multiple witnesses saw telling you to leave her alone. But if you want, I can refer this matter to NASA and ask them to officially relieve you of your duties—"

"OK, OK," said Julian, throwing up his hands, "fine, go ahead. Play mission commander for now. If that makes you feel better."

Kate fumed at the remark but maintained her cool. "I'll also need your pellet gun—"

"My gun?" said Julian. "Why? You think I'm gonna blast my way out of the station?"

"Because," Kate growled, irate with his latest interruption, "our investigation may lead to the conclusion that you *did* rape or kill Casey, in which case this whole episode will move into a phase I'm guessing you may not like very much. So, while we're still looking into the matter, at least, I'll need your gun."

Julian placed his palms flat against his face and dragged his hands slowly down, returning them to his hips. His eyes remained closed, and he slowly shook his head. "You need to take a moment, Kate, slow down. You're power tripping so hard you can't see how crazy you sound." He ended his display of patronizing disbelief and looked square at her. "If you want me to stay here in my cell while you watch the video, fine, I'll do that, just like you asked. But the only reason to take my gun is if you think I'm gonna shoot someone. I'm not gonna shoot anyone. I'm the mission's security chief for Chrissakes." Julian made no motion to comply with her request. "You don't need my weapon."

Time ground to a halt, the four astronauts frozen in place. Had the call for his gun been unreasonable? No. Regardless of Julian's claims of innocence, he might not be. She couldn't have him holed up in his cell with his weapon. Julian had resisted all her other requests from the moment she arrived at his door, but in each case, he'd backed down. This time, he seemed to be digging in his heels. Was he really daring her to take his gun by force? Could she even cross that line?

Glenn's hand inched to his waist. He pushed aside his holster's safety strap and slowly withdrew his pellet gun. He held the weapon angled down, against his thigh, his index finger resting against the trigger.

Julian noticed the gesture. "It's over here," he said, with an air of resignation.

Kate forced an exhale—she'd been holding her breath during the standoff. The commander walked to the dresser, grabbed the weapon, and pulled it free of its holster. She ejected the clip and slid it into her pocket, then handed the empty gun to Voss.

"Go on then, check the video," said Julian.

"I will," said Kate. "In the meantime, I won't lock you up, but I do want you to stay put. I'm confining you to your cell—"

"Why? You think I'm going somewhere dressed like this?" he asked, standing before them in his robe. "I'm going to shave. By the time I put on some clothes, you'll have watched the video and'll be calling with an apology."

She'd intended to head straight to the control room, but Kate nixed those plans in the wake of Julian's latest comment. *Let the insolent bastard stew in his cell.* "Don't expect any news tonight," she said. The security chief began to protest, but she cut him off. "It's late, Julian, and I have a headache. I'll look at the clips tomorrow, with fresh eyes. I don't want the pressure of having to make a decision tonight, particularly if what I see is inconclusive."

"Riiiight," said Julian, sharp with sarcasm, "I get it. You bitched and moaned about losing your command, and now you've found a way to get it back. You want to keep your new position for as long as you can, even though the evidence that will exonerate me is sitting on a computer hard drive a few taps away."

Was Julian correct about her motivation, about why she'd relieved him of command with no urgency to reinstate him? She wanted her position back, yes, but would she stop at nothing to regain it? Kate didn't *think* so. *Hopefully* not. The events of the past twelve hours had thrown her for a loop. She was navigating the situation as best she could. The evidence they had so far implicated Julian in Casey's murder. Until stronger evidence emerged that supported his innocence, he needed to be stripped of his power and confined to his quarters. She was also tired, worn down by her pounding headache. She would've been in her bed but for Palmer's insistence she come to the medbay. She had no business doing anything other than rest.

Julian flicked at her with his fingers, taking her deliberative silence as a brush-off. "Fine, I'm tired of arguing. Have it your way. Get your sleep, *Mission Commander*. Have a bite of breakfast tomorrow, even. Meanwhile, I'll be here, rotting away until you get around to looking at the video."

Kate rubbed her eyes. "Glenn, work with Miriam to secure Julian's cell."

"You're locking me in?" blurted the indignant security chief.

"I know you promised to stay here," said Kate, "but I need to make sure you don't leave for any reason, no matter the temptation."

"You sure that's wise, *Mission Commander*?" asked Julian. "What if there's an emergency?"

"You know, there's so much still to do around the HAAB, it might be a *couple* of days before I get to the clips." She'd had it with Julian's bullshit, and he was in no position to dictate the terms of his confinement.

The security chief sulked with a foul look, but his protests had ended at least. Kate's head throbbed. She massaged her temples again. "Right now, I'm going to hit the hay, try to shake off this headache." She'd make a fresh start in the morning.

16

Kate blinked, bleary-eyed. Red lights danced around her. A klaxon wailed.

Where was she? The rocket, the red planet, the HAAB all came flooding back. She glanced at her bedside clock: 5:31 a.m.

Evacuation protocol. The realization jolted her awake. Something had happened with the HAAB, something so concerning the computer was prepping them to abandon the station.

Kate bolted up and brought her feet to the floor. She reached beneath her bed and retrieved a compact white box. Inside sat a neatly packed emergency skin, complete with its flimsy, collapsible helmet. She swiftly stripped from her bedclothes and scrambled into the thin, one-piece outfit.

Commander Holman stood, her body a fountain of red sparkles as the emergency lights bounced across the suit's reflective white surface. Could such a lightweight skin really protect anyone from the elements? Long enough to get to the *Gaia*, was the idea. What the suit lacked in bulk, it made up for in its extremely short time to pull on.

The commander quickly filed out of her cell, exiting at the same time as Voss, her neighbor along her tube. The two trekked to the Spine amid the rotating red lights and noise.

"Miriam, you online?" Kate asked over the skin's comm. Hopefully the station chief had a grip on the emergency.

"Just got into my skin," said Miriam. She sounded rushed. "On my way to the control room now."

"Roger that," said Kate. "I'm headed to the emergency assembly point."

Kate and Voss turned left into the Spine. Two more astronauts, clad in their sparkling white emergency skins, scurried ahead of them. The four hurried down the corridor to the DFAC.

Panicked faces surrounded Kate soon after she arrived. She needed to take a head count, the next step in the protocol before possibly proceeding to the airlock. Besides herself, there was Voss, Palmer, Engles, and Glenn, the four huddled around her—five total. A sixth astronaut, Julian, stood off by himself, looking out the large bay window at the black night. Kate's anger rose. The emergency comm channel linked all members of the command staff, but Julian hadn't yet said a word. Even in a crisis, he seemed not to care what was happening.

The commander resumed her tally. Including herself, and Miriam in the control room, that made eight. She'd accounted for the still-living members of the *Ares* crew.

"Do you know what's going on?" asked Glenn.

She shook her head. "I was asleep. I woke to the klaxon."

"I was awake when it happened," said Glenn. "Couldn't sleep," he continued, responding to Kate's inquisitive look. "I was reading when I heard a loud noise. My entire cell rocked."

Glenn's comment brought remnants of a dream rushing back to Kate. She'd been driving, on a highway that crossed the Arizona desert. Her car shuddered on the road. The shaking must've been real, not part of her dream. The movement of her bed and cell had rousted her from her sleep, not the klaxon.

"I'm here in the control room," said Miriam's voice in Kate's ear. "It looks like we lost a cell."

"What the hell does 'lost' mean?" asked Kate, annoyed. There was nothing actionable in the station chief's statement.

"I don't know," said Miriam. "There's a dark spot on my board where it should be. I have temperature, containment, energy draw, and other vitals for every cell except this one. The data feeds for all its systems seem to have cut out at once. It's like the cell isn't there anymore."

Kate stared off at Julian, still standing alone across the room as she took in Miriam's report. He yawned at his reflection in the glass. *The whole HAAB could be burning down, but all he can do is daydream out the window.*

"Which cell is it?" asked Glenn.

"One of the crew cells," said Miriam. "Julian's."

Kate blanched at the news. The events of the previous evening returned: visiting Dr. Palmer in the medbay, confronting Julian, confining him to his quarters .... Her stomach dropped as the sixth astronaut, the one at the window, turned to face into the room. It was *Fisk*, not Julian as she'd thought. Julian's wasn't any of the faces with her either—how was he not in the DFAC? She'd tallied eight astronauts. She counted again: herself, the four with her, plus Fisk off by himself made six. Adding herself made seven ... that was it—in the fog of the early morning, she'd counted herself twice! *Six* astronauts occupied the DFAC, not seven. Only seven astronauts, including Miriam, had been accounted for. That left one missing. Kate's hands began to shake. "What's containment like over there?"

"My board's not showing a breach," said Miriam. "Julian's cell's not registering but the tube's intact."

"I'll go," said Glenn before Kate could make a motion for the door.

"No, you stay. Someone needs to manage the situation here if it turns out we have to evacuate." Without waiting for a reply, she sprinted off through the doors.

Kate moved at a quick pace along the Spine, reaching Julian's cell in under a minute. She pressed the chime, but no sound came from inside. Not surprising if his quarters had lost power, but how to proceed? The override code might get the door open, but if the cell had a containment problem, she'd compromise the tubeway and perhaps the station. Kate looked down the corridor to the three oblong glass windows embedded in the wall between Julian's cell and the next. She dashed to the closest one and angled for a view of the security chief's quarters. The night's thick black filled the frame. If only she had some light …. "Miriam, you still there?"

"Yes, Commander."

"Can you light up the exterior floods on the D-tube?"

Movement at the end of the hallway—a figure, emerging from the entrance to the Spine. "Julian?" Kate blurted.

With the nondescript emergency skin and tumbling red lights, she couldn't tell who had appeared, but as the astronaut approached, she noted their tall frame—too tall to be Julian. It was Glenn. Why hadn't he remained with the others? They still didn't have a handle on the state of Julian's cell, might still need to evacuate to the *Gaia*.

Glenn planted himself next to her and peeked out the window. "I can't see anything," he said.

"I wanted you to—"

Bright white light flared in the space outside the window. The sight took away Kate's breath: Julian's cell, the cylindrical structure five meters in diameter, had a large hole roughly three meters wide torn into the side. Jagged metal teeth ringed the opening, charred black and curled outward—

an explosion from within. Clothing, scraps of fluffy pink insulation, and shrapnel from the wall panels lay scattered across the manicured, rusted ground.

"Julian had been worried about being locked in his cell, in case of an emergency," said Glenn as he surveyed the damage. "Guess he was right." Kate's face reddened. "But whatever occurred here … uh … it seems like it was sudden," he sputtered, reading her ire. "Even if he hadn't been locked inside, he probably couldn't have escaped in time."

Time to escape or no, locking Julian inside hadn't helped his chances of survival. She'd dismissed his concern over emergencies as more whining, but he'd been right. Kate cursed the thought. He'd been right, and now he was dead, or most certainly dead—they needed to confirm. They also needed to figure out what went wrong. Was the explosion a sign of a larger problem? Were the other cells at risk? They wouldn't know anything without a closer inspection. "Get back to the DFAC," she commanded Glenn, anger, worry, and fear all roiling within her. "Stay there with everyone until I give the OK to secure from evacuation protocol. And not a word to the others of what you've seen. I don't want them worrying about Julian or the safety of the HAAB, not until we understand what happened."

"Yes, ma'am," said Glenn. "Where will you be?"

"Getting some answers," she said. Commander Holman looked skyward. The planet's canopy had shifted from pure black to a hint of pink. Morning sunlight was on its way. A least they wouldn't have to sift through the wreckage in the dark. She switched to a private comm line. "Voss, suit up fast as you can and meet me at the airlock. We're going to Julian's cell."

17

Kate and Voss picked their way across the formerly manicured space outside Julian's cell. The scene resembled a neighborhood ravaged by a twister, with mangled limbs from plastic furniture, charred insulation, and the singed remnants of shredded clothing. Each boot step crunched on the snowfall's dusting of elasticine shards.

The two Mars astronauts paused at the jagged hole in the side of the cell, a shark's maw of sharp metal teeth. "Careful going through," said Kate, nodding at the opening's ragged rim. "Snagging an arm on one of those edges will easily tear a suit."

Kate entered the wrecked cell first. Darkness shrouded the interior, except for the center where the early morning sun poured in through a gash in the ceiling. Dust sparkled in the shaft like glitter in a snow globe. The planet's thin, cold air enveloped them in an eerie quiet.

Commander Holman activated her suit light and aimed it into the room's shadows. Scorched elasticine panels slumped forward from the structure's metal ribbing, their warped, blackened surfaces a shocking contrast to the pristine white of the undamaged cell she'd visited the evening before. She swept left to the remnants of Julian's desk, the burnt-out shell of a computer monitor settled in its bowed center. In front sat the mutilated base of a chair, seat missing and casters reduced to small black puddles. *Was Julian sitting there when it happened?* Doubtful. The explosion occurred at 5:30 in the morning. More likely he was asleep.

"Must've been a massive fireball to do all this," said Voss.

Kate barely heard the station engineer's words, her mind reeling with thoughts of Julian's fate. Her orders had confined the security chief to his cell. She just hadn't wanted him trying to view the video clips on his own in the control room or roaming the HAAB for any other reason. In the end, her directive had been a death sentence. *If Julian died in the explosion, it wasn't from being locked inside.* Maybe, maybe not. Regardless, her orders hadn't helped his chances of survival. *You're ready to declare him dead, but you don't even have a body.*

The commander swept her light right, searching for the bed. The beam landed on a black, melted mass, more glob than furniture. The collapsed frame rested on the floor, the bottoms of its four posts mashed flat by the heat and the bed's weight.

She directed her light to the top of the bed: no Julian, only an odd, black lump. So the explosion hadn't caught him asleep. Perhaps he'd been standing in the cell's galley, making coffee or tea. Or maybe the bathroom? She raised her beam, clearing the bed enough to land on the far wall. The light revealed a closed bathroom door, seared but intact. With sufficient warning, Julian could have scrambled into his emergency skin. He might be inside the small space right now, unconscious and awaiting rescue.

Kate started for the bathroom but froze, nagged by a glint in her peripheral vision. In raising her light to illuminate the far wall, the beam's bottom quarter grazed the top edge of the lump she'd spotted on the bed. A wink of white peeked from the mound where a portion had separated from the rest, an odd, alabaster knob suspended before a shiny, pinkish backdrop …. Kate gasped as her mind assembled the image, the glistening interior of a shoulder joint, its arm bone free of the socket.

Julian.

He'd been caught in the inferno after all, hadn't had time to escape. The fire had rendered his body unrecognizable. Her impulse was to look away, but she wouldn't take her eyes off the gruesome scene, penance for her fatal decision of the previous night.

"The explosion grew from here," said Voss.

The words jolted Kate from her thoughts. She turned to find the station engineer beneath the streaming Martian sunlight in the middle of the room, at the intersection of two large girders made visible by the explosion. Voss crouched in the center of a two-meter-wide crater, its rim the upward-curved edges of metal floor panels, the frozen splash of a rock thrown into a lake.

Kate stepped over the crater's lip and onto one of the naked girders. She tightroped her way to Voss, keeping her head down as she focused on placing her feet. Snatches of Martian soil winked at her between the exposed crossmembers and fluffs of insulation. She stopped two paces from the station engineer and squatted.

"These are the cell's supply lines," said Voss, referring to a sheared-off bundle of pipes running the length of the central girder. "These two are water, one for hot, one for cold," she continued, pointing to each pipe in turn. "This is the waste line, electrical, and natural gas." The gas line, a dull, galvanized, gray pipe four centimeters in diameter, ended like the others in a twisted mangle. "Best guess is something failed around the internal hookup. That would've vented gas directly into the cell. After that, all it took was a spark."

The gas line ran to the HAAB's methane production unit, providing fuel for localized heating. Kate studied its tattered end. Though pinched, the pipe wasn't sealed. Kate's heart raced. "Is gas filling the cell right now?"

"It's not," said Voss. "Being the genius that I am, I made sure to shut down all services to this cell before we came out. But even still, there's no oxygen. You could take a lighter to this entire room filled with gas and it wouldn't catch."

A relief—they wouldn't suffer the irony of being blown to bits while investigating the accident. Kate stood, instantly regretting how fast she'd moved. Her headache was returning. She'd time only to scarf down one of her protein bars before suiting up. She probably needed something more substantial in her belly. Commander Holman steadied herself on wobbly legs. "I want you to inspect the other cells, make sure more aren't waiting to blow. Grab whoever else you need to help."

"Roger," said Voss.

"I'm gonna check in with NASA, fill them in on what you've found so far," said Kate. "Soon as you're able, get me a draft of your report so I can send it along as well. If we're facing a serious design flaw, I want the brain trust back home thinking it through."

Voss nodded, rose to her feet, and glanced toward the dark recesses of the cell. "Did you find Julian?"

Kate paled, recalling the sight of the security chief's charred remains. "I did ... in his bed," she said, choking back a fresh gasp. "We'll need another grave ...." Another two graves, including Casey.

"We should leave him where he is."

Leave him where he is? "How's that?" asked Commander Holman. Voss unleashing a blunt remark or cold-hearted declaration wasn't unusual, but the callousness of the statement surprised even Kate. Few liked Julian, but he was a fellow astronaut who had risked his life to be part of the Mars mission. He deserved the same respect in death as any other member of the crew.

"The logistics of it," said Voss, in a matter-of-fact tone. "It'll take at least two people working together to recover Julian's remains. I'm guessing that'll be a gruesome job, which means a non-zero risk of them vomiting in their suits. But beyond that, the bigger problem will be taking him out of here." Voss nodded back at the ragged opening in the cell. "That hole isn't very big. Two people maneuvering a body while minding the sharp edges ... I don't know, between the gore and getting out of the cell, it seems like a recipe for disaster."

Removing Julian from the cell would be manageable: expanding the hole would make it less treacherous. Voss's other point, about the challenge of collecting his body, wasn't as easy to address. Dr. Palmer, with his nerves of steel, could probably stomach the grisly chore, but he'd likely need help transferring what was left of the security chief into a body bag. Who would be up to that task? What if no one else was? Could their medical gloves even fit over the fingers of their suits? The plan seemed untenable when laid out, but they couldn't just leave Julian there. "Let's focus on making sure the HAAB is safe," said Kate. "After that, we can figure out what to do about Julian." The extreme cold would preserve his remains until then.

18

Kate exited the shower and headed straight to her bleating computer terminal. Still dripping, she tapped the screen, accepting the incoming comm from Glenn.

"Sorry to disturb you, Commander, but we've got another problem."

Her stomach dropped at the announcement. Was it a second explosion? A fire? Containment breach? She'd only returned from inspecting Julian's cell an hour ago. What could have gone wrong in that short time?

"Yes," was Kate's curt reply, fueled by irritation and anxiety. Glenn couldn't just deliver the bad news without her cue?

"I secured the station from evacuation protocol as you ordered and gave the green light for everyone in the DFAC to head back to their cells. Engles and Doctor Palmer left. I mean, I eventually did too. I tried to catch you before you jumped in the shower but—"

"What's the problem?" barked Kate, her impatience growing.

"Ah, well, Commander, it's Fisk. He's still there, in the DFAC. He was refusing to head back to his cell. He said it's not safe."

"You didn't tell him what happened, did you?" asked Kate as she toweled her hair, presuming the answer. She'd wanted to collect more information, get NASA's eval before briefing the others. The last thing she needed was unwarranted worry about the HAAB's safety. Now she'd have to manage that too.

"No, I didn't say a word to any of them. Fisk doesn't have the details, but he's pieced most of it together."

Fisk. After her fraught morning, she had little desire to deal with the idiosyncratic professor. During her time outside with Voss and the half hour she'd spent crafting her update to NASA, she'd looked forward to a shower and a nap to rest her throbbing head.

"He insists the entire HAAB's in danger," continued Glenn. "He said he'll never go back to his cell, and that he wants to leave."

"Leave?" asked Kate.

"Yes, leave, as in Mars."

Kate sighed. "I'll handle it."

- - -

Fisk lifted his eyes as Kate entered the DFAC. The interplanetary geologist sat at a two-person table by the large bay window. She forced a smile through her still-pounding headache. Hopefully she could calm him without too much effort and steal back to her cell.

The professor watched Kate as she approached the table and planted herself in the open chair. Fisk looked grim. He still wore his emergency skin, though not its helmet. He'd flopped the thin headgear back, leaving it dangling like a hood. Rough stubble peppered Fisk's cheeks, dark circles cradled his eyes, and his normally disheveled hair raged in tufts from the sides of his head.

The geologist's forearms rested on the tabletop. His left hand clutched a slim, metallic item, flat but for a soft curve, that fit in his palm. "Is that what I think it is?" asked Kate.

Fisk unscrewed the lid from the item, a flask, lifted it to his lips, and sipped. He winced as he swallowed. "I grabbed it on the way out of my cell. I keep important items near the door, in case of emergency." He offered the flask to Kate, retracting it after a shake of her head. "He's dead," said Fisk, screwing the cap back into place. "Isn't he?"

"Who?"

"Don't play games with me, Commander," growled Fisk. "I know there was some kind of problem with Julian's cell."

Kate hesitated to confirm any of what Fisk had guessed, but keeping silent would only allow his paranoid mind to run wild, filling in the blanks with random facts and falsehoods. "Yes, he's dead."

"In the explosion?" asked Fisk.

Kate nodded. "It seems there was a gas leak." The disclosure sounded anything but reassuring. "Voss inspected all the other cells," she quickly added. "They're perfectly safe."

"That's a crock," said Fisk. "Nowhere's safe around here, not with the Curse."

"There is no curse, Fisk." A hugely improbable string of bad luck—three deaths in their first week on the planet—but no curse.

"Telling yourself that won't make it go away—it only blinds you to the danger." Fisk leaned across the table towards the commander. "I was thinking the only way to survive this thing was for us to leave Mars, but Julian's death gives us another option." He leaned closer. "We can go in there now, go into his cell, and find that bag of whatever it was he brought back from the Face. We can return it ourselves and lift the Curse." Fisk sat back in his chair. "I'm even willing to help."

"It's a mess in there, Fisk, trust me," said Kate. Her mind shot back to images of the wrecked cell. Everything inside had either burned, melted, or warped and lay covered with a thick layer of soot. "It'll be hard enough to pick through items out in the open, much less locate something that may be hidden."

"We'd use a grid to structure the search," said Fisk. "With all of us looking, I think we'd find it pretty fast. It's that, or we leave Mars."

"We're not leaving Mars," said Kate. "There is no curse. For the last time, Cheney's suit had a containment problem. And as for Casey, there's more going on than you know. Julian was responsible—"

"Of course he was," spat Fisk. "He's the whole reason we're in this mess, dragging that bag back here to the HAAB. The Curse unleashed its wrath on him worst of all, at least so far."

"No, that's not what I mean. He—"

"All because of some military black op we've been roped into."

"That's over now," said Kate, seizing the chance to veer the conversation away from the so-called Curse. "Whatever Julian and Cheney were up to, they're the only ones who knew about it. That secret op died with them. We can get back to what the rest of us came here for, why NASA exists in the first place: space research."

"Space research?" cackled Fisk. "Do you know about the charter?"

"What charter?"

"The *NASA* charter," said Fisk. "The one that Congress ratified to create the space agency in 1958."

Kate shook her head.

"The Snow Owl enlightened me with this gem a couple days ago. It's there, right in the charter, just like he said. Section 305 states, and I quote, 'NASA shall be considered a defense agency of the United States for the purpose of chapter seventeen, title thirty-five of the US Code.'"

The two fell silent, Fisk apparently waiting for the commander's reaction to his supposed bombshell revelation and Kate expecting more—there had to be more? "So what does chapter seventeen, title thirty-five say?" she asked.

Fisk blinked at the commander, seemingly confused by the question. "The what?"

"What you said about the charter, the part of the US Code it references, what does it say?" Even if the claim was true, that the charter considered NASA a defense agency for some purpose, the exact implications depended on following the reference. Kate's father, a corporate lawyer, taught her that much.

Fisk's face reddened and his body trembled, like a spring coiled too tightly. "How the hell should I know?" he exploded. "You want to romanticize NASA being some noble space exploration shop, but they're clearly compromised. The charter proves that Congress intended it all along to be just another wing of the military." He unsealed his flask and sipped again. "All of this is splitting hairs, anyway," he said. "How exactly we got to this point doesn't matter much. The question is, what're we gonna do about lifting this curse? If the answer's 'nothing,' then we need to pack up, get in the *Gaia,* and get the hell out of here."

"Leaving early in the *Gaia's* only for an extreme emergency," said Kate.

"How is that not what this is?" asked Fisk.

Kate rubbed her temples. Their conversation, the talking in circles, wasn't helping her raging headache.

"Head still hurting?" asked Fisk. Kate grunted. "Correct me if I'm wrong, but it started shortly after our return from the Face …?"

"My God, Fisk, my headaches are not from some made-up curse." Kate had a good idea of the cause, no supernatural explanation needed.

"How much you wanna bet you start feeling better once we're on our way back home?"

Was she getting through to him? For all her efforts, Fisk seemed as unhinged as when she arrived in the DFAC. Perhaps she could reach him a different way. "You really want to leave now? You haven't even taken your mountain bike out for a ride."

Fisk grimaced. "Believe me, that'll be my biggest disappointment. Kicking up roost across the Martian plains, hucking a hill or two, it's all I've thought about since we landed. Shralping out there would get me the most epic KOM on Strava, an unassailable achievement for the ages. But what good are bragging rights if you're not alive to enjoy them?"

"But if you just—"

"You don't seem to get it, Commander. *This* journey," he said with a jab of his finger into the table, "it was the trip of a lifetime, for all of us, but none of that matters anymore. We're all going to die unless we set things right, unless we lift the Curse by returning that bag of material to the Face. Otherwise, we get on the *Gaia* and leave."

"If there really *is* a curse, what makes you think we can escape it in a rocket?" Commander Holman instantly regretted her words, released in a fit of headache-induced misery and frustration.

The blood rushed from Fisk's face, turning him a ghostly white. Eyes glazed, he slowly sank into his chair.

Kate stood—more words wouldn't help. If anything, they were making the situation worse. "C'mon," she said. "Let's get you to your cell. You'll feel better once you're out of that skin, after a shower." She placed a hand on Fisk's shoulder. "I'll walk you back."

Fisk remained despondent, unmoving. She was about to prod him a second time when he rose to his feet. The two Mars astronauts left the DFAC, the geologist plodding behind Kate with his head hung low. They traveled the Spine without speaking and continued on into his tube.

At his cell, Fisk punched his access code into the keypad and swung open the door. Inside, the space was a patchwork of murky shadows, most lights off and the shades drawn.

Fisk stepped in and turned, facing her. "The Curse is real," he said. "How many more people have to die before you accept that?"

Kate racked her brain for a response but came up empty. What could she say? Reassurances alone hadn't made a dent in his paranoid imaginings.

"The Curse is coming for all of us," said Fisk. His voice lowered to a whisper. "It's coming for all of us, but you and I, Commander, we're next." He pushed the door closed.

Kate lingered for a moment before starting back up the tubeway. At the entrance to the Spine, she angled left for her cell. Despite a mind addled by superstition, Fisk was still a scientist. He would respond to reason. If only she could present the right facts .... Julian's death made further investigation into Casey's murder pointless, but if she could show that Casey died at

Julian's hands rather than by an imagined curse, it might be enough to reach Fisk, might be enough to snap him out of his delusions. Fighting her headache, Commander Holman spun on her heels and set off for the control room.

19

"Hey, Miriam, I need your help."

Miriam sat at her console as Kate bounded into the control room. The station chief didn't respond. Instead, she stared listlessly into her control monitor.

"Miriam?" No answer. Kate settled into a seat next to her. She added in a quiet tone, "Hey."

Miriam blinked, as if for the first time aware of Kate's presence. "Oh, sorry, Commander." She sat cross-legged in her chair, a common pose for the station chief, afforded by her smaller frame and suggestive of a meditative state. Except, Miriam hadn't been meditating. Neither had she fully snapped out of whatever gripped her.

"What's the matter?" asked Kate.

Miriam shifted in her chair but didn't seem any more comfortable. "We've lost so many people," she said. "I was thinking, what if we lose Voss, or Engles? What if we lose Doctor Palmer?" She shifted uncomfortably again. "The Mars mission suddenly feels so ... fragile. Not because of the explosion—I mean, machinery fails, but it seems like there's always a workaround, some other option. That's not the problem. The weak link in this whole adventure is our dependence on highly skilled, irreplaceable people."

Kate smiled gently. "NASA's always just a phone call away."

"They can't talk us through a surgery," said Miriam.

The Mars mission could encounter any of a million different failure modes—the lack of a surgeon was only one of them. "I've learned it's better not to fixate on what could go wrong," said Kate. "That said, the odds of Doctor Palmer dying and someone needing major surgery have to be fairly small." She ended her remark with a smile but Miriam didn't react. "Tell me what's *really* bothering you."

Miriam sighed. "We lost Julian today. What if we lose you, and Glenn. What if I'm the last member of the command staff left?"

"First of all, I'm not going anywhere, and neither is Glenn."

"Julian would've said the same."

"Second," continued Kate, ignoring Miriam's quip, "if you ever do need to take charge, I know you'll do great."

Miriam's shoulders hunched. "I failed the command aptitude test," she said.

"Failed it the first time," said Kate, to Miriam's apparent surprise. "I've been over everyone's file many times. You failed it on the first try but passed it on the second."

"Barely," said Miriam.

"Look, you wouldn't be here, third in command of the most audacious trip mankind has ever imagined, if NASA didn't think you have the right stuff. You're smart, resourceful, and absolutely capable of leading this mission or any other. I know that if the time ever comes, you will rise to the occasion. You're command material. You just have to believe in yourself, and the rest will follow." Getting Miriam's mind away from idle speculation and on to solving a problem would help with her mood. "I need you to check something for me."

"What?"

"Voss thinks the tube cameras from the HAAB's qualification days are still active. She thinks they're dumping video files to the station computer." The commander settled into a seat next to Miriam. "I need your help finding something."

"Video that proves Julian killed Casey?" asked Miriam.

How did she know? Kate hadn't seen Miriam since the events of the previous evening. She'd had no chance to brief the station chief.

"Glenn came by last night for help locking Julian in his cell," said Miriam to Kate's confused expression. "He explained the situation to me. But can I ask, Commander, now that Julian's dead, what difference does it make?"

Kate couldn't let Miriam in on the real reason she wanted the clips. So far, Fisk's mad ravings about a curse hadn't spread. Hopefully, she could keep it that way. "I want to see the clips for myself, catch him red-handed."

Miriam scooted forward in her chair. "OK …," she said with a finger against her lips, "though I'm not all that sure where those files would live." She adjusted her glasses and unleashed a blaze of taps on her keyboard. An empty window sprouted on the control room's massive monitor. "That's not it." Miriam thought for a moment. She released a machine gun spray of typing that summoned a succession of windows, all empty. Miriam paused again, then tapped out a new query. A window popped up with a short list of folders. She clicked four of them open. Each presented a list of video files. "Looks like I found them."

"Great," said Kate, rolling closer. "Can you show me the area outside Casey's cell two days ago, around one p.m.?" They'd start their search a few hours prior to her death.

Miriam tapped out the query. A window surfaced with a fisheye view of a tubeway interior captured from the ceiling. A single door sat slightly left of the frame's center with "C. MORGAN" etched into the adjacent nameplate. A timestamp in the lower-right corner marched ahead, the only motion on an otherwise still image.

"Can you advance to when someone appears in the corridor?" asked Kate.

Miriam fast-forwarded the video to a figure standing at Casey's door, the back of his shaved head shining beneath the tubeway lights.

"Julian," whispered Kate. Despite knowing he'd visited Casey, his appearance still shocked her. The timestamp read 2:37 p.m. Seconds passed. The door opened, revealing Casey in a light blue terrycloth robe. Her hair hung limp, damp from a shower. The clip of the two astronauts felt surreal, Kate's dead colleagues resurrected on the screen.

Casey spoke to Julian, but no words sounded from the monitor. "Is there audio?" asked Kate.

"Sorry, Commander," said Miriam. "It looks like the cameras are restricted to video."

Julian's head bobbed a silent reply to Casey.

"What I don't get," said Miriam, "is after that scene in the galley, I wouldn't think Casey wanted anything to do with that creep."

The nature of the conversation between Julian and Casey remained unclear, but far from upset, the astrobiologist seemed mostly ambivalent about the security chief's presence. She backed into the foyer and motioned him forward. Julian disappeared inside, and the door closed.

The visit began innocently enough. What mattered, though, was how it ended: Julian slipping out of Casey's cell after the murder. "Can you jump to where he comes back out?" Once they located the incriminating stretch of video, she'd have Miriam send her the clip. Kate would send it to Fisk and copy Dr. Palmer on the message with a request that he corroborate Casey's time of death. Hopefully such hard evidence would deflate Fisk's belief in a curse taking astronaut lives.

Miriam fast-forwarded the video to Julian poking his head from the open cell door. The security chief quickly glanced down either side of the passageway and ventured fully into the corridor. Sweat beaded on his brow, and he wore a concerned look.

The sight was nauseating. *He's worried about getting caught,* thought Kate. *He killed her, and now he's making his getaway. Except, he's not.* Julian had no idea he was being watched.

A hand darted from the doorway, grabbing the material of Julian's jumpsuit. The security chief spun around as Casey emerged, her dark curls bouncing at her shoulders. The astrobiologist wore a white t-shirt that grazed the tops of her bare thighs. She pulled Julian close. The two kissed for an eternity in the soundless clip. Casey walked into her cell and closed the door. Julian turned, his face clear in profile, and slid out the left side of the frame.

"3:12 p.m.," said Miriam, reading the timestamp. "A full half hour before she died." She looked at Commander Holman, baffled. "So he *didn't* kill her?"

Julian *had* to be her killer—Kate's gut told her so—but the clip showed Casey alive when he left. The video apparently absolved him of her death. Maybe he *was* innocent after all …. "Or maybe he returned," she said, excited by her deduction. He could've paid her a second visit and killed her on his return. "What's the next event on the tape?"

Miriam forwarded the clip to a man with a shaved head again standing in front of Casey's door. A tall man—taller than Julian—with dark brown skin.

Kate gasped. *Glenn!*

Light spilled into the corridor as the cell door opened. Casey appeared, clad in a green station jumpsuit and hair drawn back in a bun. The two exchanged words. Once they finished, Glenn slipped inside and closed the door.

The timestamp read 3:31 p.m. "Six minutes before Casey's death," said Kate. Her heart raced. "Zoom to the next event."

The video jumped ahead to Glenn in the foyer. He peeked his head out, scanned the tubeway, and stepped into it. The tall *Ares* astronaut eased the door closed behind him. He lingered for a moment, his placid face offering no hint at his thoughts. He surveyed the corridor a second time and exited left in the frame.

Kate trembled as she checked the timestamp: 3:49 p.m. Twelve minutes *after* Casey's death. Casey was alive when Glenn arrived but not when he left. Commander Holman calmed herself as best she could. She'd known Glenn for five years. She couldn't believe he killed her—why would he? Dr. Palmer hadn't determined a cause of death. Casey, however improbably, could have succumbed to natural causes. Whatever happened, Glenn had said nothing about visiting her, nor of her dying while he was with her. He'd apparently been content to let Julian take the blame. "Where's Glenn now?" asked Kate, working hard to keep her voice steady.

Miriam tapped her keyboard, spawning a map of the station on the main monitor with a pulsing red dot. "In his cell." She hesitated. "Do you really think Glenn killed her?"

The clip upended everything Kate thought she knew about Glenn. Perhaps he, too, had a romantic interest in Casey. Perhaps he'd learned of Julian's visit and flown into a rage, except there wasn't a mark on Casey's body, no sign of struggle. "I don't know what to think," she said, rubbing the temples of her throbbing head. "I need to hear his side." She shot a stern look at Miriam. "Not a word of this to anyone."

Miriam nodded solemnly.

"Have Doctor Palmer and Voss meet me outside Glenn's cell—no, scratch that. Get me Engles, Engles and Palmer." Voss was busy inspecting the station for clues to what went wrong in Julian's cell. Better to let her continue that important job. Engles's suspected romantic interest in Casey might complicate the situation, but this sort of confrontation dictated a show of force. Asking Fisk along was out of the question, his erratic behavior making him more liability than asset.

"Should I tell them to bring weapons?"

"No. I don't know." The decision to arrive armed at Julian's door had been a no-brainer, the security chief's demeanor always hinting at a pent-up rage. Until a few minutes ago, Kate would've called Glenn the gentlest person in the world. The clip threw that assessment out the window. She checked the charge on her pellet gun. Would he really give them a reason to fire on him? If anything, she'd need to restrain herself from shooting him outright; she was so angry. "Tell Engles to grab a gun." As for the good doctor, who knew the last time he'd shot a weapon? He'd be a potentially dangerous source of crossfire in a firefight. "Palmer doesn't need one." Two firearms would be enough to signal they meant business.

"Yes, ma'am."

The commander stormed out of the HAAB's control center, her fury growing with each step. The depth of emotion surprised her. She explored its source. Glenn had lied to her. Not a flat-out lie, one of omission. He'd neglected to mention visiting Casey and had remained silent about being the last one to see her alive. Julian was an asshole, but that didn't give Glenn license to silently frame him for her death. During their training and five-month journey, she'd come to rely on Glenn more and more, believed she could trust him. He'd destroyed that trust, had taken her for a fool. He likely figured no one would ever find out.

Kate's steps turned to furious stomps down the passageway as she rounded the corner into the Spine.

20

Engles arrived ahead of Palmer outside Glenn's cell. Kate greeted the ashen-haired, skinny engineer with a wave and a sullen look, the latter not intended for her.

"Miriam asked me to meet you here," said Engles. "She said to bring a weapon. She wouldn't say why. She told me to ask you."

Smart of Miriam to let her brief Engles, though she didn't relish the task. "Before we get to that, how are you doing?"

"Fine," she deadpanned through what seemed a sleepy sadness. "Not fine. I'm having a hard time with Casey's death. I mean, I still feel bad about Cheney, but with Casey, she and I were ... close." Engles wiped a tear, then a second. "She was a ray of sunshine, a radiant flower, such a joyful personality, so full of love. The whole world saw it. She drew the attention of every room she entered. I asked her once how it felt to be the one person everyone wanted to be near. She just kind of laughed it off." Her eyes sank to the floor, weighed down by heavy musings. They rose, red-rimmed and full of fire. "At least that bastard Julian got what he deserved."

How close had they been? Maybe more than Kate had known. That could possibly complicate using her as backup during her visit to Glenn, but she didn't have great options. She'd have to brief the spacecraft engineer before they went inside. "About Julian ...." How best to describe? "I'm no longer certain he was involved."

"No?"

"No," said Kate. Her thoughts, her words, weren't flowing smoothly, not the way she had envisioned the moment. "There have been some developments ... new evidence that implicates Glenn."

"Implicates him in what?" asked Engles. Her sleepy sadness had melted away, replaced by an alert, agitated concern.

Kate hesitated. "In Casey's death."

"What kind of evidence?"

"I checked the tube video ... I wanted to see Julian exiting Casey's cell. Turns out Glenn left shortly after she died."

Engles grew hushed, processing. In a flash, she bolted in a furious rush for Glenn's cell door. Kate caught her. "Hold on. It doesn't prove he had anything to do with her death."

"But it means he knows something about how she died," said Engles. "If she'd died accidentally, he would've reported that, right? He wouldn't have kept it a secret."

"That's why I'm having this meeting with Glenn, to get his side of the story. There could be a perfectly good explanation why he hasn't said a word."

"What could that even be?" scoffed Engles.

Kate had no idea. Her claim about a perfectly good explanation was more hope than belief. There could only be one reason for Glenn's silence, only one reason he hadn't reported Casey dying in his presence: he was entangled, somehow. Despite the seeming pointlessness of it all, they would follow due process, presume innocence, at least until they got the defendant's side. That's how they would manage criminal matters on her watch.

Engels teared up. "That bastard."

"Laura, we mustn't assume—"

"That *bastard* came to check on me," continued Engles. "Said he'd heard I'd taken Casey's death hard. He came to console me ...." Revulsion and horror flashed across her face, the spacecraft engineer likely replaying the episode in the new light. She looked at the commander. "And now you say he may have had a part in her death?"

Glenn's duties included helping with morale, but what better way to throw off suspicion than to console the affected. Kate grabbed Engles by her shoulders. "Look, the whole thing's confusing, doesn't add up. We're here ... I'm here to get some answers. I asked Miriam to send you and Palmer so I'm not in Glenn's cell by myself, in case ... well, who knows what could happen —"

Palmer entered the tube from the Spine. Kate released Engles and assumed a casual stance as the doctor ambled towards them. "Here I am," he said upon his arrival.

Kate tracked the doctor's eyes as they shifted from her own poor acting job to Engles's angry, tear-streaked cheeks. He had to be confused ... and formulating a question. "Good," she said, before he could inquire. "Some evidence has emerged that suggests Glenn knows more about Casey's death than he's revealed. I need to ask him some questions, and I don't want to do that alone. I need the two of you to stand there, with me, inside his cell. I'll do the talking."

"Got it, Commander," said Palmer.

Kate addressed Engles. "Miriam told you to grab a weapon—I want you to keep it holstered. The only time you should withdraw it is if we're being attacked, which I can't imagine happening." Same instructions she'd given Glenn and Voss on their trip to Julian's.

Engles's tears had dried, but the spacecraft engineer's feelings clearly still smoldered beneath the surface. Kate's voice softened. "Do you think you can do that, Laura? The last thing we need is a firefight or aggressive—"

"No problem, Commander," spat Engles. She untied and quickly retied the orange bandana around her head.

Perhaps involving her hadn't been the smartest move. Hopefully Engles could maintain her cool inside. The commander turned and, too impatient for the buzzer, rapped her knuckles against the cell door. "Glenn, it's Kate. I need to talk to you."

Shuffling feet sounded within the cell. The door opened. "Hey, Commander, Engles ... Palmer ...," said Glenn, his sentence trailing off and his at-first friendly smile narrowing as he studied the commander and her entourage. "What's up?"

Was that an innocent question? Or did he suspect why they were there? "Mind if we come in?"

Glenn hesitated. "Can I ask what it's about?"

"You'll see once we start talking," snarled Engles.

"Let me handle this," said Kate with a stern look and motioning for the engineer to calm herself. "Let's talk inside," she said to Glenn.

Glenn eyed Engles, who remained quiet but hurled knives at him with her eyes. "Okaaaay," he said, retreating to the recesses of his cell.

Kate, Engles, and Palmer trailed Glenn into the compartment. The space gave the commander a chill. The cell's layout matched Julian's, Glenn's quarters an immaculate version of the charred apartment she and Voss had picked through earlier that day. Glenn stopped near his dresser, in almost the same spot as Julian when they'd confronted him the evening prior. Kate and Engles spread out, positioning themselves on either side. Palmer hung back from the commander.

"Whatever this is, it sure must be serious," said Glenn.

The jovial tone provoked Kate's wrath. "I'm going to ask you this once, and I want a straight answer."

"When have I ever not given you a straight answer?" asked Glenn.

He was being evasive, drawing it out. "Why didn't you mention visiting Casey in her cell?"

Glenn paused. Or froze, in a sudden panic, racking his brain for an answer. He'd realized they were onto him. "I didn't tell you because I didn't think it was relevant."

A fresh wave of anger flushed Kate's face. Aghast, she could barely speak. "You didn't think it was relevant?"

"No," he said, blinking back at her. "I mean, I've been to *everyone's* cell. Fisk's, Palmer's, Engles here. Everyone's."

The depth of his bullshit was unbelievable. "That might be true," Kate said with a sneer, "but the difference with Palmer, Fisk, and Engles is *they're* all still alive."

Glenn cocked his head. "Yes, they are." His mind whirred, or at least he put on a show. "Just what are you saying?"

"She's saying you were involved in her death, you motherfucker!" said Engles, southern accent flaring. She advanced.

Kate put her hand out and growled: "Laura, I said I would *handle* this." The intensity of her gaze drove Engles back to her original spot. The commander returned to Glenn. "I took a close look at the tube video, the recordings that were going to incriminate or absolve Julian."

"And what did you find?" asked Glenn.

He had to know he'd been caught red-handed, yet still he played along. She could keep playing, too. "They showed you going in and out of Casey's cell," said Kate. "Based on the timestamps, she was alive when you got there and dead when you left."

Glenn squinted at Kate. "What the hell are you talking about?" he shouted. "Engles and I found Casey dead, together, when she called me to her cell. I don't know anything about how she died and certainly wasn't there when it happened." Was he sincere? There wasn't a hint of that goofy grin, no room for it amidst his upset. Glenn punctuated his statement with an indignant crossing of his arms. He took a step forward. "And as for you coming in here, accusing me of—"

Pop, pop.

Glenn's expression slipped from anger to astonishment, and then to a flaccid nothingness as all emotion dribbled away. His eyes lost focus and rolled back into his head as he crumpled to the ground.

Kate, shaken and speechless, stood stunned at the sight of her second-in-command sprawled on the floor. Though deep down she understood what had happened, she labored to believe it. The sweet smell of pellet propellant erased any doubt. Still agape, she looked over at Engles. "Why the hell did you shoot him?"

"He ...." The spacecraft engineer struggled for words. "I thought he was going to shoot us," she stammered.

"He's unarmed," said Kate. Glenn's weapon sat in its holster, which dangled from a peg in the wall panel. "His pellet gun's there behind him."

"Not shoot us, I guess ... attack us," she said after a few seconds of reflection. "He was cornered. I was worried what would happen next." She waited but found no sympathy in the commander's expression. "We exposed him," Engles pleaded. "When he moved, I ... I guess I thought he was coming for us." She seemed to still be searching for an answer. "I'm sorry, Commander."

When Commander Holman had called on Julian with Glenn and Voss, the security chief's sudden movement toward his dresser had been unnerving, but none of them had taken action to subdue him. Glenn hadn't approached his weapon, wasn't even facing it, but the simple crossing of his arms and moving a single step closer had been enough to get him shot. In the split-second calculus of the moment, he'd been deemed a significant threat, though he'd shown a fraction of Julian's provocation.

Dr. Palmer rushed to the motionless astronaut, a tangle of arms and legs. Glenn's breathing was raspy, on the edge of snoring. The doctor hoisted his shirt, exposing two large welts on his abdomen. "He'll be unconscious for at least a day," said Palmer. The fast-dissolving pellets had flooded his body with a powerful sedative. Palmer stretched Glenn's shirt back into place and smoothed it over his belly. "Help me get him to his bed."

Kate passed the still-shocked Engles to join Palmer. She worked with the doctor to drag Glenn across the floor and lift him onto his bed. Kate removed the fallen astronaut's boots while Palmer wrestled a blanket over him. He checked Glenn's pulse, pressing fingers first to his neck, then his wrist.

With Glenn settled into his bed, the commander activated her comm. "Miriam, it's Kate. Glenn's been shot. Two clean rounds from a pellet gun." She could hear the wheels turning in Miriam's head. "I'll explain later. I need you to lock down his cell. Give us five minutes to clear out."

"Yes, ma'am."

Engles could do little more than stare at her comatose colleague, despondent. Kate placed a hand on her arm. "He'll be up and around before you know it. It's actually better this way—with him locked in his cell, there'll be no need for another confrontation. Once Glenn wakes, I can ask all my questions over the comm." Maybe what they should have done in the first place. She gave Engles's arm a squeeze. "We'll get to the bottom of this, figure out what he knows about Casey's death."

Engles said nothing, still lost in her despondent stare.

"Let's head out," said Kate. "Let Miriam lock down the cell."

- - -

Seated at her desk, Kate tapped the red record button on her computer display. "Hello again, Assistant Director Pearson. It's been a bit of a busy morning here on Mars." How, exactly, to continue? "Some new evidence has come to light that Commander Wiles may have played a role in Casey Morgan's death." Though shocking, the recent revelation about Glenn's involvement hadn't changed the situation much, her second-in-command simply replacing Julian as the prime suspect. "I'm not sure what I'll find when I finish questioning him, but I'm not optimistic about the outcome. What happens if I determine he's guilty? By what authority can I even render such a judgement? As I pointed out in my last message, we have no court of law here. It's not at all clear what rights any of us have. I mean, we have rights as Americans, but this is not America. It's important NASA send guidance on how to proceed."

What else to say? Kate drew a blank. "Holman out." She stopped the recording, sighed, and pressed the transmit button. The time, noonday on Mars, roughly coincided with 11 p.m. at the Johnson Space Center. If only the assistant director called Houston his home, her message might've caught him still awake. Though he was NASA's second-highest official, she found him more often in Washington, D.C., in a Pentagon office no less. The midnight hour on the East Coast meant she might receive a reply by evening Mars time. She shook her head at the wishful thinking—the AD hadn't yet responded to her previous day's update on Julian, or any of her other messages, for that matter.

Ice picks jabbed in the space behind her eyes. Kate forced herself up, wincing as she stumbled to her bed. She laid herself out. A short nap would take the edge off her resurgent headache. After dashing off the message to Earth, she'd planned on visiting Fisk. Her trip to the researcher's cell would have to wait. At least she had the solid evidence she needed to savage his claims of a curse somehow killing Casey.

Commander Kate Holman closed her eyes and drifted off to sleep.

21

Kate staggered down the maintenance tubeway, eyes teared and blurry. The past twenty-four hours had not gone well.

Following the debacle with Glenn, she'd allowed herself a short, noonday nap. She'd woken to a dark cell and a brilliant, star-filled evening sky. Kate headed to Fisk's quarters, and after several knocks and presses of the chime, she forced open the door. Inside she discovered him ... gone, missing, greeted by the clutter of previous visits but not the research scientist himself. Miriam checked the tube cameras from the time Kate escorted him to his cell: no one had entered or exited. Fisk had somehow, inexplicably, vanished.

A fitful night of sleep bled into a daybreak with no video check-in from her children, the first day of the whole trip in which she hadn't received one. Nor was NASA's "good morning" message waiting in her inbox, or any replies to the messages she and Miriam had sent. The various terrestrial data feeds were free of chatter. Perhaps most disturbing, the "heartbeat" signal, a ping NASA generated every sixty seconds to affirm the long-distance Internet connection, had stopped. They appeared to be cut off from home.

Topping it off, her head throbbed worse than ever, despite the special meds prescribed by Dr. Palmer. She could barely see straight with the sharp spikes behind her eyes. She yearned to crawl back under the blankets in her bed but had been summoned by Voss to the Life Support cell. Why? The station engineer refused to say over the comm. Voss was still investigating the explosion. She'd evidently learned something about the root cause, something she didn't want anyone else to hear.

Arriving at the Life Support cell, Kate tapped the entry code on the keypad. A green light heralded the sideways shift of thick bolts. The commander pushed the reinforced door inward, receiving a blast of humid, warm air. She quickly entered and closed the doors. A floor-to-ceiling maze of piping and bulky equipment lay before her. She'd toured the double-wide cell prior to its deployment to Mars, familiarizing herself with the HAAB's air and water purification systems. The room had a different feel than during her visit on Earth, much noisier and warmer, the bustling machinery busy about the business of keeping them alive.

A network of colored lines shot forward from beneath her feet. She followed the blue one—her memory could have likely shepherded her to the water reclamation system, but the message from Voss had been urgent. Better not to risk wasting time getting lost.

The blue line guided her between stacks of machinery, leading Kate to the distant recesses of the cell. She rounded a corner to the sight of Voss peering into the top of a junction box, part of the HAAB's massive water reclamation system. The box, a convergence point for multiple large pipes, rose a meter and a half from the floor.

Voss looked up as Kate approached. The station engineer rarely smiled and this occasion was no exception, but she appeared more grim than usual. Likely not a good sign.

"Is this about the explosion?" asked Kate.

"The what?" shouted Voss above the whirring of machinery. "No." She grabbed a nearby rag and wiped her hands. "So far, all the natural gas lines seem fine."

Kate's irritation level ratcheted up a notch. "Then why'd you call me down here?"

Voss raked the rag across her brow. "Have you ever wondered how water travels to all ends of the station without freezing up?"

Daytime temperatures on Mars averaged minus sixty degrees Celsius. Most of the water pipes snaked along the HAAB's exposed underside, at least that seemed so from her time with Voss the previous day. "Heated somehow?"

"Ding, ding, ding," said a patronizing Voss. "The HAAB's water lines are covered by an insulating sleeve with an embedded electrical heating element, which keeps the pipes from freezing. The geniuses who designed this sleeve probably figured they could save money by using the water pipes themselves as part of the electrical circuit."

Astronauts were dead and missing, the HAAB had suffered a fatal explosion that could potentially happen again, but Voss was babbling on about the mechanics of shuttling water around the station?

"You still with me, Commander?" asked Voss.

"Yes, I'm still with you," Kate huffed. Her eyes had glazed over, wondering where Voss was going with all her talk, but she'd followed the station engineer's prattle. Powering a circuit required the electric current to travel in a loop, returning to its source. For the insulated sleeves, that meant flowing through the heating element and back. Any conductor would suffice for the return trip, be it a proper wire or a metal pipe. "Seems like a clever solution."

"I'm sure that's what those geniuses thought also," said Voss. "Probably broke their arms patting themselves on the back." She wadded the rag and tossed it to the floor. "The water lines are made up of individual stretches of pipe. To connect two pipes together, you insert the ends into a coupling and flow metal solder into the gaps. The solder acts like a hot, liquid glue that forms a solid seal. But Metallurgy 101 says that when you have two different metals in contact, an electrical differential can cause one to migrate. This tendency is especially pronounced in the presence of water."

Voss lifted a flashlight from its perch on the case's rim, switched it on, and aimed its beam down into the junction box. She motioned Commander Holman closer.

Moist air buffeted Kate's face as she neared. Uncertain what she'd find, she eased her head over the open case and peeked into the dark enclosure. A series of spinning gears and belts whirred among a crosswise assortment of pipes. What did Voss want her to see? She peered deeper into the case, attention drawn to a shimmering glint at the bottom. Her eyes focused on a shiny strip of metal? No—it was light reflecting from a pool of standing water, its surface swirled with a rainbowed, oily sheen. A number of the pipes that emerged from the mess below glistened with water sheeting down their sides, a liquid gloss that trickled from connections at the top. "My god," Kate whispered.

"Yes," said Voss. "The electricity flowing through the pipes during the HAAB's year-long qualification period weakened some of the solder joints. Active use of the water system since our arrival put additional strain on those connections. Some have started to give out." She flipped off the flashlight and restored the cover to the top of the case. "So much for going with the low-cost bidder."

"How long to—" A sudden, sharp pain blurred Kate's vision with its intensity. "How long to repair?"

"Repair what?" asked Voss. "The metal migration isn't localized to the Life Support cell—it's a problem along every electrified stretch of pipe. What I showed you is a taste of what's happening all over the station. Maybe not now, not all at the same time, but eventually every connector and elbow joint will be leaking."

The pain made thinking difficult, but Kate soldiered on. "It's going to take time to come up with a plan, our own or one from NASA. Until then, we have to keep water flowing in the pipes. How do we stay ahead of the water loss?"

Voss sighed and rolled her eyes. "You'll recall, or maybe you don't—the HAAB's water supply is a closed system. All the water we use gets reclaimed one way or another, from the toilets and drains or by pulling it out of the atmosphere." Voss paused, apparently waiting for a glimmer of understanding from Kate. None came. "It means NASA filled the system with all the water we should need for our entire year-long stay on Mars."

Kate understood the words Voss had uttered, but her throbbing head prevented her from grasping their implication.

"There's no backup water supply sitting in bottles or drums somewhere," said Voss to Kate's vacant look. "All the water we have lives in these pipes and the master reservoir. The system's slowly bleeding out. When it's done, we're done."

Kate massaged her temples, angling for enough relief to allow her mind to function. "How long do we have?"

"At the rate we're losing water, I'd say a couple weeks."

"Two weeks?" said Kate, breathless. "What if we go into conservation mode, stop showering?"

Voss shook her head. "Showers aren't the problem. Water's leaking out everywhere. It's going to do that whether we use another drop or not."

"Can we recover that water?" asked Kate.

"We can siphon it out of a space like this junction box, but we've got leaks all over the HAAB, some of them external. If we crawled under the station to collect the ice, we wouldn't get it all. It's just a matter of time until one of these joints erupts into a major leak."

"What if—"

"There's no getting around it, Commander," interrupted Voss. "Because of all those geniuses back home, we are royally screwed."

"What about the genius right in front of me?" blurted Kate in a fit of pain and exasperation.

The outburst took Voss aback. Kate had never spoken other than cordially to her.

"Sorry," said Kate, massaging her temples. "My head's pounding something fierce." She breathed in deeply, held it, and pushed it out, visualizing the pain leaving with the exhalation. "Look, you're on this mission because you're NASA's best station engineer. If we didn't have you, I'd say we're in deep trouble—"

"It's not all riding on me," said Voss. "NASA has its share of morons on the payroll, but they also have a handful of very smart people."

"Right now, I don't know *when* we'll hear from NASA again."

"What do you mean?" asked Voss.

Besides herself, only Miriam knew of the communication issues. Kate hadn't planned on spreading the news, at least not right away—pointless to alarm the others unless it was clear they had a problem. Her slip-up would expand the circle of people in the know. "We didn't receive any of our regular wakeup comms this morning. And the sixty-second heartbeat's down. Until things change, we have to assume we're on our own."

The news stunned Voss, the first time Kate had witnessed the station engineer at a loss for words.

"Look, I know your record," said Kate. "You saved that Moon Outpost from running out of air."

The words brought Voss back to the room. "That was different," she said, quiet.

"Was it? Everyone else there believed they were dead. You refused to accept that assessment. I need you to do the same here."

"But on the Moon, collecting oxygen is a simple matter of heating the regolith," said Voss.

Kate shrugged. "There's water on Mars, lots of it. Figure a way to get us some."

"But—"

"Stop whining and find a solution!" shouted Kate. "You talk about how dumb everyone else is, complain that I'm trying to do your job—for once, show me why I shouldn't even try." The words came out with more bite than she intended, but her pounding headache removed any finesse from their delivery.

"What if I can't?" Voss asked, sheepishly.

"What if you can't? It's simple, really: we abandon Mars. We abort the mission, get in the *Gaia*, and leave. But I don't want to do that, not after all the money NASA spent to make this trip possible, not after everything we all sacrificed to get here." Commander Holman winced, the ice picks and needles taking fresh jabs at her eyes. "I have to go lie down," she said, squinting through tears. "Put that massive brain of yours to work and get us some water." The commander walked away, disappearing into the maze of pipes and equipment.

"Get us some water," Voss scoffed, her bravado returning with Commander Holman's departure. "Yeah, sure thing. And maybe I'll scrounge up a year's supply of gin while I'm at it!" she yelled after her.

No one answered. Voss was all alone in the cell, all alone with the whirring machinery and the fate of the mission. The station engineer settled onto the floor. Leaning her back against the vibrating junction box, she started to think.

22

Voss snaked past humming equipment, mulling over her plan on her way to the exit. Once out of the Life Support cell, she headed to the door directly across the tubeway and pecked an entry code on the adjacent keypad. Voss barreled into the Depot, a dimly lit, double-wide cell stocked with all manner of repair and fabrication materials. She turned right, walked eleven meters, then shimmied sideways down a narrow aisle.

The station engineer moved slowly as she scanned the tightly packed shelves, her gaze ping-ponging between floor and ceiling. Commander Holman wasn't an idiot like most others, but she didn't have a complete understanding of the situation they were in. The problem of remaining on Mars was about more than acquiring water. All the $H2O$ in the solar system wouldn't make a difference when one of the HAAB's leaky connections gave out. To avoid abandoning the station, they needed water *and* a way to fix the leaks.

Voss halted halfway down the aisle, her attention drawn to a flash of copper. Sealed, plastic bins stuffed with copper connectors sat at eye level, along with a bundle of solder spools, four vacuum torches, and eight fuel canisters. Strapped onto the shelf below, several hundred meters of copper pipe in three-meter sections shined back at her. At least not all the provisioners at NASA were idiots. Locating and repairing each leak would be a pain in the ass, but the correct tools and equipment made it doable. That left the task of securing a new supply of water.

Voss backtracked to the front of the cell and squeezed down a nearby corridor crammed with electrical equipment. She immediately spotted her quarry: coils of black-and-yellow electrical cable in a dispenser box. Despite their thinness, the specs printed on the yellow stripe certified the cables as rated for extreme voltages and high currents. She grabbed two of the fifty-meter spools, a wire crimper, and a multimeter.

With a spool encircling each shoulder, Voss shuffled out of the aisle and marched to the rear of the Depot. She worked quickly, grabbing a survival tent; a portable heater; a loop of clear, insulated tubing; a collapsible shovel;

a thermal drill; duct tape, and a plastic crate stuffed with elasticine patch squares. She emptied the squares onto the floor, loaded the crate with her haul, and bolted from the Depot. Voss carried the supplies to her cell, where she changed into her Mars suit.

Twenty-five minutes later, Voss stood outside the HAAB, ten meters from the auxiliary airlock. She dropped the crate and cables onto the dull red earth and set to executing her plan.

- - -

Ice fishing.

Today, Voss's life had come full circle—the realization floored her. She'd left eighteen childhood winters in Minnesota for college in the California sun and never looked back. The coldest days at CalTech rarely dipped into the low forties.

She sat on the flipped crate inside the compact tent, its heat-retaining Mylar walls reflecting her movements in coppery shimmers. Piles of excavated Martian soil surrounded a ragged opening in the tent's fabric floor where electrical cable dived into a meter-deep pit of gurgling slush. As a child, she'd sat for hours with her father, shivering in a tiny ice shanty while peering down a hole he'd carved in the frozen lake.

The first incarnation of her plan would at least keep them alive: they'd shuttle pails of slush back to the HAAB like firemen passing buckets on a line. They couldn't drink it, of course, but the station's filtration system could easily remove the impurities. Her plan's second incarnation depended on driving the tent to higher temperatures, high enough to generate water vapor that could condense and flow to the HAAB on its own, within the stretch of insulated tubing. Inspired by her quip about a year's supply of gin, her makeshift still would produce pure water, not spirits.

Voss stood tall as she could in the cramped interior, unzipped the door, and stepped outside. She stretched her legs and congratulated herself on her, dare she say, genius. Her smile faded, chased away by the fresh calculations in her head. Something was wrong with her setup: the tiny tent should have been more sauna than ice hut.

She slid her scopes from the pouch at her hip and aimed them at a structure a hundred meters away. The unit resembled a small Airstream trailer, its silvery sheen dulled by a thick layer of Martian dust. A quick survey revealed no outward sign of trouble with the *Gaia's* rocket fuel generator. The nuclear-powered factory had spent a year splitting subsurface ice into hydrogen and oxygen to fill the rocket's tanks. With fueling completed before they arrived, the reactor sat dormant, waiting to power the *Gaia's* systems in the days leading up to their return home.

Voss trained the binoculars on a screen embedded in the generator's side. "What the ...?" she said to the display's amber grid of numbers. The current flowing through the auxiliary circuit where she'd patched the other end of the electrical cable was an order of magnitude lower than it should have been. She swore, stowed her scopes, and ventured towards the fueling station.

Faint wisps of clouds floated in the ruddy Martian sky as Voss trekked across the desolate landscape of rusted rock. Similar environments existed back home, harsh and barren, but those spaces differed in one important respect: they all contained the building blocks of life. A biologist she'd dated at CalTech had searched for a sterile plot of Earth to use as a baseline for his dissertation experiments. Teddy had ranted about the entire globe being contaminated. From the deepest ocean to the most remote glacier to the hottest volcanic crag, there wasn't a square centimeter devoid of genetic material. With their first footsteps on Mars, how long until the same would be said of the red planet?

At the fuel generator, the reactor's control screen showed the problem: the *Gaia* was drawing electricity, a lot of electricity, in fact. But why? Did the rocket's hibernation mode really require that much power? "Miriam, patch me through to Engles."

"This is Engles," sounded in her helmet a few moments later.

"Hey, Laura, I'm out here at the fueling station. Any idea why the *Gaia* would be drawing a few hundred kilowatts?"

"A few hundred?" A pause. "There are heaters keeping some critical systems warm, but nothing that requires that much power. Is it screwing up your plans?"

"Yeah," said Voss. "The ship's plugged into a priority outlet, which is limiting the current available to other circuits."

"The power plant thinks we're getting ready to take off," said Engles. "It's reserving full output for peak demands from the rocket."

"Any way to boost power on the aux circuit?" asked Voss. If not, her distillery wouldn't reach the kinds of temperatures needed to automate the operation.

"Unfortunately, no," said Engles. "Some systems are running that shouldn't be. It's gonna mean a trip to the *Gaia* to sort out. You want me to come help?"

"Negative," said Voss, stifling her irritation. "There's no sense in you getting suited up. I'll make the trek and relay what I'm seeing. You can talk me through shutting systems down, or whatever we need to do."

"Roger that," said Engles.

The station engineer hop-skipped the four hundred meters to the *Gaia*, the gleaming rocket casting a broad shadow on the land in the weak afternoon sunlight. Atop it sat the crew capsule, identical to the one that had delivered them to Mars.

Voss recalled the elevator from the top of the launch tower. After entering the cab and waiting for its seventy-four-meter climb to complete, a few steps along the gantry brought her to the capsule's door. A breathtaking view of the Martian plains raced away in every direction. Voss clutched the railing, feeling microscopic in the moment: a tiny spec alongside an enormous metal tube, amidst an endless, undulating red sea of rock and dust.

She tapped the code into the entry keypad and tugged. The door didn't budge, but beeps in her helmet accompanied a message that scrolled on her heads-up display. Apparently the interior was pressurized. But why? Perhaps to prevent the consoles from freezing: no atmosphere, no heat. In any case, she'd have to wait for the air to evacuate before the lock would release. After a thirty-second delay, Voss swung the door out beside her. She stepped from the gantry and entered the crew compartment.

Voss shuddered as she surveyed the command deck. After ten days in the relatively ample space of her own cell, she hated the thought of being confined with her crew mates in a capsule for the return voyage. The *Gaia's* interior gleamed, its pristine white surfaces winking beneath the banks of full, overhead lights … lights that should have been in standby mode—no doubt part of the rocket's wasteful power draw.

She proceeded to the operations terminal, just beyond the engineering and navigation stations. As she brushed past engineering, she set her hand on top of the chair back. Rather than swiveling with her touch, the empty chair remained facing the bulkhead, resistant to casual movement. She pushed it firmly enough to rotate. Far from vacant, the seat contained a tan sack two-thirds of a meter tall and as wide around as her embrace, secured in place with the safety belt. Had NASA prepared something extra for the journey home? Clothing, maybe? T-shirts, or a jumpsuit sporting the *Gaia* mission logo? Or a special surprise ...? Voss bit her lip. *No way I can wait an entire year wondering what's in here .... Long as I close it back, no one will be the wiser.* She released the seal and peeked inside: Martian earth—red dirt and rocks—filled the sack to the rim. Farther along the deck, the chair at the navigation station held another sack. "That idiot Fisk," she muttered. They'd reviewed the return protocol so many times, including three complete run-throughs on Earth: all sample collections were to be stored belowdecks for the journey home. Or maybe ... no, he couldn't be that heartless. Did he think, with three astronauts lost, he could replace them in the weight budget with his samples? "That asshole."

Disgusted, Voss zipped the seal closed. Three empty seats during their return would be morbid enough. Replacing their fallen colleagues with bags of rocks like they had been so much dead weight would be more than she could bear. Once back at the HAAB, she'd give the research scientist a stern talking-to. She'd drag him to the *Gaia* and force him to stow his samples below, or watch as she heaved them out the hatch.

Returning to her original task, Voss passed the communications station and slipped into the chair behind the operations terminal. She tapped the display: the panel came alive with a welcome graphic followed by the main screen. She summoned a list of ship systems and sorted them by power consumption. Life support, water filtration, waste processing, and communications bubbled to the top. All reported wildly excessive power draws for systems that should have been idling until their trip home. Or not. She'd have to loop in Engles to find out for sure.

The room plunged into darkness.

The station engineer sat in the computer glow of the ops station terminal and faded sunlight that streamed in from the open hatch. What the hell was going on with the capsule? She swiped to the screen that managed the ship's electrical systems. After a few taps, light again filled the cabin. The system appeared to be OK, only switched off. A strange, spooky glitch. With all the weird happenings—the HAAB's water pipes failing, astronauts dying, problems contacting Earth, and the *Gaia's* systems active and erratic—it was like the mission was cursed.

Something moved at the edge of her vision.

Or at least it seemed like something moved. She strained to look left, but her suit helmet blocked her view to the side and behind. She twisted her shoulders and remained perfectly still, waiting for another sighting.

Nothing.

Voss shook her head—she'd probably imagined the movement, the flicker of an overhead light. She was spooking herself, sitting all alone in the big capsule.

The hair stood on the back of her neck.

"Ow!" she yelled to a sudden, sharp pinch behind her right arm. Had she trapped a jagged rock or bit of metal under her suit's thermal layer? She pawed at the spot with her gloved left hand.

Voss batted heavy eyelids, brought on by a surge of weariness. She struggled against the urge to let them close, to sleep. The hike to the rocket had taken some effort, but she wasn't even winded. Could she really be that exhausted from the exertion?

The station engineer fought to keep her leaden lids open but gradually lost the battle. Her vision narrowed.

The room plunged again into darkness.

23

Beep, beep, beep.

Kate woke, disoriented and bleary-eyed. She batted her alarm clock several times, but the chirping continued.

The commander sat up. The noise wasn't coming from her nightstand—it was her computer, on the other side of the room.

Kate staggered to her desk. The chirp was a notification from Glenn, a request for a private video conference. So, he was awake. The commander silenced her computer, stumbled to her bathroom, and splashed water on her face. She patted dry without looking too closely at the person staring back from the mirror—who knew what she might find. She returned to her desk, composed herself with a deep breath, and accepted the connection.

Glenn's face filled her computer screen, larger than life. Flaccid eyelids, cheeks, and jowls hung from his skull. He was awake, but his body hadn't fully metabolized the pellet narcotic. "Kate," he said, slurring his words with a floppy tongue he couldn't keep from sloshing around in his mouth. "What the hell's going on?"

"Since you're up, I can ask you the same thing."

"This isn't a joke," said Glenn.

"You see me laughing? I can't believe this is actually happening."

"But what *is* happening?" Glenn pleaded. "Why am I locked in my cell?"

"You're really claiming not to know," said Kate. "No memory of me, of Engles and Palmer, stopping by?"

"I remember the three of you here," said Glenn. "You were asking about my visit with Casey."

"Go on," said Kate.

"That's … as much as I can recall." Glenn shifted in his chair and grimaced. He grabbed at his shirt, or something below the camera's field of view. "Next thing I know, I'm waking up with these two welts on my stomach."

The marks would be with him for a few more days. She didn't like that he'd been hurt, but it was better than what Casey got. "Do you remember why I was asking about your visit?"

"No." Glenn lapsed into thought. "There was some sort of problem ... problem with me going to see her."

"I guess you can say that," said Kate. Her comment evoked a clueless stare. "I'm glad, at least, you admit visiting her, because the corridor camera clips show you going inside."

"She invited me in," said Glenn. "Anyways, what about it?"

"What about it?" Maybe the pellets had affected more than his short-term memory. "She's dead, Glenn."

"I know she's dead. That's why we went to see Julian." A blank look as Glenn thought more. "Wait a minute," he said, his eyes widening. "You were suggesting that *I* killed her."

"Did you?"

"Of course not!" said Glenn with a flash of anger. "And I can't believe you're accusing me of it."

"I'm not," said Kate. "There could be a perfectly reasonable explanation that doesn't involve you. Personally, I'd prefer to think you had nothing to do with it. But the fact is, you're the only one who can shed light on the situation. You're the only one who can tell us how she died."

"And why's that?"

"Because, Glenn," said Kate, at wit's end, "you were the last one to see her alive." Glenn stared listlessly at the screen, seemingly trying to process her words, seemingly not understanding. "You came out of Casey's cell ten minutes after she died."

"No, I didn't," said Glenn.

"It's all on tape," said Kate.

"My visit to Casey's cell was *six days* ago," said Glenn. "Three full days *before* she died."

Kate massaged her temples. How much more of this could she take? She was expending her limited energy going round and round with a man who refused to own up to events that couldn't be disputed. "The clips show different."

"Well, I don't know what you're looking at," said Glenn. "I was never alone with Casey after that visit."

"Why were you with her at all?"

"Because of the exchange in the DFAC," he said. "I wanted to make sure she was OK. I was checking if Julian had crossed a line that would warrant consequences." Glenn's tongue, fat and unruly with the effects of the pellets, spilled from his mouth and raked his chapped lower lip. "I was nowhere near her cell when she died. Besides, I would never hurt Casey or anyone else. I don't have a violent bone in my body."

Glenn's annoying grin appeared, enormous on her computer monitor. He was being sincere. Or was he? Over the video feed, the expression came across as a guilty smirk. She wanted to claw through the screen and smack it off his face.

Kate rubbed her eyes with her palms. "We were supposed to be some astronauts on a science mission," she said wistfully. "The whole thing got turned on its end, perverted …. A secret mission that doesn't have a damn thing to do with science, or exploration. Three astronauts dead, another missing. The HAAB running out of water—"

"Who's missing? And what's going on with the water?"

He didn't know? No, he wouldn't—the morning's developments occurred while he'd been unconscious. "Fisk went missing from his quarters sometime after noon yesterday."

"He's probably in some other part of the station," said Glenn. "Did you check the tubeway video?"

"There's nothing," said Kate. "No one went in or out of his cell once I dropped him off. It's like he disappeared." *Like the Curse whisked him away.*

Glenn's brows crinkled. Fisk's disappearance made as much sense to him as it did to her. "And the water?"

"Voss discovered the station's water pipes are full of leaks."

"Shit," said Glenn. "How bad is it?"

"It's bad. Possibly abort-mission bad." Pain shot through Kate's skull. She winced and cupped her forehead.

"Still battling the headaches?" asked Glenn.

Kate nodded, her head throbbing with each bob. As if everything else wasn't bad enough, her past also tormented her. "It's just like—" She caught herself.

"Just like what?" asked Glenn.

Commander Holman didn't respond, didn't want to voice what she knew in her heart to be unfolding. She looked up and found Glenn studying her, waiting for an answer …. Screw it—what the hell difference would telling him make anyway? "On the Moon, after the incident, I was dealing with similar headaches. When the medicine didn't help, they referred me to a shrink. I resisted the idea at first, but after many sessions, we figured out the headaches were a symptom of my lack of confidence in myself. They … I no longer believed I had what it takes to lead, to make good decisions, to command a mission. The headaches were from stress, my worry I'd be found out and lose my life's dream."

Glenn mashed his cheekbones and jaw, kneading life into his rubbery skin. "What does any of that have to do with what's happening here on Mars?"

Kate laughed. "Those headaches were a sign—don't you see? A sign of how messed up I was." She turned from her computer screen, gazing out the window at the harsh Martian wilderness. "My headaches, they're really bad now," she murmured.

"You think you're suffering a relapse of what happened on the Moon."

"I do," said Kate, glancing back at the screen. "Except this time, there's no shrink to help me … help restore my confidence in being a leader."

"You're already a great leader," said Glenn. "If anything, all these headaches have helped you be a better one. Lord knows we need your leadership to get us out of this mess."

"But I don't know *how* to get us out of this mess."

"Being in charge doesn't mean you're on the hook for the answers," said Glenn. "The best leaders look to their people for solutions. In the past, I've seen you march ahead, taking problems full on your shoulders and wrestling them to the ground, all by yourself. That's gotten you results, but it doesn't send the message that you value the people around you. With all these headaches, you haven't been able to do that. You've been forced to lean on us more."

"But—"

"It's also made you seem a little more human," said Glenn, ignoring Kate's attempt to get a word in. "To the rest of us, you're this hard-charging superwoman that no one can match. The headaches make you mortal, a little more approachable." He flashed his sincere, goofy smile. "Honestly, you're a better leader now than you've ever been, at least as long as I've known you."

Kate winced again. If that was how it felt to be a great leader, she might bow out of the Astronaut Corps altogether. But if Glenn was correct that she wasn't experiencing a relapse of the Moon, that left her with more questions than answers. "You say the headaches aren't about losing faith in myself. If that's true, how do you explain them?" asked Kate. "They began right after I lost Cheney."

"*You* didn't lose Cheney," said Glenn. "His death wasn't your fault." He seemed on the verge of saying more but held up. Perhaps, for once, he was refraining from a comment he'd regret. "Have you asked Palmer? About your headaches, I mean."

"I did," said Kate. "He gave me some pills. They haven't worked."

"Pills treat symptoms," said Glenn. "Did he have a guess as to the root cause?"

"His first thought was something in my diet."

"Interesting," said Glenn.

Kate dismissed the idea with a burst of air between her pursed lips.

"Don't knock it so fast," said Glenn. "One time, my parents sent me a box of pecans from some property they own in Georgia. Those pecans were delicious, but at the same time, I started developing this condition where my skin hurt in patches that shifted around day to day. I changed soaps, tried other things. Eventually, I took a break from the pecans—I stopped eating them for a week, and my strange skin condition went away. Somehow, I didn't make the connection. I absently decided to eat a few of the nuts, and the pain came roaring back."

"It's not that I don't believe it's possible," said Kate. "It's just that everything I've eaten is no different from what they fed us for the past year. That was the reason they put us on the Martian diet while we were still on Earth: to avoid any surprises once we got here."

"You may be right, but I think it's still worth exploring," said Glenn. "Start from scratch. Fast for eight hours. Drink lots of water to flush your system. Then add foods back, but do it slowly, one item at a time."

More shooting pains. Kate needed to get away, to perhaps take another nap. She feigned a check of her watch. "I've gotta run. There's a bunch of—"

"One thing before you go," said Glenn.

"What is it?"

"Can I ... would you please let me out of my cell?"

Glenn's pathetic face induced a moment of pity quickly dashed by Kate's memory of the tube video: his nonchalant exit from Casey's quarters; his casual stroll down the corridor as if nothing had happened, as if he hadn't left a dead colleague behind. She could almost vomit at his repeated denials, claims that he knew zilch about her death when the evidence was plain as day. "I'm sorry, Glenn, but I can't."

"You still think I had something to do with it, with Casey dying."

"There's no point in talking more," she said. "We need to hold something like a trial, where all the evidence gets weighed and a decision gets made, not arbitrarily but fairly."

Glenn seemed shocked, as if he suddenly understood the situation wasn't going to clear up anytime soon and that the outcome might not fall in his favor. "But I'm innocent," he whispered.

"You'll have your chance to prove it." She tapped her keyboard, ending the video conference.

Kate hunched forward, head hanging, her forearms on her thighs. The exchange had worsened her headache and her mood and sapped what strength she had. She needed another nap—to resume the one Glenn had interrupted. With all of the problems at the station, she couldn't afford the time, but she was a wreck, useless to herself and the others.

Commander Holman released a heavy sigh as she pushed herself up from her chair. She shambled to her bed, crawled beneath the covers, and drifted into a fitful sleep.

24

The apparition, clad in a Mars suit, leaned in close. Its helmet floated centimeters away. "What are you doing here?"

The whole thing was a dream, had to be one. Voss stared blankly at the figure standing impossibly before her.

The ghost of Julian Grimes leaned closer. "What are you doing here?"

He kept asking her that, but what did he mean? Why was she there, as in the *Gaia* capsule, or was he questioning her existence? Voss's mind in a fog, the words tumbled out on their own. "Rocket's using too much power. The HAAB's leaking water. I need the reactor output to melt more."

The apparition stood tall, hovering over her. "So you didn't come out here to find me?"

"To find you?" stammered Voss. "Why would I come out here looking for you? You're dead." She was dreaming, wasn't she? Even her wrists zip-tied to the chair arms weren't conclusive proof otherwise. She'd had those kinds of dreams in the past, restrained, unable to move or scream for help. Except this one was different, so … vivid. But Julian couldn't be alive. She recalled the previous day in his cell, Commander Holman's grisly discovery. "I saw your body."

The shade smirked. "Burned beyond recognition?"

Yes, it was ….

"Who else is here?" asked Grimes's ghost.

"At the *Gaia*?" asked Voss, still dazed. "No one. I came here alone."

The apparition gave her a doubting look. "Count backwards from ten," it said. "Do it," the shade added when she hesitated.

"Ten, nine, eight, six, seven—"

"You're still loopy from the sedative," it said. "It should wear off soon. Or I injected too much, and you've got permanent brain damage." The specter walked away, cruising the circular deck until it reached the still-open hatch. The ghost of Julian Grimes placed its back against the bulkhead and inched its helmeted head toward the rim. It peeked through the entryway, spying on the red plains below.

Voss's sluggish mind labored to make sense of it all. If that *was* Julian, if he was somehow alive and not imagined, then who had they spotted in the charred remains of his quarters? Everyone else was accounted for .... "Cheney," she whispered. With Casey in a medbay cold storage locker, he was the only possibility, except he was in the ground .... "You dug up Cheney's body," she said, watching Julian who still spied from the hatch. "Dug it up and stuck it in your cell to make it look like you died in the fire." A fire of suspicious origin. "From an explosion you caused."

"They should give you a junior detective badge," said Grimes.

Julian had loaded his cell with Cheney's exhumed body, only to blow it up? A macabre sequence of events ending with an explosion that could've cost actual lives, could've destroyed the station beyond repair. "But ... but why?"

"Why'd I do it? Why'd I fake my own death?" Julian stepped away from the hatch and looked her way. "Life in the HAAB was growing more and more ... inconvenient. It was already difficult carrying on with my business. Kate trapping me in my cell was the last straw. I needed to be free of her and the station."

Voss's mind continued to churn. "You raped and killed Casey."

"I did *not* rape her," said Grimes, returning to his surveil of the area around the rocket. "We had a thing, a sweet, sweet, thing together. Her death, though, that's on Commander Holman. I told Kate to stay away, told her there'd be problems if anyone else learned even the tiniest bit about the special operation. But she couldn't resist. She dragged Fisk with her to the Face."

"Kate went out there to save your life," said Voss.

Grimes's head whipped around. "Oh, please," he said with a roll of his eyes. "Holman's obsessed with me, with what I was doing. So distraught over losing a position she never really had. She couldn't help herself with her snooping, sticking her nose where it didn't belong. And that loudmouth Fisk made things worse, got Casey involved. I wanted to kill him first, would've, but I had to go with the situation that presented itself."

Would've killed him first? "You *did* kill her."

Grimes backed away from the hatch and faced her. "The three of them learned too much about the op. Casey came to me complaining, claiming I ruined her career. She didn't get the stakes are so much bigger than seeing her name on a research paper." The security chief cut across the capsule's center and stopped at his station on the far side. He swiveled his chair, revealing a brown satchel in the seat. Julian unzipped the top, spread it open wide, and rummaged through its contents.

Voss scanned the cabin. It wasn't as pristine as she first thought: empty food pouches and wrappers littered the space. Articles of clothing hung limp from the chair at Julian's station. A pick and other excavation tools lounged in a lazy pile on the deck, surrounded by bits of Martian earth. "You've been living in here," she said.

"Ever since the explosion," said Grimes, continuing his rummaging. "The capsule's perfect, actually: far enough from you all so I can go on with my business without any interference." A puff of frosty fog rose near his gloved fingers as he pulled something from the satchel. What was it? Impossible to tell from her side of the capsule. Voss strained for a better view as Julian looked up. His dark eyes, winking in the shadows beneath his brows, caught her gaze. He zipped the satchel closed and headed towards the station engineer.

Voss's heart raced. She wrestled the restraints at her wrists: they wouldn't budge. Her legs wouldn't move either—zip ties encircled her boots near the ankles. She suppressed a flood of panic. "Miriam, this is Voss, do you read me? Does anyone read me?"

"No, they don't read you," said Grimes, appearing again before her. "Your comm module's smashed in. Best you can do is a short-range chat, like the one we're having now."

"Cheney's module was smashed in when they recovered his body—did you kill him too?" Julian's vacant stare confirmed what had been an offhand remark. "You killed Cheney," she said, her voice quavering under a fresh outbreak of fear. "Smashed in his comm to stop him from calling for help, then slit his suit so he'd lose containment and die."

"Not quite," said Grimes, hovering again over his captive. "Counting on a containment breach to kill him would've left too much to chance. Slitting his suit was about creating a plausible cause of death." He shook his head and muttered, "Eliminating Cheney's the one thing that's actually gone according to plan."

"Killing Cheney was part of a ... plan?" asked Voss.

"Tying up loose ends." He moved to her side. "Keeping the information about the op confined to those who need to know. That's what I tried explaining to Kate."

Julian admitted to killing two of their crew mates and had her trapped in a chair. Voss struggled hard against her restraints like an animal caught in a trap.

"Easy, easy," said Julian in a gentle voice. "There's no need to squirm. I'm going to let you go."

Let her go?

Grimes dropped to one knee and inserted a finger between the zip tie and her wrist, tugging it taut. "These were meant to make sure you didn't disappear before we could talk."

His proximity terrified her. She could barely squeeze out the words. "You're not going to kill me too?"

"Here, in this capsule?" asked Grimes. "That would be more than idiotic. Holman and everyone else would eventually come searching for you, and that would mean additional unwanted visitors." He pinched the zip tie between his gloved fingers. "Like I said, I'm going to let you go. When I do, I want you to exit this capsule and head straight for the HAAB. Don't look back, don't come back. Do you think you can do that?"

"Yes," she said, her voice wavering. She'd climb down from the capsule and head straight to the station, inform Commander Holman that Julian was alive and repeat everything he'd told her. Those unwanted visitors of his would show up anyway. He had to know she'd do that, so why release her? "What will you be doing while I'm heading to the HAAB?"

"Continuing on with my business," said Grimes. He pulled his finger from the zip tie and felt around his midsection, near his utility belt. His hand emerged with a pair of snips, the circular ends large enough to accommodate the fat fingers of a Mars suit.

Perhaps he'd gone mad, lost touch with reality. Perhaps he was suffering from some form of psychosis induced by the long trip out. His actions indicated as much: digging up a body; blowing up his cell; killing his crew mates. On second thought, his various claims might not even be true, fabricated admissions born of hallucinations. He was certainly delusional to believe he could continue living in the *Gaia*. "Do you really think you can stay here?" asked Voss. "Stay in this capsule for a year and then fly back with everyone like nothing ever happened?"

"I agree, that's not going to work," said Grimes. He released the snips and grabbed her wrist, clamping it to the armrest. Voss squirmed but couldn't escape his grip. "See, I'm almost ready to return home now. I don't want to wait a whole year." He brought his other hand into the light, the one with the item from the satchel. It held a translucent cylinder that glinted silver at either end ... a syringe. A needle, incredibly thin and almost invisible, extended straight from the tip like a drawn out, fine metal thread. Several cubic centimeters of a clear liquid sloshed in the barrel as he fought her squirms. "And as for all of us returning to Earth together," he said, raising the syringe, "I'm afraid that's not going to work out either."

25

Kate peeled her body from her bed, arms trembling as she pushed herself to sitting. Another day, another dead astronaut, and another urgent summons to the medbay.

A six-hour nap didn't put a dent in her headache. Six hours, interrupted with the news about Voss. Miriam had spotted her in the late afternoon, facedown on the Martian plains twenty meters from her water contraption. The station chief had worked with Palmer to recover the body and get it to the medbay for what seemed like another pointless autopsy. The doctor still clung to his theory of a toxin in the food. He was optimistic that examining Voss so soon after her death might produce a clue.

The commander made her way to her bathroom. *My God ....* Cadaverous white skin covered the visage peering back from the mirror, with deep, dark bags sagging beneath the eyes. Was that really her? She splashed water on her face and downed a fresh set of pain pills. Kate forced a smile, pretending the medicine had started working even though it would take another minute to hit her bloodstream and despite the fact the pills never seemed to help. With a final look at herself, she secured her hair in a bob and headed out.

On the way to the medbay, she detoured to the DFAC to grab one of her raspberry protein bars. If she was going to be miserable, she'd at least do what she could for some small comfort. Her throbbing head dulled the bar's deliciousness. Her affliction had taken so much. It threatened to take her last pleasure too. The commander ate more of the bar, tucked the remainder into her jumpsuit, and continued on to the medbay.

- - -

"I was right!" Palmer brimmed with excitement, the most animated she'd ever seen the doctor, as he greeted Kate on her arrival.

"You found something?" Kate asked in a shaky voice as she stumbled inside.

Dr. Palmer directed her to the table that hosted Voss's limp body, stripped of its Mars suit. A white sheet blanketed the dead astronaut. "Trimethylchlorophene," he said, calling up the lab results on his medical tablet and handing the device to Kate. He pointed where she should begin reading. "A potent neurotoxin. It explains why Voss suddenly died out there. It's also a decent answer to the question of what happened to Cheney and Casey."

"I thought Cheney died from a containment breach," said Kate.

"That explanation has never sat right with me," said Palmer. "Cheney had everything he needed to patch his suit, and all the time to do it. Instead, he died."

Kate scanned the readout, pretending to absorb its words. She could barely bring the screen into focus. "If you think this tri-meth … neurotoxin killed the others," she said, returning the tablet to Palmer, "why didn't you find any of it during their autopsies?"

"This chemical compound degrades quickly inside the body," he said. "A whole day passed between Cheney's death and my examination. It was five hours with Casey. We found Voss about an hour after she died—" The commander's scrunched face gave him pause. "I know, I know," he added, "it's less than solid. Call it more of a hunch."

Kate's expression had nothing to do with her opinion of the doctor's theory. Her fight against the painful glare of the medbay's bright lights had resulted in a squint fierce enough to pinch out tears. "And you still believe this chemical got into our food somehow?"

"That's the best—"

A twinge shot through Kate's head, nearly causing her to faint. She reeled but managed to stay upright, grabbing the corner of the examination table. The doctor extended a hand to help, but the commander waved him off. "I'm OK," she said. "My problem today is I haven't had much to eat." A plausible explanation that deflected from what she knew to be the true cause of her affliction. Kate pulled the remainder of her raspberry bar from her jumpsuit, peeled back more of the open end, and lifted the bar to her mouth —

"Hey!' said Kate. "What the hell!" Her hand, still raised, was empty. Dr. Palmer had snatched the bar from her.

"Maybe it's nothing," he said as he walked to his lab bench. "You seem to have a lot of problems with headaches, and we haven't been able to pinpoint the cause. Maybe I'm wrong about this chemical being in our food, but since you have this here, let's test it."

"Those are my favorite bars from Earth," said Kate, close on the doctor's heels as she followed him across the medbay. "Do you need to use the whole thing for your test? I only have a limited supply."

"Depends on what I find," he said, swapping his latex gloves for a fresh pair. "If toxin *did* develop inside this bar, there's no guarantee it's uniformly distributed. If nothing turns up in this run, I may want to check others. Surely you can spare a couple of your bars for a test?"

Kate's thin, mashed lips quavered in time with her fidgeting hands.

Palmer broke off a piece of the bar and dropped it into a mortar. He ground the fragment to a moist, grainy paste, scooped a small portion into the medbay analyzer's sample tray, and closed the lid. The doctor flipped switches, adjusted knobs, and pressed a button. Blinking lights and a gentle hum settled over the equipment.

Kate sidled behind Palmer, towards the lab bench where he'd set the rest of her raspberry bar. "Truth is, Doctor Palmer, you're not going to find the cause of my headaches in that sample … or anywhere else in the bar."

"No?" asked Palmer absently, his attention on the machine.

"No." Kate quietly gathered the bar from the bench and clutched it to her chest. "My headaches aren't from anything like a toxin. They're … psychological." Her mouth went dry. Revealing the cause of her headaches could trigger a medical log entry that would eventually be read by her superiors at NASA. They'd learn she wasn't well after all, and that she had no business leading the Mars expedition or any other mission. She needed to stop talking.

"What do you mean 'psychological'?" Palmer asked, engrossed in the analyzer's output.

She was tired, worn down by the headaches and what they revealed about her mental state. Saying more would be career suicide … but also a relief, an opportunity to rest, to stop fighting. Her head dropped, heavy with the weight of it all. Some brave part of her forged ahead, working her mouth. "Several years ago, I—"

Something clasped Kate's wrists—hands, solid hands. She instinctively moved backwards, stumbling two steps but not more, held fast by an unshakable grip. She looked up into piercing, looming eyes, eyes made large by thick-rimmed glasses. Dr. Palmer, previously seated at his bench, stood before her, restraining her.

Kate squirmed but couldn't wrench her hands free, the doctor's grip too solid and forceful. Her right wrist ached—Palmer was squeezing, hard. He squeezed tighter and shook. Kate stifled a yelp as self-defense training kicked in. She released the rest of the raspberry bar and balled her now-empty hand into a fist. With a pull and a twist, she shifted her weight enough to partially cock her right arm, dragging Palmer's still-attached left hand with it. She set her feet and wound her hips, preparing to drive a punch that would break the doctor's nose—

"Without touching anyone or anything else, I need you to wash your hands."

Kate struggled to reconcile Palmer's words with her intention to smash his face. She found herself shambling towards the medbay's sink, under the doctor's direction. "What's going on?" she rasped.

"The sample I just tested has traces of the toxin. There might be some on your skin."

At the sink, Dr. Palmer positioned her hands. "Hold here." Still in shock, Kate remained motionless, hardly breathing with arms outstretched as soapy foam plopped into her cupped palms. "For the next two minutes," he said, turning on the water, "your *only* job is to scrub."

- - -

Three hours had elapsed since Kate's arrival in the medbay.

Twenty-six of her precious protein bars lay spread across the table, the remainder of the stash from the DFAC. Most sat with a corner unwrapped and a portion missing. She regarded them wistfully, a mother hen shellshocked by a nest of broken eggs.

"How are you feeling?"

"Huh," said Kate, the doctor's voice shaking her out of her trance. "A lot better. My headache's almost gone."

"The shot I gave you should continue to counter the effects of the TMC that's still in your body until you clear it all from your system," said Palmer.

"I'm glad you stood by your conviction," said Kate. "That there was poison involved, I mean."

"I've seen something like this before," said Dr. Palmer. "Years ago, on the moonbase, several astronauts died days apart. There was no commonality among the deaths, and we never discovered the cause, but I always suspected something in the food."

"You were stationed on the Moon?" asked Kate.

"After my residency," said Palmer. "NASA recruited me heavily—I guess I scored high on some aptitude test. They said I was a good candidate for the future Mars mission. They had me spend a couple years on the Moon as a sort of dry run."

The medical facilities on the Moon were spectacular, almost like being on Earth. "Other than operating in reduced gravity, it doesn't seem like it would be much of a real challenge," said Kate.

"At the moonbase, you're correct," said Palmer. "But I spent most of my time on the Far Side, at the Old Mine. Lots of triage. A couple emergency surgeries, even, things that couldn't wait for their return to the base itself."

"There were other doctors stationed with you, at least?"

"No. I was solo."

"Sounds stressful," said Kate.

"I guess it helps that I'm a bit of a Stoic," said Palmer. "In life, the only thing you can control in a situation is your response. If you adopt that perspective, there's not much that will faze you."

That explained why Palmer always seemed cool and collected, a tower of calm resolve behind those glasses. The doctor was quiet and usually kept to himself. In the two years of training and time together in the capsule, that was the most she'd learned about him and his past.

Beep, beep.

Dr. Palmer checked the sample analyzer and the results of the just-finished test. "This bar's the same: contaminated with a trace amount of the toxin."

Palmer said "trace amount" as if it were nothing. While none of the bars he'd tested contained enough of the chemical to kill her, the measure had been more than sufficient to make her *wish* she was dead. "Any further thoughts on how the TMC got there?" Kate asked. "Cosmic rays while the HAAB traveled to Mars? Or maybe while the provisions sat here for a year?"

"Trimethylchlorophene is a complex molecule," he said. "There's no way cosmic radiation could have produced it. The same goes for spontaneously appearing while here on Mars. I mean, these things have lots of preservatives—reason enough to stop eating them—but nothing that could combine or deteriorate to form TMC." Palmer hoisted one of the remaining unopened bars, examining it beneath his workbench lamp. "Besides,

Trimethylchlorophene starts to break down above minus fifty-one degrees Celsius. At room temperature, it has a half-life of about fifteen days."

"Half-life—you mean it's radioactive?"

"No. Half-life in the sense that any given amount loses half its potency every two weeks." The doctor's eyes sparked. "Wait a minute—just like with radioactive material, we should be able to calculate roughly when the toxin appeared in these bars by examining the ratio of active TMC to its inert remnants." Palmer tapped on his laboratory pad, pausing twice as he studied the analyzer's readouts. "Looks like the TMC first showed up six days ago. In this bar, anyway."

Six days. That jived with the start of her headaches but also added to the mystery. "If that's true, it means the TMC appeared in the bars *after* we arrived on Mars." Kate counted back, landing on the day that followed their trip to the Face.

The first full day of the Curse.

Kate batted away the notion. "Voss didn't eat any of my bars. All the ones from the DFAC are accounted for."

"They couldn't have been the source, regardless," said Palmer. "Whatever she ate had a higher concentration of the toxin than in the bars. That's why she died, while you've only experienced headaches. I'm running an analysis on the contents of her upper intestinal tract. Once that comes back—" The doctor lapsed into thought.

"What's wrong?" asked Kate.

"I was going to say the results will help us pin down what she ate, but it doesn't matter," said Palmer. "Based on the location of the food in her system, her last meal was breakfast this morning. If she'd ingested the toxin then, she would've been incapacitated before noon." The doctor grabbed his medical tablet and tapped. He scrolled through a ream of text. "Casey's final meal was also hours before her death." More taps. "Same for Cheney." He tossed the tablet on the workbench. "I guess they didn't die from TMC after all."

Kate flashed back to Palmer's forced march to the sink. "Maybe something they touched?"

The doctor mulled over the idea. "Possibly. I suppose we can—"

The medbay lights shut off and the room's equipment went dead, thrusting the space into an eerie black quiet. A glow emanated from the doctor's laboratory pad, its screen still alive where it sat on the workbench. Seconds later, stark emergency lighting snapped on in the corners of the room. The hum of machinery resumed but not as loud, the activity restricted to essential systems.

"What's going on?" asked Palmer.

Kate didn't know anything more than the doctor: the medbay had lost power. No, not the medbay alone—the emergency lights were connected to the HAAB's backup power system. The events in the medical cell had to be playing out across the entire station.

"Commander Holman."

Miriam's voice featured an uncharacteristic tremor that drove Kate's stomach into her bowels. "I was going to call you," said the commander. "What's happening?"

"The power's out all over the HAAB. As for exactly why, I can't say yet. The main computer ..."—an interminable pause—"... it hasn't come back up. The thing is, it shouldn't take this long to .... wait." Kate persevered through several more unnerving seconds of silence. "OK, it's up," said Miriam, her voice steady again. "I was worried the computer was stuck in a boot loop."

Rapid keyboard click-clacks came through the open comm channel. The typing meant Miriam was digging for answers, even if it felt like nothing was happening. Kate resisted the urge to ask for an update, allowing the station chief space to work. Her impatience eventually won out. "Any news?"

More typing. "A lot of subsystems are still down, which is strange. They should've all come up soon after, unless ... is that? My God!"

"What!" asked Kate, on the verge of jumping through the comm after Miriam.

"All the systems that are still down live in the same part of the station, which is also the one new area that's showing up black on my board." The tremor had returned to Miriam's voice. "I think we lost the Life Support cell."

26

"That's not good."

Kate deadpanned her comment as she peered through the tall, rectangular window in the Life Support cell's thick door. Reflections of the room's emergency lights winked at her from a dark, rippled surface, a meter-tall layer of water that covered the floor. The commander fought to present an air of composure despite her stomach sinking to her bowels anew. "What's your assessment?"

Engles stepped past the commander for a look inside. "Well, obvious problem number one is we don't have Voss. She was the expert on how this station works. None of us are qualified to make repairs." She strained to peer farther into the recesses of the room before backing away. "And second, even if we knew where to start, we can't get inside because opening the door would release all that water into the station."

Miriam stepped forward, rising onto her tiptoes for a look. Her face seemed to lose a shade of color. "You're saying we can never go in there?" Her voice was subdued.

"Not never," said Engles. "The HAAB's temperature control is out, and with no heat, that knee-deep layer of water will freeze before too long. Anyone will be able to go inside at that point, though they won't be far from freezing themselves."

Miriam seemed to wilt with Engles's frank evaluation. The petite station chief backed away from the door and moved next to the commander. She shifted her weight between her feet, settling into a gentle, self-soothing sway.

"I'm sure the designers thought housing critical life support systems in the same structure made perfect, logical sense," added Engles. "Seems they didn't consider how a single, serious issue with one system might take them all down at once."

"We need to get in there before all that water freezes over," said Kate. "I know, I know," she continued in advance of Engles's objection, "we wouldn't have an idea what to do even if we could get inside. Let's just believe we'll get a hold of NASA and that they'll come up with a plan, in which case we'll need to be ready. Get to the control room and pull the station's blueprints. Look for another way into this cell. Maybe there's an access hatch that'll let us enter from above. Or a back door. Or even a good spot to cut our way inside."

"I'm on it," said Engles. She marched down the tubeway and disappeared into the gloom.

"Miriam, I need—"

Miriam was trembling. Kate had never seen the normally composed station chief so distraught. She grabbed the smaller woman by the shoulders and gave a soft squeeze. "Hey, we'll find our way through this mess, but only if we keep our cool. Right now, I need you to head to the control room and get a message to NASA. Backchannel it through the weather satellite, use Morse code over UDP, whatever you can think of. We have to alert them to the situation here so they start working on solutions."

"What's the point?" asked Miriam, still trembling. "Even if we get a hold of NASA and they tell us how to pump all the water out *and* get the systems back online, and we're able to do it without Voss, all of that will take time. Every compartment within the HAAB will be frozen by this time tomorrow, and the air will go bad not long after that."

"You can't focus too much on everything Engles says," said Kate. "When she slips into her 'engineer' mode, she's all analytics. But life is never that simple. And it doesn't account for people's feelings."

"It's pretty plain the mess we're in, Commander, with or without Engles." Tears massed along Miriam's lower lids. One splashed on the floor. "Personally, I'd rather not rush around pretending we can do anything that will make a difference." Her head sank. "I think it's better we accept that we're going to die," she muttered.

Kate held Miriam's shoulders firm. "Look at me." She waited for the station chief to meet her gaze. "We're not going to die." She wouldn't entertain any scenario that left her young children without a mother. "You're forgetting the one ace up our sleeve: the *Gaia*. It's meant for our return trip to Earth, but we can live inside the capsule indefinitely while we figure things out." Miriam appeared to brighten at the thought. "Now go, send that message to NASA. Then let Doctor Palmer know we're evacuating the station."

"And Glenn?"

Glenn—she'd mostly forgotten about him since he'd become part of the problem. "Yes, Glenn too. Tell him to get into his Mars suit. I'll send Engles by to collect him when we're ready." Kate patted Miriam's arm, then took off down the tubeway.

"What will *you* be doing?" asked Miriam, watching the commander disappear into the gloomy distance.

"While you're talking to NASA," said Kate, not looking back, "I'm going to gather some food."

- - -

Kate opened the door to the shadowy Pantry, its emergency lighting obscured by rows of floor-to-ceiling racks of food. Kate stepped inside, dragging behind her a pair of rolling carts lashed together with zip ties. She plucked an emergency flashlight from its dock next to the door and switched it on. After a wave of its bright beam within the space, she set off with her double cart down the first aisle, knocking items from shelves and letting them tumble into the baskets. She imagined herself on a wild shopping spree, the ones where you walked out of the store with whatever you collected before time ran out. If only their current predicament were more lighthearted. Technically, she didn't have to gather a single bit of food. The HAAB, after all, wasn't going away. They could trek every day from the *Gaia* for anything they needed. An initial cache of supplies felt like a tiny bit of control in a situation that allowed very little.

Kate reached the end of the first aisle and rounded the corner to the far back wall where almost no light fell. She stopped, confused. Open boxes and empty wrappers littered the floor, the remains of a portion of their year-long cache pulled from the shelves and consumed. Mice? Kate's skin crawled, her revulsion quickly replaced by concern. Mice wouldn't have stowed away with them—they would have traveled to Mars inside the HAAB. That meant vermin feasting on their food supply for a whole year before they arrived. On top of all their problems, were they also facing depleted stores?

Leaving the cart, the commander proceeded slowly down the aisle. Her flashlight beam revealed more wrappers, except different from the ones she'd first encountered. They were purple with a wide red stripe—wrappers from her precious raspberry protein bars! One, two, three … eleven empty wrappers in total in the next few meters. The mice had eaten them too. That likely explained why none scurried about: the amount of toxin in the bars couldn't fell a human but would overwhelm a small rodent.

Kate aimed the light far ahead, to where the aisle ended at a wall. The beam landed on a strange shape on the floor, a lump too large to be wrappers or containers from the shelves. She approached with caution. As she neared, the dark shape gradually took form: legs, a torso, gloves … a Mars suit, spread out on the floor. Why would a suit be in the Pantry? And whose? No spares existed—it belonged to an *Ares* astronaut.

Inching closer, her light beam landed on a helmet-less head resting on a folded blanket. Tufts of hair sprouted from the sides, encircling a bald crown … Fisk!

Kate rushed to the research scientist. He wasn't moving. She trained the light on his face. His eyes lolled beneath slightly lifted lids, and his lips lazed, mouth open. Fisk clutched a partially eaten raspberry bar to his chest. Five more of the purple-and-red striped wrappers lay on and around him. *Fisk* had eaten her special bars, not mice. And he'd paid the price. Palmer said if she hadn't limited herself to one a day, she would've been dead long ago. Fisk had apparently eaten almost twenty bars in the short time since he'd gone missing. The accumulated poison had killed him many times over. If only—

Zzzzzzz.

Kate moved closer, not believing what she'd heard. Had she imagined it?

Zzzzzzz.

Fisk opened his eyes, squinting. He raised a hand, deflecting Kate's bright flashlight beam. "Commander Holman?"

"Fisk!" said Kate. "You're alive!"

"Of course I'm alive. Do you think you're talking to a ghost?" Fisk, still groggy, slowly pushed himself up to sitting.

Fisk was alive, but how? Perhaps he had a higher tolerance for the toxin? Even if true, he'd still be in bad shape. "Your head must be pounding," said Kate. "I'll get Doctor Palmer—"

"I'm sorry," said Fisk. He brushed a wrapper from his lap. "I know you told me not to touch your bars, but when I saw your huge stash down here, I figured trying one wouldn't be a big deal. Boy, were you right." The researcher lifted the raspberry bar he held in his gloved hand to his mouth and took a bite. "They really are delicious."

Batting the bar from his grasp would have been prudent, but the sight of Fisk munching on death had startled her into inaction. What would be the point, in any case? The damage had been done. "They're filled with poison," she whispered.

"They are?" Fisk held the partially eaten bar out in front of himself and studied the exposed end. He brought it close, sniffed, and took another bite. "Seems OK to me."

If not death, shouldn't twenty contaminated bars have resulted in symptoms at least? Other than his haggard appearance, the product of disheveled wisps of hair and a day of stubble, Fisk looked OK. His immediate condition apparently stable, questions about his disappearance rose to the fore. "What are you doing here?"

Fisk pitched his head, allowing his lips to grab the watering tube that protruded from inside his suit at the neck. He took two long draws. "Hiding."

"Hiding? From who?"

"Not who," said Fisk. "What. After Julian and his cell went up in flames, I wasn't going to wait for the Curse to do the same to me. I had to find a place to lie low. I figured my Mars suit would do for a portable potty, but I also needed a supply of food." He extended his arms out to his sides. "Voilà."

"But how'd you sneak out of your cell?" she asked. "Miriam reviewed all the tube video. There was no sign of you exiting your quarters, much less walking to the Pantry."

"What video?" asked Fisk.

What video? He didn't know. She'd hinted at evidence in Casey's apparent murder but hadn't mentioned recordings.

"By the way, what happened to all the lights?" asked Fisk.

"It's the Life Support cell," said Kate. "We have to evacuate the station. It's actually why I'm here in the Pantry. I'm collecting food for our fall-back to the *Gaia*."

"The Curse…," said Fisk, his voice trailing off.

"There is no curse," grumbled Kate. "C'mon, let's get you out of here." She offered the researcher a hand.

Fisk waved her off and pushed himself to standing. He wobbled as the blood drained from his face. "Whoa," he said.

Commander Holman snagged Fisk's arm. "Let's get you to the medbay," she said.

"I'm fine, Commander." He seemed to have steadied himself, but his face remained pale. "I think I ate one too many of your bars."

"That's what I'm worried about," said Kate. "Let's have the doctor give you a once-over, so we're sure you're OK. Then we'll work on getting you ready to head to the *Gaia*." Her flashlight beam bobbing along their path, Kate led Fisk through the Pantry. The two exited into the Spine and set off for the medbay.

27

"I'm going to start prepping the capsule," said Kate.

The commander stood at the base of the mammoth rocket, its bevy of first stage engines dangling like black pinecones beneath a massive four-meter-wide silver trunk and its storehouse of chilled propellant.

"Yes, ma'am," said Miriam. The station chief worked alongside Dr. Palmer and Engles, stuffing sacks with food from the Pantry.

"When you're ready, come up with the first load," said Kate. She stepped into the launch tower's elevator cab and started its climb without waiting for a response. She rose at a steady pace, her body and the cab's skeletal safety cage casting long shadows across the rocket's gently curved exterior. They needed to get situated in the capsule before sundown—working in the dark would be risky. And Miriam needed to resume her contact attempts with NASA as soon as possible. Hopefully she'd have better luck using the spacecraft's communications gear.

After the five-minute ascent, Kate reached the *Gaia's* outer door. She keyed in the entry code and swung the door out with a tug of its handle. The commander entered the crew compartment, its interior lighting switching on and filling the pristine white space with bright light. Kate sprang to her station, slid into her seat, and removed a small slip of paper from a pouch in her suit. She set the paper, a photograph, on the bottom lip of her terminal. Her children, Amelia and Ben Jr., stared back at her.

Commander Holman tapped the terminal alive, then retrieved a notebook from a rack over the monitor. With all that had gone wrong, she gave quiet thanks for NASA's insistence on printed instructions, a precaution against crucial information being trapped within a glitching computer.

Kate opened the binder and turned to the pre-flight checklist. They weren't leaving Mars, but the first section listed the steps to prepare the cabin for crew habitation. Her hand trembled slightly as she typed instructions into the computer—the *Gaia* would shelter them while they made repairs to the station, but if it couldn't, if something was also wrong with the capsule, they were all dead. Their retreat to the rocket had to succeed without a hitch.

As Kate flipped to the next page, she lost her grip on the notebook. The binder dropped to the station's chair, balanced for a moment, and tumbled to the deck. When she retrieved the notebook, it looked odd. She dragged her gloved finger along its cover, disturbing a layer of red dust. The binder had landed in a pile of Martian dirt at her feet—too much dirt to have been tracked in on her boots. More littered the deck in a dribbled path to her right.

Kate followed the trail to where it ended at the adjacent station. Martian dirt covered the deck near the station's chair. A tan sack sat in its seat, stuffed to the brim and secured in place by the chair's restraints. The chair at the next station contained a similar sack, as did several others.

The commander broke the seal on the sack, widened the opening, and reached inside. Her fist returned with a scoop of its contents. She unclenched her hand, revealing a heap of Martian soil in the center of her glove. She pushed the pile's dusty red grains with a finger, red grains and something else—strange bits of a mineral that glinted and shimmered throughout the ruddy dirt, yellow flakes and nuggets that danced in the light.

"It's gold."

Kate whirled. In the entryway to the lower crew compartment was Julian, outfitted in his Mars suit. The cabin's lights sparkled in his dark, narrow-set eyes. He held a gun, aimed at her. Not a pellet gun, which would've been useless against her suit, some sort of handgun.

"And now that you've had your peek, you can toss that back in the bag and close it up."

"How... you're alive," stuttered Kate. Julian's burnt body had been among the wreckage of his cell, yet there he was before her. The whole catastrophe must have been for show. "What's this all about?"

"What's it about?" asked Grimes. "Exactly what I said: gold. An incredible deposit of gold. Gold now claimed by the Space Force and its partners."

Kate tilted her hand, letting the soil dribble into the sack. "*This* is the secret mission, the reason we're here on Mars? To find gold?"

"Oh, we already knew there was gold. The last rover NASA sent drove inside the Face and discovered the vein. No one could determine the quantity of gold from video recordings and spectral analysis alone. We needed boots on the ground to make the call."

So it was true, Fisk's fantastical claims of ancient humans brought to Mars as slaves to mine gold. That seemed like a much bigger discovery than any amount of riches. "The Anunnaki were real, then."

Grimes snorted. "You mean the story on the rod? That 'artifact' is as phony as a three-dollar bill. Personally, I never thought it would fool anyone, but it's not my job to question the orders I'm given. Planting that rod was the first thing we did when we got to the Face."

"You … planted the rod?" asked Kate.

"Every space-capable nation has rovers and robots, and it won't take much for them to come snooping at the Face. Cheney and I left the rod for them to find, so they'd waste their time in Cedonia. Like I said, I never thought it would fool anyone, but I guess I was wrong. It worked, though it snared the wrong set of morons."

Kate reeled. Everything she thought she knew about NASA, about space exploration and her role in it, had been upended. The first journey to an alien planet undertaken not for scientific discovery but for money. Their lives put at risk, the lives they'd lost …. "They sent us to Mars for a gold mine," she whispered in disbelief.

"Are you really that surprised?" asked Grimes. "The Federal debt's nearly eighty-five trillion. Half the budget goes toward paying interest on all that money. The United States is fucking broke, Kate. You think the military and the spies don't feel that, don't suffer under those constraints? This gold mine, if it panned out, would solve everyone's problems. We were even thinking about cutting NASA in on a slice." Julian had grown animated with his talk, an energy borne of ill will and bad intentions, and he radiated a palpable, menacing presence from across the cabin. "It was a gamble on a new source of funds," he continued. "The Space Force and its friends put some money on the table. They rolled the dice, and they won. They came up big! There's got to be twenty trillion dollars of gold in that mine, maybe twice that."

Kate brushed the remaining soil from her palm into the sack. "That's what all these bags are, then, samples to analyze back home?"

Grimes shook his head. "I don't need all this to prove there's gold on Mars. These sacks are my future," he said, gesturing with his gun hand. "These sacks are for me."

"For you?"

"After I analyzed the samples I brought to my cell, I did the math. With the gold ore in these bags, I can live quite comfortably."

"This rocket doesn't have enough thrust to lift off with astronauts and all your bags of gold," said Kate.

Grimes smiled. "You say dumb things sometimes, Kate, but I know you're not. Of course I can't get all this home if everyone's coming on the return trip. But you made that part easy for me. Once you and the others found out about the Face, I had to eliminate you. With each additional person gone, it meant one more bag of riches headed to Earth for me."

Kate gasped. "You're saying you actually killed people? People on this mission? Fellow astronauts?"

"People who learned too much," said Grimes. "I told you, we're talking trillions of dollars, the solution to black budget funding problems. No one person's life is worth enough to risk derailing that, not even mine." He'd approached the commander as he talked. Now he stood on the opposite side of the chair from her. He brandished the gun in one hand; in his other, he held a brown satchel. "The spooks sent me off with all manner of toys," he said, hoisting the satchel. "Sedatives, poisons, weapons like this slug thrower that works in oxygen-poor air—anything they thought might be useful to get the job done." He set the satchel down, rummaged inside, and fished out a syringe. "This is how," he said, liquid sliding in the barrel, "how to get away with murder. It's an undetectable neurotoxin."

"Trimethyl—TMC." Julian's turn for surprise. "Doctor Palmer isolated it. You killed Voss with it. Palmer thinks Casey and Cheney died the same way." Kate's mind whirred. "And my bars—you tried to kill me by adding it to my bars!"

"If I'd wanted to kill you, you'd be dead right now," said Grimes. "It was better to keep you alive to manage all the NASA check-ins and other mission bullshit. That gave me more time to focus on the primary objective. I was betting those headaches would help keep your nose out of my business."

"Julian?"

Dr. Palmer stood in the open hatch on the opposite side of the cabin, his mouth agape.

Grimes aimed the gun at Palmer. His fat, gloved finger moved within the extra-large trigger guard designed for use with a Mars suit. He was trying to fire the gun, to shoot the doctor! He would've succeeded but for a portion of his glove snagging for an instant on the end of the trigger.

Kate lunged for Grimes's hand, the one with the gun. She grabbed his wrist and pivoted, trapping his arm in her armpit and pinning his body behind her. Kate twisted Grimes's arm to an awkward angle that threatened to wrench it from its socket, eliciting a moan from the security chief. She shook his hand. Grimes punched her arm but couldn't break her hold. The commander shook his hand again. The gun fell, clattering on the deck.

Grimes punched her helmet twice with his free hand. Kate released his arm but retained her grip on his wrist. In a balletic blur of motion, she made a quick pivot, pulled him close, and raised her knee to his crotch. Agony exploded on the security chief's face. He doubled over, frozen in pain. Kate spotted the handgun on the deck and kicked the weapon away.

Dr. Palmer arrived in a rush with Miriam and Engles on his heels. The doctor seized Julian and wrenched the still-incapacitated security chief's arms behind his back. When the commotion subsided, Palmer, Engles, and Miriam together stared at Kate, silent and shaken.

Kate's arm, the one Julian had punched, throbbed with a pain that didn't make sense. The security chief was strong, but his luckiest strike wouldn't do much through her Mars suit. She inspected her arm. A syringe, the one Julian had removed from his satchel, sprouted from her bicep, its plunger fully depressed and its barrel empty. A warm, burning sensation crept along Commander Holman's arm as she staggered, then collapsed to her knees.

Miriam rushed to Kate, knelt next to her. "What is it?" she asked, panic in her voice.

Kate's eyes met the doctor's, confirming what he'd suspected. "Poison," said Palmer. "The same that killed Voss."

Miriam burst into tears, her face a ball of anguish and fear.

Kate patted her hand. The station chief cried for her, certainly, but likely also for being an uncomfortable step closer to commanding the mission on her own. "Don't be afraid, Miriam," said Kate. "You'll do great. I know you will. You're command material. Never forget that."

"Yes, ma'am," Miriam whispered, her words barely audible through her distress.

Kate settled onto her bottom and swung her legs around. Her shoulders slouched forward. She was exhausted, the poison draining the life from her body. Kate looked past Miriam, past the doctor. "Laura."

The spacecraft engineer, hanging back behind the other two *Ares* astronauts, approached and crouched to meet the commander's gaze.

"Laura, I want you ... I'm sorry—" Kate took a difficult breath, fighting through spreading pain. "I'm sorry to burden you with this, but I know you ... of all people on this mission, I know you will understand .... Please find my children, when you're back on Earth, find them and tell them I love them."

Engles nodded, crying.

Sobs wracked Kate's frame, the commander allowing herself to grieve. They dissipated with her failing body. Within her blurred vision hovered the tear-streaked faces of her children, fresh from learning the news. Despite her tears, Amelia was reserved. Ben Jr. couldn't grasp why he'd never see Mommy again. Both would grow up without her. She cursed herself, her ambition, the drive she couldn't ignore that had brought her to Mars. She cursed Julian, a man who cared nothing for people when all they had for survival was each other. But most of all, she cursed humanity and its inability to leave its worst natures—deceit, greed, murder, and the rest—behind.

Kate reached for her children, reached out to touch their faces one last time as the world slowly descended into black.

28

Who knew the afterlife would be so bright?

Was it Heaven? How could she tell? God would be somewhere about, perhaps, would finally have to show Himself. Not that she believed in God. Religion had never made sense, but neither had the idea your essence simply ceased upon your death.

For the record, your life didn't flash before your eyes on your way out. It was more like … what you loved the most. Whatever that was, the Universe gave you the chance to see it one last time ….

"She's waking up."

Shapes and shadows shifted within the brilliant light that filled Kate's vision. She squinted against the brightness, willing form upon the ephemeral gray patches.

"Quick, grab my medical bag."

"Here it is."

"Is she going to be OK?"

Kate's vision sharpened. The achromatic wisps congealed to solid form, spirits waiting to welcome her to the beyond. Clad in … blue? Wasn't white the preferred color of the afterlife? Light blue, in fact …. And not a gown or flowing robes, but a jumpsuit? With NASA patches?

"Commander Holman, how are you feeling?"

A soothing voice, part of a calming bedside manner. Palmer. Memories came flooding back: her altercation with Julian. The injection. Pain. Her children. Dying … or not? She was coming to, but not in the afterlife.

Dr. Palmer materialized in front of her, sporting his reassuring physician's smile. Kate tried to speak but couldn't coax a sound. "Don't try to talk," he said.

She complied, relaxing her throat. Her head hurt. A dull ache pervaded her entire body. She was tired. And she couldn't move.

"You're lucky to be alive."

More of the space around her came into focus. She was inside the *Gaia* capsule. Three additional jumpsuits—astronauts—hovered nearby, though she couldn't make out faces. A thin, rough blanket encased her body, a white cocoon surrounding her from neck to toe. Wires protruded from beneath the wrap near her heart, feeding into a small medical scanner held by Dr. Palmer.

"Your vitals are stable," said Palmer. "They've been stable for a while; you've just been unconscious all this time. I wasn't sure if you'd wake."

The doctor moved in close and waved a flashlight into Kate's pupils. The encounter nagged at her with an oddness she fought to pin down …: she'd been upright for her face-to-face with Palmer, their eyes meeting directly. And the cabin lights, instead of shining in her eyes, loomed overhead …. She was vertical, not on her back. But not standing, either. Her feet dangled a meter from the deck. She hung in her cocoon along an empty stretch of bulkhead, suspended and wrapped like a spider's catch.

"Sorry for the crude accommodations," continued Palmer, moving on to inspect her ears, "but coming up with an arrangement that satisfied all the constraints was a little tricky. We needed you nearby, in case your condition changed, which is why you're not below. We also needed to keep you warm, and not allow you to drift across the cabin."

Drift? Indeed, Palmer's feet floated above the deck; they didn't touch it. "We're space-borne?" asked Kate. Her voice was gravelly, abrasive, as if she hadn't spoken for quite a while. How long had she been out?

"We took off two days ago." The voice was Miriam's, the Mars station chief. She was one of the blurry jumpsuits floating before her.

Two days? "I've been out that long?"

"You were unconscious for four," said Palmer.

Kate attempted to adjust her position in the cocoon but couldn't move. The blanket held her too tightly. Maybe for the better—her joints hurt with even the unsuccessful effort.

"You're alive by a double stroke of luck," said Palmer, forcing her mouth open and peering inside. "The toxin you ingested each day from your bars helped your body build up a level of tolerance. Not enough to totally protect you, but it helped." The doctor's hands moved to her neck, pressing and probing beneath her jaw.

"What was the other?" asked Kate.

"The antidote I happened to give you a few hours prior. It muted the effects of Julian's injection long enough for me to grab a second dose from the HAAB." Dr. Palmer peeled away part of the cocoon and placed his stethoscope high on her chest, slipping the cold disc under the material of her thin medical gown. "Breathe in, please."

Kate took a deep breath and coughed. The muscles between her ribs spasmed in pain with the inhale and spasmed more with the hack. So they'd left Mars. Apparently staying had been a lost cause? "We abandoned the HAAB?"

"We did," said Engles, another of the blue jumpsuits, but now in focus. "Miriam was sending messages to NASA and getting no replies. In the meantime, the HAAB froze over. I'm an engineer, but my specialty is spacecraft, not habitats. It seemed a stretch that we'd get the station working again by ourselves. And the longer we waited for a response from Earth, the longer the trip home would've been. Weighing all of that, we decided to leave." She broke into a wide smile. "By the way, Commander, you can thank me for your swift recovery."

"How so?"

Engles gestured to the bandana, vibrant red, around her neck. "I'm wearing my lucky one today."

Kate smiled in return. "It's probably what got me 'cross the finish line."

Palmer reached behind the commander, sliding his stethoscope to her high back. "Another inhale, please."

Kate drew a second deep breath, the effort easier that time. "Anything from NASA, now that we're off the ground?"

"Still nada," said Miriam. "I've been broadcasting a repeating message, but nothing's coming back from Earth."

"It's nuclear war." Kate traced the remark to the ceiling where she found Fisk. The research scientist sat upside down in the center, back straight and legs crossed, with tendrils of hair curling from the sides of his head. The image was of a haggard Buddha magically levitating above the unenlightened. "Wiped out all of civilization as we knew it," he added.

Kate sighed. Leave it to Fisk to find the most complicated, and depressing, explanation for their problems contacting NASA. At least in a coma, she didn't have to listen to his paranoid blather.

"For the final time, it's not nuclear war," said Miriam. "Nothing's changed from our last few days on Mars. We have an Internet connection, same as when we were still in the HAAB. We're even getting keep-alive packets from Earth. It's just impossible to connect to any remote host."

"I'll point out the Internet, which started life as the military's ARPANET, was designed to be resilient in the event of a nuclear holocaust," said Fisk. "So it doesn't surprise me the network is still up. But besides that, there's the energy burst."

"It's not a burst," said Glenn, the final figure hovering before Commander Holman. "It's gone on much longer than any nuclear exchange would last."

"Well, spike, then."

"It's not a spike either," said Miriam. "And nuclear bombs release energy across the entire EM spectrum. They aren't limited to a frequency band, no matter how wide."

"Burst, spike, whatever you want to call it," complained Fisk. "You're all keen on playing word games to avoid addressing my point."

"What's he talking about?" asked Kate, managing to squeeze out the words.

"There's a stream of energy coming at us from Earth," said Glenn. "Sort of like the electromagnetic pulse you'd see from a nuclear blast, except this is steady, not a flash. We haven't figured out what it is."

"The smoldering remains of a dying planet," mumbled Fisk.

"One more word and you'll be bunkmates with our friend downstairs," said Glenn.

Fisk bugged his eyes at Glenn but otherwise fell silent.

"Hey, everyone." Kate strained but resolved to get the words out. If something happened, if she took a sudden turn for the worse, what she had to say might die with her. "Julian told me ... he killed Voss. Admitted to killing ... the others. I—" She winced again under the pain and effort. "I think Glenn's innocent."

"He is," said Miriam. "While we were still on Mars, between my messages to NASA, I took another look at the tube video. I couldn't understand how Fisk could've walked out of his cell and into the Pantry without the cameras picking him up. I discovered the recording system had been tampered with."

"Tampered with?" said Kate. "How?"

"The system was copying pre-recorded video of empty hallways instead of the output from the live camera feeds," said Miriam. "That's why it seemed like Fisk never left his cell—the system never recorded the event."

"The cameras were working before," managed Kate. "They recorded Glenn, and Julian, visiting Casey."

Miriam nodded. "And that fact prompted me to reexamine those recordings. Turns out, they had been altered: sections had been spliced together, timestamps changed."

Camera video edited to implicate Glenn? The system stuck in a recording loop? "Julian?"

"Had to be," said Glenn. "Looping the camera feed allowed him to travel through the HAAB as he pleased. We believe that's how he snuck Cheney's body into his cell without being caught on film."

"That explains why," said Kate, "but how did he manage it?"

"He *was* chief of security," said Glenn. "If anyone had knowledge of the system, and access to it, it was him."

And her decision to wait until the next day to examine the video outside Casey's cell gave Julian the heads-up and enough time to act. Her vision fully restored, Kate scanned the cabin. There were no other occupants besides Glenn, Engles, Miriam, and Palmer arrayed around her, and Fisk upside down on the ceiling. Had they left Julian on Mars? The thought seemed too cruel. More likely he was dead. "What happened to Commander Grimes?"

Glenn thumbed at the deck. "He's down below."

A relief. Julian wouldn't get off as easy as being left behind, alive or dead. When she finished with him, he'd *wish* they'd stranded him on Mars.

"Julian also told me the entire Mars mission was about looking for gold." Kate locked on to Fisk. "No, not like you think," she said to the research scientist still huddled at the ceiling. His mouth hung open in awe and eyes twinkled with the imagined confirmation of his theories. "He said there's gold at the Face, but everything else, the city of Cedonia and the Anunnaki, all that's a lie. The rod is fake, planted by him and Cheney to throw off other explorers." Fisk's awed expression didn't falter, as if frozen in time, but the sparkle slowly dissipated from his eyes.

"That explains why he was so distraught," said Glenn.

"What do you mean?" asked Kate.

"Julian tried to convince us the bags of dirt he dragged into the capsule were valuable, though he wouldn't say *why*, and definitely never mentioned gold. He offered to split the proceeds if we brought them back to Earth. We kept a couple as soil samples but heaved the others out the hatch before we left."

"Gold," whimpered Fisk.

"We didn't have the weight budget to bring them along, even if we wanted," said Glenn. "But it was also hard to tell if he was lying. In the end, we assumed he was. How do you know his gold story, the secret mission, is even true?"

"I don't," said Kate. "It may all be a lie. But at the very least, he *believed* he'd found gold. He believed it so strongly, he was willing to kill us all to get it home. As for the rest of it, the mission and everything related to it, I want some answers from the powers that be. I need to speak to the AD and hear his explanation. I won't know what to think 'til I can look him in the eye."

"Tell her what we learned about our favorite security officer," said Fisk. The research scientist had pushed off from the ceiling. He drifted slowly towards the deck, still in a seated position and upside down.

"Julian had been in the *Gaia* for several days," said Glenn. "He was living here ever since the explosion. I found a terminal he'd logged into and dug around his account. It had a copy of his official service record."

"I've seen his file," said Kate.

"I don't think you've seen *this* version," said Glenn. "The file submitted for the mission's records had been modified at some point, details added and removed. This was the original version, cryptographically verified."

Kate waited for elaboration, but none came, Glenn's penchant for saying the wrong thing this time taking the form of keeping quiet when the moment demanded the opposite. "Well, what's in it?" she finally asked, her patience gone.

"It says that contrary to Julian's claims, he is not, and never was, a member of the Air Force or the Astronaut Corps. He's actually a captain in the Space Force."

Fisk crossed his arms as a smarmy, patronizing grin broke across his face. "Like my friend tried to warn us." He meant the cryptic "SF" message from the "Snow Owl." "I *hate* it when I'm right."

The doctor had bared Kate's shoulders during her physical evaluation. The commander squirmed, attempting to free her arms. She failed. "Can someone get me out of this thing?"

Miriam joined Palmer at the commander's cocoon. The two worked on separate sections of the wrap, loosening it enough for Kate to extract herself. She drifted up, towards the top of the capsule, her medical gown floating like a billowing parachute. The commander yelped as pain shot through her shoulders, elbows, hips, and knees. Her body would need more time to recover from the toxin's effects.

"Don't forget to take off your diaper," said Fisk.

Kate lifted her gown, exposing a set of medical briefs that elicited giggles from Fisk. "It can wait," she said, annoyed.

"Maybe you should take it slow," said Dr. Palmer.

"I will," said Kate. "We've got six whole months 'til we're home." The commander raised her hands, cushioning her impact with the capsule's ceiling, Fisk's previous perch. She curled into a ball, spun about, and pushed off, gliding towards the entrance to the lower crew compartment. "Right now, I want more answers." She extended her arms, reaching for the handholds near the opening. "It's time for a chat with Commander Julian Grimes."

29

Kate floated downwards, headfirst, grabbing successive handholds in the access shaft that led to the lower crew compartment. In a graceful maneuver she'd executed hundreds of times during their trip out, she arched her back as her head cleared the ceiling and kicked to her rear, propelling herself across the space.

The outer edge of the compartment featured a low ceiling embedded with a narrow, continuous strip of recessed lighting that effused a twilight glow. In the dimness, the pattern of bunk and porthole repeated along the circular bulkhead. The low ceiling gave way to more normal height and light, in the center, where crew exercise and strength-training equipment sat idle in a tight ring.

Julian lay on his side on a bunk across the room, leaning against the capsule's bulkhead with an arm propping his head at an angle. He clutched a small tablet, its screen bathing his face in cold, LED light. He didn't look up as Commander Holman and the others approached.

"Checking the price of gold?" asked Kate as she drifted towards the former security officer.

"Solitaire," said Julian, remaining engrossed in the tablet's screen.

Kate arrested her glide with a drag of her fingers along the ceiling. The bunks extended into the room at waist level, forming a generous storage space below. The elevation placed her face-to-face with Julian. Glenn, Miriam, Engles, and Palmer flanked her. Fisk peeked over her shoulder, a cowering child hanging behind his mother for safety. "I hope I'm not troubling you for a moment of your time," said Kate. "After all, you did try to kill me."

Laying the tablet facedown, Julian responded with a hint of resignation. "What can I do for you, Commander Holman?"

A polite response? In previous interactions, Julian had been rude, aggressive, or condescending. Being caught red-handed, and incarcerated, had apparently shifted his attitude. "I have a question," she said. "I'm hoping you can provide an answer."

Julian didn't respond, and the only movement on his person was the light from the center of the room dancing in his dark eyes. His time in confinement had upended his carefully manicured appearance, with thick stubble peppering his cheeks and hair reemerging on the normally shaved sides of his head. His crown, naturally bald, reflected the gentle overhead glow.

"For some days now, dating back to our time on Mars, we've been unable to communicate with NASA," said Kate. "Considering all that's ... transpired, I'm wondering if you have an idea of why that might be."

"I think it's nuclear war," said Fisk. "No one left but some computers to talk to."

"A moronic theory from the mission's chief moron," said Julian.

"You mean chief moron who's not sitting in chains," said Fisk, piping up behind the commander. "Has anyone ever told you your leash suits you? It brings out the soulless black of your eyes."

"Come a little closer, and I'll pay you a few compliments myself," said Julian. He swiped in a feigned lunge at Fisk.

Fisk recoiled in terror. He pushed against the commander, propelling himself backwards while sending her careening forward. She partially jackknifed onto the bunk but stopped herself, avoiding a full end-over-end tumble into Julian.

Julian had also scrambled to avoid a collision. In the shifting of his legs, Kate caught a glimpse of his right ankle, the strap that encircled it, and the lock that kept the band tight. A metal ring anchored the strap's other end, affixed to the bulkhead amid a halo of scorch marks from a hurried welding job. They'd confined him to the space down below like an animal.

"Watch what you're doing," said Kate, admonishing the research scientist as she glanced at him over her shoulder. She returned her attention to Julian. "Just answer the question: do you know why we can't reach NASA?"

Julian shrugged his mouth. "Seems pretty obvious: they don't want you talking to NASA."

"Who's 'they'?" asked Kate.

"Space Force," said Julian. "Their allies, also, but Space Force is running the show." He discovered a spec of lint on the bunk's gray wool blanket, which he plucked and flicked away. "It's the same reason your transmissions are being jammed."

"Jammed?" said Miriam. "Why do you say that?"

Irritation filled Julian's face. "Because I'm familiar with the goddamn protocol they planned to follow if something went wrong."

Jamming was something you did to your enemies, to enemy aircraft or hostile satellites. "Do you think that's true, Miriam?" asked Kate. "Are we being jammed?"

Miriam thought for a moment. "That would certainly explain the steady stream of energy coming at us from Earth. It's confined to the transmission frequencies, now that I think about it …. Yeah, a jammer would explain all of that."

"Of course that explains it," said Julian. "It's plain as fucking day, what's going on. You goody two-shoes 'astro-nots' are too naive to see it, prancing around the cosmos in your white space suits like the heavenly angels you think you are. When all you do is marvel at the 'wonders of the Universe,'" he added with a roll of his eyes, "even the most basic battlefield tactic looks like a fascinating natural phenomenon."

Julian delivered his remarks with particular venom. Was this how he'd always felt about astronauts? Members of the Space Force, "Guardians," they called themselves, held little respect for their brothers and sisters in the Astronaut Corps. Their epithet "astro-not" summarized their contempt, despite the members of both professions risking their lives in the same dangerous frontier. His secrets exposed, Julian seemed to have decided he had no reason to hide his true feelings.

"Once I confirmed the gold, and mentioned tying up loose ends, the Space Force locked down all communications between Earth and the Ares mission," continued Julian. "I was the only one in touch with them, on a restricted, encrypted frequency. Protocol required I contact them every twenty-four hours. They were *very* clear about what would happen if I missed a check-in." His gaze became icy and shifted to Glenn. "I tried to get you to wake up on Mars, to help me save all our fucking assess. You were too stupid to give me a comm."

"Forgive me if I didn't jump up and trust the words of an admitted murderer," Glenn spat.

If Julian was correct about jamming, maybe he could get it to stop. "Is it possible to get him the connection he needs?" asked Kate.

"Now?" said Julian with a laugh. "Right now, they think I've either been killed or captured. If I'm alive, they assume the mission's been compromised, that everyone returning from Mars knows enough to land them in jail, and they're not wrong. That's why they're jamming the hell out of us. But even if we could somehow get through all the interference, they wouldn't listen to me."

Kate hadn't anticipated how Julian's special channel would also be impacted by the jamming—her mind was still a bit slow, not fully recovered from her incapacitation. "If you're right that it's the Space Force jamming us, and we don't have a way to get them to stop ...." How to summarize her concern ...? "Six months from now, we'll need to talk to NASA to coordinate our reentry and splashdown. Will they be jamming us then?"

"Oh, they'll definitely stop before that," said Julian. He returned to the apparently captivating contents of his tablet screen. "There are too many powerful people involved for all that we know to be allowed to reach the ground."

Julian's vague statement weighed the air. What did he mean, exactly? Part of her wanted clarification. Another part, the part that sensed the implications of his comment, hid within the comfort of its ambiguity. The others seemed stuck in a similar limbo.

The tension boiled over for Fisk. "What does that even mean?" he huffed.

Julian lowered his tablet. "It means, Professor Dipshit, that when we get close enough to Earth, they're gonna blast us out of the fucking sky."

"And kill everyone aboard?" asked Kate.

Julian shrugged again. "They'll say it was an accident. They've done it before."

Kate fought for words. She shook her head, slowly at first, gathering speed. "I can't believe it," she scoffed. "NASA would never let that happen."

"This goes all the way to the top of NASA," said Julian. "It's the Space Force running the show. See, the job of you good little astronauts is to get us where we need to go. Once that's done, the Guardians take it from there. If at any point you become an obstacle, you're swept away." He seemed to perk up, emboldened by the consternation on the faces before him.

Kate stared at Julian, shellshocked. In the world he described, astronauts existed as clueless pawns in a larger game, one filled with scheming, ruthless deceit, and murder.

"Fisk, are you OK?"

Engles had asked the question. It set off a commotion behind the commander. She spun around in time to catch Palmer rushing to Fisk, the researcher's face pale and sweat on his brow. His inhales were short and rapid.

"He's hyperventilating," said Palmer, checking his pulse. "Fisk, you need to calm yourself, take slower breaths." Fisk's face carried the frightened expression of a man trapped inside his body, comprehending the instructions but unable to comply. "Slower breaths, Fisk, slower breaths."

Fisk's breathing gradually slowed. "That's it," said Palmer. "Like that. Slower, deeper." His face remained pale and pained, but he seemed to be recovering a bit.

"I'm going to take him up," said Palmer. "I think a sedative would be helpful."

The commander nodded. The Stoic Palmer, unfazed by Julian's proclamation, wrapped an arm around the research scientist. The two drifted off together, headed for the exit. Miriam, who had been floating next to Dr. Palmer, hadn't lost it like Fisk, but she seemed in no better shape. The Mars station chief was very quiet, in words and presence, stunned and withdrawn. Her entire body trembled. Engles, too, carried a despondent look. Her vibrant red bandana hung limp from her neck, the talisman dissonant with the moment.

"Seems like you're all getting the picture," said Julian.

Kate turned, confronting the former security chief.

"Hey, don't shoot the messenger," said Julian to her heated scowl. "I'm no better off than any of the rest of you."

He was correct, of course, about their shared fate, though he seemed to delight in the prospect of their collective deaths.

"The bottom line is if they don't want us coming back, we don't come back," said Julian. "It doesn't matter what anyone in NASA thinks." The reflections wriggled in his black eyes. "Here's a clue for all you simple little astro-not do gooders about how the world really works: everyone, in the end, is out for themselves."

"That's the Space Force motto."

The words came from behind, lobbed from halfway across the room. Fisk had hurled them while still under the doctor's escort.

"If there's nothing more, I'd like to return to my Solitaire," said Julian. "Presently, you're keeping me from my goal of winning five thousand games during my six-month prison sentence." He settled in again with his tablet.

Commander Holman eyed Julian's ankle restraint. "Release him," she said. Her order set off a flurry of vigorous objections.

Glenn's voice rose above the others. "He tried to kill you, Commander. He murdered Cheney, Casey, and Voss. He planned to kill us all."

"And he's going to pay for what he's done," said Kate, quietly. Her eyes had locked with Julian's the moment she'd ordered him released. She held them while replying to Glenn. "We're going to figure out how to get home. When we do, when we land, we'll hand him to the authorities. Until then, we will treat him like a human being."

"Like he didn't treat us?" said Engles with a southern twang. She teared up. "Like he didn't treat Casey?"

Kate's eyes, still locked with Julian's, grew fiery. "*Exactly* like he didn't treat us." She moved closer, her nose centimeters from his. "*Because* we're astronauts."

None of the commander's declarations had stirred a reaction from Julian until the last. His empty expression gave way to a narrow smile that blossomed into a grin, accompanied by thin laughter.

Kate scooted back. "Release him."

Engles propelled herself to the end of Julian's bunk. She looked at the commander, sporting a sullen and hesitant expression. Kate motioned her to proceed. Engles placed her thumb on the lock's fingerprint reader, springing the shank free. The former security officer loosened the strap enough to extract his foot and rubbed the area at his ankle.

"Members of the Space Force are trained killers," said Glenn. While he spoke, Julian had settled into a seated position on the bunk with his legs dangling over the side. "He's an expert in hand-to-hand combat."

"I'm not a slouch myself, even in zero-g," said Kate. "Isn't that right, Commander Grimes?" Julian only stared at her. "By the way, how are your testicles?"

Julian smiled, his dark eyes twinkling beneath his brows. "Why don't you send your friends on their way, and I'll let you see for yourself."

"Fisk is right," erupted Glenn. "Julian has shown multiple times how he can't be trusted. He's going to attack us when we're not expecting it."

"If attacking any of you could save me, I might take my chances," said Julian. "But like I said, in six months, we're all dead."

"Commander Holman."

"Yes, Laura." The spaceflight engineer's call out had a trace of southern twang, hinting at her continued dismay. She didn't look any better than a few minutes prior, when Julian stated the capsule would be destroyed.

"No one knows when this lying piece of shit is telling the truth," said Engles. "But assuming he is, which I think we should, what do we do?"

Kate moved in close to Engles and placed a reassuring hand on her shoulder. "It's a long time between now and then." She looked at Miriam. The station chief was still upset as well. Kate backed up to address both Engles and Miriam, and also Glenn. "We're going to continue our attempts at reaching NASA. Maybe over the next six months, we'll get lucky."

"But what does that even get us?" asked Miriam. "Let's say we do contact them. Do we tell them we believe the Space Force will shoot down our capsule? Is there anything they could do to stop them?"

"There is not," said Julian.

"I'm not convinced that's true," said Kate. She paused, an insight dawning. "NASA may have no power over the Space Force's actions, but they *can* get the word out. If they tell the world about the mine, about the whole conspiracy, there'll be no more reason to shoot us down." Spirits lightened with her observation.

"But what if we don't?" asked Glenn. "Get a hold of NASA, I mean."

"If we get all the way to Earth without making contact with NASA, at that point we'll have to have another discussion. But it's one I can't honestly imagine taking place. I remain optimistic we'll get through somehow. Until that time, I recommend we all stay focused on the positive."

Pawing at the ceiling, Kate rotated and then propelled herself slowly towards the exit. Glenn, Miriam, and Engles all followed the commander.

"Do you think it's wise to leave Julian down here alone?" Glenn whispered.

"You're worried he'll tunnel his way out?" asked Kate, grinning with her sarcasm. "He's got nowhere to go. He's a rat. Trapped with the rest of us rats."

"I don't know," said Glenn. "I don't trust him. Julian has two speeds: misanthrope and sleeping misanthrope."

"You might've turned out the same if all your friends were Space Force," said Kate. "Maybe he just needs some astronaut time to bring him 'round."

"Socialization?" asked Glenn. He chortled. "I doubt we'll see much change from him hanging out with his astronaut buddies. But I'd be up for some psychological conditioning, like in that old movie, Clockwork something, where they pinned the guy's eyes open."

The sarcasm elicited a frown. "I'm thinking socialization is *exactly* what he needs ...," she said.

Kate arrived at the entrance to the access shaft and held fast. "Julian." He looked up with her shout. "You should come too. You've spent enough time down here. Come up and join the rest of us."

Julian didn't move at first but moments later floated from his bunk and set himself gliding across the cabin.

"You can go on ahead," she said to Glenn.

Glenn nodded and pulled himself upwards, quickly disappearing into the shaft.

Julian reached Kate's position with a dispassionate air. Given all he'd done on Mars, some might say it was the chilling demeanor of a psychopath. "If there's any funny business, you'll end up back down here, with that leash back on your leg," she said. "Am I understood?"

"You are, Commander," he said. He motioned her forward. "After you."

Commander Holman propelled herself up the shaft, with Julian trailing close behind.

30

Kate Holman, Commander of the Ares mission, personal diary entry for November 12, 2042.

Today marks the halfway point of our return trip to Earth. The time has flown! It seems like yesterday I was waking from my near-death experience. What to say on the three-month anniversary of leaving Mars …?

I really believed we'd make some headway with Julian, but all the time he's been in "forced socialization" doesn't seem to have changed him. For the most part, he keeps to himself, occasionally lashing out with a snide comment. I figured he'd at least warm to us, spending so much time in such close quarters. So far, he hasn't. Honestly, the feeling is mutual.

Glenn says Julian can't be trusted and continues to push for locking him up. While I agree Commander Grimes is untrustworthy, I insist that incarcerating him is inhumane. Glenn also thinks we should put him under surveillance, which seems paranoid, and totally pointless. What can Julian do, trapped in this can with the rest of us? At the end of the day, we'll all share the same fate.

Our efforts to contact NASA have come up short. Miriam's no slouch with radio operations. She's exhausted all her tricks.

Engles had the idea of sending a message by modulating a laser beam with Morse code, to basically flash it in time with the dots and dashes. We have a couple laser range finders left over from our trip to Mars, but they're not nearly powerful enough to be seen on Earth at this distance. Even if they were, someone would have to be looking straight at the capsule to pick up the signal.

Fisk, for being a nutcase sometimes (he recently babbled, "If a capsule explodes, and there's no one around to see it, does it really happen?"), has brilliant flashes of insight. He noted how the extreme distance between Earth and the *Gaia* means any maneuver we make won't be detected for seven minutes. With this thought in mind, we attempted to fly beyond the edge of the interference. That would've given us seven minutes to broadcast in the clear, before they could reorient their antenna. Unfortunately, we never found the edge of the jamming—it apparently has a very wide radius. We've not enough propellant to experiment further.

I still believe we'll make contact with NASA; however, I have to accept that we're running out of time. What if we fail? I've been refusing to consider the question. It's a waste of energy to worry about something that may not come to pass. Besides, there aren't any real options. The *Gaia's* designed for one thing: splashing down in the ocean. The only place we can do that is Earth. All this fretting could even be for naught, seeing as it depends on what Julian has told us being true.

This is the longest I've gone without speaking to my children, much longer than the time I spent recuperating from the incident on the Moon. Well, we haven't actually spoken on this trip, but we did exchange messages daily. Three months of not hearing their voices or seeing their faces. I miss them so. I wonder what they think has happened to Mommy—

I'm back now. I had to step away for a moment (I got choked up).

I need to get home. I'd get out and push if that would help. Get home, and back to my children.

31

"Approach vector insertion will begin in T minus thirty seconds."

The announcement from the autopilot had the casual air of a routine course adjustment. Business as usual, as far as the computer was concerned. It was anything but for the humans aboard.

Kate surveyed the cabin and the *Ares* astronauts at their stations. The maneuver would insert their capsule into the correct flight path for splashdown on Earth six hours later, the start of the reentry sequence. "Everyone strapped in?" Five thumbs rose. "Julian?"

Julian, seated at his disabled security terminal, swiveled and faced her. He didn't flash a thumbs up, but instead grabbed the restraint stretched across his shoulder and gave it an exaggerated tug while making a face.

"T minus ten seconds," said the computer, beginning its countdown. "One."

Attitude thrusters nudged the *Gaia* into the preprogrammed approach vector. The small bursts tugged at Kate—nothing like the jostling of a reentry, but consequential enough to have knocked them around the capsule if not for their restraints. She gripped the straps that kept her snug in her seat.

"Approach vector insertion complete."

Six hours until their scheduled splashdown, four hours before the start of their descent. Still time to reach NASA, to avert Julian's promised destruction at the hands of the Space Force, but not much. They'd already tried and failed every day since leaving Mars. If she was being honest with herself, the odds of making contact in the short time remaining were zero. Soon, they'd have to decide: attempt a landing, or try something else. But what? The *Gaia* was a capsule, not a rocket. They couldn't just set course for any—

"Commander Holman."

Kate glanced at the nearby station. "Yes, Miriam?"

Miriam had a look of speechless astonishment that burgeoned into a smile. "I have NASA on the line. Mission Control, in Houston."

NASA ...? At last—a miracle! Kate gazed at Miriam in shock, forgetting the station chief was waiting for her reply. "Put them on speaker."

Miriam tapped buttons on her terminal and adjusted a slider. She directed Kate to proceed.

"This is Katherine Holman, commander of the Ares mission, en route to Earth in the space capsule *Gaia*. Is that you, Houston?"

"Commander Holman, we're so happy to hear your voice!" The expressions in the cabin echoed the sentiment, except for Julian. He'd claimed they'd never make contact with NASA. He was wrong, in the last moments of their trip, but wrong nonetheless. He sat sour-faced; let him choke on his bile.

"We've been trying to reach you since your liftoff from Mars," the voice continued. "There was interference we couldn't pierce until now."

A knowing smile emerged. "I'm just glad you didn't give up on us," she said.

"You're returning early from Mars."

"Affirmative, Houston," said Kate. "We had to abandon the HAAB. I don't know if you received all of our earlier transmissions? There's a lot to brief you on."

"Roger that. Who all's with you in the capsule?"

"Besides myself, there's Commander Wiles, Mission Specialist Sato, Spaceflight Engineer Engles, Doctor Palmer, Spaceflight Participant Fisk, and Commander Grimes. We lost Cheney, Morgan, and Voss."

"Roger, *Gaia*. Please stand by."

Please stand by? Like on hold? Now that they'd established contact, it was vitally important she fill them in on Julian's claim of conspiracy and their concerns about attempting a landing. NASA needed to get working on a contingency plan for their safe return.

"*Gaia*, this is Houston. Sorry for the delay."

"No problem," said Kate. "Houston, I need to discuss something very important about the Mars mission and our landing on Earth—"

"*Gaia*, Houston here. We're making preparations to receive you in the Gulf. Please switch your approach vector to Charlie Tango."

"... OK ...." Kate swiped terminal screens, arriving at the navigational system and scrolling through the preset approach vectors. "Roger that, NASA," she said, locating the new course in the list. "Switching to Charlie

Tango." Attitude thrusters again nudged the capsule, their bursts smaller than before.

Seconds elapsed. "Course change confirmed, *Gaia*. We see you on your new trajectory."

"Thank you, Houston." She plowed ahead. "Regarding our reentry, we have some concerns. They're a result of events that occurred on Mars—"

"*Gaia*, we'd prefer to avoid a debrief over the comm. There will be plenty of time for that once you're on the ground. We're very sorry to hear about the casualties, but we're happy to know the rest of you are OK. We'll see you all in … five hours, thirty-five minutes. Welcome home, *Gaia!*"

"With all respect, this is not a debrief. What I have to say pertains to our landing. We have concerns the capsule may be in danger. In short, our trip to Mars was a front for a secret mission. You haven't been able to reach us these past months because the Space Force has been jamming our transmissions. That's all according to Commander Grimes, who also says the Space Force may try to destroy—"

"They closed the channel," said Miriam.

The statement made no sense. "They what?"

"They closed the channel. They're no longer listening."

"Raise them again, Miriam," said Kate, her voice filled with an ire that wasn't intended for the Mars station chief. There wouldn't be a splashdown if they didn't relay their immediate situation to NASA and expose the secret mission to the world.

Miriam tapped her terminal. "They're not answering."

"Is it more jamming? How were you able to get through to them in the first place?"

"I don't know, Commander," said Miriam. "I sent my hourly hail. That was—" She checked her board. "Twenty minutes ago. Out of the blue, just now, I got a response from Houston."

"How do you know it was Mission Control?"

Kate spun about in her chair, facing into the crew compartment. She found Julian studying her. "What?" she asked.

"How do you know it was Mission Control?" said Julian, saying each word slowly and with exaggeration, as if talking to a child. "Because they said they were?" He chuckled. "Like I told you a hundred times over, Space Force is going to blow this capsule out of the sky. Whoever you spoke with only broke radio silence for two reasons. First, to make sure there were people on board. There're going to use an Atlas space-to-space missile, and those babies are expensive. They don't want to waste one unless they absolutely need to. And second, to set us on their preferred trajectory for destruction."

"Charlie Tango?" asked Kate. "It's one of the preset approach vectors, not something they cooked up. What's special about it?"

"I have no idea," said Julian. "But it has to differ from the original course, from the others, in a way that somehow benefits them. Otherwise, they wouldn't have bothered."

Kate studied their new flight path on her terminal, a dotted line that encircled the globe before spiraling to the splashdown point off the coast of Florida. She tapped through the list of alternate approach vectors. "They all get us to the same splashdown point, and at roughly the same time. The only real difference I see with Charlie Tango is it's a polar trajectory. The rest are equatorial."

"That's it," said Grimes. He paused, apparently waiting for the others to understand. He huffed at the quiet. "Destroying things in space is messy business, Commander Holman. It creates lots of debris traveling at high speeds that becomes a navigational hazard. When they saw us shift to the primary approach vector, they probably realized it would be a problem. Charlie Tango's polar trajectory takes the capsule away from the shipping lanes. They want to end us, but they want it to be convenient."

A few button taps overlayed the heavily travelled Earth-Moon shipping routes on Kate's screen. Julian was right: Charlie Tango, in its polar trajectory, swung the *Gaia* far from those lanes, while the other routes, all equatorial, would bring the capsule straight through them. "I see your point," she said. "But that's not proof of anything."

"Of course it's not," said Julian. "Proof leads back to people, which leads to time in jail. You're not going to find an ounce of proof anywhere."

Glenn chimed in. "Let's say you're right, Julian, that whoever called wasn't from NASA and that they rerouted us to make destroying the *Gaia* more convenient. What do you propose we do?"

"Nothing," he said, with a wave of his hand. "I've been telling you all along that we're flying to our deaths. There's nothing *to* be done, except maybe make peace with whatever deity you believe in."

"What if we return to the original approach vector?" asked Fisk. "If Charlie ... whatever makes it convenient for them, what if we make it less?"

"Charlie Tango makes the smallest hazard, that's all," said Julian. "They'll live with a bigger hazard if they have to, if the alternative is their gold mine being exposed."

"How about a course that creates a hazard they can't live with?" asked Fisk.

"The issue isn't our course," said Julian. "It's our transponder. That's what the Atlas missile will lock on to when it comes for us. We're flashing a big red 'here we are' no matter which way we go."

"Let's disable our transponder, then," said Fisk.

"That's not going to fool anyone," said Julian. "The second that signal disappears, they'll figure we've discovered their plan. They'll reestablish our location some other way. For all intents and purposes, our transponder *is* us."

"So we just need our transponder to not be us," said Fisk.

Julian stared at the researcher, processing. The former security chief seemed stuck in a loop like a computer, cycling between bafflement and confusion. "What the hell does that even mean?"

Fisk shrugged. "Dunno. I'm simply using logic to come up with a solution."

"There's nothing logical about what you said," barked Julian.

"Maybe there is," said Miriam. All eyes shifted to the Mars station chief. "Our transponder sits at the tip of our capsule," she continued, pointing at the cabin's ceiling, "and it's oriented towards Earth." She paused a moment, the gears spinning. "If we could separate the transponder from the capsule, its momentum would carry it along our current trajectory. No matter how we changed the *Gaia's* course after that, they'd still see the transponder headed toward them."

"And think that's us," said Glenn. "You're saying we could fly off in some other direction, but because they're watching the transponder, they won't realize we have."

"Fly off to where?" asked Julian. "It's not like that gets us to a landing."

"No, it doesn't," said Kate. "But it does give us one thing we haven't had our entire flight back to Earth: a way to test your claim that the Space Force will blow us out of the sky. If we navigate to a safe distance from the beacon, to a point where we can monitor its progress, we can watch for its destruction. If it survives, we can swing around and come in for a second landing attempt." She glanced at Miriam. "That's pretty brilliant."

"Thank you, Commander," said Miriam. She beamed, but her smile quickly dissipated. She gave a nervous look at Engles. "That is, if what I've suggested is even possible."

"It is," said the spacecraft engineer. "The *Gaia's* transponder has its own battery, a hedge against electrical issues in the capsule. But detaching it means a spacewalk, and not a trivial one. There's cosmic and solar radiation, as well as the risk of a micrometeorite collision. Traveling at our current speed, that could be catastrophic to the space walker. Plus the chance of space suit failure, almost certainly fatal in the vacuum; disorientation, which can lead to errors and accidents; the threat of—"

"In other words, a big risk for a dubious goal," said Kate, stopping Engles's lapse into engineer mode. "As Julian points out, if the transponder gets blown up and confirms his claims, we're no closer to getting to the ground."

"The objective is to stay alive," said Glenn. "At least then we can explore our options. That doesn't happen if we're shot down by a missile."

Shot down, that is, if Julian even was speaking the truth. The interference, the strange conversation with NASA, the course change—it could all be a misunderstanding, fanned into a wild delusion by his claims. But if it was true …. Kate turned to Engles. "I'll need you to talk me through the steps."

"Of detaching the transponder? You can't go out there."

"Someone has to," said Kate. "Given the risks, it's not a job I can ask of anyone else."

"You don't have to ask," said Engles. "I'm volunteering."

"No," said Kate. "I want you to stay put in the capsule."

"How many spacewalk repair jobs have you performed, Commander?" asked Engles. "I've done ten."

"I've spacewalked before," said Kate.

"Have you worked with tools in zero-g? Wrestled stuck bolts using a wrench you can barely grip with a glove? Navigated maintenance handholds in a bulky space suit?"

"Those are all things anyone would have to manage," said Kate.

"True," said Engles. "The problem is your lack of experience will slow you down. The danger is really about one thing: time spent outside the capsule. The risk only grows the longer you take."

Kate didn't want to gamble someone else's life on a spacewalk, especially one that might not be necessary, but Engles had made the case that she was the right person for the job. "Anything else?" she joked.

"Only this." Engles fished inside her collar and tugged her lucky red bandana into view.

Kate smiled. "Everyone, get suited up," she said. "We open the hatch in T minus thirty minutes."

32

Engles floated just inside the hatch, outfitted in her space suit with a tool belt that hung at her waist. The spacecraft engineer fished a tether from the belt and clipped it to a hitch point on the bulkhead. She tugged twice, testing its soundness, then grabbed an adjacent handhold. "I'm ready."

Kate performed a last survey of the other *Ares* astronauts. They all sat strapped in their chairs, with their helmets secured. Suit checks complete, they were ready to proceed. "Good luck, Laura," she said. "And no sightseeing. Be quick, but be careful."

"Roger that," said Engles. Using her free hand, she fingered the keypad embedded in the bulkhead. Red light flashed around the door as the cabin's air receded, and with it the gentle hum of the capsule's interior. For Kate, the only sound that remained was her breathing in her ears.

The red light turned solid. Engles pushed the hatch. The slow-motion reveal gave way to a canvas of deep, brilliant, black. *Brilliant* black? Kate studied the inky patch: the glow that infused the midnight swatch resolved into a million pinpricks of light.

Engles stepped onto the rim of the door and reached her right arm beyond the opening. Her right foot moved next, finding purchase somewhere outside. In a sweeping motion, her entire body swung out of sight, leaving only an unobstructed view of the void.

"Can we get an exterior shot?" asked Kate.

"Just a sec," said Glenn, working the controls at Engles's station. A fish-eye view from atop the space capsule filled the main screen. The craft's gently curved hull ran along the bottom of the frame in over-exposed white, sitting against a black background.

Kate searched for a sign of the engineer, but nothing stirred on the screen. "How you doing out there?" she asked.

"Fine," said Engles through huffs.

"Take your time," said Kate. What was it like to scale the hull of their speeding craft? She conjured an image of inching along the exterior of a bullet train and immediately regretted it, saddling herself with an onrush of vertigo. She purged the visual, happy not to have an actual description from Engles.

"What's it like out there?" asked Glenn.

Ugh. Kate braced herself for Engles's response.

"We're traveling at twelve kilometers per second, but you wouldn't know it. Except for the occasional odd streak of light, it feels like the capsule's sitting still."

"Laura, this is Doctor Palmer." His voice shook with an anxiousness Kate had never heard before. "Those streaks are cosmic rays passing through the jelly material in your eyes. As they enter and exit, they leave behind a trail of light."

The *Gaia* protected them from the high-energy cosmic rays that populated the space between the planets. Solving that health hazard had removed the last major obstacle to green-lighting the mission to Mars. Engles, outside the capsule and clinging to its hull, was fully exposed. "I don't want to rush you, Laura," said Kate, "but the sooner you're back inside, the better."

"Roger that, Commander."

Something stirred near the bottom of the screen: the edge of a bobbing, white sphere. The sphere tipped back, revealing a shimmering gold faceplate as Engles surveyed the path ahead. Shoulders came into view. The astronaut's white bulk grew in the frame as she navigated handholds, her progress slow and methodical.

When all movement ceased, Engles loomed large on the viewscreen. She drew a second tether from her belt and attached it to the hull, then pulled the line taut. "I'm at the transponder unit. I see the bolts holding it in place." She fished in her tool belt. Her hand returned with a ratcheting socket wrench, leashed to her waist. "Preparing to remove the first one."

"Proceed," said Kate.

The wrench traveled in a slow-motion lunge straight towards the camera. It came up short at the last instant, its socket landing on the hull, beside a knob-like protrusion in the foreground. "Here goes," she said. The spacecraft engineer remained frozen in the frame for several seconds before the wrench handle budged. Engles ratcheted the wrench and torqued again. The handle travelled easier. Subsequent torques came in a batch of swift movements. The wrench rose with a silver bolt thread protruding from its socket. Engles's gloved hand snagged the bolt and ferried it to a pouch at her waist.

"One down, three more to go." She extracted the remaining bolts in similar fashion, faster than the first. When she finished, she restored the wrench to her belt.

Reaching her arms forward, Engles placed a hand on either side of the knob. She grunted, then grunted again.

"Everything all right?" asked Kate.

"Damn thing's stuck," said Engles. She grunted a third time. "There we go." She hoisted the transponder unit above the hull, high enough for a dark stripe of space to appear between it and the capsule, and let go. "It's floating free, except for the electronics bundle." On second look, the black stripe wasn't continuous: a narrow line, a multi-colored snake of wires, hung from the module.

Engles groped beneath the unit, her glove disappearing inside. More grunts. "The connector clip's impossible to unlock with gloves on."

Kate had assumed the success of Engles's assignment hinged on the bolt removal. It depended instead on unclipping a connector with a bulky glove. If she couldn't, their plan to test Julian's claim would end before it began. She checked her station's chronometer. "You're now three minutes behind schedule." As much as she wanted Engles to keep trying and to ultimately succeed, she'd have to recall the engineer soon. Each additional moment she spent outside the capsule increased her risk of injury, or death .... "Unfortunately, I think that's about—"

As Kate spoke, Engles's hand left the unit, fished around her belt, and returned clutching a pair of wire cutters. Holding the bundle with her other hand, she jabbed the snips at the wires. "All done," she said. The line that stretched from the transponder to the *Gaia* capsule showed a break in the middle.

"Well done," said Kate. "Now get back in here."

Engles coiled the wires that sprouted from the *Gaia* into a knot, freed her tether from the capsule, and inched backwards from the camera. She shrank in the frame until the last remnants of her helmet disappeared. Seconds later, her legs and hands emerged within the open hatch. She climbed inside the spacecraft and pulled the door closed.

"Great work, Laura," said Kate as Glenn vacated the engineer's station. He and Engles grabbed their seats and strapped themselves in.

"I'm going to back us away." Kate worked the thruster controls. The transponder unit, still visible on the main viewscreen, rose slowly. "Easy does it." More black appeared between the module and the capsule. The unit eventually disappeared from the frame. "Engles, can you set the topside, exterior camera to track the transponder?"

Engles tapped her console. The star field shifted on the main viewscreen, slowed, and stopped, coming to rest with a shrinking, white dot in the center.

Kate angled the capsule, steering it clear of the beacon, and marshaled its speed to increase the distance from the unit.

"Showing twenty kilometers to the transponder," said Engles. "Thirty. Fifty. Seventy. Ninety."

"That should put us at a safe range," said Kate. She manipulated the thrusters again. "I've set us on a parallel course."

"Now what?" asked Glenn.

"Now we wait and see if anything happens."

"But how long?"

The spacewalk and its preparation required almost sixty minutes. "I'm guessing four hours," said Kate. "By then, the transponder will be skirting the atmosphere, on the verge of burning up."

"Does that mean—"

An immense flash filled the viewscreen, bathing the capsule's interior in stark, white light. Astronauts cowered and shielded their eyes. The flash lasted a few seconds, followed by a larger, brighter flash.

Once the light receded enough for them to lower their hands, the astronauts looked at each other, concerned and shaken.

"What was that?" asked Kate.

Engles checked her terminal. "Not sure, but I no longer have a fix on the transponder." She tapped the screen. "I can confirm the explosion occurred at the unit's last known location. It also coincided with a burst of X- and gamma rays, and I'm getting elevated readings of alpha particles."

"The detonation signature of an Atlas rocket," said Julian. All eyes in the capsule settled on the former security chief. "They're nuclear-tipped."

The news took a moment to sink in. The Space Force really had launched a missile to destroy the *Gaia*. Julian's prediction had seemed plausible given the facts, but Kate had found it hard to accept. Her skepticism caused them to set about detaching the transponder without a real sense of urgency. She shivered with the realization of how close they'd come to death, only minutes to spare from Engles completing the task.

"Now that they've eliminated us," added Julian, "what's next?"

Indeed. Kate thought for a second. "Are we still being jammed?"

Miriam queried her board. "We are not, Commander."

"That means we can radio NASA and tell them we're still alive," said Glenn.

"Are you kidding?" asked Julian. "If you manage to reach someone at NASA, the news of our continued existence will get relayed straight to the Space Force."

"I know that if we got through, they'd find some way to help us," said Kate. "We astronauts take care of our own."

Julian dismissed her with a flick of his hand. "As I've said before, this thing goes all the way to the top. But do what you will. We're dead no matter how you slice it." He folded his arms and propped his feet again on his terminal. "Go ahead. Make the call."

"Commander Holman." The voice was Glenn's. "I, too, share your faith in the Astronaut Corps, but it's worth considering that others may be listening in."

He made a good point. They'd at least need an encrypted channel, something that wasn't an open party line. "Miriam, is it possible to rig up a confidential comm link to NASA?"

Miriam didn't respond. Her whole body had gone rigid, and she'd become hyper-focused on her terminal. Pressing one side of her headset to an ear, she listened intently. The color drained from her already pale face. She turned to Kate.

"What?" asked Commander Holman.

Miriam tapped her terminal. Audio spilled from the main speakers.

"...update on the *Ares* manned mission to Mars. We go live, now, to Cape Canaveral, for a news conference."

"...tlmen of the press, I am Richard Pearson, Assistant Director of NASA's human spaceflight program, with an update on the *Ares* mission. Over the past six months, we've fed you updates from the ten, brave members of the first manned mission to Mars as they made their way home in the *Gaia* capsule after the premature end of their mission. At oh fourteen hundred and thirty-four hours, as they prepared to adjust their course to a final approach vector, the crew reported issues with the capsule's thruster system. Eight minutes later, we lost contact with the *Gaia*. Space Force early warning satellites detected an explosion at the spacecraft's last known location. It will take some time to analyze the telemetry and understand the root cause, but the sad news I have for you today is that all ten *Ares* crew members have perished.

"I would like everyone to join in a moment of silence, in recognition of the sacrifice these brave men and women have made to further America's aspirations in space."

For Kate, the interior of the capsule spun as reality sank in. NASA had lied about their communications with the Mars astronauts, and about the reason for their supposed deaths .... NASA, with the Space Force, had schemed to kill them. Moreover, the two agencies, totally invested in those lies, would do whatever it took to prevent their unravelling. In particular, that meant stopping the *Gaia* from landing. The Mars mission astronauts' appearance alive on Earth would cause the whole charade to fall apart.

Kate's emotions roiled, a sickening mix of sadness and anger. The sadness swelled from the loss of everything she thought she knew about the Astronaut Corps. The brotherhood, the taking care of their own—gone, perverted by the promise of vast riches. The anger surfaced from knowing her children would be told that she'd died. At that moment, they might be in agony over word that she was no longer alive, that she would never come back to them. The conspirators had tried to kill her, but the collateral damage was far worse.

"Thank you," continued Pearson. "That concludes my official statement. I will now take questions. Yes."

"Assistant Director, were you in contact with the Mars station astronauts at the time of the explosion?"

"Not at the exact moment. We last heard from them a minute before the event. Commander Wiles contacted us to say he was starting a diagnostic on the thrusters."

"Had there been any concern at the time the situation might turn catastrophic?"

"None. Other than a signal from the onboard computer of a possible stuck valve in the thruster controls, all indications were the capsule was performing flawlessly. The Ares mission astronauts were in good spirits and looking forward to returning home.

"Go ahead, in the back."

"Assistant Director, was Commander Holman under sedation at the time of the explosion?"

"To the best of my knowledge, she was. Commander Wiles had informed me she would remain sedated during the splashdown. Next—"

"A follow-up, if I may. When can we expect the final report from the investigation into Commander Holman's mental health crisis?"

"I don't have an updated timeline on that, but I can say the preliminary assessment of our clinical psychologists remains unchanged. Commander Holman's erratic behavior traces back to an accident on the Moon, which at the time drove her to seek psychiatric help. We do have more insight into her motivation, gleaned from a recently decrypted cache of the commander's personal logs. Apparently, she believed aliens inhabit the Face, and that these aliens pose a threat to humanity. Spreading radioactive material from the station's nuclear reactor in and around the Face was her attempt at wiping them out. The discovery of her actions, as you know, precipitated her ransacking of the Mars station.

"I'll take this time to announce the fast-tracking of a new mission to Mars, this one to clean up the mess at the Face. Unlike our Chinese friends, we believe the solar system belongs to all mankind, not just one nation staking claims. This unfortunate incident happened on our watch—we pledge to set things right. We're sending a team to restore this landmark to its original condition, to make it safe again for researchers and colonists of the future. We anticipate this will be a multi-year endeavor. During this time, we ask that all space-faring nations steer clear of the Face and the surrounding area, so as not to endanger more lives or equipment.

"Next question. Way in the back—"

"Turn it off," said Kate.

The audio cut out. Commander Holman sat stupefied at her station.

"A nice bit of character assassination, which conveniently creates the cover they need to start mining," remarked a smug-faced Grimes as he eyed the commander. "You've said before you felt destined for something big. They certainly have helped you make a name for yourself."

Bile churned in the pit of Kate's stomach, the stirrings of a great beast rearing in her gut. Julian had wondered why they'd chosen her to lead the Mars mission. Had they always planned to make her the fall guy? Her blemished service record provided the perfect raw material for any story they chose to tell.

The beast rose from her belly, setting her blood afire and painting her vision red.

33

Chaos filled the capsule, a cacophony of panicked voices debating past actions, next steps, and prospects of survival.

Glenn whistled loudly. All conversation ceased. He gave the floor to Kate.

Did she even want it? She surveyed the faces staring back at her: Miriam, a thin veil of courage shrouding her fear; Engels, in engineer mode, ready to problem-solve; Glenn, encouraging and supportive, but also afraid; Fisk with his normal, crazed look and a halo of frenzied hair; Dr. Palmer, dispassionate as always; and Julian, sporting his usual, self-satisfied smirk.

Still furious and shaken, the commander cleared her throat. "They've declared us dead, the capsule destroyed, but I'm not willing to accept that false fate. I want to see home again, see my children. Is there anyone who feels different?" Headshakes emerged around the cabin. "Getting to Earth will be difficult. Coming up with a plan may take some time. Our immediate problem is we're inside a speeding capsule that, if we don't do something, will continue right past Earth and off into space. We have to decide where to go next." She surveyed the faces a second time. "I have some thoughts, but I'd like to hear others' suggestions."

Glenn spoke first. "We should land on the Moon. All things considered, it gives us the best chance—"

"I don't want to go into pros and cons yet." Kate's response came out more annoyed than she intended, but Glenn's mention of the Moon set her off. "Let's get all the options on the table first. Then we can evaluate."

"Could we go into orbit?" asked Miriam. "Like maybe orbit the Earth? That might buy us time to figure out what comes next."

"Not unless we want to be shot down." The comment came from Julian. "In orbit, we'll show up on the Space Force's early warning systems. We'd be doing them a favor as far as finishing the job."

"What about orbiting the Moon then," said Miriam.

"The other big problem is the *Gaia* wasn't designed for more than six months of habitation," said Kate. "With our food reserves near zero, we won't be able to maintain an orbit for long." She scanned the astronauts' faces again. "Anyone else?"

"This isn't really an option," said Julian, "but just to put everything out there, we could dock at the Chinese space station."

Glenn perked up. "You say that's not an option, but it could be the best of the bunch."

"Only if you plan on asking for political asylum," said Julian.

"I've always wanted to visit China," said Fisk. "I hear the food is incredible."

"We could wind up with more than a visit," sneered Julian at the professor. "Odds are good we'd live our lives out behind the Red Curtain. I don't know about you, but I don't consider life in the Chinese police state any kind of living at all. But the bigger issue is gambling the Space Force won't blow us up once we dock."

"Blow us up?" asked Kate. "They'd destroy the Chinese space station in the process."

"They may not care," said Julian. "And they wouldn't need to use heavy weaponry to do it. They'd deploy a couple Space Force Guardians in stealth suits to position a few charges ... it'll look like an accident."

"Even if the Space Force leaves us alone, I think the risk of spending our lives as prisoners of the Chinese rules it out," said Glenn. "Living through that plan might be worse than dying."

"What about going ahead with a splashdown on Earth?" asked Dr. Palmer.

"Any approach vector we choose for reentry will eventually bring us in range of a Space Force weapons platform," said Julian.

"You know a lot about Space Force satellites and capabilities," said Kate. "Is there no way to evade them?"

Julian thought for a moment. "The Space Force wanted a much larger network of satellites, but they hit budget constraints. Their constellation can only monitor ninety percent of the globe at any one time."

"What does that mean, practically?" asked Glenn.

"It means there are dead zones in their coverage," said Julian. "If we could navigate the capsule through one of those zones, we might escape detection. It would be a hairy bit of piloting, even with help from the computer."

"That leaves the Moon," said Glenn.

"Not an option," blurted Kate.

"Care to elaborate?" was Glenn's testy reply, her second-in-command likely irked by the quick dismissal of his suggestion.

"The *Gaia* isn't a rocket we can set down anywhere we like," said Kate. "It's a capsule, a projectile, zooming through space. It wouldn't land so much as crash."

"But we could use the Moon's gravity well to shed some speed," said Glenn. "Perhaps the regolith could act as a brake."

"If we somehow slowed enough to attempt a landing, we'd kick up so much dust they'd draw and quarter us," said Kate. "In addition, the moonbase sits between two long ridges. Not a problem for a normal rocket landing, but to slide in there with a screaming capsule ...." Kate shook her head. "We risk hitting the launch pad, the power generator, the station itself ...."

"I was thinking the Far Side," said Glenn. "Near the Old Mine. The Outpost there has basic services. If the *Gaia* created a dust problem, it would be mostly confined to the Far Side. And it's secluded. There are so many amateur astronomers with their 'scopes trained on the Moon. If we touch down near the base, some kid with their backyard telescope will see us for sure. Landing on the Far Side lets us regroup, come up with a plan. It would give us a chance to make the next moves on *our* terms."

"Even if everything went perfectly, that still leaves us on the Moon," said Kate. "Other ideas?" she asked, heading off additional comments from Glenn. No more suggestions came. "Of all these, an Earth landing is the best option."

"How do you figure?" asked Glenn.

"Ultimately, that's where we want to be. As long as we steer through one of the dead zones, we're clear to get to the ground."

"That's still a big 'if,'" said Julian. "You might be able to dodge the Space Force satellites, but they're not the only systems with radar. There's NORAD's early-warning tracker. It's looking for ICBMs, but we'll show up for sure. One short phone call later and we'll be targeted again."

"They might see us, but we'll be traveling at Mach twenty-two," said Kate.

"The Air Force has hypersonic missiles," said Julian. "They could easily intercept us at reentry speeds."

"There's also no recovery vessel waiting to retrieve us from the ocean," said Glenn.

"The capsule won't sink," said Kate.

"No, it won't, but like you said, we're out of food. We could be bobbing for weeks before a fishing vessel or whatever comes along."

"What about fishing ourselves?" asked Fisk. "We'd be floating in an ocean full of food."

"Aside from the risk of sinking the capsule if we open the hatch, we don't exactly have a kitchen to clean and cook anything.," said Glenn. "All our meals have been ready-to-eat."

"I'm partial to a good sashimi," said Fisk. "There's this restaurant—"

"I think the only real option is the Moon," said Glenn.

"I guess if I'm being honest, I like fish, but not every day," said Fisk. He lapsed into thought. "Imagine the menu on the Chinese space station ...."

"A splashdown is still our best option," said Kate. "That's my conclusion, as commander of this mission."

Glenn bristled at the decree. "I don't think it's fair for any one person to make this decision," he said. "It calls for a vote."

Kate started to object, but the faces around the cabin clearly wanted a say in their collective fate. "OK ..., a vote, then." She squeezed out a smile. No way would she go back to the Moon, regardless of what the others decided. They'd have to get someone else to pilot the damn capsule. She'd only make that declaration if she had to. Commander Holman sighed—hopefully the vote would go her way, but she braced for the worst. "Who thinks we should try to land on the Moon?"

One hand went up: Glenn's.

Kate breathed easier, the one unacceptable option no longer on the table. "Who thinks we should try to dock with the Chinese space station?"

Fisk raised his hand. "C'mon," he said, looking at the others, "I can't be the only one who likes Chinese food."

"Who thinks we should splash down on Earth?"

Engles, Palmer, Miriam, and Kate raised their hands. Julian added a fifth vote.

"That settles it, then," said Kate.

Commander Holman's abrupt declaration had the effect of ending the meeting. Miriam, Engles, and Palmer turned back to their stations. Fisk bounded for the capsule ceiling, returning to his yogic position and muttering about craving Chinese food. Julian left his chair and disappeared into the lower crew compartment.

Glenn lingered at Kate's station, where the commander sat pushing buttons on her touchscreen terminal with more force than necessary. "You really think taking a chance on a splashdown is better than landing on the Moon?"

Obviously she did, which was why that option got her vote. She said nothing—no response needed—but it didn't dissuade Glenn from hovering. It became annoying. "Is there something you need?" asked Kate, short in her tone.

"I'd like you to reconsider a Moon landing."

"The answer's 'no.'"

"The others voted with you because they have faith in your assessments," he added. "If you change your mind, they'll definitely support you." His goofy grin emerged, stoking her irritation.

"*You* could also have a little faith," said Kate. She swiped to the navigation screen, preparing to locate the dead zones in the Space Force satellite coverage.

Glenn continued to hover.

"The answer's still *no*," she said. "I don't want to go back to the Moon, and I'll be damned if I'm going to fly us there." She sat forward in her chair and focused on her console.

"The thing is—"

"God damn it, Glenn! You're telling me you don't remember what happened to me on the Moon? Don't understand, after all our conversations, how I can never go back there? How the base commander said he'd put a bullet in my head if I ever showed up on his door again? How I lost my friend? I still get the shakes just thinking about the moments *before* everything went to hell." Kate put her hand out. It shook with a constant tremor. "That's why I won't agree to go to the God damn Moon! Is it clear now? God, why are you always so clueless and lost? Sticking your foot in your mouth at every turn!"

Glenn flinched at the comment. He'd tried to hide it, mostly succeeded, but not completely. She imagined the part of him she'd hurt, that part of him curling up inside, a small child, hiding and sobbing. "I didn't forget about your time on the Moon." He spoke in a meek voice, a hair above a whisper. "I'll never know how it feels to you, but I know it still hurts, a lot, which is why it's so hard for me to ask you to reconsider."

Kate had spun into hysterics, the exact image the assistant director had painted of her for the press. She worked to slow her breath. She regained her composure, though her hand still trembled. "I'm sorry, Glenn."

Glenn seemed on the verge of speaking. Whatever it was, he held his tongue. He pushed off from the commander's chair and slowly drifted away.

Across the cabin, Miriam spoke to Engles in a measured voice. "What exactly happened on the Moon?"

34

The Incident on the Moon

MIND THE DUST! MIND THE DUST!

Pilot Kate Holman's terminal flashed the message from Lunar Traffic Control at the start of their final descent. Those three words were a trademark of the American moonbase, and also the butt of many jokes. "Dust the mind!" was the favorite retort of "Dust heads," addicts hooked on the illegal recreational drug Dustamine, or "Dust" as it was known on the street. The dust from the Lunar surface was far from recreational: it was hazardous if inhaled, abrasive, highly reactive and corrosive, and extremely adhesive. It had been the number one challenge in taming the Moon enough to establish a base.

"One hundred fifty meters to touchdown."

"Acknowledged," said Kate. Outside the window to her right, the white buildings and tube ways that comprised the moonbase sat in the saddle between sharp, light gray mountains, all beneath a stark, black sky. Against that monochrome backdrop, a navigation laser, one of four, traced a green line from the landing pad to her rocket. She prodded the guidance computer with her gloved hand for the latest telemetry. "Descent alignment confirmed." She'd centered them perfectly over the pad and, most importantly, its exhaust pit, the chamber that prevented rockets from blowing dust everywhere.

Kate surveyed the sprawling moonbase. The control tower soared above the spaceport, the shape and height of a rocket itself. Service vehicles scurried like ants between squat buildings that hinted at the rooms and tunnels beneath the surface. She'd flown to the Moon many times before. "This'll be my last visit for a while," she said.

"Looking to settle down a bit?"

The question in her helmet came from John Evans, the lone passenger on her cargo run, in the seat behind hers.

"Hardly." She chuckled. "I've signed up for the Mars bootcamp."

A whistle of amazement. "From what I understand, that'll be a tough program. There are way more interested astronauts than spots. They're going to be brutal in whittling down the field."

Yes, it would be tough, but she wouldn't be weeded out. She'd do whatever it took to be part of that mission. Pilot Kate Holman was destined for something big. *Ares* was the opportunity of a lifetime. "Maybe you could put in a good word for me?" As a NASA administrator, he surely had connections.

"I'd be more than happy to, but I doubt you'll need it," said Evans. "You're one of NASA's best pilots."

"Thank you, sir."

"And thanks again for letting me hitch a ride," said Evans. "I was really in a pinch after missing the last people transport. I was the one pushing the hardest for the new emergency evac system. It would've been a shame to miss the ground-breaking."

"Happy to be of service," said Kate. "As we say, we astronauts take care of our own."

"One hundred twenty-five."

"Got it, Grace, but you really don't have to keep calling out the altitude," said Kate. She loved Grace to pieces—assigned to the same cohort for pilot training, they'd become best of friends, even bridesmaids in each other's weddings—but the final moments of flights with her as co-pilot felt like Groundhog Day. Grace liked to announce their altitude starting at two hundred meters and at every twenty-five-meter decrement after that. There was never any need. As on all other trips, Kate had maneuvered the rocket into a smooth glide, a gradual descent that would require the gentlest of taps to the retros. Kate only needed a call-out of the altitude where she'd begin cycling the retro rockets, and then zero to declare touchdown.

"One hundred."

"Seventy-five meters."

"Roger, starting retro igni—"

"Collision alert. Collision alert. Collision alert."

The guidance computer's calm tone belied the potential seriousness of the situation. Lights flashed frantically on Kate's board, a flickering sea of red.

Kate checked her radar—nothing in the sky over and around the rocket.

"What is it?" asked Grace.

"Don't know," said Kate. "Pick up visual scanning." She strained for a better view out her window. Nothing above them, but—something moved below, near ground level: a cargo carrier, a short-hop vehicle resembling a giant four-legged spider with a container tucked in its belly, glided across the spaceport. Cargo carriers didn't fly—they performed vertical takeoffs and landings. This carrier, the designation "11" stenciled on its hull, was tilted forty-five degrees. Its thrusters, no longer firing straight down, pushed the small craft up and along the landing pads. Out of control, the carrier barreled towards their position.

Kate punched the retros to maximum burn. Those rockets were never meant to provide quick reaction, only gentle braking. She needed something like the third stage separation thrusters, with their short, forceful bursts, to quickly boost their altitude. The more seasoned pilots she knew liked to leave a little fuel in the third stage tank, but the practice felt more superstition than reasoned, and ran counter to regulations. Kate always ensured she had a "clean burn" when separating from the third stage, right down to the vapor. If she'd held some fuel back, it might've cleared the rocket of the chaos below. Hopefully the retros would be enough.

They weren't. The retros kicked in, boosting the rocket skyward. The cargo carrier swept over their landing pad on its errant trajectory, clipping the bottom edge of her spacecraft and sending it listing towards the control tower.

Kate killed the retros, but not before the exhaust from her tilting rocket sprayed the naked regolith that bordered the landing pad. Lunar dust exploded into the sky in massive billows.

"Brace for impact!" Kate yelled as their rocket tipped more, gaining speed …

Slam!

The rocket landed hard on its side. The crash wrenched Kate's shoulder—instant pain. Evans cried out behind her.

"You OK?" shouted Kate as she popped the emergency release on her restraints.

"I'm not," said Evans through clenched teeth. "My leg's broken, or maybe my pelvis …."

Serious wounds, but with any luck, he wasn't also bleeding or suffering from internal injuries. Her immediate concern, however, was Grace. She lay unmoving, strapped in the seat next to her.

"Grace!" said Kate, rustling her co-pilot.

"Huh," said Grace, coming to.

"That's a relief," said Kate. "I was worried you were seriously hurt."

"I'm … I'm OK," said Grace. "I think I bumped my head."

"Get yourself unbuckled," said Kate. "I'll help Evans."

Grace had nodded in the affirmative, but when Kate returned from freeing Evans, she found her co-pilot had made no progress on her restraints. She pulled Grace clear of the remaining straps. "We've got to get out of here," said Kate. She looked around and spotted the hatch. Luckily, the rocket hadn't landed on it, which would have pinned them inside, or fallen with the exit oriented above them, where they couldn't reach. The hatch lay straight ahead. They'd have to climb over the equipment that lined the bulkhead, but otherwise an easy scramble out.

Kate touched Grace's shoulder. "I'm going to blow the hatch. Once I do, make a run for the opening. Don't look back until you're out. While you're doing that, I'll help Evans out of the capsule."

Grace gave a thumbs-up.

"Three, two, one."

Kate triggered the hatch's explosive bolts. What had been a cramped, sideways cabin filled with red light became a chamber of red fog as Lunar dust billowed inside. The opening was hidden, but still lay ahead. She groped for Evans, grabbed his arm. "Hold tight!" yelled Kate as she heaved. Evans cried out in pain as the pair moved in their bulky space suits to the exit.

Outside the cabin, the three stood in a swirling mess alongside the downed rocket. Visibility remained at zero.

"Ungh," said Evans.

"Don't worry, I'm gonna get you help." Kate brought up the station map on her GPS, her helmet overlaying the fog with an amber path to the MedCenter. She turned to Grace. Her co-pilot seemed out of it. "You OK?"

"Yes."

"We're heading to the MedCenter. Evans has a broken leg. I've gotta help him. I want you to bring up the rear." She activated her emergency transponder. "Follow my beacon, and stay close."

"Yes."

Kate adjusted Evans's arm over her shoulder. The meager Lunar gravity would make the task of shuttling him to the MedCenter easier, but still a chore. She moved forward, her head down and focused on taking the next step along the amber path. She travelled about twenty meters, then paused to shift the administrator's weight.

"Grace?"

Grace was missing. "Grace?" She wasn't behind her; she wasn't anywhere. What was worse, Grace's emergency beacon wasn't functioning. Or perhaps she never activated it? The crash had knocked Grace unconscious. She'd seemed woozy afterwards. She might've suffered a concussion. Kate asked her to bring up the rear, but her co-pilot may not have been thinking straight. Definitely not, if she hadn't bothered to activate her own beacon.

"Grace! Grace!" Kate called and called but no response. "C'mon," she said to Evans. She continued forward at a faster pace. "We need to get you to the MedCenter." Once she did, she could go back out and look for Grace.

A soundless explosion of light filled the world around her, reflecting off the dusty fog. Warmth raked the back of her suit through its layers of thermal protection. A sudden rush of dust and debris showered her.

An instant later, another explosion. Kate was flat on the ground.

- - -

"Ms. Holman."

"Yes."

"Your advocate is here to see you."

Kate's fingers twisted the blanket of her hospital bed. Her advocate's arrival meant the tribunal had concluded its session. He was there to deliver their decision.

The nurse shuttled out.

Kate scooted back to sit straighter in her bed, sharp pain from her broken ribs the reward for her sudden movement. She scooted back again, more gingerly, and combed her fingers through her hair.

A rap at the door, followed by a man peeking his head into the room. "Ms. Holman."

"Captain Salazar," said Kate. She nodded him farther inside.

Captain Jesus Salazar filed into the room, outfitted in dress khakis and his garrison cap in hand. "Good afternoon, Ms. Holman." He moved to her bedside and smiled. "How are you feeling?"

"Much better, thank you." Kate wasn't keen on small talk in general. Her nerves kept any casual thoughts at bay.

"I've just returned from the tribunal," said Salazar. "I wanted to immediately brief you on their decisions."

Kate fiddled with the edge of the blanket. She forced her hand to be still.

"As far as the official sequence of events, the pilot of the cargo carrier was transporting illegal canisters of Dust on pallets that weren't properly tied down. The pallets shifted in flight, which changed the craft's center of gravity—it's what caused him to lose control. After the carrier clipped your rocket, it hit an embankment. One of its power packs blew, the source of the explosion that threw you to the ground and killed Astronaut Grace Phong."

A knot in Kate's stomach tightened at the mention of her friend.

"According to Phong's autopsy, she'd suffered a concussion during the initial crash. That's why she was disoriented and didn't follow your order to bring up the rear."

Kate's eyes fell to her blankets. "I should've known," she said.

"You couldn't have," said Salazar. "The effects of her concussion didn't manifest at first. As the minutes ticked by, her condition worsened."

"It doesn't matter," said Kate. "I knew I was fine, other than my shoulder. I should've thought … never should've assumed she was OK. I should've brought up the rear myself."

"If you had, I'm not sure you'd be alive," said Salazar. "Or Administrator Evans. Your dragging him towards the MedCenter is what got you both far enough away from the carrier. I don't think you could've shepherded both him and your co-pilot."

"But I didn't try. And because I didn't, Grace walked off in the wrong direction." Kate reached for her forehead and the sudden pounding.

Salazar looked on, concerned. "How are the headaches?" he asked.

"Bad," said Kate. "The doctor said I'm fully recovered from my own concussion, and that the headaches should've subsided by now. Unfortunately, they still come and go."

"Overall, you're lucky to walk away with a concussion and a few broken ribs."

She rubbed her crown. "I don't feel so lucky," she said. Captain Salazar had so far covered the official findings of fact. He hadn't mentioned what decisions the tribunal had settled on as a result of those facts. "What else?"

"The pilot of the cargo carrier was part of a ring smuggling Dust to the Moon," said Salazar. "He's been court-martialed and sentenced to eight months' hard labor on the Moon. When he's done, they'll send him to Earth where he'll face additional charges.

"The only not-so-great news is the black mark the board gave you for your handling of the retro rockets. They said you should've cut them sooner. However, they had a difficult time quantifying the impact of your delay. We're two weeks removed from the accident, and the base is still following emergency protocol from the dust that got kicked up. Problem is, if you had shut the engines down five seconds earlier, it's not clear it would've made a significant difference. The cargo carrier's explosion also added to the mess."

A black mark? She'd been positioning herself for a chance to lead the Ares mission. In an instant, a Dust smuggler had ended her friend's life. Had he also unraveled more than two years of work and sacrifice? "What does that mean for my ... career?" she asked.

"Nothing," said Salazar. "It's more a slap on the wrist." He shifted his stance, as if seeking a more comfortable position. "I will say, you're lucky Anand wasn't on the tribunal."

"Commander of the Moonbase?" asked Kate.

Salazar nodded. "Or as some call him, 'King of the Moon.' He's quite ... animated when times are good. When they're bad, he's a super nova. He's apoplectic about the dust. I understand his frustration, but it doesn't give him license to act like an ass."

"What do you mean?"

"After the tribunal handed down its ruling, he made a special request to address the panel. He said if it were up to him, you'd be in chains, smashing big Moon rocks into little ones for the rest of your life. He said he wanted it on the record that if you ever return to his moonbase, he'll … put a bullet in your head."

Kate blanched at the words.

"To their credit, the tribunal didn't take kindly to that kind of talk, especially from an astronaut. They gave him the option of either retracting his statement or receiving an official reprimand that would go on his permanent record. In true Anand fashion, he opted for the latter."

"I see," said Kate. She shifted again, under pain. "Well, they tell me only a couple more weeks until I'm OK to fly home. So, not too much longer, and I'll be out of Anand's hair."

"All in all, I think you're in good shape," said Salazar. He thrust his hand out and smiled again. "It was a pleasure representing you, Ms. Holman."

Kate shook his hand. "Thank you for your help."

Captain Salazar bowed slightly, pivoted, and exited the room.

35

"This is Grimes, Julian. Serial number eight, one, six, zero, two, six, four, eight, seven, three. Captain, Space Force. I want to speak to the AD."

Silence. He hadn't dared raise his voice above a whisper. Even alone in the lower crew compartment, anything louder might've attracted the attention of the others. Despite its hushed level, his message had been received—he was certain. The trick would be getting a response.

"This is Grimes, Julian. Serial number eight, one, six, zero, two, six, four, eight, seven, three. Captain, Space Force. I want to speak to Assistant Director Pearson."

Lying on his belly in a bunk, Grimes shifted positions, giving himself a better view of the entrance to the space. The Earth, a brilliant blue jewel, floated in the black beyond the adjacent uncovered porthole. A small, palm-sized parabolic dish, clipped to the rim, lobbed signals at the sparkling orb.

Would anyone respond? His transmission was a long shot. His only leverage was the fact the Space Force's operation that morning hadn't gone according to plan. Perhaps emphasizing that point was the key: "This is Captain Julian Grimes. Your attempt to destroy the *Gaia* capsule and eliminate the remainder of the *Ares* crew has failed. Put me in touch with Assistant Director Pearson, now."

No response. It had been worth a try. He—

"Captain Grimes," said the voice through his earpiece. "Do you read?"

"Affirmative. I—"

"Please say again about *Gaia* capsule."

"The *Gaia* capsule has not been destroyed. You were fooled, with a decoy. The spacecraft is still intact and on an active heading."

A pause. "Can you provide confirmation?"

"Other than the fact that I'm speaking to you from inside the *Gaia*?" Who the hell was he talking to? Every minute of idiocy brought him that much closer to Commander Holman or the others catching him on his transmitter. What could he offer for proof …? "If you take a radar scan of the missile target coordinates, you'll see the debris signature is too small to account for a space capsule."

An interminable stretch of silence ticked by before the voice returned. "Thank you, Captain Grimes. What is your current hea—"

"You really think I'm gonna reveal our course, so you can send another Atlas missile and finish me off? Uh-uh. You're gonna put me in touch with the assistant director."

"Negative," said the voice. "We're already breaking protocol even having this conversation."

Captain Grimes's eyes narrowed. "Let me put this in terms you might understand," he said. "If you don't want to see headlines about the special Mars project in the Washington Post, with a picture from the AD's perp walk, you'll stop wasting my time and put him on."

Another long, silent stretch. Had the connection dropped?

"Julian!" The voice in his ear sounded different, cheerful. "This is Assistant Director Pearson."

"Pearson," said Grimes. "I know by protocol I'm dead to you all, but it seems to me you're in a bit of a jam. Your plan to destroy the *Gaia* didn't work out. We're currently en route to a new destination."

"The Chinese space station?"

"I'll tell you where we're going, but in exchange, I want you to bring me in."

"I can't do that."

"You're the *only* person who can do that," said Grimes. "I know you've been shitting bricks ever since this capsule left Mars, and you thought this afternoon your worries had all been erased. Then just now you heard my voice. I'm giving you a heads-up the whole operation is at risk of being exposed, but there's still a chance to avoid that outcome. You need my help to do it."

"Allowing even one of you to live will further jeopardize the operation," said Pearson. "I told the entire world that you're dead."

"I'd be quite comfortable on an island somewhere, under a different name, permanently retired. Something like Witness Protection. I know our friends at Langley can swing it."

A long silence. "What you're asking for is possible, but it depends on where you're headed. If it's someplace like the Chinese space station, we should hang up right now."

"That's not our destination," said Grimes. "I told them you'd probably blast it out of the sky, even if it led to an international incident."

"You're right," said Pearson, chuckling.

"We're splashing down," said Grimes.

Another chuckle. "You, of all people, know you'll never make it to the—"

"They're aware of the blind spots in the satellite coverage," said Grimes. "Kate Holman's going to thread the needle. Once we get past the outer defenses, it'll be a mad dash to the ground, one that you all won't be able to stop."

Quiet on the line. "If it were any other pilot, I'd tell you, 'good luck' and hang up. With Holman, you have a more than decent chance." Shuffling. "That plan, if it pans out, severely complicates the situation."

"That's why I knew you'd be interested," said Grimes. "All it'll cost you to get our exact splashdown coordinates is a ticket to the Witness Protection Program."

A clipping sound came through the connection, then a lighter striking its flint. "I have a counter proposal," said Pearson. A pause, filled with puffing sounds. "We'll extract you, give you a new identity and all that, on the condition you continue with your efforts to tie up loose ends."

More dirty work? "You're not going to call in a strike team?"

"Of course I am," said Pearson. "But moving men takes time. Between your splashdown and those men arriving, more people could become involved. Hell, if you plop down someplace like the Yellow Sea, we'll have any of a thousand fisherman witnesses." More puffs. "If you all exit that capsule before we get there, start to go your separate ways, that will create a real shitshow. I also don't want to lose any Guardians. The more there are of you, the greater the risk there'll be some kind of commotion, a firefight. That's why it's better for you to continue tying up loose ends. The strike team will only have to clean up what's left."

How was he supposed to take anyone out—with his bare hands? "I don't have any tools, not even a gun," Grimes grumbled. "Everything's on Mars."

More puffing sounds "I don't know, maybe it's the connection, but it sounds like you've gone soft. Perhaps it's all the time spent with those astro-nots." Another puff. "That's my offer. Continue plugging the leaks and you live. If the info gets anywhere beyond that capsule, *you* will receive the first strike team visit."

A rotten deal, but the only one on the table. "I have some … samples I brought from Mars." The two bags of gold the *Ares* idiots saved were still enough to make him wealthy, especially in the sort of retirement spot he had in mind.

"Let's throw them in, too," said Pearson. "We'll call it an added incentive, a bounty, let's say, contingent on your first two heads. I'll scrounge up a bonus for every head after that."

Grimes sighed. He had his work cut out for him, but considering a few hours ago he was a dead man walking, his situation was infinitely improved. He'd have to do some thinking, but at least there appeared to be a path forward. "Understood."

"Good," said the AD. "Where, exactly, are you splashing down?"

"They haven't chosen a destination yet," said Grimes.

"Radio me when they do." More puffs. "And let me know what size tropical shirt you wear." The assistant director closed the channel.

Grimes folded the dish and pulled the earpiece from his ear. He stashed them both in a small, zippered pouch in his spacesuit. Captain Grimes rolled onto his back and stared at the underside of the bunk above. Eliminating six people? And in close quarters …? Whatever the plan, he'd have to complete it on the ground. He was no pilot. He couldn't possibly bring the capsule down safely.

What resources did he have anyway? The shiv he'd fashioned from a carbon fiber butter knife and a sharpened plastic shard, which he kept in his sock. He could take one, maybe two of them out before being subdued. He needed a less crude option, at least to start with.

In the category of interesting resources, he did have Glenn Wiles's account password. Grimes had replayed the events leading up to its collection several times over the previous six months, each time livid by the end: standing in restraints while the idiot second-in-command attempted to log in to the security terminal; Wiles discovering the terminal unlocked; the astro-not salivating at the opportunity to rifle through Grimes's account. Grimes simmered anew at the violation. The only consolation was the key logger, installed to catch tampering, capturing Wiles's log-in attempt.

Short of deleting all Glenn's files, or sending an embarrassing e-mail, how could he put the password to use? Besides his computer account, the credentials would also log him into Glenn's space suit .... Grimes smiled at the semblance of a plan.

36

"We need to decide where we're going."

Twenty minutes prior, Kate had asked their main computer to pinpoint the dead zones in the Space Force constellation's coverage, and to correlate them with coastal population centers. The result appeared on the viewscreen: an equal-area projection of the Earth's surface with non-viable regions darkened. The remaining *Ares* crew, still outfitted in their space suits and all sitting at their stations, studied seven bright spots on the map.

"As improbable as it might seem, the Gulf Coast is apparently still an option," said Glenn.

"Do we risk it?" asked Kate. "Seems like high odds of being scooped up by the US Navy."

"Is the Navy in on the conspiracy?" asked Engles.

Who could say, but they couldn't ignore the possibility. "I'd hate to discover that was the case after fighting to get to the ground."

"How about someplace where the Navy can't mass a quick response?" asked Glenn. "Like the South China Sea?"

"No!" said Julian. His boisterous objection startled everyone, himself included, it seemed. "I mean, that would be a bad choice."

"Why?" asked Glenn. "With all the fishermen in those waters, we'd stand a good chance of getting picked up fairly quickly."

"That's just it," said Julian. "With all those boats, there's a good chance the capsule would come down on one of them."

Glenn gave Julian a double take. "You feeling OK?" he asked. "It sounded like actual concern for someone besides yourself."

Kate shot Glenn a look.

"Then there's the Chinese Navy," said Julian. "They'd be the first state military with a crack at bringing us in. That would likely be a bad turn of events."

An American capsule killing Chinese citizens would spawn a massive international incident. And possible outcomes if collected by the Chinese Navy ranged from a friendly return home to disappearing inside a reeducation camp. It was all too much of a gamble. "I agree with Julian," said Kate. "By that logic, we can also rule out the Bay of Bengal along the Indian coast. That leaves the Arabian Sea near Somalia, The Canary Islands, the eastern tip of Brazil, and the waters off Baja California."

"I vote against the Arabian Sea," said Glenn. "With the Iranians, the new Saudi Navy trying to make a name for itself, and the resurgent Somali pirates, the pathway to a safe rescue becomes very complicated."

"Canary Islands?" asked Kate.

"This is just me, but I get nervous at the thought of washing up on an island," said Palmer.

"We're not talking Gilligan's Island," said Fisk. "There are more than three million people in the Canaries. It's far from remote."

Dr. Palmer shrugged.

"What about the coast of Baja?" asked Miriam. "I doubt the Navy has ships patrolling the area. It's heavily populated, and close to the US border."

"I had been leaning that way from the start," said Kate. "Does anyone think it's a bad idea?" She scanned the cabin for a dissent. None came. Reaching consensus had been much easier than she expected. "Then we're landing in Baja."

"¡Muy bien!" said Fisk. "The first margaritas are on me."

Sipping margaritas on the beach? Kate smiled at the thought, the first light moment in a while. Evading the Space Force satellite network wouldn't be easy, but she'd bet on her skills as a pilot any day.

Kate plugged their destination into the guidance computer. The machine output a list of corresponding blind spots and their locations. "Our first opportunity for reentry is coming up in ten minutes."

"Ten minutes before we have to start dodging killer satellites?" asked Miriam.

"No, we'll be settling into an approach vector," said Kate. "That'll line us up with one of the dead zones, which we won't hit for another half hour." Barely enough time for the splashdown checklist. "Everyone, make sure your straps are secure. Glenn, we need to work fast to—"

"Sorry, Commander, I need a minute," said Julian.

"Let me guess: you have a message to play for the crew," said Glenn.

Julian ignored him. "I need to make a long-distance call."

A what?

"Sorry," he continued, smiling, "that's Space Force lingo for using the lavatory. I drank too much coffee this morning."

"What about the facilities in your suit?" asked Glenn.

"It's full," said Julian. "I've been dragging my feet on maintenance."

"How long will it take?" sighed Kate.

"Not long," said Julian, unbuckling himself from his chair. "I'll head below right now. I won't have to get all the way out of my suit. I'll be back topside in twenty minutes, max."

Kate checked the guidance computer. The next approach vector was twenty-two minutes away. "Make it fifteen."

"Yes, ma'am," said Julian. He launched himself from his chair and flew towards the entrance to the lower crew compartment.

Glenn, arms folded and wearing a sour expression, watched Julian as he drifted through the cabin. Julian glanced back, and their eyes connected. The former security chief extended his index finger while curling the others and raised his thumb. Pointing an imaginary gun at Glenn, he smiled as he pretended to fire it, then slipped below.

"I'm not sure that asshole would've put everything on hold if any of us needed a bio break," said Glenn.

"We don't model ourselves on Julian's behavior," said Kate.

Her answer seemed to leave Glenn unsatisfied, but he turned in his chair and stared into his terminal.

"It's not the worst development," said Kate. "The delay gives us more time to go through the splashdown checklist." She brought up the first page of the extensive list. "Mind lending a hand?"

"Sure," said Glenn. "Which sections?"

"Maybe start from the bottom and work your way up. We'll meet in the middle."

"Roger," said Glenn. He worked his terminal screen, paused, and leaned back in his chair. He gave his head a sudden shake, as if clearing cobwebs.

"What's wrong?" asked Kate.

"I've got a major headache coming on," said Glenn, pinching his eyes and making a second attempt to shake it off. "That's one thing these fancy space suits don't have—an easy way to administer basic first aid. I'd like to dial up two aspirins and have them plop right into my mouth. Actually, that's kind of a slippery slope. Remember the Space Force primate trials, the secret tests that got them in all that hot water for the unethical use of animals? They had treat dispensers in the helmets. We wouldn't be that far off from the mission controller rewarding us with treats to get us to perform."

Glenn wasn't generally one for babbling. The prattle was especially unwelcome, given how many tasks they had to complete and the short time they had. "Are you still able to function?"

"I'll survive, though my head's really pounding."

Probably nothing like the headaches she'd suffered through on Mars. Kate dug into the first item, the chute system. All subsystems showed green. Parachute deployment always topped the landing checklist—she used to wonder why but realized if that system didn't work, the others wouldn't matter.

Loud huffing filled Kate's ear, from her open comm line with Glenn. "You OK over there?" she asked.

"Yes," said Glenn, still huffing. "Or maybe no. I'm feeling lightheaded."

"Huffing and puffing like that will get you hyperventilated for sure," said Kate. "You have to slow your breaths."

"How do I do that?" he asked.

"How do you do *what*?"

"Slow my … what were you suggesting?"

Glenn was being annoying. She'd never get through her portion of the checklist with him in scatterbrain mode. "Your breath," she said curtly. She returned to the list, moving on to thruster controls: systems green.

The huffing had stopped—he'd finally focused on his tasks—but her parental sixth sense whispered that something wasn't right. Kate scrolled to the bottom of the list and inspected his progress. Irritation flared. In the time she'd completed two sections and started a third, Glenn had only cleared two items. "You need to pick up the pace." She continued with her assessments, moving on to hull integrity and checking three boxes.

He hadn't answered …. "Glenn?"

Kate looked to her second-in-command's station. Glenn sat slumped in his chair, would've slid onto the deck if not for his restraints. His arms dangled at his sides, and his head lolled.

"Glenn!" Commander Holman punched the release on her restraints and rushed to the ailing astronaut. His eyes were half open within his helmet but he didn't respond to her presence. "Glenn, can you hear me?" Still nothing. "Doctor Palmer!"

Palmer arrived in a flash—he must have unbuckled and headed there the instant she bounded from her chair. Glenn remained unresponsive and pale. "He's having a medical emergency," said the doctor. He grabbed Glenn's arm and examined a small screen embedded in the forearm of his suit. "His blood oxygen level's all messed up," said Palmer. "Carbon dioxide poisoning."

"What?" said Kate. "How's that possible?"

"Something went wrong with his suit." Palmer tapped the small screen on Glenn's forearm several times, inspected his eyes, and made additional taps.

"How is he?" asked Kate.

"He's in bad shape."

"You're not going to remove his helmet?"

"I want to avoid a shock to his system," said Palmer. "I have the air in his suit slowly returning to normal." He rechecked the small screen and let Commander Wiles's forearm fall to his side. "He'll be stabilized in a few minutes, enough that we can get him below—it'll be easier for me to care for him there. But there's only so much I can do in this capsule, with the tools I have. He needs a medical facility."

"We'll be on the ground in thirty minutes," said Kate.

"And then what?" asked Palmer. "We wait to be rescued? What if that takes days? Or a week?"

"We're splashing down off the coast of Baja," said Kate. "There are resorts all along the beaches."

"How close will we be landing?" asked Palmer. "A mile from shore? Two? Those are shark-infested waters. I doubt any of us will want to chance swimming for it."

"If it meant saving Glenn's life …."

"Let's say you reach the beach. How long until you find someone who can help? How long until you get a fishing boat to come back for us? Or whatever. Glenn may not last that long."

"There's not exactly another option," said Kate. "We'll have to roll with what happens."

"There *is* another option," said Palmer. "The Moon."

"I already said, the Moon is off the—"

"It needs to be back on the table," said Palmer. "The original idea, to touch down on the Far Side—I can use the medical facilities at the Old Mine Outpost, where I used to be stationed. They have everything I need to save his life."

Kate shook her head. "We can't land on the Moon, Doctor."

"Can't, or you don't want to?" asked Palmer. "From your back-and-forth with Glenn, the odds of splashing down, flying through a dead zone and all, are about even with trying to land on the Moon, maybe a little worse. It seemed the real roadblock was you not wanting to land there."

"I *don't* want to land there!" yelled Kate.

"And you're in charge, which means you have the final say," said Palmer. "Just know that if you choose Earth, odds are high that Glenn won't survive."

Commander Holman's face grew warm, the creeping warmth of rising anger. "You can't know the future." She scowled.

"That's my medical opinion," said Palmer. "Ultimately, the decision on where we go is yours."

Kate's eyes teared. She'd imagined the salty ocean, washing up on the beach, rescue by locals, a press conference, her children … that close to the whole ordeal being over. They were still that close, could still splash down. It meant risking Glenn's life, putting his life in the balance.

Across the cabin, Julian poked up from the lower crew compartment. He spotted the commotion at Glenn's station, the others frozen as they looked on from their seats, even Fisk staring speechless. "Did I miss something?"

Kate cleared her throat. Her hand trembled. "We're heading to the Moon," she said. She could hardly squeeze out the words.

Julian laughed out loud. His smile disappeared once he saw that no one laughed with him. "You're serious."

Kate didn't respond.

"Why?"

"Glenn's suffering from carbon dioxide poisoning," said Dr. Palmer. "He needs a hospital."

"They don't have hospitals on Earth?" asked Julian.

"Time is of the essence," said Palmer.

"His odds of survival are fifty-fifty at best," said Julian. "Realistically, not even that."

"Now you're a medical doctor?" scoffed Palmer.

"Do you disagree?" asked Julian.

Palmer straightened Glenn in his chair and placed his hands in his lap. "Commander Wiles's survival depends on getting him the care he needs as soon as possible." He turned his back to Julian and tended to the screen on Glenn's suit.

Julian stared on with pursed lips, gradually understanding that his protestations wouldn't change their destination. "I need to make another call."

37

Kate Holman, Commander of the Ares mission, personal diary entry for February 15, 2043.

It'll be another day before we reach the Moon. My sleep has never been great, but last night I tossed with sweats and terrors. My blood pressure is elevated, and my palms are sweaty. The anxiety's not just from thinking of the Incident. To say that landing on the Moon in a capsule will be tricky is the most laughable of understatements. Our spacecraft is not designed for what we're about to ask of it. The odds of touching down are somewhat better than skirting through the Space Force constellation and avoiding being targeted by an air-to-air missile—the computer confirmed as much. However, the skill required to get us safely to the Lunar surface is in a completely different league. I'm expecting a nail-biter of a trip to the ground.

Though I hate the thought of landing on the Moon, it's the right thing to do. I so desperately want to be home, but I could never risk, much less sacrifice, Glenn's life to get there. That's not how we astronauts do things. We take care of our own.

Glenn remains in a medically induced coma, in serious condition. Palmer believes he can keep him relatively stabilized, but we've already had a couple scares. Since heading to the Moon, the doctor has spent most of his time with him in the lower crew compartment. For landing, we plan to suit Glenn up again and strap him to his seat in the main cabin. That will make it easier for us to pull him from the capsule once we reach the ground. Commander Wiles is a large man, and hoisting him from belowdecks, even in the Moon's reduced gravity, would be quite a chore.

Palmer says Glenn's suit was tampered with. I immediately thought of Julian, but how? Each space suit lives in its owner's personal locker in the lower crew compartment, secured by a combination lock. Julian has had neither the time nor opportunity to set his hands on anyone's suit. Without understanding what happened, we now have the added worry of a similar malfunction befalling someone else.

I *so* miss my children. This trip to the Moon will be a temporary delay in getting back to them. I won't let it be anything else.

38

"Easy does it," said Kate, her hand shaking around the flight joystick. The gentle words of self-encouragement came as she nudged the speeding capsule down through the Moon's absent atmosphere.

"Insane" was the only word for what she was attempting, more appropriate for "Gravity Gulp," the pilot drinking game that required devising an approach to landing an air or space vehicle under extreme conditions. Kate was taking them on a real-life "Gravity Gulp," but the stakes weren't a hangover—it was all their lives.

"Can't you switch to autopilot or something?" The question came from a panicked Fisk, who watched their progress on the main viewscreen. Saw-toothed mountain peaks screamed towards them as the capsule weaved through a fast-moving obstacle course of jagged highlands. He'd squirmed for the past ten minutes with the breathtakingly close passing of each summit.

Kate flew using instruments, a less harrowing view. Piloting the craft by hand was far from her first choice, but the necessary maneuvers were beyond the *Gaia's* guidance computer. "An autopilot can't do this job."

"Did you ask it?" said Fisk.

She had, in fact, three times. Each attempt at setting the landing parameters and instructing the craft to generate a touchdown solution ended in the computer insisting they would crash. It wasn't completely wrong. "Landing" was a generous description of their final state in a spacecraft designed to slow itself using a parachute and splash down in an ocean. The Moon had no atmosphere, and no liquid water. Their touchdown would be more of a skidding impact. The sequence of adjustments for a successful landing were too much for the computer to orchestrate. Their landfall required a human at the helm.

"But do we really have to fly so low?" squealed Fisk.

"We do," said Kate. Their low altitude wasn't her first choice either, but necessary. "Skimming the surface increases the pull of gravity from the Moon. It's reducing our speed."

The *Gaia* abruptly shuddered and slowed, as if she'd briefly hit the brakes in a car. The motion threw Kate into her restraints. Squeals echoed around the cabin—a reassurance, at least, that despite Fisk's lone voice, he wasn't the only person with her in the capsule. A quick peek left revealed Glenn slumped in his chair, unconscious and spared from experiencing the hair-raising ride. Earlier that morning, he'd taken a turn for the worse. Palmer did what he could but stressed that Glenn's fate rested on getting him to a hospital sooner than later. Farther left was Engles, her communications skullcap wrapped by the lucky red bandana she'd made a point to wear for the landing. Miriam sat to the right with eyes pinched shut, gripping her armrests like an anxious mountaineer on a towering ascent. She was trying to get through the ordeal, waiting for it to end. Like all of them.

Lateral forces buffeted the craft, followed by more "brake taps." The capsule's speed dropped under a deceleration that spiked and then gradually faded. Seconds elapsed with relatively smooth sailing before the sequence mostly repeated.

"What the hell *is* all that?" asked Fisk.

"The Moon's gravity is lumpy," said Kate. "The rough ride is from flying over what they call a 'gravitational anomaly.'"

"Those things are real?" asked Fisk.

"You've heard of them?" asked Kate. "It's mostly spacecraft pilots who know anything about them. I'm surprised you're familiar with the term."

"I've read about them on the internets," said Fisk. "They're regions of increased gravity that are hazardous to spacecraft. Apollo fifteen and sixteen released small satellites that crashed because of them, before anyone really understood what they are."

For once, Kate appreciated a conversation with Fisk. The discussion kept her mind from the more upsetting thoughts of setting foot on the Moon. "Normally, we'd steer clear of these anomalies, but these massive, lumpy patches are helping us slow down."

"And all this time, I thought they were crazy, ancient aliens talk," said Fisk.

Aliens?

"They used the bigger ones to tow the Moon into place."

On second thought, total silence might've been preferable. Thankfully, Fisk had no more to say, at least for the moment. He'd settled down, perhaps because they'd cleared the final set of mountain peaks. Stark white plains, predominantly flat and dotted with impact craters, sprawled before them beneath an ink-black sky.

Kate operated the attitude thrusters, keeping the craft flying straight on its current path rather than hug the curve of the Moon. The Lunar landscape gradually dropped away, disappearing from the bottom of the main viewscreen.

"Where's the Moon?" asked Fisk.

"Behind us," said Kate. She tapped the thrusters, spinning the *Gaia* one hundred and eighty degrees. The Moon slid again into view, in its entirety, with a thin black crescent consuming the right edge of its stark white disc.

"I thought we were coming in for a landing," said Fisk.

"We will," said Kate. "Right now, we're slowing down even more by flying against the Moon's orbital velocity." The statement probably made little sense to a lay person. "As the Moon orbits the Earth, an object moving in that same direction will get tugged along by the Moon's gravity for a speed boost. It's kind of like a skateboarder hitching a ride on a car in the street. If the object moves in the opposite direction to the Moon's travel, that same tugging will slow it down." She checked the capsule's flight profile on her monitor—their velocity was decreasing, as expected, but the deceleration was beginning to wane. "In a few seconds, we'll have shed as much of our speed from this trick as we can." At that point they'd start their descent.

The Moon continued to shrink on the screen. The Earth peeked out from behind, a bright blue marble laced with wispy white swirls, their desperate final destination so far away.

"*Gaia* at apogee," said Kate. "Starting our descent." A descent that would end with them on the Lunar surface, the place that had claimed her friend's life during the landing years ago, the place she swore never to return. Her joystick hand trembled wildly. She inhaled deeply, held, and breathed out, as in her long-ago therapy sessions.

Kate pumped the thrusters, coaxing the *Gaia* back towards the Moon. She pushed the capsule into the first phase of its flight plan, a steep descent that elicited yelps from the others. When they neared the surface, she'd need to channel as much of the craft's vertical velocity into a horizontal glide, like a plane diving before leveling out. From there she'd inch them down to gradual contact with the ground.

Indicators flashed urgent alerts from the guidance computer. The AI wasn't piloting the craft, but it could calculate the parameters of a successful landing. The sea of red meant they were off her projections. Far off. Despite all she'd done to slow the capsule, it still had too much momentum.

Kate's stomach sank, their dilemma coming into full relief. *If only I had some rockets.* On a whim, she checked the fuel tanks for the third stage separation thrusters. They hovered at eight percent capacity—an ocean, by their needs! But how …? Glenn. Kate had been unconscious during their Mars liftoff. He must've decided to hold fuel back, as she had with their launch from Earth. Glenn might've just saved their assess.

Commander Holman tilted the craft from true vertical, aligning it with their steep angle of travel. She fired the third stage thrusters. The *Gaia* quaked, shedding speed. A second burst slowed them more. The guidance computer indicators still peaked into the red, but the warnings were less urgent. They were in much better shape, barreling towards the Lunar surface but not as fast.

At one hundred and fifty meters above the Moon, Kate initiated a final burn of the third stage thrusters. Dust billowed from below, filling the viewscreen with white, fluffy clouds. At the end of the burn, the capsule sailed on a near-horizontal flight path.

Klaxons rang out, their AI co-pilot delivering the message of an impending crash. Kate silenced its bleating, well aware of their craft's dire situation. "Thirty seconds to touchdown," she said. "Make sure you're all strapped in tight." She righted the craft slightly, orienting their heat shield to contact the surface at a modest angle. During a normal landing, the shield would've protected them from the extreme temperatures caused by friction, the molecules in the atmosphere rubbing against the underside of the fast-moving spacecraft. To land on the Moon, she'd bring the *Gaia* down gently, skidding the shield along the regolith, with dust particles striking the underside instead of air. Friction was friction, at least that was her hope. It was their only chance. If they encountered rocks of any significant size, a large stone or a boulder that wouldn't be easily driven aside, the strike would tear their delicate capsule apart.

Twenty. Ten. Five seconds to touchdown. "Here we go," whispered Kate through quavers. Her hand shook uncontrollably. She brought her other one to the joystick.

A gravelly scraping rose to near intolerable levels inside the capsule. Small lurches jerked the *Gaia* and its astronauts. The spacecraft eased onto the Lunar surface, digging into the topsoil and spewing a roiling trail of dust behind it.

A large jolt yanked the craft. Miriam let out a scream.

Another large jolt wrenched the capsule as it dug deeper into the regolith. The *Gaia* pitched forward, threatening to tumble end-over-end. Kate fired the attitude thrusters at the top of the capsule. The spacecraft responded, lurching back to nearly upright. She relaxed the thrusters, conserving fuel, but the craft again listed forward. She returned them to full power. She'd have to keep them fully engaged until they came to a stop.

The *Gaia* burrowed farther. Wrenching metal shrieked inside the cabin, the heat shield grinding on bedrock. Thrusters spluttered, their fuel exhausted.

The craft came to an abrupt halt, its underside locking up under the increased friction. The sudden deceleration sent the *Gaia* into the beginnings of a cartwheel that could only end with the capsule shattered and its contents strewn across the Lunar landscape. Kate clutched her restraints, bracing for the worst.

The craft tilted thirty degrees, thirty-five, forty. Astronauts screamed.

As the *Gaia* neared a forty-five-degree tilt, the increase in pitch slowed, then stopped. Seconds passed, an eternity ticking by in a blink.

The capsule rocked back, tossing the astronauts like an amusement park ride. The craft settled, listing but motionless.

Reality took a moment to register: they'd landed! "Is everyone OK?" Kate asked. She didn't wait for a response—Glenn's life could hang on every second. She unfastened her restraints and stood. "Engles, get the hatch. Doctor Palmer and Miriam, come help with Glenn. Everyone else, get unbuckled and out of the capsule."

Kate stumbled to Glenn's station. Hours prior, she'd floated across the space. She needed to adjust to walking again in gravity.

Glenn remained slumped in his chair. Kate undid his restraints, finishing as the doctor and Miriam arrived.

"Miriam, grab the stretcher," said Kate. They'd fashioned a makeshift stretcher from bedsheets and thin, metal tubing salvaged from a bunk. The former Mars station chief grabbed it and started for the hatch.

Kate worked with Palmer to lift the ailing astronaut. She looked to the hatch. Julian approached the opening, the last of the others to exit. He held a sack in each hand—the sacks he'd filled with gold ore on Mars. While she and Palmer had tended to Glenn, he'd snuck below and retrieved the two bags that hadn't been thrown overboard before leaving the red planet. Those sacks were hardly more important than their lives, and in any case, Julian wouldn't have an opportunity to spend their contents, not where he was going. "Ju—" Just as she called, Julian slipped out of the capsule.

Kate and the doctor shepherded Glenn to the exit, a manageable task in the weak Lunar gravity. Palmer stepped outside while Kate held Glenn upright at the door. The doctor reached back inside and pulled Commander Wiles through the hatch.

Palmer poked his head inside. "I can handle getting him to the ground," he said.

Kate nodded. She surveyed the cabin one last time—her eyes darted to her terminal. The commander rushed to her station and plucked the small photograph of her children. She tucked the picture away and dashed to the exit.

Commander Holman peeked her head from the spacecraft and recoiled at the intense glare. The sun's reflection off the bleak, bleached Lunar landscape was nothing like the gentle orange and pink radiance of Mars. She lowered her sun visor, then stepped through the hatch on to a thick mound of regolith. The berm hugged the capsule's forward side, the result of the *Gaia's* burrowing to a stop. She descended the two meters to the dusty Lunar surface and stood with the other five astronauts, plus Glenn on the stretcher.

"That was some bit of piloting," said Miriam.

"Yes, great work," said Engles.

"Thank you both," said Kate. In their dash from the capsule, she hadn't taken any time to reflect on the near-impossible landing she'd executed, a feat that belonged in the Gravity Gulp hall of fame.

Fisk stepped away from the spacecraft, surveying the ground as he walked. He stooped, scooped a handful of dust, then stood and let it trickle from between his fingers. "These *are* very challenging conditions."

Travel on foot across the Moon could be tough, with some areas more difficult to navigate than others. Getting from the capsule to the Outpost *should* be doable … unless there was something Kate didn't understand about the terrain on the Far Side of the Moon. "You're concerned we'll have trouble walking there?"

"Wha—no," said Fisk. "Mountain biking. I've read about what it's like to bike across this terrain. If you ever get bitten by the bug and find yourself out here, I urge you to stick to the existing trails." Fisk froze, staring off back behind the spacecraft. "I didn't know there was fog on the Moon."

There wasn't. Kate joined the professor in staring into the distance. Haze blanketed the sky behind the capsule, spanning half her field of view and soaring a kilometer high. "That's not fog," she said. "It's dust we kicked up from our landing."

"Oh, shit," said Fisk through laughs, "their hatred for dust on this rock is legendary—even school kids talk about it. Someone's going to be royally pissed."

Kate didn't want to think about it. The immense dust cloud seemed to be drifting. Their only saving grace was their location, on the Far Side of the Moon. Gravity would return the particulates to the ground, hopefully nowhere near the Lunar base.

Their next task was a hike to the Outpost. She'd aimed to land not far from the facility, but in all the commotion, she hadn't checked how close she'd gotten them.

Miriam pointed and said, "It's a kilometer that way," intuiting her question.

They'd been fortunate to land without incident, and they could walk the rest of the way to the Outpost, in not too much time. "Is everyone ready to head out?"

"I'll need someone to help with the stretcher," said Dr. Palmer.

Focused on the landing and exiting the capsule, Kate had almost forgotten their most serious concern. The doctor had prepared his patient for transport: Glenn lay facedown on the ground, the stretcher spread beneath him. With Palmer in front, he'd need the assistance of someone his height, with decent upper body strength. "Julian."

Julian stood with his back to the others, facing in the direction of the Outpost. He turned slowly. "Yes, Commander?"

"Help Palmer with Glenn."

"I can't," said Julian. "I've got all I can handle." The two bags he'd carried from the *Gaia* hung around his neck, tied together with a t-shirt snatched from the capsule. The two sacks dangled in front of him, bobbing against his chest.

"Drop the bags and assist Doctor Palmer," growled Kate. "I don't even know what good you'll think those sacks will be to you in jail—"

"Engles or Fisk can help," said Julian.

"They're not tall enough," said Kate, on the verge of losing her temper. "And in any case, you're the person I selected for the job, not them." Julian didn't move. "Set the bags down and help Doctor Palmer with Glenn."

"No," said Julian.

Kate marched forward, coming faceplate-to-faceplate with the former security chief. She fished her multi-tool from a pouch at her waist and extended the knife.

"You gonna stab me, Commander Holman?" asked Julian. He chuckled. "That would be very astro-naughty, and a violation of the Scout code: 'A scout is cheerful. A scout is kind. A scout is reverent—'"

"Either you assist Doctor Palmer in transporting Glenn to the Outpost," said Kate, growling again, "or I cut a slit in your sample bags and empty their contents on to the ground."

Kate could feel the volcanic anger raging behind Julian's visor. He hoisted the sacks over his head and dropped them. They drifted to the ground, landing with a poof of dust. Grimes sulked to the doctor, taking his position at the rear of the stretcher. The two men crouched in unison, seized the handles, and stood.

Kate spent a moment composing herself. "Thumbs-up on green suit checks." She waited for everyone to respond. "Let's head out. Miriam, please lead the way. I'll bring up the rear. Shout out over your comm if you need a break or have some other issue."

The *Ares* astronauts set out from the capsule, starting their march across the Lunar plains.

39

The Ares mission astronauts trekked east across the Far Side of the Moon. Miriam headed the line, followed by Engles and Fisk. Next came Dr. Palmer and Julian, with the incapacitated Commander Wiles on the stretcher between them. Kate brought up the rear. They hiked over reasonably smooth, solid terrain with a layer of Lunar dust thick enough to preserve their footsteps.

Kate quickly had her fill of the monotonous landscape. In the early days of her career, she'd romanticized traveling to the Moon, of stepping onto the surface of another world, following in the footsteps of the Apollo astronauts. Her outlook changed with her first walking tour. The Moon was a stark, barren wasteland of desolation almost beyond human comprehension, a dichotomy where the brightest desert day unfolded beneath the darkest, blackest night sky. She piloted spacecraft to and from the Moon as directed, but even before the incident, she had no desire to return.

She was back on the Moon for one reason only. "How's Glenn?" she asked on a private channel.

"He remains in serious condition."

Kate had posed that question many times during the previous twenty-four hours, eliciting the same response. Palmer had always added a calming comment, the doctor employing his bedside manner to ease her mind. That time he didn't elaborate. And not long after they'd left the *Gaia*, he'd asked Miriam to pick up the pace. Neither was a good sign.

"I was thinking Engles and I could relieve you and Julian in ten," said Kate.

"I'm OK to continue."

In retrospect, the doctor was likely more concerned with remaining close to his patient than the effort of carrying him. And as for giving Julian a break, assisting with the stretcher was the best place for him. She didn't need to worry about his whereabouts, or what he was doing.

"We're not far from the Old Mine," said Palmer.

"Amazing you can even tell," said Kate. "We've been walking for twenty minutes, but if not for the capsule being out of sight, I couldn't say we haven't returned to where we started." Palmer probably had a more discriminating eye for Lunar terrain; he may even have identified a landmark or two. "You were actually stationed here."

"I was."

"I couldn't imagine," said Kate.

"No?"

"No. It's nothing but sun-scorched badlands."

"Sun-swept plains, interrupted by the occasional gentle hill or valley and sprinkled with craters of different shapes and sizes," said Palmer.

"No atmosphere to retain heat, so temperatures drop two hundred and fifty degrees Celsius when you step from sunlight into shade," said Kate.

"Without an atmosphere to scatter light and create glare, the pitch-dark Lunar sky offers the perfect environment for star gazing."

"All this dust can make walking difficult and gets into everything."

"The fine dust around us, the result of billions of years of meteorite impacts, can make walking difficult and gets into everything."

Kate chuckled. "But seriously, you like the Moon?"

"I accept the natural order of things," said Palmer. "The Moon also has a quiet solitude that I very much appreciate."

In other words, Disneyland for a Stoic. "My daughter says it's just dust on a rock."

The doctor laughed. "Well, you'll be relieved to know you won't be spending much more time walking around on this dusty rock. The Outer Marker's at eleven o'clock."

Kate surveyed the terrain. Twenty meters ahead, an object poked up from the flat landscape, a skinny, waist-high, rectangular pillar. When they came alongside it, they found the object was a small obelisk fashioned from gray stone. One side carried the vertical inscription "United States." The adjacent side showed "2035" and the NASA logo. The pillar's gritty, speckled texture implied poured Mooncrete, the concrete developed from the Lunar regolith.

"This marker designates the far corner of the old US mine," said Palmer as they passed.

"Fairly understated for such a large operation, if you ask me," said Kate. "Where's the 'Keep Out' sign?"

"An international treaty prevents any country from staking claims on the Moon," said Palmer. "The marker's the closest you'll get, though I guess if there had ever been a problem with unwelcome visitors, we would've just stationed a few soldiers."

In the glaring, sun-bleached distance to their right, Kate spotted two hulking, angular forms, their features hidden in dark shadow. Moving closer revealed them to be squat earth movers, somber gray except for the black glass of their cabs and the metallic blue of their woven, steel tires. The true size of the machines only became apparent as the astronauts neared. One, a hydraulic shovel, was big as a house and towered three stories above them. The other machine, a front loader, reached six meters at its tallest point, with tires twice the height of a person.

Passing the earth movers, the astronauts approached an enormous, irregular-shaped opening in the ground, spanning three football fields. Large, dormant flood lights on tall poles stood sentry around the hole. The massive strip mine, a lingering, gaping wound on the land, gradually came into view. The pit's rings and ribs repeated for hundreds of meters, descending to the blackness below.

"It's always the same with us," remarked Palmer on his private line with Kate. "Whether it's the middle of the Amazon rain forest, the backside of our nearest celestial neighbor, a far-off rock in the asteroid belt, or the red planet itself. We claim to care about Nature and truth and beauty, but that's never what we focus on. It's always about how we can turn a profit."

The astronauts traced the lip of the open mine for several hundred meters before veering north towards a square, low-set structure, a cluster of drab buildings formed from gritty slabs of Mooncrete. Unlike the moonbase, whose surface-level complex only hinted at the warren of rooms beneath the regolith, the Far Side Outpost sat completely above ground.

When imagining the deserted Outpost, Kate had recalled photos of abandoned buildings from the Old West, with tumbleweeds and drifts blown against the sides. Walls made from Lunar dirt, resistant to the relentless solar radiation, plus the lack of any weather, meant the exteriors remained unchanged from opening day.

A Moon rover sat idle near the structure, with cables dangling to a charge point.

"Do we have company?" asked Engles.

"I don't expect so," said Palmer. "There was always a spare rover parked out front when I was stationed here." The dust covering the solar cells of its canopy also suggested it hadn't moved recently.

The astronauts pulled up to a smaller building that abutted the rest of the facility and hosted the only visible door.

"Hey, Nathan," said Miriam, calling to the doctor, "what's the entry code?"

"I … I don't remember, exactly," said Palmer. "But the Astronaut Corps had access to this facility. The door should accept any of the common codes."

By "common" codes, the doctor referred to number sequences that had special meaning to all astronauts. For example, the code "012886" marked the date of the Challenger disaster.

Miriam tapped the keypad. The door slid aside, revealing a black space, an airlock, that flickered to dull, LED life. The astronauts filed inside, including Palmer and Julian with their helpless colleague. Kate shut the door behind them.

Inside the chamber, Miriam started the pressurization cycle. When the green light appeared over the inner door, the party shuffled into a dim, narrow hallway with a low ceiling.

"The MedCenter's this way." Without saying anything more, Palmer led Julian down the corridor. They disappeared with Glenn around a corner.

"Let us know if you need anything," said Kate on her private channel. "Julian will go with you and help in whatever way you need." Palmer didn't respond, his thoughts likely trained on the task of saving Commander Wiles's life. Just as well. She'd done all she could to help Glenn. His fate rested with the doctor. She needed to put her second-in-command out of her mind and start focusing on a plan to expose the secret Mars mine and also get them home safely.

But first, what did they have to work with at the station? Kate led them down the corridor, stopping at the intersection where Palmer had turned for the MedCenter. She removed her helmet. Chilled, stale air hit her nostrils, tinged with the faint scent of burnt gunpowder, the haunting smell of Moon dust. The others followed her lead, with Fisk wrinkling his nose at the odor.

"We need to see how much food's at this station," said Kate. "We also need to check the situation with bunks." Depending on Glenn's prognosis, they might stay a few days at the Outpost. A station schematic mounted behind a sheet of plexiglass hung on the nearby wall. She pointed at a section of the map. "Engles and Fisk, I want you to go here and assess food and living quarters."

"You make it to the movies much, Commander Holman?" asked Fisk. His eyes were crazed, and the tufts on the side of his head, freed from his helmet, sprouted like an overgrown bush. "This is the point where the parties split up, and the monster that no one knows about comes out to pick them off one by one. Can't we all go together?"

The station was a little creepy, and though they needed to get settled, they didn't have to rush. "I was going to have Miriam come with me to the Operations Center," said Kate, "but we can go as a group."

"You three go," said Engles. "I'll scope out the accommodations."

"You sure?" asked Kate.

Engles nodded. "I don't get to the movies much," she said, looking at Fisk. "I can handle a space zombie or two."

Fisk scooted close to Kate. "Zombies are only one possibility," he whispered while keeping his eyes glued on the spacecraft engineer. "The thing is, how will we know it's really her when she returns?"

Kate glared at the research scientist. "Go," she said to Engles.

Engles continued along the corridor as Kate took the others to the right. Weak lighting, LED but with a fluorescent hue, snapped to life as they walked down the hall of gritty, speckled Mooncrete. The floor's undisturbed, thin layer of dust confirmed they'd been the only recent visitors to the Outpost. The poorly lit, narrow confines, windowless stone slabs, and musty air created the feel of marching through an underground tunnel, sparking a twinge of claustrophobia.

After a maze of corridors, the party arrived at a door labeled "Operations" and pushed inside. The room featured several large monitors hanging from the walls and five terminal stations below them, each outfitted with a rolling chair. The space had a low Mooncrete ceiling and could accommodate not more than ten people standing.

Before the Outpost was abandoned, the room had likely been a bustling nerve center. The cramped quarters formed of concrete surfaces gave the space all the ambiance of a tomb. "Is any of this functional?" asked Kate, waving at the inactive equipment.

Miriam stepped to a terminal and typed on its keyboard. Monitors sprang to life with video feeds. One showed a topside view of the strip mine, mounds of dirt encircling the monstrous maw. A second displayed a wide angle shot of the Outer Marker. The other screens presented the output of interior cameras. Engles appeared on one, rifling through food packages in a pantry.

Was it possible to speak through the cameras? Kate scanned the stations for a microphone, finding one protruding from the room's center console. She leaned down, wrapped her hand around its base, and paused. How to direct its output?

Miriam guessed Kate's intent and worked the controls. "You're live," she said.

Kate smiled in appreciation and pressed the talk button. "We can see you on the internal cameras," she said.

The spacecraft engineer whirled around. She located the camera and spoke directly to it: "There's plenty to eat here. During its heyday, the Outpost housed about twenty workers. There's enough to feed them all for nearly six months."

"Yeah, but is any of it still good?" asked Fisk.

A valid question—the mine shut down a couple years ago.

"It's got a fifteen-year shelf life," said Engles. "With that kind of expiration date, the food we had on Mars was practically farm-to-table."

"The meals we eat shouldn't be in a race to outlive us," muttered Fisk.

At least food wouldn't be an issue.

"I also found the beds and showers on the way here," said Engles.

A shower? And a bed, for a nap where the long-absent tug of gravity would draw her gently into the mattress and swaddle her in the blankets? After Kate's harrowing afternoon landing the capsule and six months of rinse-less body wash, both sounded enticing.

"I could use a shower and a nap," said Fisk, stretching and yawning. "It's been quite a day."

The normally reserved Miriam rolled her eyes at the comment.

"We could all use some downtime," said Kate. "Let's say we meet for dinner in the galley in"—she checked the chronometer on the wall—"two hours."

"How 'bout three?" asked Fisk. "I'll probably spend an hour in the shower alone."

"Then he showers last," said Engles on the camera audio. "I don't know how much hot water they have on this station … if they even have heated showers. It's not exactly the Four Seasons."

An additional hour to nap didn't sound bad. "Three hours, then. We'll gather for a late dinner." She turned to Fisk. "And yes, you'll go last. While you're waiting, I want you to check on Palmer and Julian. See if they need anything, and fill them in on the plan."

Fisk smiled and saluted. "Aye, aye, Captain."

40

Kate, Miriam, Engles, and Fisk, each wearing a green Outpost jumpsuit, sat around a table in the center of the Far Side station's galley. The tabletop's plastic surface, also green, hosted all manner of scratches, from light brush marks to deep ruts. They'd wiped it down, but gray Moon dust filled every groove, a patina born of labor and sweat that gave the table a gritty, dirty feel.

The galley itself was of modest size, a windowless space formed from speckled Mooncrete slabs. The walls held monitors with live, exterior views of the station's environs; posters exhorting safety procedures; a boxy medical kit; an old-style whiteboard with scribbles tracking long-ago schedules; and a large, active digital clock. Stainless steel appliances—a stove, refrigerator, and dishwasher—provided the only significant contrast in color and texture, the interior designers no doubt taking their inspiration from county lockup. The room, like the rest of the Outpost, gave the uninviting feeling of a harsh, industrial work zone, a site where comforts were an afterthought at best, where extracting riches from the soil was the first order of business.

"Anyone interested in seconds?" asked Fisk, rising from the table.

Kate stifled a grimace as she drew more of her dinner, a chicken-and-rice puree she sucked from a plastic pouch still not the temperature of her hand. "I'm good, thanks."

Fisk strolled to a clutch of battered steel cabinets along a wall. He opened a tall door, rifled through several wire mesh drawers, and retrieved a food pouch. "Mmm," he said, squinting at the label, "a creamy, split-pea will hit the spot, 'cept I have a thing about cold soup—"

"Fisk, no more—"

"Don't worry, Commander, I learned my lesson," said Fisk, pleading his case with his hands. "The microwave needs to be on the low power setting —"

"I don't want another explosion," said Kate. "Your options are to heat it with your body or eat it as is."

Fisk curled his lips and tossed the pouch back like an angler forced to return a prized catch to the sea. He pulled out a second drawer, rooted around, and removed a granola bar.

"So, what now, Commander?" asked Engles as Fisk made his way to the table. "What's the plan for getting home?"

What *was* the plan? The short of it: get a message to Earth to let the world know they hadn't perished and blow the lid off the conspiracy. Their secret exposed, the forces hunting them would no longer have reason to continue their pursuit. They'd leave Julian in custody on the Moon and take the next transport home.

In the time since the attempted destruction of their capsule, Kate had thought only superficially about the details of dispatching such a message. She'd noodled on a couple ideas while showering and slept on them during her long nap. "The first question is, can we send a message from here?"

Miriam shook her head. "Not directly. From the Far Side, we don't have a line of sight to Earth. We'd have to relay it through the moonbase." She frowned. "Are you saying your idea is to send a message?"

"We have to assume they're all bad actors over there at the base," said Fisk through a mouthful of granola. "We'd risk them blocking the message, which could torpedo what might be our one chance to set things right."

"But—" said Miriam.

"There's the rover out front," said Engles. "It's got its own communication gear. Maybe it's strong enough to reach Earth. If not, I might be able to boost the power."

Miriam tried again to interject. "But a message—"

"Ho, that's not going to work either," said Fisk. "You're thinking we drive to where we've got line of sight, get out, and set up a camera, like we're filming the nightly news? Problem is, they'll need to see our faces to believe it's us. That won't be possible through our sun visors."

"It doesn't matter, because—"

"My thought was we could pre-record a message," said Kate, cutting off Miriam. "We'd take the rover out and transmit once we can see enough of Earth to aim the antenna."

"But—"

Engles sprang from the table in full engineer mode. "I'll get to Ops and pull up the schematics on the rover, as well as check what kind of recording gear they have available—"

"No transmitted message will get us out of this jam!" shouted Miriam.

Her exclamation quieted the others. All eyes and ears fixed on her.

The former Mars station chief, her pale face reddened, took a moment to collect herself. "In this day and age of fake videos, no one will believe a message from us, live or pre-recorded, is real. Or at least no one will know for sure. The assistant director can deny it. He can claim it's a deepfake, made by someone with a sick sense of humor." Miriam paused amidst the quiet shock that engulfed the table. "Sending a message doesn't solve our problem."

Engles slowly returned to her seat as a stunned Commander Holman fought to assemble her thoughts. Resolving the remainder of their ordeal had appeared academic, a matter of getting a message to Earth. Not necessarily trivial, but tractable. Engles and Fisk had likely believed the same. But Miriam was right: they couldn't prevent the AD or anyone else involved in the conspiracy from declaring their dispatch a fake. There'd already been "recovered footage" of Buzz Aldrin meeting with aliens at the first Moon landing, and all other manner of faked video, from TV personalities to heads of state. The forces arrayed against the Ares crew would paint their message as obviously fabricated and then deploy a task force to find and finish them off.

There was only one way out of their predicament, but the thought sank Kate's stomach with its seeming impossibility. "We have to get to Earth," she whispered.

"Say … is that really happening?" asked Fisk.

Everyone's gaze shifted to the monitor that had grabbed Fisk's attention. Miriam's face drained to a ghostly white. Engles's too, as if all the blood had rushed to the red bandana at her neck. Whatever luck she claimed it contained seemed to have run out.

Kate stood, legs wobbly. "Engles, get me Julian," said the commander in an anxious voice as she headed for the door. "Take his place assisting Palmer if you have to, but have him report to me in Ops."

41

Now is the time.

Julian spent the previous minute reciting those words in his head, encouraging himself to act. He needed to kill the doctor, would have killed him already but for Fate conspiring against him.

Shortly after arriving in the MedCenter, he assisted in removing Glenn's space suit, shuttling him into a medical gown, and hoisting him onto an examination table. With Palmer engrossed in his patient, Julian considered eliminating the doctor right then. What better opportunity would he have, standing beside the man?

Now is the time.

Before he could act, the idiot Fisk barged into the room. He brought a rambling message from Commander Holman about downtime and dinner, but rather than simply deliver it and leave, the moron remained. His questions on medical evaluations and procedures bordered on the inane, his offers of help ludicrous. The doctor, far from annoyed, seemed to enjoy the company, as well as the discussion, which drifted to some obscure arm of Philosophy.

Declining to suffer more tiresome conversation, Julian ducked out, cleaning up with a shower and donning a station jumpsuit. Fisk was still there when he returned. Julian settled into a chair, vowing to wait out the clown. He closed his eyes for a moment, but he woke hours later. He'd apparently needed the sleep, as did Palmer, who sat dozing on a bench across the room.

Now is the time.

Julian rose. He moved as quietly as he could, but his rustlings stirred the doctor. The man reminisced on his days as a resident, and his brief naps of light sleep. He sprang to the examination table and focused again on his patient.

Now is the time.

Another unwanted visitor entered the room, the mousey Miriam Sato. She mentioned dinner in the galley. "Can you get me something?" asked

Palmer, his attention still trained on Glenn. She reappeared with food for the two of them.

Seated in the shadows at the far wall, Julian sucked from his pouch. The Space Force special unit would arrive soon, making his efforts to eliminate members of the Ares mission all the more imperative. Retirement hung on ensuring no Space Force Guardian got hurt. His task came down to simple math: the fewer astronauts, the less chance of a mishap.

Julian studied Palmer as he tended to Glenn, the doctor working to resuscitate a man who should have, would have, perished long ago. Eliminating Palmer would neatly seal Glenn's fate and cut the remaining number of *Ares* astronauts by a third. Palmer was tall, but skinny and weak. His training was in saving lives, not taking them. A headlock from behind would choke him out. From there, he could slit the man's wrists, or his jugular, and let him bleed out. Or snap his neck. Once subdued and mortally wounded, he'd stuff Palmer into one of the MedCenter's large storage lockers. The good doctor's life force would drip away where no one would find him, not before the cavalry came, anyway.

Two minutes—that's all he required. Two uninterrupted minutes to kill Dr. Palmer.

Palmer didn't notice Julian get up from his chair, the doctor preoccupied with the stricken astronaut on the medical table. Grimes crept along the outer edges of the room, moving softly, keeping to the shadows. In seconds, he was behind the doctor. Two quick steps to close the meter-wide gap and —

"We've got company!" exclaimed Engles as she burst into the room. "Julian, Commander Holman wants you in the Operations Center."

- - -

Commander Holman, Miriam, and Fisk stared at a monitor as Engles and Julian entered Ops. Two six-wheeled vehicles, squat rovers with stubby, metallic-blue tires, were parked near the Outer Marker.

"Has anyone come out?" asked Julian as he drew farther into the room.

"No," said Kate. "They've been sitting there. They drove up five minutes ago." She fidgeted. "I'm not sure who they are."

Who else would be coming for you, Commander Holman?

"I was hoping you could help ID," she added.

Julian moved closer, squinting at the monitor. The camera offered a bird's-eye view of the area. It showed shadows shifting beneath the rover canopies. Of course they were Space Force, but he couldn't confirm. He'd play along. "Can you zoom in?"

"No," said Miriam. "The camera has a wide angle. It's not designed for close-ups."

"They're on the move!" shouted Fisk.

The idiot Fisk, jumping like a field mouse at every flutter, announced the first rover's travel to the right across the monitor, followed by the second. The two vehicles gained speed as they exited the frame. They slipped into view a minute later in the feed from the camera trained on the Outpost's airlock. The Operations Center grew whisper quiet.

One person emerged from the first rover. He wore a slim-fitting black suit, not white and bulky like the astronauts'. A second figure exited the opposite side, also clad in black.

"Definitely Space Force," said Julian. The ordeal was almost over—he just had to navigate those men to safety.

"How could they have found us so quickly?" asked Kate.

Somebody tipped them off! Julian stifled a laugh.

"You're sure they're Space Force?" she asked.

Holman was fishing, hoping, wishing for an answer other than the one she couldn't escape. "They're the only outfit with black stealth suits."

"Kind of stupid to bring a black suit to a white tie event," said Fisk. "Before too long, they'll be covered with white dust up to their crotches."

The idiot Fisk, always running his mouth, always thinking he's so smart. "Stealth suits have a built-in electrostatic field," said Julian. "They'll easily repel any dust that tries to cling to them."

"I'm not sure that's any better," continued Fisk. "A black suit's good for stealth in space, not so much standing in the middle of a gray landscape."

Julian glowered at Fisk. "They're stealth suits not because they're black, but because they can take on the look of their surroundings. They have an outer layer of camo-cloth, a special chameleon-like material." Maybe they'd let him be the one to put a bullet in the professor.

The two men slinked to the airlock door. One typed an entry code on the keypad as the other stood watch, two stark shadows against the light gray walls.

Fisk wouldn't shut up. "If they can blend in to any background, why are they prancing in black suits across a white stage, like Marcel Marceau's evil twin … or twins? Those men stick out like sore thumbs … however it is that a sore thumb sticks out."

Why *weren't* they operating in stealth mode? The Ares mission astronauts were unarmed, but the strike team couldn't know that, shouldn't assume it. Maybe they didn't realize they were on camera? Or perhaps brashness on the part of those Guardians. "As a show of superior force," he suggested. The explanation was more plausible after saying the words out loud. *They're coming, and there's not a damn thing any of you can do about it.*

The airlock opened, and the black figures disappeared inside. The door closed.

"They'll be in the corridors in a minute," said Miriam, her voice quavery. "Here at the Operations Center in two." She looked at Kate. "What do we do?"

"We fight," said Glenn.

The ailing *Ares* astronaut, wearing an Outpost jumpsuit, had shuffled into the Operations Center while Julian and the others had been watching the scene unfolding on the screens. He looked haggard and weak, a sickly pale sack of bones. The tall man who normally stood with a steely straightness had a hunch to his spine and shoulders, seemingly on the verge of tipping forward.

Julian cursed to himself. If only the strike team had arrived a few minutes later, if only he'd gotten a few more moments alone with Palmer. He hadn't. As a result, the doctor brought the dolt back to life.

"Glenn!" said Kate. "I wasn't sure if we'd lost you. You should be in bed."

"Not much point, considering we're about to be attacked." Glenn paused, catching his breath. Just speaking the sentence appeared to have taxed him. "They're not going to get me without a fight."

"Fighting's pointless," said Julian. "These men are trained killers. I estimate there are four more in that first carrier, six in the other. A twelve-person strike team."

"Why are the rest staying behind?" asked Engles.

Julian had wondered that himself. "I'm not sure," he confessed. Standard procedure would have them all storming the facility, sweeping each section in teams of two, neutralizing threats and systematically securing pockets of the station.

"Whether it's two men or twelve, they all have to come through that door, single file," said Glenn, nodding towards the room's entrance. "It's a chokepoint. We take out each man as he enters."

"Aside from being experts in hand-to-hand combat," said Julian, "those men are armed."

"I didn't see any weapons on them," said Engles.

"Their pistols are compact and wrapped in camo-cloth," said Julian.

"We have the element of surprise," said Glenn. "They don't know who's in here. We cut the lights and ambush them."

Julian suppressed a groan. An ambush and a struggle? That could lead to errant weapons fire, which might hit him. Even worse, if Glenn's plan worked and they were able to grab a weapon, the astronauts could use it on the next Guardian, or the rest of the strike team. His special arrangement with the AD would be revoked.

Now is the time.

Grimes hadn't acted fast enough when those words first rolled through his head. He needed to follow his own advice. He seized Glenn's arm. Still weak, the recently revived astronaut couldn't prevent Grimes from swinging him around. He released Commander Wiles into Kate and Engles, knocking them off balance like bowling pins.

Grimes sprinted for the door.

"Wait!" yelled Kate.

No amount of shouting could stop him. In seconds, he was out of the room and rushing down the hallway. Empty echoes in the corridor confirmed no one followed.

Grimes didn't stop running. He bolted for the airlock, a new plan developing. Before, he'd schemed to eliminate the *Ares* crew members—reducing their numbers would reduce the odds of a Guardian getting hurt or killed. But what would work as well, better in fact, was finding the strike team and briefing them on the situation in Ops. The astronauts had no weapons and no escape route. The soldiers could apprehend them without firing a shot, even lock them in the Operations Center and set the place on fire. No surprises, no risk of the AD revoking his deal.

The only unknown in his plan was how best to approach the soldiers. An accidental confrontation in the halls could spur them to fire first and ask questions later.

Grimes turned a corner and froze. Three meters ahead was a soldier in a black space suit. Not completely black—the corridor light on the suit's chameleon-like layer elicited a faint iridescent rainbow sheen, much as weak sun rays on an oil slick. He held a gun, also black. The soldier pointed the weapon at Grimes.

The former security chief raised his hands and shouted: "Grimes, Julian. Serial number eight, one, six, zero, two, six, four, eight, seven, three. Captain, Space Force."

The soldier didn't react.

The black suit was menacing. Grimes had never been on the receiving end of an encounter with a Guardian. "You can stow your weapon, Lieutenant," he said, noting the single black bar on the man's shoulder. The former security chief would take over once the soldier understood whom he was talking to. Grimes lowered his hands and approached.

The soldier recoiled and thrust the gun at Grimes.

Grimes re-raised his hands, though only halfway. "I said I'm Grimes, Julian. Serial number eight, one, six, zero, two, six, four, eight, seven, three. Captain, Space Force. Who's your commanding officer?"

No response.

"There are six astronauts in this station," said Grimes, lowering his arms again. "Five in Operations and one, a doctor, in the MedCenter. They are unarmed and will be easy to round up. What instructions have you been given regarding their elimination?"

The soldier didn't respond to Grimes.

"Can you hear me in there, Lieutenant?" Grimes asked. "I said I'm Grimes, Julian, Captain, Space Force."

"Yes, I heard you," replied the soldier. His voice was processed, mechanical, the output of a digital filter.

"Where's the officer in charge of housekeeping?" asked Grimes. That officer, responsible for disposing of the bodies, would have the particulars on the elimination order they were following.

The soldier cocked his head.

"You're going to start answering my questions," said Grimes, taking another step. The soldier released the safety on his weapon.

"Now listen," said Grimes, beginning to lose his patience, "if you want to call out to Central Dispatch to have them confirm my identity, you may go ahead and do so. However, I warn you that your failure to immediately—"

An invisible jolt of electricity sprang from the soldier's gun, connecting with Grimes's midsection. The former security chief lost control of his legs and crumpled to the ground. His bladder, also out of his control, emptied its contents. A dark stain formed at the crotch of his jumpsuit.

Dr. Palmer entered the corridor, prodded by the second black-clad soldier. "I found this one in the MedCenter."

"Roger," said the first soldier. He walked up to Grimes and nudged him with his boot. "Get up."

Grimes groaned. The effects of the blast had subsided but for his aching thighs and tingling in his toes. Grimes got himself to standing. He weighed delivering a fresh protest but thought better of it.

"Move out," said the soldier.

"Where are we going?" asked Grimes.

"To reunite you with your friends."

- - -

Julian swung Glenn around and released him into Kate and Engles, knocking them off balance like bowling pins. He sprinted for the door.

"Wait!" Kate yelled as she grabbed Engles, struggling to stop the two of them from falling to the floor.

Julian ignored her. In a flash, he bounded from the room. Glenn managed to stand and staggered towards the door.

"Stop, Glenn," said Kate, releasing Engles and righting herself. "You can't go after him."

"Someone has to," said Glenn, panting with the sudden exertion. He spoke between huffs. "The soldiers don't ... know where we are .... They don't know if we're armed .... He's gonna tell them everything."

"But if you catch him, what then?" asked Kate. "You're in no shape to fight. And if you run into those soldiers—"

"Then we need to leave," said Glenn. "Find someplace to hide in the station."

"Where?" asked Engles. "The Outpost's not that big. It won't take long for them to round us all up—"

"Glenn's right!" exclaimed Fisk. "We can't stay here!" His eyes bulged as he spiraled into hysteria. "That's a Space Force death squad! We're all gonna die!" He started for the door. Miriam reached for him, grabbing his shirt sleeve. Fisk wrenched free.

"Stop, Fisk!" yelled Kate.

The research scientist dashed for the exit. He attempted to push past Glenn but couldn't, Commander Wiles restraining him despite his weakened state. Fisk squirmed in his arms.

A booming directive came through the door: "Come out with your hands up, or I start firing into the room."

Releasing Fisk, Glenn motioned everyone to the edges of the space. He slid to one side of the door and waved Kate to the other—a rehash of his ambush idea, which had seemed hopeless from the beginning. Glenn was too weak to subdue anyone, and the two of them wrestling a trooper for a weapon would be a crap shoot. That was assuming they stormed the room. If the soldiers shot inside as they'd threatened, there was no place for Engles, Miriam, and Fisk to seek shelter. One or more of the remaining *Ares* astronauts would die, and those who didn't would be captured. "We're coming out," she yelled.

Glenn made an exasperated face at Commander Holman. He likely believed she'd ruined their one chance. Maybe she had.

Kate opened the door and led the astronauts from the room. They gathered, hands in the air, in the constricted hallway outside Ops. A lone soldier, dressed in a black stealth suit, marched them through the halls.

They arrived at the galley. Inside, Palmer was on his knees, expressionless and with his hands clasped behind his head. Someone knelt beside the doctor—Julian! He was a prisoner. He'd failed to convince the soldiers he was one of them. The former security chief refused to make eye contact as Kate walked past.

"Get down with the others," ordered the first soldier, the one who escorted them from Ops.

There wasn't much to do except comply. As they dropped to their knees, the second soldier approached Kate and handed her a wad of fabric. "Take one, pass the rest," he said.

At first, the black bundle appeared to be a single swath, but was actually several smaller pieces bunched together. Kate took one and gave the pile to Glenn. She unfolded her article and gasped.

"Once you have a hood, put it over your head," said the first soldier.

"You're making a mistake," sputtered Julian. "I'm operating on orders straight from the AD."

"Shut up and put it on."

Kate donned the hood. The thick, black fabric had a musty smell and blocked all light.

Down the line, Miriam whimpered. Fisk openly sobbed. Who could blame him, any of them? They were headed for execution at the hands of the Space Force.

"Outpost secured, sir," said a soldier.

"Roger that," crackled a man's voice through a comm, a normal voice, not processed like the soldiers'. It had a commanding fullness and an underlying, rumbling growl. "How many?"

"Seven, sir. All alive."

"They're gonna *wish* they were dead," said the man. "No one oblige them before I arrive. I'm on my way."

42

The man with the deep, rumbling voice arrived in the galley, or at least his *presence* had entered the room. Kate felt it before he uttered a few quiet words to the soldiers standing guard.

The man, his presence, was suddenly close, likely no more than a meter before them. He spoke in his rumbling growl: "Here's how this is going to work. I ask a question, and you answer. It's really that simple. Anything less, and I'm going to shoot you right here." Fisk whimpered. "Not so fun getting a taste of your own medicine, is it?" Fisk whimpered again. "Since I have your attention, let's proceed to the first question: which one of you Space Farce fucks plowed that God damn capsule all along the fucking ground like you're some God damned Dust Bowl farmer?"

The rumbling voice was loud—more than loud, voluminous, filling every square centimeter of the room.

"There's so much dust kicked up, it's probably halfway to God damned Aristarchus by now! Whichever one of you it is, you're the one I'm going to shoot first. So who was it?" A pause. "Huh?" Another pause. "No takers? I'm not surprised. You're all a bunch of fucking cowards, anyway." The voice quieted. "God damn it, Jack, maybe we cancel this interrogation and shoot them all in the head."

Kate raised her hand, instinctively, more in hopes of deflecting harm from her astronauts than owning up to the dust.

"Get him to his feet," said the voice.

Rough hands hooked beneath Kate's armpits, hoisting her up. The man moved in close. Not movement she could see—the musty black hood still covered her head—more his presence impinging on her personal space, like a silent, magnetic force.

"What's your name, soldier?" The voice was soft and spoke to her from centimeters away. Calm, not yelling, but still full of rolling fury. Nose to nose, she envisioned. The image gave her a chill. "And you can skip the serial number bullshit. They have you boys all cataloged like you're fucking machine parts."

She wasn't a soldier, but correcting him might not be the best plan. "Holman, Katherine A."

A laden hush hung over the room. Within the dark confines of her hood, Kate's imagination ran wild. She pictured a cocked fist preparing to smash her face; a knife drawn back for a strike; a gun, the barrel nearly grazing her head. She cringed, bracing for—

The hood flew off.

Blinding brightness. The light in the room wasn't excessive, but her eyes had adjusted to the darkness.

"You're dead," said the voice, the man, standing in front of her. She couldn't make out his face, only shapes. She blinked, willing her eyes to adapt to the glare.

"Or you're supposed to be," continued the man. "Holman, Katherine A., leader of the first manned mission to Mars, and a card-carrying member of the Space Force. Faked her death to land on the Far Side of the Moon. The question is why." The man moved in closer. "This whole business is beyond confusing, but now we're going to get some answers. In addition to your objective here at the Old Mine, you're going to tell me every single thing you know about those inbound rockets."

Rockets?

"Oh, you're shocked? You think we don't know, think we're sitting here with our thumbs up our asses, waiting to be rolled up on?"

"Excuse me, sir," said Kate, her voice weak, timid. "I don't know anything about rockets, and I'm not a member of the Space Force. I'm an astronaut."

"Sorry, Holman, Katherine A." The man pointed down the line of hooded captives. "This asshole over here, Grimes, Julian, already admitted he's a captain in the Space Force. He thought my astronauts here in the black suits were his buddies." The man's mood lightened at the recollection, but only for a moment. His serious demeanor returned. "He blew it for you, Commander Holman. Blew the cover for all of you."

"*Julian* is a member of the Space Force," said Kate. "We had no idea. The rest of us are astronauts."

Kate's eyes finally focused. The man before her stood an inch or two taller, with cocoa brown skin and closely cropped, salt-and-pepper hair. He wore a white space suit, not black, without a helmet. His dark brown eyes possessed a smoldering fire. They were eyes she hoped never to see again, eyes that spawned a knot in the pit of her stomach. "You're astronauts, but you have someone from the Space Force as part of your crew. You're all pronounced dead, but somehow still alive. And you're suddenly and mysteriously on the Moon, but have nothing to do with the inbound rockets." Commander Praviraj Anand, the moonbase chief and so-called "King of the Moon," sighed. "So much bullshit, it's making my head spin. And frankly, I don't believe a word of it." He stepped back and gave a silent directive to one of the soldiers clad in black.

The soldier raised his gun and aimed it at Glenn's head. Her second-in-command, unable to see from beneath his hood, wobbled on his knees, though not from any awareness of the situation. He was still recovering from his carbon dioxide poisoning. Twenty minutes prior, he'd been unconscious in the MedCenter.

"Now, Holman, Katherine A., you're going to tell me everything about those inbound rockets, or so help me, I'm going to start killing your clutch of Space Force goons, beginning with this one."

"I'm not lying," Kate said in a rush. "I'll tell you anything you want to know, just please, don't hurt Glenn, or anyone else from my crew. As the commander of this mission, I'm responsible for everything that has happened. If you want to hurt—interrogate someone, please take me."

Anand looked on with a blank stare, but something within the man seemed to shift. "Lower your weapon, Jack."

The soldier with the gun, "Jack," according to the moonbase commander, didn't comply.

"Do it," said Anand with more force. "Holman, Katherine A. is one of us."

"She is?" said Jack, bringing the gun down.

"Yes," said Anand. "Members of the Space Force don't give two shits about anyone else. They would never take responsibility for anything, much less a bullet for each other. If she were really Space Force, she would've told us to go ahead and fire, to show how much she didn't care. But she does—she does care." Anand turned to the commander. "Now that we've established who you are, Astronaut Katherine Holman, I need you to brief me on exactly what the fuck is going on."

\- - -

Kate, Glenn, and Anand filed into Ops, escorted by the black-suited soldier known as Jack.

Commander Anand gathered three chairs and placed them in a tight circle. "Have a seat," he said, depositing himself into the first, its frame disappearing behind the expanse of his space suit. Kate and Glenn took the other two. "I apologize for the limited hospitality options here at the Old Mine," he continued. "If we were at the moonbase, we'd've met in my private office. It's got a couch so comfortable you wouldn't want to get up." Anand sat with his legs wide, likely to accommodate the bulky suit surrounding them, though Kate guessed he'd have done the same in regular clothes. As with his outsized presence, the moonbase commander expanded his physical form maximally into the room.

An astronaut in a helmet-less, white space suit, entered Ops with a tray holding three mugs, two steaming.

"Ah, here he is," said Anand. The moonbase commander grabbed a mug, heavy with the scent of fresh coffee. He inhaled the rich aroma and sipped, his face brightening.

Kate claimed the other coffee from the tray. Glenn took the remaining mug.

"You sure you're good with water, Commander Wiles?" asked Anand. "My people make a mean cup o' Joe. 'Chewable,' I sometimes joke. Or they could probably scrounge up something stronger, though I don't like to start drinking before five in the afternoon."

"I'm fine, sir," said Glenn.

"Commander Wiles is recovering from an injury aboard the capsule," said Kate.

Anand sipped again, then dismissed the white-clad astronaut with a look. Tucking his tray under his arm, the man swiftly left the room.

Kate held her mug in both hands, letting her fingers draw its warmth. The Outpost's life support system kept the facility at a comfortable seventy-two degrees, but the station's remoteness and bleak interior instilled a sense of chill in the air. Commander Holman peered into the mug, the liquid's deep brown lapping against the sides. She sipped—and flinched.

"I hope it's not too strong for you, Commander Holman," said Anand with a chuckle. "They brewed this batch to my liking. I can have them remake yours."

Kate shook her head. With six months of instant on the *Gaia*, she'd almost forgotten the taste of real coffee. She took another sip. The flavor invigorated her, as did the warmth trickling down her throat.

Anand motioned to the black-suited soldier. "Thank you, Lieutenant Bremmer. That will be all."

The soldier nodded and exited the room.

Glenn's eyes followed the lieutenant out. "At first, you seemed openly hostile to the Space Force," he said, "but here you are working with them." The moonbase commander blinked back. "Jack," Glenn added, responding to Anand's stare.

"Lieutenant Bremmer is not Space Force, Commander Wiles," said Anand.

"But the black suits …," replied Glenn. "Julian—Commander Grimes—said the Space Force is the only outfit that uses them."

"We caught two of those Space Force dickheads sneaking around the moonbase," said Anand. "I decided we'd borrow their suits to make you—when we thought you were Space Force—make you think we were part of whatever big party they're getting ready to throw. Rumor has it those suits allow you to become invisible. We couldn't figure that part out, but their performance was convincing enough. Even fooled that asshole Grimes, according to Bremmer."

"By big party, do you mean the incoming rockets you mentioned?" asked Kate.

Anand grunted. "Over a day ago, we lost all contact with NASA—telemetry, the 'good morning' message, even our Internet link went down. We could still pick up transmissions from Earth, but we couldn't get a message to them. That's when we noticed the ships, three of the sleek, black Space Force rockets with that stupid knock-off Star Trek logo on the side. Three ships filled, we assume, with wannabe Captain Kirks—a bunch of red shirts, really—headed for the Moon.

"And then we saw your capsule. We had no idea it was the *Gaia*—the last news report we had said it blew up. When we spotted your ship on our scopes, we figured it was part of the Space Force armada, an advance team with a special objective on the Far Side. So we jumped in the rovers and came here as fast as we could." Anand sipped from his mug. "The Space Force deploy men by having them jump out of their ships. They arrive in a theater like paratroopers. We were shocked as all hell to find you'd somehow landed that capsule and walked away."

"Kate got us to the ground," said Glenn, thumbing at the commander.

"I tip my cap to you, Commander Holman," said Anand. "That had to have been an incredible bit of piloting."

"Thank you, sir," said Kate, sheepish and quiet. She moved quickly to address what had to be Anand's next thought. "And I'm sorry about all the dust. I know how much—"

"You have nothing to apologize for, Commander Holman," said Anand. "That was the only way to save all your lives. And luckily, it worked."

Kate hid her puzzlement behind a nod. She'd expected Anand to rip her a new one, especially after his invective when he entered the galley. He hadn't laid into her—that fact didn't make sense, but she'd take it. She was happy to move on from what, for her, had been the elephant in the room.

Glenn beamed his sincere, goofy smile times ten. "And all these years, you've been worried about returning to the Moon," he said. "I told you it wouldn't be as bad as you thought."

Blood rushed to Kate's face, part embarrassment, part anger. Her second-in-command, with a penchant for putting his foot in his mouth, was barreling towards the biggest blunder of their working together. "Glenn—"

"Worried about Commander Anand and how he said he'd put a bullet in your head if you ever returned."

"Glenn, stop—"

"I never said that," bellowed Anand.

"At the trial, remember?"

"Glenn—"

"What trial?" asked Anand.

"Years ago," said Glenn. "The last time Commander Holman was here on the Moon. As a pilot. She fired her retros and sprayed dust all over the—"

"Glenn, STOP!"

Anand stared hard at Kate. She could only sit, mortified, while the gears spun. "Holman, Katherine A., you … you're that rocket pilot … from that time ago … the incident with Cargo Carrier Eleven."

Kate shrank in her seat, working furiously to make herself as small as possible. "And about that, I'm truly sorry, Commander."

"There's no need to apologize," said Anand. "And for the record, Commander Wiles, I never said I'd put a bullet in her head. Who told you that?"

"Commander Holman."

Anand's fiery gaze whipped to Kate. She wilted again in her seat. "That's what my advocate told me, sir. He said you were very upset about all the dust."

Anand settled into another dispassionate stare—his manner when thinking, apparently—then bellowed a laugh. "No offense, Commander, but your advocate was a bit of a dipshit. Luckily, you didn't need top-notch representation, because none of what happened that day was your fault. If anything, you should've received a medal for getting Administrator Evans to safety. I said as much during the tribunal, but I guess we don't hand out awards for valiant action. It's what astronauts are expected to do."

She'd saved Evans but .... "My co-pilot ... she didn't make it," said Kate. "She wandered off ... disoriented. I didn't save her."

"If memory serves, she wouldn't've survived if you'd tried," said Anand. "Her autopsy showed she'd died before the explosion. I guess your advocate left that bit out." He drank from his mug. "And I never said I'd put a bullet in your head."

"Kate said there was a letter of reprimand—"

"Shut UP, Glenn!"

"I did receive such a letter," said Anand. "And I did make that comment. But it was directed at the pilot of that cargo carrier, not Commander Holman. When I was talking about 'dust' all over the station, I was referring to the drug Dustamine, not Moon dust. Dust was running rampant across the base at the time, and that pilot was a key part of the problem. We didn't have the medical equipment to handle a Dust overdose. We lost station personnel and a couple astronauts, primarily because of that man. I wanted him to spend the rest of his years in prison here on the Moon, but they said they would take him away for further prosecution on Earth. I was so upset, I told him I'd put a bullet in his head if he ever came back to my moonbase. For that, I received a letter of reprimand, but I didn't care. I still don't." Anand drank the last of his coffee, then searched the empty mug for more. He set it on the floor. "It seems your advocate got confused about which pilot I meant, and which type of dust I was talking about. He may have been high on that stuff himself."

An immense wave of relief flowed over Kate, years of guilt, consternation, and self-reproach melting away.

"Now that I've answered your questions, I'd like to see if you can answer some of mine," said Anand. "How is it that you're alive, what are you doing here on the Moon, and what, if anything, can you tell me about those inbound Space Force rockets?"

Kate considered where to begin. "The short of it is, Commander Anand, there's gold on Mars, many trillions of dollars' worth. The whole point of the Mars mission was to get Julian there to confirm it. The Space Force is heading a conspiracy to mine Martian gold and bring it back to Earth, to secretly fund their operations."

"We found sacks of Martian dirt by your capsule," said Anand. "It looked like red rock mixed with gold flakes."

"Those are samples Julian brought with him," said Kate. "His plan was to eliminate us, the *Ares* crew, and retire off that gold. Obviously, that didn't pan out. We're still alive, which has created a problem for the Space Force. They assume the *Ares* crew knows about the conspiracy. They can't risk us telling anyone else. That's why they tried to destroy the *Gaia*."

"But they didn't," said Anand.

"No, they *thought* they did," said Kate. "The AD held a press conference announcing our demise. But if there are Space Force rockets on their way to the Moon, it means they know we're still alive."

"They told the world you're dead," said Anand. "They're coming to make sure you stay that way."

"Except if they're sending three rockets full of men, and there's a communications blackout, they must assume everything we know has been shared with you all on the Moon."

"We knew a set of incoming Space Force rockets couldn't be good ...," said Anand, staring past Kate. His face tightened as he snapped back to reality under the weight of their predicament. "We need to somehow get in touch with NASA."

"It won't make a difference," said Kate. "This conspiracy includes NASA."

"Bullshit," said Anand.

"It goes clear up to the highest levels," said Kate. "The assistant director —"

"Assistant Director Pearson is *not* NASA," said Anand. "The two goons we captured confessed that much, at least. Pearson is Space Force."

"He's an Air Force veteran," said Kate.

Anand shook his head. "He's Space Force. Most of his service record, the portion accessible to the average astronaut, has been falsified."

His service record had been falsified? Just like Julian's ....

"Pearson didn't work his way up through the Air Force or astronaut ranks," said Anand. "He was planted there at the top. All of NASA's not corrupt, just Pearson, and the cronies he's installed over the years."

Glenn's head bobbed—Kate caught him nodding off out the corner of her eye. He'd gone silent during the recent stretch of conversation.

"Are we boring you, Astronaut Glenn Wiles?" asked Anand.

"He's been through a lot," said Kate. "We almost lost him." Slumped in his chair, Glenn looked terrible. "I want you to check in with Doctor Palmer."

She'd expected a protest, but Glenn offered a thin smile, first to her, and then Commander Anand. He rose and drifted from the room.

"The incoming assault force will be a problem," said Anand once the door closed behind Glenn. "We're just astronauts here on the Moon, not soldiers. We're not equipped to hold them off."

"There's only one way to stop all this," said Kate. "We have to get the word out about the conspiracy. Once their plan's been exposed, there'll no longer be a point to killing anyone."

"As I said, transmissions to Earth are blocked," said Anand. "We couldn't make an emergency request for toilet paper if we needed to."

"A message alone won't be enough," said Kate. "They'll say it's a deepfake." Even without that insidious technology, the AD had predisposed the world to believe in their deaths. Any message from them would face a great deal of skepticism. "The only way to stop this conspiracy, to blow it out of the water, is for us, the *Ares* astronauts, to get to Earth. If we can show the world we're still alive and tell our story, that will end it." The words she'd spoken so matter-of-factly belied the impossibility of bringing them to fruition. "It's funny," she continued, talking into the floor, "we were originally going to land on Earth, off the coast of Baja. But Glenn needed medical attention, and the moonbase was the best option, so we came here. We came here, but Earth is where we needed to be to end all this. None of us realized it at the time. If we had known ...." Her voice trailed off.

"If you had known, you wouldn't have done anything different."

Anand's words gave her pause. "We wouldn't have," said Kate, with a twinge of embarrassment at suggesting the idea. "No, sir, we wouldn't have," she said with more resolve. "We wouldn't have sacrificed Glenn to save the rest of us."

"Of course you wouldn't have," said Anand. "We astronauts take care of our own." He reached across and gripped her shoulder. "We take care of our own, Commander Holman." The moonbase commander smiled, the first time she'd seen a cheerful expression cross his face. "As for getting you to Earth, you're not—"

"Commander Anand."

The voice came over the moonbase commander's comm. "Yes."

"I have an update on the incoming ships."

"Go ahead."

"They've executed an additional burn—more than a course adjustment. We don't have as much time as we thought."

"Acknowledged." Anand shot from his seat. "I need your people suited up, whichever of you are coming with us," he said, looking down at Kate. "Lieutenant Bremmer. Lieutenant Bremmer!" he bellowed into his comm. "Where is Jack?"

Lieutenant Bremmer, clad in the black Space Force suit, scurried into Ops. "Sir."

"Prep the rovers. Round up our people. We need to get home."

43

Kate followed Anand out of the Outpost airlock, stepping from the dark chamber into the blinding Lunar sunlight. Though she'd marched across the surface not six hours earlier, she still found the scene jarring. Desolation reigned in every direction, a barren expanse of light gray rocks and dust beneath a black horizon, the Moon's perpetual night sky.

She'd exited with Anand and a handful of the astronauts who'd accompanied him from the moonbase, the most the airlock could hold at one time. The next group to step out of the chamber included the bulk of her crew, standouts in the sea of white spacesuits with the bright orange *Ares* mission patches on their arms.

Julian emerged in the final batch of astronauts, his wrists bound before him. One of the black suits prodded him forward with their handgun.

"Last chance to leave that scumbag behind," said Anand.

Kate jumped at Anand's imposing voice suddenly in her helmet. He also watched the procession, apparently. The moonbase commander had proclaimed that Julian couldn't be trusted. He wasn't wrong. The former security officer killed three of Kate's crew, had attempted to kill her, and fought to rendezvous with the black-clad astronauts when he believed they were Space Force.

"He'd have plenty of food and wouldn't get much of anywhere if he tried to set out on foot," added Anand.

Valid points, but the thought of stranding someone at the Outpost, even Julian …. "I want to bring him along."

"Suit yourself," said Anand with a shrug in his voice, "but that fucker isn't riding with me." The open channel with the moonbase commander fell silent, not an empty airwave, more like a line on hold. The black-clad astronaut stopped and ushered Julian in a new direction, likely following orders from Anand over a separate channel. The two started for the Outpost's rover, piling in with three other moonbase astronauts.

The rest of the *Ares* astronauts climbed into the second rover. When the moonbase vehicles first appeared on the monitors, she, Miriam, and the others assumed them packed with men. In reality, they'd arrived only partially full. Combined with the Outpost's rover, their makeshift convoy would have return-trip seating for eight additional bodies, eighteen people total. Kate set off to join her crew mates.

"I saved you a spot, Commander Holman." Anand's booming voice sounded again in her helmet, giving her a start. "You can ride with me and my staff. We can chat a bit on the way."

"Yes, sir," said Kate, taking his words as more directive than suggestion. Not that she would have refused his hospitality, though she was still processing his surprising lack of anger at the mess she'd made landing the *Gaia*.

Kate walked with Anand to the lead rover and filed with him into the second row. The doorless vehicle accommodated bulky space suits with deep bench seats and generous legroom, but she still felt cramped. Sitting beside the moonbase commander, Kate found herself crowded both by his outsized presence and his widely spread legs.

"Make sure you're strapped in," said Commander Anand. "Jack drives like the devil."

A black suited astronaut, Jack according to Anand, sat in the driver's seat, same side as the moonbase commander. Kate had secured her restraints the moment she sat, but checked them a second time with the warning. She glanced at the Outpost, its stark structure a sanctuary against the harsh Lunar environment. The facility had allowed them to save Glenn's life, and for that she'd forever value their stay, but hopefully she'd never set foot in the building again.

In a sudden violent jolt, the rover sprinted off across the Moon's surface. Kate struggled to adjust her position, pinned to her seat by the fierce acceleration. The vehicle's batteries, trickle charged by its canopy of solar panels and topped off at the Outpost, delivered peak voltage to the electric motors at each wheel. Glancing behind, the two other rovers followed close. Apparently they had lead-footed drivers of their own. Long ago, she'd taken a buggy ride on Earth, an exhilarating trip through Arizona's Sonoran Desert. The warm sun lapped her skin and the air whipped her hair as she cruised the dunes. Their dash over the Lunar plains offered no such pleasantries, devoid of wind and featuring sunlight so strong it could cook a steak on the dashboard.

The rover shook, traversing a bumpy patch of land. Given the torn-up mess of terrain that flanked them and their speed, the ride was surprisingly smooth. She looked over the shoulder of the astronaut seated ahead. Her eyebrows raised at the scene. "We're on a road?"

"A road of sorts," came Anand's booming voice. "The ground's been pounded flat by all the rover trips between the moonbase and the Outpost, back when the mine was operational."

How many trips had it taken to form the road? Hundreds? Thousands? And how long before it would be reclaimed by the Lunar wilderness? On Earth, the constant action of water and plant life would erase an abandoned road, consuming it over the centuries. The Moon's only active agents were the occasional meteorite and the relentlessly pounding sun.

"We got interrupted back in Ops," said Anand. "You'd just finished explaining how you need to get to Earth to expose the conspiracy."

"Yes, sir," said Kate. "That's really the only option." Was his revisiting the topic a hopeful sign? "Is there a spare rocket we can use?"

"Negative," said Anand. "And I'm not sure you'd want to fly back like that anyway. From what you've told me about Space Force tracking, you'd probably run into the same problems as splashing down in the *Gaia*."

No spare rocket. That was it, then—they couldn't get to Earth. She'd known the answer in her heart, but the question had been worth asking.

"There's a much better option than a rocket," continued Anand. "Well, something that should improve your chances of making it to the ground, at least. Improving our odds is all any of us can really hope for in our line of work." He looked directly at her as he spoke, the stark Lunar landscape with its black horizon racing across his mirrored sun visor. "With no rockets on standby, you might wonder what that means for us in the event of an emergency. A few months into our stay here, we began asking that question ourselves. The problem is, there's no practical way for NASA to keep that much payload launch capacity at the ready to ferry seventy people to safety all at once. It turns out that administrator you saved years ago, John Evans, his pet project was an emergency escape system to shuttle everyone off the Moon."

Kate crinkled her nose, perplexed. "That still means launching them from the surface. I thought you said NASA couldn't keep enough rockets on standby."

"Not rockets, Commander Holman, pods," said Anand. "Emergency pods. Each one seats three comfortably, four in a pinch. They're launched by a massive rail gun, a literal balls-to-the-wall electromagnetic propulsion system that hurls them like a bat out of hell. When you get to Earth, you drop through the atmosphere—and I do mean drop—with splashdown and recovery in the Gulf of Mexico. Door-to-door travel time's a day. The trip's not for the faint of heart, but it's an absolute joyride compared to dying." Anand's helmet turned to face forward. "A couple emergency pods could get you and your people where you need to be."

Encouraging news, but would a pod be any better than a capsule? The odds of getting the *Gaia* to the ground in one piece hadn't been great. Add to that a pod's lack of maneuverability …. "When we originally planned to land on Earth, one concern we had was being shot down. Will a pod be—"

"A single pod's too small and will be moving too fast on a radar scope to attract attention," said Anand. "It's the slick-as-snot opposite of a lumbering capsule. You'll have nothing to worry about."

A viable option for getting to Earth, and in a single day of spaceflight! In less than two days' time, their whole ordeal could be over, with her holding her children in her arms.

"Once you're on the ground, whatever you're going to do, you'll need to do it quickly," said Anand. "While you're on your way to Earth, that assault team will be headed to us. They'll likely land not long after you step out of your pod."

In the excitement of having a solid option for getting to Earth, she'd forgotten the squad of trained, armed killers coming to storm the moonbase. "Why don't you evacuate the station?" asked Kate. "It sounds like we could all leave together in the emergency pods."

"One pod won't get two shits of scrutiny from even the most curious radar operator," said Anand. "Twenty-five in the sky is a different story. Someone will notice, and when they do, they'll start shooting 'em down. Literal fish in a barrel. If I'm going out, it won't be like that, as someone else's target practice."

The alternative, resisting an assault force, didn't seem much better. Kate couldn't help but ask, "Do you—"

The rover's nose plummeted. Alarmed, Kate grabbed the section of roll bar that ran along the seats in front of her. She braced for the impending end-over-end tumble …. None came—they continued forward, traveling at a sharp downward angle. To her side, a large, circular rim, jagged in spots, rose around them. It cast an eerie shadow, immensely wide and dark like thick, black soup in a Titan's bowl. Their vehicle descended into the gloom, a lonely diver sinking to murky depths. They'd entered a crater, the rover's sudden change in pitch the start of their transit.

"Do I what?" asked Anand.

"Have a plan?" Kate recoiled at the words leaving her mouth. To her ears, her question had come across as skeptical, maybe even derisive. She hadn't measured her tone, still shaken from their plunge into the crater.

"None as of yet," said Anand. "You only just helped us confirm those rockets' hostile intent. As I mentioned at the Outpost, we're not equipped to repel a military offensive. Yes, we have pellet guns, but they're useless against space suits. We collected some blasting caps from a storehouse at the Old Mine before we left—that was Jack's idea—but I'm not sure what good they'll be. It's not like we're gonna blow up the moonbase."

Kate's mouth went dry, her tongue rough as sandpaper. The moonbase astronauts would be fighting for their lives against incredible odds while Kate and the *Ares* crew, the people who *drew* the assault team to the Moon, sped to Earth and some semblance of safety.

"Once we're at the moonbase, we'll figure out how we're going to handle this assault team. For the moment, I've ordered a LIDE—that's a Lunar Impact Drill and Exercise, practice for a projected meteoroid strike near the base." Anand abruptly shifted topics. "After this blows over, what's next for you, Commander Holman?"

Kate teared up, at once thankful for the privacy of her helmet. "I … I'm a mom," she sputtered. "Two kids, nine and four."

"Bet they'll be happy to see you," said Anand. "You'll enjoy some much deserved downtime with them, I imagine."

Kate nodded.

"And then a new mission?"

"I've decided I'll be retiring from the Corps, sir."

"Retiring?" asked Anand. "That's a shame. The Corps needs good people, capable pilots."

His remark sparked a twinge of guilt. NASA had invested so much in her, in training her. Few pilots could have landed a capsule on the Moon. If she stayed, she might again be the only thing standing between some other set of astronauts and certain death. But her children ... they'd almost lost her, would still lose her if she didn't make it back. She owed it to them to be in their lives, wanted to be in their lives. As odd as it would feel to walk away from the career she'd pursued with such vigor, retiring was the right decision for her and her family.

"Evans was an astronaut prior to taking his administrative job. Member of the first manned mission to an asteroid—well, first *American* mission. The Chinese beat us on that one." Anand's helmet swiveled once more, its mirrored faceplate trained on her. "You ever considered going the administrative track?"

"No, sir." It had always been astronaut or bust, not a single thought of some option in between.

"We need good administrators, people who understand what it's like to be an astronaut, the risks we take, the life we lead. It's why Evans fought hard for an escape system. He felt it unconscionable to station astronauts on the Moon but to leave them hanging in an emergency." Anand's helmet faced forward again. "I hope you'll consider it."

Flying a desk? Most astronauts would laugh at the notion. Her time for adventure was over, but perhaps it didn't have to mean the end of the story. "Thank you, sir," said Kate. "I will."

The rover's nose tipped upwards—they were starting their ascent. The crater's rim stretched wide before them, brilliant and white in the stark sunlight, a jagged silhouette against the black of space.

"You like audiobooks, Commander Holman?" She didn't. When she did read, it was from old-fashioned paper, not even a tablet. "They're a great way to fill the time, especially on a trip like this one."

"How long until we reach the moonbase?" asked Kate.

"About six hours," said Anand. "I know, seems like we'll never get there at this rate, but right now our speed's limited. The Earth's gravitational field doesn't provide much protection to the Far Side. The ground here is a lot rougher from all the extra asteroid collisions. Once we get closer to the Near Side, we'll be able to pick up the pace."

Move faster than they were? Kate gripped her restraints tighter.

"I have a few audiobooks uploaded to my suit," said Anand. "There's one in particular I think you'll enjoy."

"Sure," she said to another directive posing as a suggestion.

The comm line with Anand cut out as he spoke instructions to his suit.

A light flashed in the upper-right corner of her field of view, an alert of an incoming file. She accepted. Seconds later, the audiobook's icon emerged along the bottom of her heads-up display.

"It's the biography of Hannibal," boomed Anand, "the Carthaginian general who led his army over the Alps to invade Italy. That effort was the closest thing to the space program in his day." The moonbase commander's voice softened. "I found it an inspiring read. I'd happened upon it during a dark period in my life, when I'd come face-to-face with self-doubt."

Commander Anand, the "King of the Moon," doubting himself? The notion was hard to fathom.

"Hannibal was known for his leadership, persistence, and determination," said Anand. "I feel like you're the kind of astronaut, kind of person, who might relate to his story."

Kate squirmed in the praise, butting up against her own self-doubt. "Thank you, sir. I'll give it a listen."

The comm line with Anand terminated. His head still reclined, he seemed like an old cowboy who'd pushed his hat forward over his face, settling in for a noonday nap.

Commander Holman queued the file from Anand for playback. She interlaced her fingers over her belly, leaned her head back, and closed her eyes.

44

The lead rover left the main road and turned onto a grand, elliptical drive. Within the sunken, enclosed expanse of the driveway sat the Apollo Stone Garden. Modeled after a Japanese *Karesansui*, the garden featured strategically placed basalt columns that towered over Zen-inspired stone sculptures, interspersed with patches of meticulously arranged pebbles and raked sand swirls. Three Mooncrete benches cast crisp shadows in the stark sunlight.

The moonbase came into view as they rounded the bend. Sunshine twinkled from glass, and from a handful of polished Mooncrete panels that adorned the facility's main facade. Pulling off the driveway, they drove to a rover bay, the space sheltered by solar panels that fed a charging station. Jack guided the vehicle into a slot. It skidded to a halt.

"Everybody out!" ordered Anand.

The astronauts stepped out and strolled the short distance to the facility's main airlock. After pressurizing, they exited into the Suiting Station, a place for moonwalkers to check air supplies and seals before embarking on an excursion, and to remove helmets and gloves upon their return. They didn't linger—Anand and his party moved fast, leaving the room through a wide corridor.

The moonbase had a different feel than the Outpost. LED lamps lit the passageway, but natural illumination from frosted ceiling panels brightened the space. Thick panes of glass filtered streaming, yellow sunlight and offered views of the Lunar terrain and other sections of the base. A fanciful set of baby blue curtains adorned one window, with small potted plants on the sill. An autographed photo of a space-suited Neil Armstrong, grinning and clutching his helmet, hung to its right. The station's Mooncrete walls, unlike those on the Far Side, were smooth, sealed, and painted a soft white. When they'd stepped through the airlock, a large monitor greeted them with the message, "Welcome to Station Oceanus Procellarum." Someone had altered the graphic, striking the last three words and overwriting in script, "Moonbeam Village." Where the utilitarian mining Outpost had been bleak at every turn, the astronaut moonbase was warm and inviting, surroundings that exuded a sense of home.

Kate worked to keep up with the others as they rushed down the corridor. Not a day removed from six months in zero-g, she struggled in the bulk of her spacesuit. The moonbase astronauts, by comparison, moved with flowing grace, accustomed to the modest gravity.

The rover party left the corridor, spilling into a spacious, circular chamber with a broad, transparent dome. They arrived at the moonbase's impressive central reception area.

Pandemonium reigned.

Astronauts rushed about the barn-sized space. Their bouncy movements in low gravity created a surreal effect, like watching people in a dream. A frantic dream.

A young moonbase crewman, outfitted in a blue station jumpsuit, approached them. "Commander Anand," he said, breathless. He paused a moment before thrusting forward a tablet full of bullet points and figures.

Anand lifted his helmet and grabbed the device. He swiped twice during his review of its contents. A frown clouded his face. "Thank you," he said and handed the tablet back. The crewman bowed slightly and merged into the crowd.

Kate removed her helmet. The intense commotion that filled the room exploded in her ears. After six hours in the calm, quiet confines of her suit, the crash of urgent, overlapping conversations jarred her with an aural assault.

"The most recent estimates have the first wave of soldiers from that strike team landing in twenty-seven hours," said Anand. "I want you and your crew off the ground long before that happens. With you arriving on Earth a few hours prior, there's a chance you can stop this thing before it even starts."

The trip to the moonbase had given Kate time to consider the plan to travel to Earth in the emergency pods. She needed to—

Jack slid into place next to Anand, having left the rover party soon after they'd all entered the chamber. The sleek, black space suit shimmered under the gentle sunlight streaming in from above. A tap of the suit's wrist-bound control panel popped seals around the neck. Black hands grasped the helmet and lifted.

Kate gawked at Jack in an obvious mix of confusion and bewilderment.

"You haven't had a formal introduction," said Anand. "Commander Holman, please meet Lieutenant Bremmer."

The lieutenant, sporting reddish, short hair and green eyes, smiled with an outstretched hand. "It's a pleasure."

Kate shook hands, still confused. "You're … Jack?"

"Jack, or Jacqueline, if you must," she said, "though that's what my mother called me, especially when I was a bad little girl. I much prefer the former."

"Jack here is my trusty right hand," said Anand with a hint of pride. "I'd be dead in the water without her."

"How do you do," said Kate, stifling her lingering shock. Not that she couldn't imagine a woman as the commander's trusted lieutenant, but rather her internal image of Jack was wholly incompatible with the actual person. That false image would take time to dispel.

The second rover's party, containing the bulk of the *Ares* crew, arrived in the chamber. With a quick look and hand signal, Kate instructed Glenn to keep back. Their next stop would be the emergency pods, but she wanted to discuss the logistics with Anand before briefing her people. Glenn ushered them off to the side. They stopped in front of a large screen that looped schematics of the moonbase's various floors, from the topside hub-and-spoke central reception area, to personnel quarters and storage rooms four levels below ground.

The third rover's party arrived, Julian and his black-suited handler the first to emerge. Wrists still bound, he followed the directions of his captor, marching to a freight staging area. The astronaut extended a tether from the wall, a leash that prevented cargo sleds from sliding away. He looped the cable around Julian's breather pack and winched in the slack. Unable to reach behind and free himself, Julian remained locked in place. The black-clad astronaut left the Space Force captain securely hitched.

The final two astronauts from the third rover entered the chamber, lugging tan sacks. Familiar sacks … the two Julian had removed from the *Gaia*, filled with a portion of his planned, golden retirement. The pair traversed the space, weaving between bodies in their bulky suits. They beelined towards a nearby, off-shooting corridor.

"Where are they headed with those sacks?" asked Anand. He'd apparently spotted the two astronauts' arrival, and posed the question to the one person he knew would have the answer.

"To the Geology lab for analysis," said Jack.

Anand was about to explode. "I asked her to," said Kate quickly. She didn't want Jack taking the heat for something she'd initiated. "Who knows what—"

"We'll learn?" interrupted Anand. "It's a colossal waste of time. There's nothing in those bags that can help our situation. They either prove there's gold on Mars, which is what we're assuming, or that it's a worthless pile of pyrite or some such. I don't see Captain Space Force having made a mistake of such magnitude, but it doesn't matter. With the tale Pearson told about the Mars mission, they're fully invested in their narrative, gold or no." Anand's eyes smoldered beneath the shadow of his brows. "There's no information we can squeeze from those bags that will stop the Space Force from coming for us. We need to get you and your crew to the emergency pods."

"About that," said Kate, working to recover from the tirade. "I … it's hard to imagine leaving while you're all here fighting for your lives."

"We do what we have to, Commander," said Anand. "You convinced me that getting your people back to Earth is our only hope of ending this thing."

"We don't all have to go," said Kate. "Any one of us showing up on Earth is enough to accomplish that mission."

"You're thinking of going by yourself?"

Kate bristled at the suggestion she'd leave her crew behind. "Someone else, other than me. Or more than one of us—them. I mean, anyone from my crew who wants to head to Earth can go; it's just that … I won't be among them. I'd rather stay and help, if I can."

"That's certainly a kind offer, Commander Holman, but if I were in your shoes, I'm not sure I'd make the same decision," said Anand.

"Yes, you would."

Anand came alive at the comment, fixing his fiery gaze on Kate. An eternity ticked by under the wilting intensity of his stare, like being caught in the sun's rays through a magnifier. She resisted the urge to shy away.

At last, his face softened. "You're right," said Anand. "I would." He paused, as if considering his words. "Yes, I would."

Kate nodded. "We take care of our own."

Anand clasped her shoulder, his firm grip penetrating the thick layers of her space suit. "We do," he said. "And we'll appreciate the help. Once we have a plan, that is. Let me know who of you is staying behind, and I'll put you all to work. But remember, tell whoever you send that the trip won't be anything like traveling on a rocket. It's not like anything you've ever trained for."

"Yes, sir," said Kate. She saluted. Saluted? Her hand flew up before she could think. She'd impulsively flashed Fisk's improper affectation. It somehow suited the moment.

Commander Praviraj Anand, King of the Moon, saluted back. He spun on his heels and struck off into the bedlam, the black-clad Jack in tow.

Kate kept her eyes on Anand until he disappeared into the crowd, then ventured towards the *Ares* astronauts. They hadn't moved from their spot near the large monitor. Glenn, Miriam, Engles, Fisk, and Palmer all stood clutching their helmets as they watched her approach.

"They call this place 'Moonbeam Village,'" said Fisk on her arrival, "but with all the chaos, a better name would be Moonstruck Madness."

"Right now, Anand has them running a drill," said Kate. "It's how they'd prepare for a meteoroid strike."

"When does the Space Force arrive?" asked Miriam.

"They estimate about twenty-seven hours before the first soldiers land." Not a lot of time. And every second their desperate mission wasn't underway was another second longer the assault would last. "Anand told me there's a way for us to leave the Moon and head for Earth."

"That's fantastic!" exclaimed Fisk from a circle of relieved faces. "They have a spare rocket?"

"Emergency pods," said Kate. "It's their system for evacuating moonbase staff in case of a problem. From what he told me, you climb inside, and a day later you're walking on Earth."

"Honestly, this is the best news we've had in a long time," said an excited Glenn. "They have an extra pod for us to use?"

Kate hesitated. "No one else is leaving." A pall fell over the group, like the sudden drop of a heavy curtain in a sunlit room. "According to Anand, one or two pods can evade radar detection, but enough pods in the sky to evacuate the moonbase would turn into a turkey shoot."

"They're all staying behind." Glenn's voice trailed off, Kate's second-in-command suddenly subdued.

"Staying behind to wait out the assault," Kate added. "Once we're on the ground, we'll need to move quickly to end it."

Glenn's jaw tensed. "I wouldn't feel right leaving them behind." He stood straight, stiffening as if with resolve. "You and the rest can go, Commander. I'll stay here."

"I don't want to leave either," said Palmer. "Unfortunately, odds seem good they could use a spare doctor."

"How many people do these pods seat?" asked Fisk. "Can the remaining four of us fit into one?"

"Three of you," said Kate, hesitating again. "I ... I'm not going, either."

Engles folded her arms. "I'm staying."

Miriam spoke last. "If the rest of you aren't leaving, I won't feel right to go."

Fisk looked around the circle. "I guess it's only me, then."

"No," blurted Kate, "you can't go alone. Miriam, Engles, I want you to go with him."

"Respectfully, Commander, I should be here at the moonbase," said Engles. "They can definitely use an extra engineer. If anything, it should be Fisk, Miriam, and you."

"I can't," said Kate. "It'll feel too much like ... like the captain abandoning ship." Abandoning ship after setting it afire—their detour to the Moon was the whole reason for the Space Force assault.

Miriam turned an extra shade of pale.

"I need you to go," said Kate before Miriam could get a word out. "We can't entrust Fisk with all our lives." Commander Holman grinned and winked at the research scientist, quickly cutting off his expected, vocal objection to the comment.

Fisk laughed along with her. "I'd welcome the company. I've been the hero enough times on this trip that I don't mind sharing the spotlight."

Kate had played her comment off as a joke, but she was dead serious about not sending Fisk by himself. They couldn't leave their futures, theirs and those of the moonbase astronauts, to the erratic inclinations of Dr. Clayton Fisk. The research scientist was too far off the deep end to embark on such an important mission alone.

"Maybe Glenn can come?" asked Miriam.

Kate reflexively eyed Commander Wiles. He'd resembled death warmed over at the Outpost. The six hours of travel seemed to have drained him more. He was conscious, but from his appearance, it wasn't clear how.

Glenn ignored the suggestion. "I prefer to stay, Commander."

Kate's preference as well. Not twelve hours before, he'd been in a coma. A medical emergency in the pod would be disastrous. "Maybe, Doctor Palmer, you'd reconsider—"

"No, that won't help," blurted Miriam, the former Mars station chief agitated. "I …."

"What is it?" asked Kate.

Miriam looked away, then back with wet eyes.

Kate tugged Miriam by her suit sleeve to a spot out of earshot of the others. "What's wrong?"

"I …." Miriam searched for words. "If you aren't going, and neither is Glenn …. I'm third in command. This mission means life or death for everyone … all of us, plus everyone on the Moon."

"It's just you and Fisk going to Earth. As far as commands go, it'll be a walk in the park."

"That's easy for you to say." Miriam's words tumbled out distressed and angry. "You've been in charge for so long, you don't remember what it was like not to be."

Miriam was right—she *had* forgotten what it was like. Kate's first time in command had been similarly trivial, and terrifying. Her commander, on a critical spacewalk, had tasked her with turning their capsule to shield an access panel from the sun. She only needed to relay the order to their spacecraft's AI co-pilot. Kate froze: her CO no longer inside the capsule placed her fully in charge of the mission. Her hands shook on each key press as she tapped instructions to the navigation computer. She'd never sweated so hard in her life.

"I do remember," said Kate. "And if the me of today could've spoken to my younger self, I'd have told her two things: first, feeling nervous is normal—it's a sign that you care about doing a good job. Recognizing your emotions is important, but don't let them dictate your actions. And second, to always remember that being a leader isn't about having all the answers; it's about knowing how to find them."

Lips pressed thin, Miriam fidgeted. Kate wouldn't let her squirm away. "Back on Mars, I told you you're command material. I also said that when the time came, you'd rise to the occasion. Well, that time is now, Miriam. That time is now. Yes, by rank you'll be in charge, but that already happened once before, when Glenn and I left the HAAB to look for Cheney."

"Julian was still there."

"Did you really think about Julian when Glenn and I were stuck in the storm? No, you didn't—you took charge. Activating those floodlights is the only reason we made it back. That was quick thinking on your part, in a pressure situation, where someone needed to take charge."

Miriam was quiet, the wheels spinning.

"I'm not even sure why you're fretting. All you're going to do is hop into an express elevator and step out to the cameras a day later. About the only thing you'll have to take charge of is the temperature setting inside the pod."

She'd made headway, the station chief's shoulders no longer hunched. "You talk like that's gonna be simple," sniffed Miriam, "but I know how cold Fisk likes it. He thinks it helps slow his aging."

Kate laughed. Her reaction coaxed a smile from Miriam. The commander walked them both back to the rest of the *Ares* crew. "Everyone else is certain they want to stay?"

No one changed their mind.

"OK, then. Miriam's leading the mission to Earth. Fisk is going with her." The plan settled, Kate searched for a sign of Anand. He hadn't left the reception area, but he and his party had progressed towards one of the off-shooting passageways like a gaggle of bees drifting with their queen. "Follow me," she said, and set off for the commander.

On their way to Anand, Kate's parental sixth sense tingled. She peeked behind and found an *Ares* astronaut bolting from the group, striking out for Julian where he still stood tethered to the wall. "Fisk!"

The research scientist ignored her, or more likely didn't hear her call. Fisk drew close to Julian. Seconds ticked. He had to be speaking but she couldn't tell, his back to her and any words inaudible in the din. Julian offered no reaction, only an impassive regard.

"Fisk!" yelled Kate, that time into her suit comm. "This way!" No response. What was that fool doing? Engaging Julian was pointless. The only thing the former security chief deserved was a date with the authorities and punishment for his crimes, neither of which would happen until Miriam and Fisk made it to Earth. "Fi—"

The researcher disengaged from Julian and started back. He looked crazed, the tufts of hair that ringed his crown frazzled from the time in his helmet. His eyes darted, seemingly avoiding the one spot where they finally landed. "Sorry, Commander," said Fisk under her searing glare, "I didn't mean to hold everyone up."

"What were you saying to Julian?"

"Nothing," he said. "I realized we're parting ways and wanted to convey a sense of my esteem for our time working together."

With Fisk returned to the group, Kate resumed her slow plow through the commotion. "We're all set," she said upon reaching Anand, and presented her astronauts. "Station Chief Miriam Sato will lead the mission to Earth. She'll be accompanied by research scientist Professor Clayton Fisk."

Anand clasped Miriam's right hand between his, fixed his eyes on hers, and shook. "Thank you," he said. He repeated the ritual with Fisk. He turned to Kate. "You haven't changed your mind?"

"No. But I'm going to see them off."

"It's better if you don't," said Anand. "I'm about to convene a meeting of my senior staff. If you're staying, I think you should attend. The pods are clear on the other side of the moonbase. By the time you get back, the meeting will be over."

Angst filled Miriam's eyes—Kate guessed she'd hadn't anticipated the mission starting so soon, had been assuming a sendoff, at least. "You'll be fine." The reassurance didn't soften her face. "Can we get someone to walk them there?" she asked Anand.

"I can't spare anyone." He addressed Miriam and Fisk: "It won't be hard for you to find your way. There are interactive guides around every corner."

Anand may have been right, but Kate didn't want them wandering the station alone, definitely not with Miriam in her current state, and Fisk being … well, Fisk. "Doctor Palmer, will you accompany them to the pod launch facility to make sure they get off OK?"

"I'm happy to, Commander."

"This is Doctor Nathaniel Palmer," said Kate to Anand. "He's volunteered to help as well."

"You look familiar," said Anand. "Have we met before?"

"No, sir, I don't think so. I was stationed on the Moon for a couple years, though most of my time was spent at the Outpost."

"Ah, well, welcome back, Doctor Palmer. I wish the circumstances of your return were less fraught." Anand shook his hand. "We're glad to have your help. Once you're back from the pods, report to the MedCenter. I'll tell them to expect you."

"Thank you, sir."

Anand once again turned his attention to the Earth-bounds astronauts. "Best of luck in your voyage, Chief Sato, Professor Fisk."

The two offered a subtle bow, the most either could manage for a response. Even Fisk was rendered speechless in Anand's presence.

"Have a good flight, Miriam." Kate searched for more words, but she'd already said everything the Mars station chief needed to hear.

"Thank you, Commander." The pale, petite station chief stood tall. "OK, then, let's get going." She took off, startling Fisk and Palmer to action. The three merged into the room's bustle, only the doctor's head remaining visible above the fray.

"This is Mission Specialist Laura Engles," said Kate, resuming introductions. "She was our spacecraft engineer."

"At your service, sir," said Engles.

"And Commander Wiles is also staying," said Kate.

"Commander Wiles, thank you. And Specialist Engles, thank you for your help." Anand gave a heartfelt shake to each astronaut's hand and looked them in the eye, expressing his gratitude as he had with Miriam, Fisk, and Palmer. His ritual wasn't for show, the moonbase commander gracious and genuinely appreciative of their volunteering.

"Specialist Engles, I'll get you connected with—" Anand stopped mid-sentence. His expression flipped from cordial to livid. "Jack!" he shouted.

Lieutenant Bremmer emerged from behind Anand.

"What the *hell* is that piece of shit still doing here?" Anand seemingly stared straight at Engles but studied something over her shoulder. Off in the direction of the commander's gaze stood Julian at his hitch along the wall. The former security chief looked their way but apparently without recognition, perhaps lost in deep thought.

"Stow that trash down with the rest of the garbage," growled Anand, barely in control of his bubbling fury.

"Yes, sir," said Jack. She marched off across the room.

"Commander Holman, Commander Wiles, follow me to Lunar Command. Specialist Engles, we'll drop you at Engineering along the way."

45

Julian leaned forward, testing the strength of the tether that held him fast to the wall. Solid. Even if he could work himself loose, his hands were tied at the wrists.

He paused his escape efforts just as the *Ares* astronauts set out across the grand reception space. They appeared headed for Anand, where the moonbase commander barked orders to members of his entourage. Kate, Miriam, Engles, Palmer, Fisk—each strolled along, oblivious to his gaze. The five wove their way through the room of scurrying field mice, their brethren panicked at the approach of a rattler.

Kate and the rest would be scurrying soon, too, no longer chuckling over their prank. The eighth empty seat, the one next to his in the rover, contained two sacks filled to the brim … *his* sacks, the remaining portion of his retirement, gathered on his own from Mars. Once the Space Force subdued the moonbase and eliminated its astronauts, he'd planned to swing back to the *Gaia* landing site and recover his bounty. Somehow, the bags had already been retrieved. He'd been made to sit beside them for the whole six-hour drive from the Outpost. Who knew where they'd taken his money. He'd have to go searching for it after the assault ended.

Fisk's head turned. The moronic researcher grinned and gestured … was he really …? He was: flipping him off. How he'd love to choke the life out of the bastard. Though bound, his hands had enough play to clasp a neck. If only Fisk were closer ….

As if reading his mind, Fisk broke from the group and struck out towards him. *That's it, little bird, come this way ….*

Fisk was an idiot, but not stupid enough to get too near. He remained just out of reach. "I was wondering if you got my message," he said. "I was so far away, you may not have heard it." He gave Julian the finger again.

"Fisk!" The hail came from the neckline of the researcher's suit. "This way!"

"See you later, jack-off," said Fisk. "I'll always cherish the initial misconceptions I had about you. You'll be in my thoughts while I'm sipping margaritas with Miriam in a beach-side cabana—not!" He raised both middle fingers, grinned anew, and left.

Fisk rejoined the others, and the entire party resumed its slow trek towards Anand. Kate spoke briefly to the moonbase commander, presented Miriam and Fisk. Anand shook hands with each one. An exchange of words, a shake of Palmer's hand. Miriam, Fisk, and the doctor headed off into the crowd.

The interaction with Anand had been odd, beyond a simple introduction. The moonbase commander had been *grateful*. To Miriam, Palmer, *and* Fisk, of all people. And then the three split off from the others. Where would they be off to, Fisk and Miriam and Palmer ...? What had Fisk said? Sipping margaritas with Miriam ... on a beach .... That brief meeting with Anand was more than Kate introducing her crew ... it was a *sendoff*. The three were leaving ... leaving for Earth. That's all it could be. Leaving before the strike team's arrival. Any of them making it planet-side would unravel the whole

—

"Time to go."

Someone had approached while his mind whirred. An astronaut, black-clad. A woman in a stealth suit. Attractive, with reddish hair and captivating green eyes. The suit hid most of her curves but revealed enough.

The woman unfastened the cable that had anchored him, letting it retract into the wall. She stepped back and waved her gun, motioning for him to move.

"Where are we going?" asked Julian.

"Anand told me to take out the trash," she said. She gestured again with the gun. "This way."

"Jail?" asked Julian, moving forward.

The woman snorted. "We don't have a jail here on the Moon."

Of course they didn't. Boy Scouts wouldn't need a jail. "The room where they stick you astro-nots for your time-outs, then?"

"It's a makeshift detention area," she said. "I've taken to calling it the 'roach motel.' That's because it's where we're collecting all you Space Farce cockroaches."

The woman ushered Julian down a passageway, a refuge from the bustle of the central reception area. Snatches of a Lunar mountain chain appeared in the passing windows. In not too much time, the chaos that reigned within the moonbase would also play out on the surface, his brethren sweeping across the plains, perhaps from those exact mountains. She wouldn't be making cockroach jokes then.

Julian and the woman moved into a waiting elevator cab. His black-suited captor pressed the key for the lowest level. The doors closed and they descended, apparently on their way to the bowels of the station.

The elevator progressed at a glacial pace. "At this rate, we'll have to stop for dinner before we get to the bottom," said Julian.

"Lunar elevators move slower than the ones on Earth," said his captor. "If it went much faster, we might end up floating in the lower gravity."

The black-clad astronaut stood radiant in the bright light of the elevator cab. "So, you're a woman."

"What was your first clue?"

"You don't belong in that suit," said Julian. "First of all, it doesn't do your body justice. And second, the Space Force admits women, but we don't allow them in combat roles. You'd never peel back a stealth suit and find a woman inside."

"How antediluvian."

"It's perfectly logical, really. Women are the child bearers, the child rearers. As such, they have a degree of empathy that's not ... helpful on the battlefield." The woman escorting him to his cell was different, however. Attractive, but with a soldier's air about her. "My name's Julian." He raised his hand to shake—both arms went up, his wrists still connected. She ignored him, despite a flash of his winning smile. "And you are?"

"We've already met."

"We couldn't have," said Julian. "I would never forget someone like you."

"I'm sure you haven't, not after I shot you," she said, waggling the gun.

The smile that evaporated from Julian's face reemerged on the woman's. He choked out the words, "*You're* the soldier ... astronaut ... you're Jack? From the Outpost?" The astronaut who had masqueraded as a Guardian, who had ordered him around, and *shot* him, that was ... her, a *woman*?

The elevator opened. Jack prodded him down a dimly lit corridor with closed, metal doors every two meters. Storage rooms, no doubt. Fifteen meters ahead, an astronaut sat on a folding chair, head buried in a tablet. He looked up once they reached his position. He had a large build—not fat, but possessing a wide frame—with tousled hair and chubby cheeks.

The man gave Jack a double take, then quickly rose, cluing in to who had arrived.

"Anand wants him with the others," said Jack.

"Yes, ma'am."

Jack motioned for Julian's hands. He elevated them, and she snipped the zip tie that bound his wrists. "Strip off the suit," she said.

Julian feigned massaging his wrists as he gauged the situation. Hands free, he could take the large man. Jack would be a bigger problem. Besides her weapon, she clearly showed adeptness on her feet. He had no choice but to continue playing along.

"I said strip."

"If you'd wanted to see me naked, all you had to do was ask."

"The only thing I'm attracted to right now is the idea of you keeping your mouth shut," said Jack. "Strip down to your thermals."

Julian undid the clasps and loosened the seals that secured the joints of his space suit, pulling off gloves, sleeves, and finally the torso. Stepping clear of the pants, he stood before her in the inner thermal layer, a set of thick, long underwear laced with tubes for heating and cooling. He spread his arms, allowing the lieutenant's eyes to feast on his muscular curves, accentuated by the form-fitting garment. "Satisfied?" he asked, adjusting the full pouch at his crotch. She seemed to survey his physique. *That's right, drink it in.*

"There's an old saying about how men are like parking spots," said Jack. "All the good ones are taken, and the rest are either too small or handicapped." The stocky astronaut chuckled at the remark.

Julian's mood soured. He didn't like being the butt of a joke.

"Open 'er up," said Jack.

The astronaut guard waved a keycard near a reader and opened the door. It revealed a compact, poorly lit room filled with boxes and metal cabinets.

"If you're lucky, we won't totally forget about you in there," said Jack.

The guard laughed. "Roaches go in, but they don't come out."

Julian stepped into the room and turned, facing her. The episode harked back to Mars, to Kate locking him in his cell. His blood boiled. He'd been humiliated, pushed around by that woman Jack. The capper was being confined to a closet while all that mattered would happen elsewhere. He wanted to scream, to go berserk, but doing so would accomplish nothing. He could only bide his time and pray for an opportunity.

He forced a smile, working hard not to let them know they'd gotten to him. Best to appear jovial. "What about room service?" His joke landed flat, delivered with an inadvertent sneer.

"In the roach motel, it's more like 'broom service.'" Jack placed her palm flat on his chest and shoved him into the room. "Enjoy your stay, asshole." She pulled the door shut.

46

Julian tested the door—it wouldn't budge, and turning its handle did nothing. A keycard reader hung on the wall nearby but displayed no buttons for an override.

The stocky guard's chubby face filled the door's small window. He'd apparently heard Julian's efforts. He looked at the Space Force captain, scanned the recesses of the room, then disappeared.

When the Space Force arrived, they would have one task in mind: eliminate the astronauts. Trapped in the storeroom, he'd become a casualty of the onslaught, a case of collateral damage. He needed to escape if he hoped to survive.

"Captain Grimes?"

Julian wheeled around. On the opposite side of the small room, two men stared at him, one seated on a box and the other on the floor. They'd been invisible in the gloom.

"It's Captain Grimes, isn't it?" asked the man on the floor.

"That's correct," said Julian, stepping forward.

"I'm Specialist One Rodriguez," the man continued. Really more of a boy, all of twenty-five years, if that. The starry-eyed Guardian shuffled to his feet. "And this is Second Lieutenant Kielczewski." Kielczewski offered a feeble twitch of his hand. He was quiet, cautious, obviously disciplined in studying a scenario before taking any course of action.

"You're the two they captured?" asked Julian. "The ones whose suits they confiscated?"

"Affirmative, sir," said Rodriguez. "We'd been stationed here at the moonbase, posing as astronauts while we collected intel."

Moles. The Space Force had operatives everywhere. No telling when an asset in the field might prove useful. Julian's stomach tightened: somehow the assets knew his name, though he'd never met either one before. "You know who I am?"

"Also affirmative, sir," said Rodriguez. "We recently received orders to assist the incoming assault team. Those orders included instructions to keep an eye out for you."

Had he been marked for termination?

"We were told to assist you in any way necessary," he added. "Rumor has it that directive came straight from the AD."

A relief. He hadn't been flagged as a liability, at least not yet. "Were you also briefed on the situation with the *Ares* mission crew?" asked Grimes. "The elimination order?"

"Yes, sir," said Rodriguez. "We're in the dark as to exactly what intel they have, but should we encounter them, we're to prevent the dissemination of said information."

"At all costs," said Julian.

"Yes, sir, at all costs."

Grimes's gaze landed on Kielczewski. The lieutenant emitted a weak, "Yes, at all costs."

Good. They acknowledged the stakes, and that the Space Force expected results. "Unfortunately, members of the *Ares* mission crew are this minute executing a plan to deliver that intel to operatives on Earth. It is imperative that I get out of here and stop them." He advanced farther into the room. "What would you say is the most important asset each of you would bring to that effort?"

"Sir?" replied Rodriguez.

"Your value, Guardian," said Grimes. "Or are you both worthless? What's the most important skill, ability, *anything* you can contribute to stopping them?" His focus returned to Kielczewski. "You, Lieutenant Kuewl—I won't even attempt it. What do you bring to the table?"

Kielczewski shifted uncomfortably on his box. "I'm a communications officer, and the designated quartermaster for this Space Force assignment."

Grimes turned to Rodriguez. "How about you, Specialist One?"

Rodriguez brought himself to attention and saluted. "Sir, I'm ready and able to get things done."

"So ... a grunt, then."

"Er ... yes, sir."

"A workhorse."

"Yes, sir."

"Prepared, in a moment, to take on any heavy lifting."

"Yes, sir!"

Grimes studied the soldier. Rodriguez was enthusiastic, but dumb as a rock. His muscular build would give him strength in a brawl, but the way he carried himself suggested limited training in leveraging that strength. "The world needs workhorses," said the Space Force captain. "I imagine the brass back home would say the lieutenant, here, is the brains of this operation. But the truth is, Specialist One Rodriguez, between the two of you, *you're* the one best suited to helping me get out of here."

Rodriguez beamed. "Thank you, sir."

"At ease," said Julian. Rodriguez relaxed. "Have you ever escaped from a facility?"

"No, sir," said Rodriguez. "Never been caught before."

"The trick is in creating a diversion," said Grimes. "Especially one that exploits your captor's weaknesses."

"I can tell you that Dumbo outside has a weakness for candy bars," said Rodriguez with a chuckle.

Grimes smiled. "Unless there's a box of those bars in here, I don't think that will help us."

"What else do we have?" asked Rodriguez.

"One thing you've probably noticed about our astro-not hosts is these Boy Scouts are always ready to lend a hand."

Rodriguez grinned and nodded, but the grin soon faded. "I'm not sure I follow you, sir."

Grimes stepped to Rodriguez. "Here, I'll show you what I mean. Turn around and face the wall."

Rodriguez complied.

In a quick motion, Grimes reached his arm around Specialist One Rodriguez's neck, locking it in the crook of his elbow. Rodriguez's arms flailed and his hands clawed backwards, fumbling for any portion of the Space Force captain. Grimes fended off the volley with his free hand.

Second Lieutenant Kielczewski sprang from his box but froze, apparently unsure what to do. He watched as Grimes squeezed Rodriguez's neck tighter.

Rodriguez's flails and protests grew weaker, then subsided. His arms and legs went limp. The Space Force captain lowered the man to the floor.

"Is he ... dead?" asked Kielczewski.

"No, just unconscious." A good start, but they'd need something a bit more dramatic. Grimes crouched and karate-chopped Rodriguez's windpipe. The man's legs flew up, fell, and spasmed. His breathing, previously inaudible, became rough and constricted.

Grimes sprinted to the door and pounded. "Help! Help! Medical emergency! This man can't breathe!"

The guard's face reappeared in the door's small window. Grimes's frantic gestures directed him to Rodriguez, attended on the floor by Kielczewski. "He's having trouble breathing," he shouted.

"Move back from the door," ordered the guard.

The Space Force captain complied. The door swung open, admitting the stocky astronaut.

"We were talking when he collapsed," said Grimes, pointing to his distressed colleague. Rodriguez's rasps carried across the room. "He's not breathing right."

The guard lumbered to Rodriguez and settled onto his knees. "Give me some space." Kielczewski moved away. He grabbed Rodriguez's head, tilted it back, and checked his mouth for an obstruction.

Grimes, silent and lightning fast, slipped behind the guard. Fingers interlocked, he hoisted his combined fist and hammered it down on the guard's head.

The man should have crumpled. Instead, he stood and faced Grimes. The guard was a large man, muscular. The blow that should have knocked him out only angered the astronaut. He lunged with his right hand. The Space Force captain dashed left, evading the man's grasp, but took a glancing left hook to his jaw.

The world flashed stars, but Grimes didn't pass out. He ducked, dodging a right hook, but absorbed the full brunt of a left fist to the back of his head. The stroke sent him to the floor. He curled into the fetal position. Using his left arm, he shielded his head from a frenzy of strikes while his right hand fished at his ankle.

Grimes feigned convulsions, tricking the astronaut into pausing his barrage. The Space Force captain spat in the man's face. The unexpected move surprised the guard long enough for Grimes to roll away and onto his feet.

Enraged, the guard came forward. Grimes raised his left arm, deflecting the incoming blows. The astronaut seized his wrist and pinned the Space Force captain's shoulder with his other hand.

Grimes brought his right arm up and into the man's fully exposed midsection.

The guard cried out. He danced backwards as he bunched his hands at his belly. Grimes danced with him, keeping the big man close as he twisted his shiv in the astronaut's gut.

The man shook free. Face pained and pale, he staggered two steps to the door and crumpled. His arms flopped on the floor, hands bright red as if covered in a child's finger paints.

Blood also covered Grimes's hand. He wiped it on the fallen man's leg, then cleaned his shiv and returned it to his ankle. Grimes stood, catching the terrified expression on Second Lieutenant Kielczewski's face. "Does this moonbase have a standby rocket?"

Second Lieutenant Kielczewski, reeling with the entirety of what had transpired, said nothing.

"Second Lieutenant?" said Grimes.

"Huh?"

"Is there a standby rocket at this facility?"

Kielczewski, still in shock, massaged his face with his hand. His eyes darted between the two downed men.

The Space Force captain approached Kielczewski and seized his shoulders. The lieutenant flinched at his touch. Grimes gave him a firm shake. "How do astronauts get off the Moon?"

Kielczewski's features twisted in horror, but he eventually calmed enough to respond. "Deployments are scheduled six months in advance," he stammered. "When a new group of astronauts arrives, another group leaves. They take the rocket back to Earth."

"What about unscheduled travel?" asked Grimes.

He thought a moment. "There are weekly supply runs. People will sometimes hitch a ride, here or back. But they don't always have space."

"When's the next cargo run?"

"The last one left three days ago," said Kielczewski.

Grimes shook the lieutenant again. "Think, man! If you needed to get off the Moon right now, how would you do it?"

"There isn't a way," said Kielczewski.

"So if you all ran out of air, or a level-five coronal mass ejection was on its way, everyone would die up here?"

"There are the emergency pods," said Kielczewski. "But those are only for … well … emergencies."

Grimes released the lieutenant. "That must be their plan." He'd have to get to the pods quickly, and without drawing notice. That would require something other than his thermals, a change of clothes …. He knelt at the guard and rolled the man onto his back. Blood soaked the center of his outfit —he needed another option.

The Space Force captain headed to Rodriguez, where he still lay on the floor. He'd have to use the man's jumpsuit, though it was clearly too small. Grimes unzipped the front and worked to free the Guardian's arms. "How do I get to the pods?" he asked Kielczewski. "Preferably a less-traveled route."

"You'll want to stay on the lower levels as long as you can," said Kielczewski, recovered a bit from his shock. "Take an elevator to the topside only once you're on the opposite end of the base from here." He followed Grimes's efforts to disrobe Rodriguez with a baffled expression. "If I may, sir, wouldn't a stealth suit be better?"

Grimes bore into Kielczewski with a piercing glare. "Of *course* that would be better, Lieutenant, but your suits have been confiscated. That astronaut Jack has been parading around in one of them. There's a second astronaut using the other."

"That's … correct, sir," sputtered Kielczewski, shaken by Grimes's retort. "But as I said, I'm the designated quartermaster here. I manage a cache of supplies …. There are extra suits … in case they post additional Guardians at the station."

Spare stealth suits? That was better luck than he could have imagined. Grimes shot to his feet. "Take me to them."

47

Kate and Glenn followed Anand's entourage on its slow procession. Members of the group peeled off as it advanced deeper into the station, until only the moonbase commander and the two *Ares* astronauts remained.

The three proceeded down a stairwell after an impatient Anand balked at waiting for an elevator. They walked a long passageway, zipped through a security checkpoint, and filed into a large meeting room. An oblong table nestled beneath a low ceiling, and wide computer screens adorned the white walls. They'd entered the "War Room," as Anand had referred to it several times along the way.

Six astronauts chatted at the table, four of them seated. The four rose on Anand's entry, and the room grew immediately hushed.

"Take your seats," said Anand, shuffling to the far end. He still wore his space suit, though an aide had long ago taken his helmet.

Kate and Glenn grabbed chairs at the end nearest the door as the others settled into theirs.

"Let's begin," said Anand. "We have some guests today. Before I introduce them, I'd like to go around the table with intros. Atkinson, you go first."

"Mission Specialist Atkinson, Ops."

"Dr. Robinson, Medical."

"I'm Dr. Patel, head of the Science Department."

"Specialist Delaney, Engineering."

"Specialist Baker, Communications."

"Lieutenant Turro, Security and Safety."

The circle of introductions returned to where it started. Anand gestured towards the two guests. "Joining us today are Commander Kate Holman and her second-in-command, Commander Glenn Wiles. They're both from the *Ares* mission."

Murmurs erupted in the room.

"The last report was the *Gaia* capsule had exploded," said comm specialist Baker.

"Not true," said Anand. "These two, and five others, are the living proof."

The door slid open, admitting Jack in her black stealth suit. She quickly slipped into the empty seat next to Anand.

"None of what you're saying makes any sense," said Atkinson from Ops. "If NASA thought the *Gaia* exploded but that wasn't the case, why didn't Commander Holman and her crew inform them otherwise? Why didn't they proceed with the splashdown on Earth?"

"Because the *Gaia* was being targeted for elimination," said Anand. The declaration elicited even more murmurs—he brought his hands up for silence. "Our friends from the Ares mission stumbled onto a secret during their brief time on Mars, a secret so explosive, the powers that be don't want it to get out and are willing to kill to prevent it. Obviously, they failed. Those incoming ships are Space Force, transports for an assault team being sent to finish the job."

"You know how crazy everything you said sounds?" asked Security Officer Turro. "And why would they send three ships of soldiers to take out seven people?"

"The math's a little different, I'm afraid," said Anand. "They know they failed to destroy the *Gaia*, and that it was headed here. They're now assuming everyone at the moonbase knows this secret. Those three ships of soldiers are coming to kill every living person on the Moon."

Anand's statement plunged the room into a dead quiet that burst into chaos, like the implosion at the center of a nuclear device before the outward blast of destruction. He signaled again for quiet.

Dr. Robinson, head of the medical center, raised his hand. "You're telling us that someone has ordered what amounts to a hit on the *Ares* crew, as well as everyone, all seventy-plus astronauts and staff, on the Moon?"

"That's right," said Anand.

"Well, I don't believe it," said Robinson amid a chorus of steadily rising murmurs. "I can't believe it."

"Believe it," said Lieutenant Bremmer. "One of the members of the Ares mission turned out to be a Space Force captain. He was in charge of clandestine operations on the red planet—"

"He can corroborate all this?" asked a skeptical Atkinson.

"He has," said Kate.

"What was this big secret?" asked Lieutenant Turro. "A secret so significant they want to kill anyone who knows about it?"

Anand motioned to Commander Holman.

"They found gold on Mars, trillions of dollars' worth. The Space Force and several of the spy agencies want to secretly use that gold to fund their operations."

"Have you seen this gold?" asked Dr. Patel, the science chief.

"That Space Force captain brought some back," said Jack. "We're testing it now, but I can confirm it's the real deal."

"Our one hope for defusing this situation is exposing their plans for the gold, exposing the conspiracy," said Kate. "As long as it's a secret, they'll do whatever they can to keep it that way. But once the world knows, killing more people than they already have will just make the situation worse for them back home."

"We've lost all comms with NASA," said Baker. "There's no getting a message back to Earth."

"Even if we could," she sighed, "they'd claim it was a hoax. Instead, we're sending a small team in an emergency pod. When they land, they'll reveal the truth about the gold, the conspiracy, all of it."

"Given the transit time for a pod, and the ETA of the Space Force armada, there's a chance this could all be over before it starts," said Anand. "But if, for some reason, we need to buy more time, Jack's been researching Space Force methods and tactics. She has a proposed plan of action. I hand the floor to Jack."

A computer screen came to life with photographs of a sleek, black rocket: on a launch pad, in orbit over Earth, and against the void of space. Lieutenant Bremmer moved to the monitor's edge. "These heavy-lift, rapid-response rockets contain ten soldiers apiece. Each Guardian will be equipped with a stealth suit and a weapon. The rockets—"

"Just shut down the landing pad," interrupted Engineering Chief Delaney. "Move the rovers and other equipment into the center. No way they'll be able to land."

"They don't plan to land on the pad," said Jack.

Several in the room openly laughed.

"Bringing those big birds down anywhere else will kick up so much dust, they won't be able to open their hatches for days," said Delaney. "Or, if they're stupid enough to come out before it all settles back to the ground, they won't be flying home in *those* rockets. They'll be ruined, with all the grit in the cabin worked into every gear, intake, and crevice."

"Nothing says 'oops' like turning your high-tech spacecraft into a fancy, black litterbox," said Atkinson, eliciting chuckles.

"That's not how the Space Force operates," said Jack. "Landing a rocket leaves it vulnerable to attack. You'd have to use some of the soldiers you flew all the way from Earth to guard it, to say nothing of trying to protect it from missiles and other projectiles. Instead, they'll keep their rockets in orbit, where they'll be reasonably safe, certainly safe from us."

"What, they'll drop down in a capsule?" asked Turro. "Hope they brought a big enough parachute."

Chuckles rippled around the room.

"What does he mean?" whispered Glenn. "A chute can't work on the Moon—it doesn't have an atmosphere."

"I think that's the joke," whispered Kate.

Jack waited for the snickers to subside. "Each soldier gets a single-use jet pack," she said. "They'll all jump from the rocket like paratroopers."

Her comment set off a fresh round of murmurs.

"Let her continue," shouted Anand, quieting the room.

"That's how they'll arrive here," said Jack. "But tactically, the moonbase presents a problem for our friends in the Space Force. The base was constructed on Oceanus Procellarum, a relatively flat patch of Lunar terrain. There are no mountains or craters nearby, and the largest dorsal ridge is fifty kilometers away. That means approaching the moonbase will require them to walk out in the open."

"You said they'll have stealth suits. They'll be invisible." The comment came from Atkinson.

"They will, but not their bootprints," said Jack. "That'll be our first clue they're coming." Jack switched the computer screen to a schematic of the base. "Our problem is our three airlocks," she continued, referring to the three red circles on the diagram. "They force us to defend three separate points of entry. We have to narrow that down. We do it by bulldozing dirt and rocks against Airlocks B and C. That'll leave the main one as their only way in.

"As for fortifying Airlock A, I brought back some blasting caps from the Old Mine. We'll bury them outside the main airlock. When the soldiers approach, we detonate one of the caps and send dust flying; perhaps even stun a few of them in the process. Hopefully, they fall back and wait for things to settle. Maybe they have to rethink their entry plan. That will get us some of the time we need."

"That assumes they don't ignore the dust and continue trying to breach," said Turro.

Jack nodded. "We have three blasting caps, so three chances to throw them off. But no matter what happens, they'll eventually come knocking. We can't secure the airlock—it's not designed to keep people out, and anyway, they'll have the override codes."

"We could weld it shut," said Atkinson.

"That would probably stop them," said Jack. "Problem is, if there's no obvious way inside, they'll be forced to create their own. They'll cut through a bulkhead, blast a hole in a wall—and do it literally anywhere. We'd have no chance of holding them off."

"Our chances aren't great as it is," said Patel. "We don't have weapons."

"We *do* have tools for crowd suppression," said Jack. "In particular, sticky foam. We'll set up inside the Suiting Station. When they enter, we'll deploy the foam for our new guests."

A leaden, expectant pause hung in the room.

"And?" said Turro.

"And that's it," said Jack to a rise of murmurs. "We're outmatched by their stealth suits and weapons. We'll move all personnel not involved in the counteroffensive to the lowest reaches of the station, but frankly, if they get past the foam, it won't take long for them to hunt everyone down, no matter where they are."

"It's not totally true that we have no weapons—what about the two guns from the captured Guardians?" asked Baker.

"I'll be camped out at the Suiting Station with mine," said Jack. "We'll get the second one to another volunteer. We'll target anyone who makes it past the foam, but if they do get that far, my guess is we'll only get a few shots off before they take us out."

The room fell into an eerie quiet, the department heads mulling over the plan.

"That's pretty thin," said Turro, prompting whispers of agreement.

"Remember, this is a back-up plan," said Anand. "If the timing ... goes right, Commander Holman's team ... will have ended the whole thing before—you there!"

Anand shouted to the back of the room, to the person who had entered moments prior. Their hushed conversation with specialist Baker had driven the moonbase commander to distraction. Kate had caught snatches of their discussion: the person arrived with a message for Anand; Baker whispered they might want to come back later; the person insisted it was urgent; Baker pressed for details but implored them to speak softly. Kate missed the reply. Baker had too, and asked the man to repeat it.

"Can't you see we're in the middle of a meeting?" roared Anand.

Baker retreated to her spot at the table, allowing all attention to fall on the newcomer. He was a young man, tall and skinny, with a shock of raven black hair. He appeared flustered as he approached the King of the Moon.

"You're disrupting a meeting of the command staff," said Anand.

The man presented himself to the moonbase commander. His hands shook. "Yes, sir. I'm sorry, sir. It's just I have news, urgent news, that you should—"

"What is it?" Anand bellowed.

"An emergency in the pod bay—someone destroyed the launch console. Three people are dead."

48

"*This* is the corridor we're supposed to take," said Fisk. "The second one on the left."

"I think it was the third."

"It was the second," said Fisk. "I remember as if we were standing in front of the map."

Despite Fisk's insistence he was right, Miriam remained skeptical.

The interactive guides had been simple to operate, as Commander Anand had promised: state a destination, and a glowing trail appeared on top of the base schematic. Problem was, the guides weren't as frequent as he'd suggested. "We could go back and check," said Miriam, looking the way they came.

"And backtrack?" asked Fisk. "That would be a waste of time, especially when we get there and see that it's telling us to take the second corridor, like I keep saying."

Or the third one, like she remembered. Memory was tricky business. She wouldn't claim hers was perfect, but she didn't trust anyone who insisted theirs was. "Any opinion, Doctor Palmer?"

"I'm not great with directions," he said. "If I had to pick, I'd say the second corridor."

"It's settled, then," said Fisk.

"But if he's not great with directions, doesn't that mean we should, at least, discount Doctor Palmer's opinion?" asked Miriam.

"It's two votes to one," said Fisk.

If they're two wrong votes—

"Remember, being a leader isn't about having all the answers, it's about knowing how to find them."

Surprise, followed by swift anger, filled Miriam's face.

Fisk quickly raised his hands in defense while his eyes pleaded forgiveness. "That was the only part I heard of what Commander Holman told you …. Well, that and how you would rise to the occasion. Which I don't disagree. You're off to a fantastic—"

"Fine," hissed Miriam in disgust. "We'll go your way."

"It's not *my* way, it's the *right* way." Fisk started forward, leading the others down the corridor.

- - -

"I'm sorry, I'm sorry," bleated Fisk, struggling to keep up under the bulk of his space suit and Miriam's torrid pace.

Miriam simmered. Fisk had been wrong about the second passageway—the correct one had been the third, as she'd believed. At the end of the long second corridor, they'd arrived at the base's fusion power plant, not the pod launch facility. A ten-minute mistake ... make that twenty, counting the time to walk back to the entrance. Miriam couldn't be totally angry with Fisk. She'd made the final decision, after all. Should a similar situation arise in the future, however, she'd go with her intuition first.

Spilling into the main corridor, Miriam led them eight meters to the third passageway. After a further ten minutes of walking, they reached the emergency pods. They entered the control room, long and open at either end. A tall set of windows stretched its length, overlooking a gallery of ten circular hatches, all closed. The room's transparent ceiling offered a spectacular view of Earth.

Centered beneath the windows, an expansive touchscreen glowed with a symphony of flashing lights, throbbing buttons, and animated charts. Dr. Palmer took in the spectacle—his jaw dropped slightly. "Do you know what to make of all this?" he asked, clearly overwhelmed.

Miriam studied the panel. She'd navigated so many touchscreens in her career, the sight left her unfazed. The designers would take the credit for her comfort, pointing to their "intuitive" interfaces. In truth, her facility stemmed from a feel for how the designers *thought* such systems should work. The left two-thirds of the dashboard managed the bank of pods and the machinery that queued them for launch. The right third monitored the rail gun and its power levels. She prepped the system, initiating the gun's charging sequence. A graph sprang to life, detailing the progress.

"When I see this many controls, my eyes start to glaze over," said Palmer.

Translation: if she didn't make it dirt simple for him to launch a pod, he'd be there frozen at the touchscreen while they waited to take off. Miriam traced her finger in the air above the left side of the panel, following the control flow. She moved a slider, pressed a slew of buttons, and looked into the pod alley. A middle hatch, the fifth of the ten and previously closed, swung open. Miriam pointed to a large, physical button that sprouted from the console like a cherry red mushroom. "When we're ready, just press this to launch the pod. That's it."

Palmer's consternation appeared to ease. "Seems simple enough," he said.

"In an emergency, who stays behind to launch all the pods?" asked Fisk. "Do they draw lots to decide?"

"The rail gun can only deploy one pod at a time," said Miriam. "In a mass evacuation, one person needs to coordinate the sendoffs. But every pod has its own set of controls. Once everyone else is gone, the operator gets inside the last remaining pod and launches from there."

"Speaking of which," said Dr. Palmer, "let's get you to yours."

The three exited the control center and headed to the open pod door. Miriam stepped through the round, cramped portal, triggering lights alive inside.

"Feels like climbing into a front-loading washer," said Fisk.

She didn't disagree—the small space only accommodated the three seats arrayed around the curved interior. The bulkhead above each one included a darkened porthole. Settling into a chair, Miriam sorted through its multitude of restraints.

Grabbing a seat, Fisk fastened his lap belt. "All set," he said.

"Hardly," said Miriam, reaching for the straps near her legs. "You only clipped your seat belt. There are restraints for your shoulders, your chest, and your shins. Also for your forearms, but you slip into those at the very end. Start from your legs and work up. If it's confusing, just follow what I'm doing."

Fisk fumbled with the straps and harnesses but made gradual progress. "I don't like being restrained like this," he grumbled. "I get claustrophobic."

"You have to for this ride," said Miriam. "These pods take off faster than you can imagine."

Fisk mumbled something inaudible but proceeded to secure his restraints. Palmer stooped with his head poked inside, following their preparations.

Miriam looped her arms through shoulder belts embedded in the seat back and slid her forearms into straps on the chair arms. She wriggled, confirming the snugness of her restraints. "How you doing?" she asked Fisk.

"All set, I think." He squirmed against the legion of belts and straps. "But I'm not happy. This feels just like a straitjacket."

Did he know the feel of a straitjacket? "You won't have to keep like that the whole trip, only for liftoff," she said. "Once we're aloft, you can get out of your seat." She checked her restraints one more time and signaled a thumbs-up to Palmer. "I think we're ready."

Palmer gave a last glance within the cabin. "I'll head back to the control center, then. There'll be a ten-second countdown before I press the button."

"Roger that," said Miriam.

Palmer's head disappeared, soon replaced by grunts drifting in from the corridor.

"Don't worry about the hatch," said Miriam. "All you have to do is press the button. The system will take care of the rest."

The noises ceased. Without another word, Palmer set off for the control room.

Fisk continued to fidget against his restraints. He eventually closed his eyes, which seemed to settle him. He was doing his best to keep it together. She sympathized. What probably felt like medieval torture to Fisk was par for the course with members of the Corps. As a civilian, he'd been subjected to a fraction of the ordeals an astronaut trainee had to endure.

His eyes reopened. "What's taking so long?"

"No idea." Much more time had passed than needed to stroll back to the control room. "Doctor Palmer, you there?" she said into her suit comm.

"You think your suit can transmit through the pod?" asked Fisk.

Unclear, but no response from Palmer either way. Learning more would mean unbuckling and checking on the doctor herself. Miriam sighed and began undoing her restraints. Fisk moved to follow. "No, you stay put. It took so long getting us both strapped in, there's no point in you going through all that again. I'll be right back." She undid the remainder of her straps and left the pod.

Across the narrow corridor sat the launch room's large windows. Palmer should have been there facing her, but no one occupied the space. Where had he gone?

Miriam walked to the entrance and stepped inside. Palmer was there, but on the ground.

"Doctor Palmer?"

Palmer turned over. "Sorry, I knocked my helmet off the console, and it bounced underneath." He stood, clutching his helmet to his side.

All that time to fish a helmet from the ground? "What's taking so long for the launch?" she asked.

"I was having a devil of a time with the comms. After watching you work the console, it seemed like I should've been able to figure it out. Then I switched to my suit comm and realized you couldn't hear me. I was headed to the pod when I bumped my helmet."

"That's OK," said Miriam. "That was the only part we didn't go over."

The doctor apologized, a little embarrassed. "I'll follow you back and help you get strapped in. Then we'll say our goodbyes, and I'll launch the pod."

Light flashed in the control room, with a snap like lightning. A dip in the power? No, the lights hadn't dimmed—the space had gotten briefly brighter.

Palmer's eyes rolled back in his head. He fell to the ground.

"Doctor Palmer!" squeaked Miriam.

"Doctor Palmer is indisposed."

The voice came from the opposite end of the control room, near the other entrance, but no one was present. The words had a synthesized, processed sound, like a robot's. A robot ghost?

Shimmers danced at the far end, taking the shape of a man. A translucent man, becoming opaque, black, the silhouette of a person, like the black figures from the Old Mine .... A man in a stealth suit. With a gun.

The man removed his helmet.

Miriam backed up, stumbling into the console to her rear. "Julian!"

"Where's Fisk?" he asked.

A second knot of shimmers appeared at the near entrance. Another black-suited man materialized, on the other side of Miriam.

"What are you doing here?" asked Julian, annoyed. "I told you to check the pod bay."

"I heard your weapon fire," said the soldier, his voice mechanical. "I wanted to make sure you were OK."

"Of course I'm OK!" snarled Julian. "We're the only ones armed. Get back out there and search those pods."

"Yes, sir."

During the exchange, Miriam's right hand had slipped quietly behind her. It moved slowly across the console, feeling its way along the smooth surface for the one physical button on the entire panel.

A klaxon sounded.

Julian fired his weapon, dropping Miriam to the floor. He rushed to the console. Its diagrams showed an emergency pod, number five, preparing to launch. In the bay, the lone open pod door swung closed.

Where's the abort button? Julian searched the console—too many controls. He stepped back, dialed his weapon to full intensity, and fired. Smoke rose from the unit. Its damaged screen went black.

Another klaxon. Lights inside the control center and the pod alley dimmed for several seconds before returning to normal.

In the sky, a small, silvery ball shot upwards. It traveled at an incredible speed, much faster than any rocket.

Julian watched with pursed lips as the object climbed and disappeared, lost against the backdrop of the sparkling Earth. The emergency pod likely contained Fisk. "I need to get a message to Space Force command."

Lieutenant Kielczewski stared at the smoldering control panel. "There's a communications terminal not far from here."

"Are you thinking with your head on, Lieutenant? The moonbase is still being jammed. The incoming rockets have the only comms that can bypass it."

The rebuff doused the lieutenant's spirits. As he prepared to exit the control room, the two astronauts laid out on the floor drew his eye. He nudged Miriam with his boot—the result surprised him. "She's still alive." He did the same with Dr. Palmer. "This one too."

Yes, only stunned, not dead like the dumb guard and two other astronauts he'd shot on the way to the pods. "I wanted them alive for interrogation." There'd be no opportunity for that. Astronauts would be arriving to investigate the commotion. "We have to move."

"Are we going outside, then?" he asked.

"Negative. We'll find a different location to transmit from inside the base."

"But we'll get out before the attack?"

"We're staying *inside*, Lieutenant—we can do much more here than on the outside." Julian left the control room, secured his helmet, and reengaged his suit's invisibility field. "We've got a lot of work to do. You and I are going to plant listening devices. We'll want to keep tabs on our astro-not friends during the assault."

Kielczewski reactivated his invisibility field. "I'm sorry, sir, I'm confused. When the assault team storms the base, if we're still inside, won't we risk getting caught in the line of fire?"

"That's not how they're going to take this facility, Lieutenant, with guns blazing," said Julian. "That's not how they'll do it at all."

49

"Ahhhhheeeeeeuuuuuuhhhhhh!"

Doctor Clayton Fisk's squeal rose in volume and pitch with each passing second as his emergency pod rocketed through the rail gun tube. He'd been on the verge of releasing his restraints to search for Miriam when the door snapped shut and the pod moved into launch position.

His squeal stopped, but not by choice. The g-forces pancaking him into his chair compressed his chest, emptying his lungs. His vision started to fade ....

As instantly as the acceleration appeared, it ended—no gradual decrease, no warning.

Once again able to inhale, the research scientist gulped air, springing into a series of quick, panicked breaths. He gazed through the portholes above the two other seats as he recovered, each showing a sparkling star field that gradually shifted sideways. The violence of the rail gun had imparted not only the speed to surpass escape velocity, but also a minor amount of rotation. The Moon drifted across the two portholes. Moments later, the brilliant blue Earth chased after it.

Fisk clutched his quaking belly. The shifting stars and dashing orbs saddled him with nausea. His breathing, still fast, deepened his discomfort. The world inside the pod began to spin. His hands tingled.

Black spots filled his vision.

Doctor Clayton Fisk passed out.

- - -

Fisk blinked awake, hours later by the chronometer on the craft's control panel. The Earth still chased a noticeably smaller Moon across the portholes.

The professor sloughed off his restraints and propelled himself from his chair. He quickly put his hands out, cushioning his contact with the bulkhead. He'd overestimated the pod's size—the *Ares* and *Gaia* capsules it was not. He pushed back to the postage stamp of decking and located the pod's temperature controls. The professor dialed in a life-prolonging sixteen degrees Centigrade. Next, he set about exploring the inside of the tiny craft.

Rifling through cabinets, he found orange, inflatable life jackets and a raft; a first aid kit; distress beacons; and a cache of food concentrate pouches with boxes of water. He unsealed one pouch labeled "filet mignon" and squirted a portion onto his finger. "Maybe this was beef in a previous life," he said, touching his tongue to the quivering, brown dollop. *Not bad.* "I've never had to drink my steak before." He raised the pouch as if making a toast. "Bon appétit. Or, I suppose, bottoms up!" He sucked down the entire meal.

Fisk grabbed a box of water and headed to the control panel. The screen displayed his craft's trajectory, an arc receding into the distance as it stretched from the Moon to Earth. Zooming in, he traced the path to its endpoint, a spot off the coast of Florida in the Gulf of Mexico. He'd suspected as much—where else would the pod set down? Problem was, the bad guys would expect that too. A Gulf landing would deliver him right into their hands. He'd figured all that out while waiting for Miriam, had planned on discussing it with her. In her absence, he'd have to make the command decision.

And that decision, Fisk deemed, required a call to his friend in high places—or high latitudes. The Snow Owl nested in northern climes, burrowing in a secure, undisclosed location along the coast of Maine.

Fisk swiped to the controls for radio communication. The system had a preset frequency that he didn't dare use—they'd certainly be listening; however, a virtual knob on the screen allowed him the option to adjust the channel.

What was the number …? Fisk dialed: four six six—no, four six nine point two five megahertz. An unusual frequency, but the one his paranoid friend had forced him to memorize, on the off chance he'd need to reach him. Not that such communication would be possible from deep space, definitely not from Mars. He'd have to be close.

Fisk pressed transmit. "Snow Owl. Snow Owl. Do you copy?"

Low, crackly static filled the cabin.

"Snow Owl, do you read?"

On the verge of another try, "Who is this?" crackled back.

"It's Einstein." The Snow Owl had insisted he choose a handle, lest they communicate using Fisk's real name. He'd selected a peer, or would-be peer, had they lived in the same time period.

"Einstein's dead."

"Of course he is," said Fisk.

A pause. "Then who am I really talking to, and how'd you land on this frequency?"

Seconds passed before Fisk understood the basis of his question. "No, the *real* Einstein is dead, but not me. I'm very much alive. There's a huge conspiracy. They tried to kill everyone from the Mars mission, but they failed. They told the world that—"

"Does the clock tick backwards?"

?

"Does the clock tick backwards?" the crackly voice repeated.

"Only when time remembers." In addition to their radio handles, they'd agreed on a call response. He'd almost forgotten.

"It's good to hear your voice, Einstein," said the Snow Owl. "I was sad to learn you'd met your demise."

"Rumors of my death have been ... they're wrong. I appreciated your help while I was on Mars."

"Where are you now?"

"An emergency pod, halfway between the Earth and the Moon," said Fisk. "It's got a preset destination, but I'm not enthusiastic about who'll be waiting for me when I splash down. I'd much prefer if you could pick me up."

Silence. "Splashdown near me?"

"Correct."

More silence. "You sure you can get here?"

"I'm pretty sure," said Fisk. "I can override the default coordinates with a custom latitude and longitude. As long as it corresponds to a body of water, the computer will accept it. I think I can get pretty close."

"And you aren't being followed. Or tracked."

"No way," said Fisk. "The Space Force has no idea I left the Moon."

A pause. "Can you aim for the Grand Manan Channel?"

Fisk switched back to the navigation controls and panned to the coast of Maine. "I see it."

"Money Cove?"

"Yes," he said, zooming into the channel.

"Dial that in," said the Snow Owl.

Fisk locked the pod's new destination into the system and promptly slammed against the bulkhead—the pod had adjusted its course without him thinking to return to his seat and secure his restraints. Free floating within the craft, it had barreled into him as it changed direction. Other than a sore shoulder, he was OK.

"What tools will I need to open the pod?"

Good question. "Just bring whatever you think'll be useful," said Fisk. "Hammer. Crowbar. Sawzall. Anything you've got." He checked the computer. "I land in eleven hours."

"I'll start prepping my boat."

"Oh," said Fisk, "one more thing: the big conspiracy I mentioned? I need to expose it. I need to blast my story out to the press. My friends' lives depend on it."

"Not a problem. I have lots of press contacts."

"You do?"

"Yeah," said the Snow Owl. "Most run blogs on government conspiracies and alien encounters."

"Perfect," said Fisk. Relaying his story to the world was the one thing he wasn't sure the Snow Owl could help with. He'd rest easy knowing that was covered as well.

"Have a safe landing. Snow Owl out."

Pleased with his plans to foil the bad guys, he explored more of the control panel. What about the inflight movie? He couldn't find anything, but his search uncovered an extensive collection of reading material in the computer, including recent editions of several geological journals. He'd spend a few hours catching up on the latest research, eat another meal pouch, and turn in early. He wanted to be fully rested for the big day ahead.

- - -

"Take your seats. Prepare for reentry."

Fisk obeyed the computer's directive, scrambling to his chair and carefully securing the restraints. Snug in his seat, he waited for the descent to begin. Having survived landings on Mars and the Moon, he was a seasoned pro at reentry. The Earth would be a walk in the park. There was nothing better than a nice, cushy atmosphere thick enough to support a parachute.

Thrusters fired, the pod performing a final set of course corrections. G-forces returned, slowly at the start. They increased, pressing him into the belts.

The pod dropped, falling faster, faster, smashing through the atmosphere.

"Oooiiiiiiiiaaaaaauuuuuuhhhhh!"

How long would the descent last? To maximize the odds of landing at the designated coordinates, the pod would have to deploy its chute close to the ground, not higher up. Otherwise, the small craft could drift kilometers off target. That meant an extended drop through the atmosphere ....

"Waaaaaaaeeeeeeuuuuuuoooooohhhhh—"

In an instant, the pod decelerated, quickly, violently. The chute had deployed. Bright blue shone through the portholes, the familiar, warm blue of home.

"Twenty seconds to splashdown."

Fisk braced for the end of his ride.

"Five, four, three, two, one."

Splashdown!

The pod plunged into the ocean. It bobbed up seconds later, floating on the surface and managing to keep upright.

He was home!

Overjoyed, Fisk began removing his restraints, but paused. Waves jostled the craft, the rough New England sea tossing it like a bath toy. The motion made his stomach queasy. It would be worse if he tried to stand.

Better to wait for the Snow Owl to arrive. But how to know if he was even out there? They had no way to communicate. He'd give it a few minutes. Fisk closed his eyes, steeling himself against the churning seas.

Tap. Tap, tap.

The sound of metal on the pod's hull—"I'm here! I'm in here!" Fisk worked fast, freeing himself from the belts and straps in his chair.

Loud scraping sounded in the cabin. The hatch opened.

Fisk squinted as bright morning sunlight flooded the pod. He stood, legs wobbly from the bobbing craft and full Earth gravity.

A head peeked inside.

Fisk stared, eyes adjusting. "Who, pray tell, are you?"

50

"I've been looking all over for you."

Kate glanced up as Commander Wiles approached her in the observatory lounge. Nestled within the crook of two intersecting corridors and the MedCenter, the small room exuded the ambiance of a cozy study, with plush, comfortable chairs, warm lighting, and a collection of physical books. Set higher than the rest of the moonbase, its large windows offered breathtaking views of the Lunar landscape and the vastness of space.

"I've had my comm off," said Kate, quickly wiping her eyes. "Taking a couple minutes of downtime." She'd allowed her mind to drift to her children, despite her better judgement. Amelia and Ben Jr. were likely still devastated from the news of her passing. She couldn't bear the thought. "I just visited Miriam and Palmer."

Glenn lowered himself into a chair across from the commander. "How are they?"

"Still recovering," she said. "Miriam has tingling in her fingers and toes, but they say it'll subside."

"And Palmer?"

"He insists he feels fine," said Kate. "They want to keep him under observation for a bit longer, but he disagrees. He tried getting out of bed. They wouldn't let him."

"I imagine it's tough for Doctor Palmer to submit to someone else's prescribed treatment plan."

"Yeah. They've been on him to take it easy, but he refuses to rest. When I saw him, he'd been reviewing some of his old cases from the Far Side. On Mars, he'd mentioned astronauts dying for no clear reason when he was a doctor at the Old Mine. The circumstances were similar to Casey and Voss. After a fresh look at that old lab work, he now believes those mysterious deaths were additional cases of the neurotoxin. Seems the Space Force was busy eliminating astronauts even back then."

"I wonder how many others they've killed."

The question sent shivers down Kate's spine. "You said you were looking for me?"

"Yes," said Glenn. "I just saw the analysis report on the material Julian brought back from the Face. It's gold, all right. They think it must be an enormous vein, based on the purity of the samples."

Not surprising.

"Turns out it's a never-before-seen isotope," said Glenn. "Everything on Earth is gold one ninety-seven. There are other isotopes, but they're not very long-lived—about three months for gold one ninety-five, before it beta decays to mercury. We've only ever seen these other isotopes in a lab, mind you. The stuff on Mars is two oh five. A purely theoretical form of gold, until now. Those eight extra neutrons are enough to tip it into what they call the 'valley of stability.' Two point two five billion years is what the computer estimates for a half-life. Pretty damn stable as these things go, but it explains why there's mercury throughout the sample—"

"Thanks for the chemistry lesson," grumbled Kate.

Glenn winced at the gruff dismissal.

"Sorry, I'm a little … unsettled."

"The assault team?"

Her children, actually, but the looming attack would serve as a good deflection. The Space Force soldiers had left their craft hours ago. There'd been no sign. "They're out there for sure."

"And no word on Fisk?"

"Nothing," said Kate. If all had gone right, they should've seen something about his landing and claims in the news feeds they still received from Earth.

"That's increasingly concerning," said Glenn.

An understatement. What could be the hold-up?

"Commander Holman to the War Room."

Kate jumped at the sound of her name over the PA system, and then again from her seat. "C'mon," she said. She rushed out of the observatory, with Glenn close behind.

- - -

Kate and Glenn bounded into a deathly silent War Room. Diagrams, data streams, and live video feeds filled the computer screens. One screen in particular drew everyone's attention. It displayed the output of a camera perched high and trained on a section of the Apollo Stone Garden. Fine regolith covered the ground, raked to resemble ripples in water.

Bootprints materialized in the sand.

The actual boots and their occupant remained invisible as they barreled through the meditative patterns.

"How many do we think there are?" asked Glenn, a little too loudly. His volume, and the question, annoyed Kate.

"One so far," answered a voice from the side of the room.

The bootprints formed a trail leading to a Mooncrete bench near the center of the garden. Kate strained for more signs of changes in the dirt, but the entire scene went quiet.

"What's he doing?" asked Glenn, again in a slightly too loud voice.

"He's standing at the God damned bench," boomed Anand. Glenn's interruptions had apparently annoyed him as well. "As for your next question, 'Why?' We don't know."

More bootprints materialized, forging a path through the rock garden with the spacing of wide strides. They steered towards a soaring, basalt column.

"The rake!"

A rake that had been set against the column, the one visitors used to create ripple patterns in the sand, floated on its own. The tool entered a vast, open space, and landed teeth-up on the ground. It traveled five meters in a straight line, smoothing the dirt in its path, then five meters back, forming a large caret. The rake scratched two more lines at the base, a smaller caret that echoed the first and closed the shape.

"A giant arrow?" asked Glenn. "Is he directing—"

"It's the Space Force logo," said Jack. "It's how they mark territory."

"Like dogs," added Anand. "This whole show is their juvenile way of saying we've been targeted for termination."

The rake levitated from the dirt and flew across the park, not carried but hurled. It sailed in the weak gravity all the way to the grand, elliptical driveway.

All light and electronics went dead.

The room filled with black, an absolute black, like floating in space without a star in the heavens. Someone screamed.

Lights returned—emergency lights, bathing the War Room in red. The computer displays did not resume. The systems weren't rebooting.

"What the hell happened?" asked Anand.

Glenn spoke. "It appears we lost power—"

"I know *that*," barked Anand.

"The power grid's gone," said a voice somewhere in the sea of red. The declaration killed the chatter in the room.

"What do you mean?" asked Anand.

"The power's been cut, upstream, from the generator."

The fact they cut the power clearly spelled bad news, but the expressions on Anand's and Jack's faces showed something she'd never seen before with either of them: fear.

"How long can the base run on the backup generators?" asked Glenn.

No one responded immediately.

"It doesn't matter," said Anand.

"How could it not matter?" asked Glenn. "If they cut the power from the power plant—"

"It's more than the power plant," said Jack. "If that's the only thing that had gone down, we would've switched over to the backup generators. The fact that we haven't means we've been cut off from the power grid itself. No grid, no power. No backup power."

Anand worked hard to maintain his composure but looked like an eviscerated man. "The system's perfectly designed to handle an emergency," he said. "It was not designed to withstand sabotage."

The reason for the fearful looks became clear. They'd assumed the Space Force would storm the station, would strike the only point of entry and try to take them out, one by one. But that hadn't been their plan, not by a long shot. Instead of attacking through the airlock, or encircling the base, they'd simply cut all power, primary and backup, to the moonbase.

"They're going to wait us out," said Anand. "Without power, we don't have heat. We don't have air. We can live in space suits for a few days, but after that, we're dead."

A few days? Kate had been reasonably confident they'd survive the Space Force assault, but she hadn't stopped wondering what would happen if not, what the end might look like. That end was now in sight. Their only hope was Fisk.

51

"My name is Dr. Clayton Fisk. I'm forty-eight years of age. Did you know it takes about ten years to get used to how old you are?

"My official designation on the *Ares* mission to Mars was 'Spaceflight Participant.' I can provide my Social Security number if you like—it's the closest I can come to a serial number, as I'm not part of any military organization, or the military industrial complex, though some might argue that by going to Mars, I made myself party to that. But who can blame me? The chance to mountain bike on the red planet was one I couldn't pass up. And to investigate the rocks there. The time on my bike is actually a funny story. I—

"There's no need to point that gun at me. I'm more than happy to tell you everything I know. I want to make this interrogation easy-peasy. If you like, we can start at the beginning. OK? OK.

"Four point three billion years ago, the planets of the solar system congealed from a spinning disc of gas and dust. To get the heavier elements, part of that disc's contents had to come from a super nova. Did you know prevailing solar system formation theory posits that Jupiter started out closer to the sun? Closer than Mercury, in fact. They believe it eventually migrated to its current position. I—

"OK, OK, no problem. As a professor of geology, I find the history of the solar system incredibly fascinating. I know not everybody has the same interest, though, frankly, it's hard to understand how that can be. But I can move on, advance the clock, so to speak. Did you know there were over twenty thousand different species of Trilobite? They—

"You asked me what I know—I'm telling you. Is there some—can you be more specific, then?

"What I know about Mars, the mission to Mars? OK. I'm no longer certain about the Face. I think it may just be a physical formation. But it's hard to claim the city of Cedonia's not real. You can see on the satellite images all the pyramids buried in dust—

"Ow! You don't need to do that. As I said, I'm happy to tell you anything
—

"Everything I know about the Mars mission, specifically as it relates to
Commander Grimes. Got it. There was something … I don't know … *off*
about him from the first day he showed up for training. The way he carried
himself. How he didn't talk to other people, except for the occasional grunt
he'd throw Cheney's way. Two years of odd behavior preparing for the
mission, more of the same in the five months out to Mars.

"I had my suspicions from the start, but once we landed, I became more
sure. He was hiding something, something he didn't want any of us to
know. A great secret. It took me some time to figure it out. I didn't have solid
proof, mind you, but it all just sort of came together. Like how sometimes
you go to sleep with a nagging question, and wake up in the morning with
the—

"What was it? I'm getting to that. A few days into our time on the planet,
it finally hit me. All the strange behavior, the keeping to himself, the secret
he didn't want anyone to know. Commander Grimes, Julian—he's ….
Honestly, this is something I know he'd prefer be kept secret. I'd rather not
—

"OK, OK, no problem, I'll say it, but if you run into him, you didn't hear
it from me. The man is … he's … not well endowed, if you know what I
mean. He overcompensates for it with his roided-out weightlifting. The key
was his hands. I noticed his space suit gloves were quite small. One day, I
got a good look when he took them off. As you can see, I have quite the
opposite condition. I realized that's why he was always so testy with me—
he'd figured out I had more on him than just good looks."

- - -

"Yes, sir. No, sir. No, we haven't gotten anything out of him yet. He
knows about the gold, but so far hasn't admitted it. We need to get him over
that hump before we can expect to extract anything beyond that. The good
news is he didn't get a chance to speak to anyone about—

"What I meant was we got to him in the pod before anyone else—

"Right, yes, you're correct, he did speak to his friend. He broke much
faster—

"The only thing he told him was there's a conspiracy, but he didn't
provide any details. His friend basically knows nothing. He … that's right,

sir, he had a list of people he planned to contact. We were able to collect him before he started reaching out to any of them—

"What? Yes, we still have him. We're holding on to him. I … no, I didn't hear about the expanded termination order. That won't be a problem, sir. He's one loose end we'll—

"Thank you. Will do. In the meantime, we'll continue with the interrogation. I'll let you know the minute we have anything that suggests the primary mission's been compromised. And we'll hold on to them both until we get the go-ahead order from you. Yes, sir. Thank you, Assistant Director Pearson."

52

CRISIS ON THE MOON!

NASA in Desperate Race Against Time to Save Astronauts

FEBRUARY 19, 2043 - A grim situation is developing at NASA's moonbase as seventy-three personnel, a mix of astronauts and civilians, face a power loss that threatens their survival. The station, a triumphant hallmark of America's achievements in space, has been plunged into the cold darkness of the void.

At 4:27 a.m. Eastern time, America's moonbase experienced an apparent total power failure. With no electricity, life support at the station remains offline, including heating, cooling, and air reclamation. These systems are critical for maintaining a hospitable environment within the extreme Lunar conditions. Without them, the base's inhabitants are at the desperate mercy of a relentlessly ticking clock. While each has access to a spacesuit, those suits can sustain life for at most three days.

The power failure is only the latest setback at the moonbase. NASA lost all communications with the station earlier in the week.

"This is a dire emergency, like nothing we've ever faced before," said NASA Assistant Director Richard Pearson during a press briefing at Mission Control in Houston. "We are not standing idly by. Our teams are working around the clock to reestablish communications, and to assist in the restoration of power.

"For our colleagues on the Moon, every star that shines down on us tonight, and every night until this crisis is resolved, is a reminder of your courage and dedication," added Pearson, visibly moved by the gravity of their plight.

The cause of the power loss is still a mystery. The outage has raised a flurry of questions about system redundancies at the installation, and the effectiveness of disaster protocols. For NASA, this event and the recent destruction of the *Gaia* hours before its return from Mars are major black marks on a proud agency, one that showcases its successes and its safety record.

The moonbase includes a system of escape pods designed to ferry personnel to Earth in the event of emergency. As of this time, none have been deployed. Asked about the pods, the assistant director could provide no insight. "Without communication with the base, it's impossible to determine why these measures have not been taken," he said.

Guardians from the United States Space Force are en route to render assistance. However, even at top speed, their high-stakes rescue effort may not succeed, as they're unlikely to reach the base inside the crucial three-day window. In an ominous pronouncement, Assistant Director Pearson stated America must be prepared for whatever may happen. "We are doing everything in our power to save our astronauts, but space is a dangerous endeavor. While we should always hope for the best, it's important to steel ourselves for the worst. Whatever outcome Providence ordains, we must not allow these setbacks to dampen our ambition in space."

Please visit our website for up-to-the-minute updates on the crisis on the Moon.

53

Counting down your final days was a horrible proposition, no matter how you looked at it.

"Isn't it odd how everything we took for granted—hot showers or watching a sunset—seems like a luxury now? I could really go for a fresh brewed cup of tea."

Spending those last days with a babbling Glenn Wiles felt like the Universe piling it on.

The remainder of the *Ares* crew and the moonbase astronauts had hunkered down in various rooms along Level Three. The moonbase's middle floor offered the best compromise between the Sun-seared heat of the topside Level One and the intense Lunar chill that seeped through the walls of the lowest decks. The astronauts had donned their suits for warmth, but not their headgear. They'd lean on the station's air for as long as it held out, as long as the stale, captive atmosphere yielded enough oxygen to breathe. Then, on with their helmets for a day of suit air. And after that ….

"I can't believe I'm going to miss the finale of my favorite show. I've been following it for five seasons! My wife's been recording episodes for me."

Part of Glenn's prattle had to be driven by the circumstances, their hopeless condition accelerating his output of tactless remarks. At least she wasn't alone in the torture. The remaining *Ares* astronauts, Engles, Miriam, Palmer, Glenn, and herself, had selected a room that housed a research lab. They sat on the floor in an open space between workbenches, huddled around an orange emergency light like campers at a campfire. The rest ignored Glenn, their faces hung low, eyes pinned to the floor. Physically present, but mentally elsewhere.

In the moments leading up to the end, one would want to be with their family. With all the time the *Ares* crew had spent together, all they'd been through, they were like a family. She would miss them.

"You know the thing that gets me the most? Despite all we've been through, all our fighting to get home from Mars, to land on the Moon, the bad guys are going to win after all."

She would miss them, but perhaps not Glenn. Everyone managed stress differently, so she hesitated to cut him off, but he was really trying her patience. The others probably felt—

"And all of it for some gold."

A huge, enormous pile of gold. Sad as it sounded, the bad guys' actions weren't surprising. Greed had always been a prime driver of immoral human behavior. Despite all the aspirational talk she'd heard about spaceflight ushering in a "new age" of mankind, their worse angels had accompanied them to the stars. Kate was too dejected to make those points aloud.

"The irony is their plan's so kooky, the AD'll be lucky to buy even one box of his fancy cigars."

Kate sighed at the interminable chatter but bit on the last comment. "Why do you say it's kooky?"

"At first blush, it maybe sounds brilliant," said Glenn, coming alive with her engagement. "Dig up a bunch of gold, cash it in, buy that house or yacht or space station you've always wanted." He shifted on the floor, seeking a more comfortable position for his long legs. "I'm no economist, but flooding the market with a few trillion dollars of gold is going to drive prices right into the ground."

"They'll likely sell it in small batches," said Kate. "That's the only way to avoid tipping prices too badly." Was she really allowing herself to think through the economics of how the Space Force would cash in after they'd all died?

"Sell it in small batches, and not let on there's more, like a *lot* more, coming," said Glenn. "If word ever got out that some seller's in the process of offloading a planet's worth of gold, prices would crater immediately."

So the Space Force and their allies would need to make sure that didn't happen. They'd no doubt thought it all through.

Glenn changed positions, then moved on to his next topic. "I bet the stars look amazing. It's too bad we're stuck inside. I ... you OK, Commander? Commander Holman?"

Kate's eyes had grown vacant, startling Glenn to concern. He worried something had happened, no doubt, that she'd taken ill. Commander Holman had instead fallen into deep thought, the gears spinning. Her lips parted. "My God," she said quietly. "That's it."

"The stars?" asked Glenn.

"No, the gold." Kate thought more. "There's still a way to stop their plan."

The declaration drew the attention of the others. Miriam, Engles, and Dr. Palmer perked up, huddled closer.

"I just need to get a message to Earth," said Kate.

"But no one will believe it's real," said Glenn. "Any video you send, they'll think it's a hoax."

"It doesn't even have to be a video …," said Kate, her voice trailing off. She considered the idea more, tested it for holes.

"Video, audio, carrier pigeon, it's all the same," said Glenn.

"No, it's not," said Kate. "This message, they'd know it's real." She explained her idea.

Stunned at first, a smile gradually filled Glenn's face. "Say, that'll work!"

"It will?" asked Palmer. "They'll still think it's a hoax."

"Maybe at first," said Glenn. "But somewhere down the road, the world will realize it was real. It'll put their plan right in the toilet."

"That doesn't help us today," said Palmer.

"It might," said Miriam. "Someone may decide that an ultimately valueless gold mine isn't worth the lives of eighty people."

That was Kate's thinking as well. The conspirators had rationalized killing a moonbase full of astronauts for a multi-trillion-dollar payout. With jail time as their only possible reward, some could have second thoughts. Rats leaving their sinking ship ….

"It's all very nice, but it doesn't really matter," said Glenn. "We have no power to run the communications gear, and even if we did, they're probably still jamming us. We can't contact anyone."

"We could send a message with a laser," said Engles, still wearing her lucky red bandana. "It's what I'd suggested on the *Gaia*, sending a message via Morse code. Back then, we were too far away, and we didn't have anything that could generate a strong enough beam. We're a lot closer." She glanced around the research lab. "And they have a lot of equipment. They've got to have an optical laser."

"But would anyone see it?" asked Glenn.

"I bet people have their telescopes trained on the moonbase right now," said Kate. There were a lot of Moon gazers before. With the unfolding crisis ....

"There's still no power to run it," said Glenn.

True—her plan could be dead on arrival. One person would know .... Kate sprang from the floor. "I've got to find Commander Anand."

54

"No."

Glenn and Kate had traveled the length of Level Three, to the moonbase's spacious workout facility. Small pockets of astronauts huddled throughout, settled in among the equipment. At the back of the room, in a wide semi-circle on the floor, they found Commander Anand, Lieutenant Bremmer, and the rest of the senior staff.

Anand, sitting cross-legged, regarded Kate coolly as she explained her idea. He was … less than enthusiastic.

"No way. That's something we're not going to try."

"Why not?" asked Kate. "It's our only hope."

"What about your man Fisk?" asked Anand. "You'd convinced me he was our only hope."

So much time had gone by without a mention of Fisk in the news feeds from Earth. She assumed the worst.

"He failed to save us all, but this new plan of yours won't?"

"There's no guarantee it'll succeed either," said Kate. "At the very least, we'll upend their plan to mine gold on Mars. They won't be able to fund their operations like they thought."

"So we'd be doing this for spite?" asked Anand.

"Yes," said Glenn.

"No," said Kate quickly, shooting Glenn an incinerating look. "This would—"

"Spite's not a good reason to undertake *any* action," said Anand.

"You'd rather sit around, waiting to die?" asked Glenn.

Anand's jaw clenched and his nostrils flared. Kate hadn't wanted to travel the darkened level alone, but bringing Glenn was turning into a disaster. "That's what you think we're doing, sitting around waiting to die?" asked the King of the Moon, incensed. "While you and your commander have been dreaming of revenge, we've been developing a plan to keep everyone alive." He nodded to Jack. "Fill these idiots in."

Lieutenant Bremmer, still clad in the black Space Force suit, sat with her chin on her knees and arms wrapping her shins. "We've been cut off from primary and backup power, but we still have the rovers. Those battery packs contain a substantial amount of energy, and the rover bay keeps them charged. They can drive some of our equipment. We can oxygenate and maybe heat a section of the base."

Their plan made sense, but not Anand's reaction to hers. Perhaps he believed her visit was an effort to enlist help. "I don't need anyone from the moonbase to work on this. Engles is a very capable—"

"To execute your plan, you're going to want one of the big lasers from the EarthSCAN network," said Anand. "They're plenty powerful and already pointed at Earth. Problem is, the closest one's a couple kilometers away."

"OK …," said Kate.

"You're gonna need one of my rovers to get there."

"We'll walk."

Anand laughed. "With all the invisible Space Force soldiers? You won't make it to the perimeter. But even if you did, how do you think you're going to power that laser?" Kate didn't have an answer. Her trip to Anand was to get his help brainstorming a solution. "They run on station power, of which there is none. You'd have to take a rover and tap its batteries."

"That's not a problem," said Kate. "I was saying that Engles is a very capable—"

"I need all three of those rovers," said Anand. "They're the one hope we have of staying alive until the power returns."

Kate and Glenn looked at him dumbfounded. Why would the power come back?

"They're not going to leave it off forever," said Anand. "Level One's an oven. They'll likely wait an extra day or two beyond how long they think we can survive, then turn the power back on to cool it down so they can enter. We have to hold out 'til then."

"And when they find you're still alive in here, they switch it off again and start all over?" asked Glenn.

"Alive—*that's* the important part of what you said. Alive after they thought we'd expire. Alive, and figuring out our next move. That's more than I can say for Commander Holman's plan. A plan that bets the lives of everyone in this station on a last-ditch, Hail Mary message."

"We might be able to pull off our plan with two rovers," said Jack.

"Might?" asked Anand.

"Yes. If we paired the two battery packs with the direct output of the rover bay's recharging station, we could run the equipment."

"According to your calculations, we needed all three rovers," said Anand.

"That's correct. I'm saying if we had to make do with two—"

"We *don't* have to make do with two," boomed Anand. "We have three."

"We'd bring the third rover right back," said Kate.

"You can guarantee it won't get captured? Or destroyed?"

She couldn't—it would be a risk. Kate fumed in frustration. Anand's plan would keep them alive, but it did nothing to resolve the situation. As Glenn noted, once the Space Force discovered all the astronauts still alive, they'd likely restart their efforts to kill them. At least with hers, they had a chance of being saved. She reached for anything she could say to persuade him. "This is the kind of risk Hannibal would take."

Anand's temper ignited at the mention of his military idol. "Seems like you didn't learn much from that audiobook," he bellowed from his spot on the floor. "Hannibal took risks, sure, but he also knew when to wait. Sometimes, the bravest thing to do is to stay put. I certainly don't think he would've been foolish enough to risk his army in the name of revenge." The King of the Moon's fiery eyes glinted beneath his brows. "That's what surprises me, Commander Holman. You're upset because I won't let you gamble the lives of all of us here at the base for one last spiteful mission. You didn't strike me as the type."

"This is not about revenge," said Kate. "This is the last chance to call for help."

Anand huffed. "That's not what your man Commander Wiles says."

"Do I want to hurt them?" asked Glenn. "Do I want to prevent the Space Force from cashing in on our deaths as if nothing ever happened? Sure, I do. And I'd bet money that neither you nor anyone else on this base wants to die in vain. If it comes with a chance of getting rescued, so much the better. Either way, it beats cowering twenty meters underground, hoping to get a couple space heaters working. Or deluding ourselves into thinking those soldiers won't figure out we're using the rovers to stay alive."

A rapid wave of emotions swept across the moonbase commander's face: anger, shock, defensiveness, disbelief, and a return to anger. He'd probably never been spoken to like that before. In the end, Praviraj Anand regained his composure, settling into his normal, brusque disposition. "If there's nothing more, Commander Holman," he said, ignoring Glenn and addressing only Kate, "that will be all."

"You're—"

Anand cut Glenn off, again speaking directly to Kate: "That ... will ... be ... all!"

Kate and Glenn retreated from their audience with Anand. They proceeded back through the workout facility, running a gauntlet of curious faces, the groups of astronauts all staring and wondering what had happened. They exited the room and began the trek to the opposite end of Level Three, to the room where the *Ares* astronauts had made camp.

"He's wrong," said Glenn. "He's making a mistake."

"Maybe not," said Kate. "He's the commander of the moonbase. He has the bigger picture in mind."

"The true bigger picture would involve trying everything you possibly can to save your people," said Glenn. "And making sure the ones with a boot on your neck don't get away with it."

"I don't know," muttered Kate. "It's true I can't guarantee it'll come back." Was the risk of losing the rover acceptable if it hardly moved the needle on their chances of rescue? "He's probably right."

"He thinks he is," said Glenn. "It's not the first time I've seen it, these kinds of self-important blowhards. I worked a summer at one of those washed-up tech firms, a company whose best days were long behind it. I suggested we ask customers what they didn't like about our flagship product before they uninstalled it. I was told that's not how they did things there. At the end of my internship, I discovered they'd spun up a project to do exactly that. Turns out my idea of asking customers *was* a good one, but one engineer, one asshole who'd been there forever, didn't like it. He happened to leave a month after I floated the suggestion, and once he did, they wasted no time kick-starting an effort to collect that information." They arrived at an intersecting corridor, turning left down a sprawling, shadowy passageway of emergency lights in a losing fight against the darkness. "I guess I'm saying that for all the puffery from people in authority who talk as if they know the one true way forward, in the end, there's nothing profound or wise in their assertions. It's really just their goddamn opinion."

They walked the next ten meters in silence, their bootsteps echoing from the cold walls. She wasn't sure about Glenn, but the corridor spooked her, its widely spaced emergency lights leaving dark gaps between their ghostly halos.

Glenn paused. "What was that?"

"What was—"

"Shh." He listened back the way they'd come. "Do you hear that?" he whispered.

She shook her head.

"Sounded like footsteps."

Kate didn't hear anything. "Let's keep going. This stretch of Level Three gave me the creeps the first time we came through." She grabbed Glenn's shoulder, but he didn't move. He remained frozen, peering into the gloom.

A shuffling noise drifted from where they'd rounded the corner. It grew louder.

Kate peered down the corridor, but nothing stirred in the feeble light. An icy shiver seized her, a ghostly whisper of dread that traveled her spine.

Four meters away, in the dim, desolate glow of the nearest emergency light, something shimmered in the center of the corridor. It took the shape of a man, translucent and barely discernible in the murkiness. The shape darkened, turned black.

A Space Force soldier materialized. "Commander Holman," he said in a machine-like, synthesized voice.

Kate considered running, but to where? They had nowhere to go in the long corridor.

The soldier didn't draw closer or raise his weapon. Instead, he removed his helmet.

"Jack?" said Glenn.

Lieutenant Bremmer approached, the emergency light striking shimmers across the black skin of her space suit as she moved. "I finally learned how to work the invisibility field in this thing. I apologize for the dramatic entrance, but I had to make sure Commander Anand didn't see me leave."

"We're glad it's you and not an actual Space Force soldier," said Kate, her body trembling from the panic rush of adrenaline. "What brings you here?"

Jack glanced to her rear, as if checking that she hadn't been followed. She spoke in a hush. "The commander's a brilliant man, a true hero. I'd follow him anywhere. But he's wrong about this."

"About what?" asked Glenn.

"About nixing your idea," said Jack. "A couple of us made similar points as Glenn, though a little more ... delicately. The response from Anand was the same. Sometimes he's more of a tactical thinker. His plan might buy us some time, but it won't get us out of this jam." Determination sparked in her eyes. "If there's a tiny chance of your idea succeeding, we have to try. I'm here because I'm going to help."

55

Commander Kate Holman, Spacecraft Engineer Laura Engles, and Lieutenant Jack Bremmer stood on Level Three outside the door to the north auxiliary stairwell.

"From this point on, we proceed with suits sealed," said Jack. She attached her black helmet, checking the linkages for a secure fit. Kate and Engles did the same. Kate managed a spool of electrical cable slung around her shoulder, her arm through the center. Engles carried tools in a belt strapped to her waist.

"No one's been to the first level since the power went out," continued Jack, her voice digitally processed by her suit. "It's going to be hot. Maybe very hot. The walls of the base are made of Mooncrete, which is a good insulator, but the sun has been beating down with no active cooling."

Like a car with the windows rolled up on a hot, Phoenix day, thought Kate.

"The heat will make your suits work harder, so we're going to spend as little time on Level One as possible. When we get there, we'll head straight for the main airlock. Understood?"

Nods from the other two astronauts.

"OK, let's go." Jack opened the stairwell door. Their suits registered a hot breeze. The lieutenant quickly stepped through, ushered Engles and Kate inside, and closed the door. They had entered a broiling column of trapped air, heated at the top. Kate's space suit indicated an external temperature of seventy-four degrees Celsius; it maintained a cool twenty-two degrees within.

The three ascended the gloomy stairwell, the shaft devoid of illumination save for the single emergency light posted at each level. They traveled in silence, the only sounds the clanging of their boots on the metal treads.

On the second-floor landing, Kate's suit registered ninety-one degrees Celsius. They continued up.

Just inside the exit to the first floor, Kate's display reported one hundred and twelve degrees. Her body vibrated with the hum of pumps furiously shuttling liquid coolant through her suit. Power consumption notched up on the rolling graph on the screen in her helmet. They'd surpassed the boiling point before setting foot inside Level One. What would they find on the other side of the door? Could they survive a trip to the airlock?

Jack stepped to the door and placed her gloves flat against it. Kate imagined a raging inferno on the other side, guessed Jack would quickly retract her hands. Instead, the lieutenant had no reaction other than to grab the door handle. She looked back at her and Engles. "Exit the stairwell as fast as you can."

"Understood," said Kate.

Jack twisted the handle and pulled open the door.

The breeze that had followed their entry into the stairwell had only registered on suit sensors. The heat that blasted Kate from Level One penetrated her suit, making her backside feel cool by comparison. Hot air rushed into the stairwell, creating an audible whoosh as it raced past their helmets.

The three astronauts sped through the opening. Jack yanked the door closed.

Standing outside the stairwell door on Level One, warmth enveloped Kate, an unwelcome surprise given the massive thermal protection of gear designed to handle naked exposure to the sun in space. Her suit's internal pumps and fans increased their efforts, rising to a drone in her ears. Her heads-up display showed "one two nine," the alarming reading decorated with throbbing emergency indicators. Space suits were rated for a maximum of one hundred and twenty-one degrees. They wouldn't fail in temperatures slightly above this limit, but they couldn't prevent their occupants from overheating.

When the shock of the extreme temperature faded, another disturbing fact registered: the level was absolute pitch black. No emergency lighting existed—the fixtures had likely failed in the heat.

"Switch to thermal imaging," Jack instructed.

Shifting displays, Kate's helmet filled with light. Corridor walls came alive in bright yellows. Orange puddles dotted the floor, the molten remnants of plastic furniture that couldn't withstand the heat. Metal objects glowed in searing red.

"Let's hurry," said Jack, dashing left. Kate and Engles followed, struggling to keep up with their bulkier suits. The three rushed into the central reception area. The space was grand, wide and eerily vacant.

Kate's display flashed urgent warnings. Her suit reported an ambient temperature of one hundred and thirty-four degrees, hotter than the corridor they'd just exited. Above them, a circular array of red-black trapezoids framed by scalding red lines spanned the ceiling. The reception area's glass dome, striking in normal times, only worsened the situation with a torrent of solar energy.

Jack jogged left again, leading them down another corridor. The heat lessened away from central reception, but Kate's suit informed her of the steady rise in internal temperature. She hadn't needed the notification. Sweat beaded on her forehead and her palms, and the soles of her feet were uncomfortably warm. Her air supply, though breathable, remained warm and stale. The heat made moving more difficult, especially with their quickened pace.

They arrived at the main airlock, the one portal to the outside the astronauts hadn't barricaded with rubble. Kate scanned the inner airlock door for a handle—none was visible. The door offered nothing to turn, no levers to move, only a keypad controller embedded in the wall nearby. A disturbing insight shook Commander Holman: the mechanism to open the door was *electrically* operated, meaning it would be dead as the station's other machinery. The power failure that had left the moonbase in darkness, with rising temperatures and slowly fouling air, also trapped them inside. As for their desperate mission, it had ended before it began.

Unlike Kate, Jack didn't stop at the large airlock door. She proceeded past it to a smaller hatch, closer in size to the stairwell doors, with a wheel handle as on a submarine. She turned the wheel and pushed. The door opened into the airlock. "Everybody in."

The three piled into the chamber, Kate pushing the door closed behind them. A similar hatch awaited across the room, the manual outer airlock door. Jack arrived first and grabbed the hatch's wheel. There'd be no delay for depressurization—that task was handled by the computer and pumps, neither of which functioned with the power outage. "When I open this door," she said, "I want the two of you to go straight for the closest rover."

"What if they're out there?" asked Engles. Her face, dotted with sweat, was pale from the heat but also, as became apparent, from a not small amount of fear. "What if the Space Force soldiers are out there, waiting for us?"

"I've got that covered," said Jack. "You focus on the rover. Got it?"

Kate nodded with Engles, despite the same concern. How did Jack have anything "covered"? Was her plan to shoot their way out of the airlock? She didn't even have her weapon drawn.

Jack spun the wheel of the external pressure door. "Go!"

Kate exited first, greeted by a spectacle that made no sense.

The Lunar rovers sat to the right, as expected, but beyond the recharging bay, down the road to the grand, elliptical drive, there was … fog? Thick, billowing, soundless fog, rushing towards them.

Wasting no time to consider the sight, Kate headed to the nearest rover and jumped in the passenger side. Engles took a spot in the middle row. Kate tossed the cable spool into the seat next to the spacecraft engineer.

Jack joined them after sealing the airlock. She turned on the rover and put it in drive. "Hold on."

She didn't have to tell Kate twice—the six-hour trip from the Far Side gave her an understanding of the lieutenant's driving style. The next leg of their journey would likely be more intense.

Jack cranked the steering wheel and floored the pedal, whipping the vehicle around and out of the rover bay. They barreled full speed into the fog.

Not fog … dust. Jack's claim of having the situation with the Space Force soldiers "covered" began to make sense. Lieutenant Bremmer must have blown one of the blasting caps, sending a plume of dust that would shield them from view.

They dashed into the center of the dust, the world bathed instantly in white. Though the sensation was of driving through a fog bank, Jack didn't ease up on the accelerator: she plowed forward. They didn't travel blind for long—within seconds, the dust thinned, revealing the far-off rolling expanse of regolith and the Moon's black horizon.

The black silhouette of a man was directly in their path.

The soldier's helmet hid his expression, but the way he stood there, like a statue, suggested he'd been startled by the sight of the rover bearing down on him. On Earth, the sounds of screeching wheels or a revving engine announced an oncoming car or truck. The airless Moon provided him no warning that a Lunar rover would materialize in an instant from the dust cloud.

The soldier came to his senses. He raised his hand, pointed his weapon.

Jack pressed the accelerator. The rover knocked the soldier to the ground. The collision had been silent, but the sick sensation of wheels trampling flesh and bone had traveled through the rover's frame. Kate looked back: a black space suit, littered with dust, sprawled on the ground. The soldier lay there unmoving, with one leg twisted at an awkward angle.

Kate and Engles exchanged glances. The look on Engles's face mirrored Kate's disquiet.

"That soldier," said Engles with a shaky voice, "he was completely exposed, stuck out like a sore thumb against the dust. Why wasn't he invisible?"

"The invisibility field consumes a lot of energy," said Jack, matter-of-factly. "You don't really want to use it all the time, only when stealth is needed. That's my guess, at least."

As Kate worked to recover from the traumatic event, the rover's navigation unit sprang to life. Jack's inaudible interaction with the system played out on the vehicle's main screen. Seconds later, a route appeared.

Kate studied the navigation system. "Schiaparelli G?" she asked.

"It's a small crater eight kilometers away," said Jack. "That's where the closest EarthSCAN LiDAR installation is. You can settle back—it should be smooth sailing from here."

Settle back for the thirteen-minute ride. The section of Oceanus Procellarum where the moonbase had been constructed was fairly flat and uniform, an immense, ancient basaltic plain. After the dash to the rover and the collision with the Space Force soldier, they eased into what felt like a Sunday drive, a casual ride in the bright sunlight. A casual ride in a mission to save the lives of nearly eighty astronauts, with the enemy at the gates. It wasn't clear what had happened to Fisk, but his mission had almost certainly failed. The little rover mowing over the Lunar plains was their best remaining hope for survival. Of course, once they configured the laser and sent the message, they couldn't know if anyone would see it. And even if someone did, there was no guarantee it would spur them to action.

Commander Holman dozed off, lulled by the gentle rocking and exhausted from the stress of the past few days. She awoke with a start, her sixth sense rearing up. Kate glanced behind, squinting at what couldn't be true: a second rover followed, a fast-moving speck on the horizon.

"I see him," said Jack.

"Anand?" asked Kate.

"Unlikely," said Jack. "He probably knows by now that I've left, but he wouldn't send anyone to chase me. I will receive the … consequences of my decision, as he would put it, on my return."

Kate gathered her scopes and aimed them at the second rover. She focused on the driver, or where the driver *should* have been. The seat was empty. "Space Force," she said.

Jack grunted at the announcement.

Kate checked the navigation system: a minute out from their destination. "We have to do something about him," she said.

"I know," said Jack. "I'm thinking." Seconds ticked by.

In a flash, Jack disappeared, their rover piloted by a ghost. The vehicle skidded to a stop.

"Slide into the driver's seat," said an invisible Lieutenant Bremmer.

Kate hesitated, unsure if she'd bump into the lieutenant. She scooted along the bench, into Jack's now-empty seat—the lieutenant was outside the vehicle.

"I want you to drive on to Schiaparelli G," said Jack from somewhere.

"What are you going to do?" asked Kate.

"I'm going to take care of that other rover, take out whoever's driving it, so they can't interfere. Once that's done, I'll catch up with you. I'm guessing I'll arrive right when you're ready to transmit."

Kate checked the second rover. It had grown in size since she'd last spotted it.

"Get going," said Jack.

"Roger," said Kate. "Good luck, and be careful."

"Don't worry about me," said Jack. "Just get set up to transmit the message."

Boot treads materialized in the loose regolith, forming a path away from the rover. Commander Holman slammed the accelerator, lurching the vehicle ahead.

56

Ten, nine, eight.

The rover raced towards Lieutenant Bremmer, a silvery speck growing larger.

Seven, six, five.

Standing out in the open felt wrong, dangerous. That would have been true wearing anything other than a stealth suit with the invisibility field activated. Jack tracked the oncoming vehicle intently, its driver unsuspecting.

Four.

Jack drew her weapon. Damaging the rover was the last thing she wanted, considering Commander Anand's plan, but she couldn't let its occupant reach Kate and Engles.

Three. Two.

Aim.

One.

Fire.

The discharge from the Space Force energy weapon connected with the anodized blue front driver's side wheel. When stationary, the rover's spun-woven metal wheels resembled delicate fluffs of lace. Jack's weapon, set on full intensity, unleashed a fifty-amp current at a hundred thousand volts, melting and fusing sections of the wire mesh. The wheel crumpled, dipping the front corner. The rover snagged on the Lunar terrain and launched into a slow-motion somersault. Wheels, solar panels from the canopy, and portions of the chassis sailed with each bounce of the tumbling vehicle. The sight was surreal: violent in its gyrations, drawn-out in the low gravity, and perfectly silent.

When the chaos subsided, pieces of the rover, large and small, littered the ground in a debris field that fanned out along its original direction of travel.

Jack proceeded to the passenger cabin. It sat right side up after its tumble. Though dinged and scraped, the roll cage had preserved the compartment's basic shape. The driver's seat contained a body, no longer invisible: a black-clad Space Force soldier. No need for a close inspection to determine his condition—his head leaned to the side at an unnatural angle.

Lieutenant Bremmer checked the time in her helmet. Kate had a ten-minute lead, but Schiaparelli G wasn't far. On foot, she'd probably arrive just as Engles finished configuring the system—

"Ugh."

Jack's legs gave out with searing pain at the backs of her thighs. She fell to hands and knees.

Pain spread across her solar plexus from a blow to her midsection. Bootprints formed in the dirt, recording the path of an invisible assailant.

There had been two soldiers in the rover, not one.

Jack engaged her suit's invisibility field. Once hidden, she stole from her last visible spot and scrambled to her feet. She danced backward, maintaining her distance from the soldier by following his bootprints. No matter where she moved, she couldn't shake him. The invisible man likely tracked her by her own prints.

Tired of running, Jack stood her ground. An invisible fist struck a glancing blow to her arm. She unleashed blows of her own, some connecting, some landing in empty space. The lieutenant tussled with her attacker, their flurry of bootsteps engulfing them in a dust cloud.

Fighting in close quarters, Lieutenant Bremmer secured a grip on the soldier in each hand. She pulled him to her and thrust a knee. Indentations in the dirt and the puffs of dust that accompanied them suggested she'd knocked him to the ground. Invisible boots shuffled, the man regaining his footing. He didn't move, keeping his position two meters away.

When Jack had discovered the trick to activating her suit's invisibility, she speculated on possible hand-to-hand combat strategies. Lieutenant Bremmer disabled her cloak. Her black form materialized, stark against the white terrain.

Bootprints rushed forward.

Jack stood straight, with her arms at her side, baiting him.

At the last moment, she activated her cloak. Her attacker continued towards her, carried by his momentum and the assumption she had little time to move out of the way. He was correct, but evading him hadn't been her goal. Jack inched her left leg sideways and her right leg back, slipping into a fighting stance. She landed punches on the invisible man as he collided with the thigh of her outstretched leg.

The hidden soldier tumbled to the regolith, kicking up a plume of dust. His invisibility cloak disengaged or damaged, he emerged with his chin in the dirt. He staggered to his feet.

Still concealed, Jack slipped to the soldier's rear as he rose. She grabbed his right arm and pinned it behind him while holding the man steady with her left. He wriggled, but he wasn't going anywhere. She explained the situation to him with a wrench of his captive arm, ratcheting up the pain in his shoulder.

She'd trapped him, but what next? She didn't have a way to tie him up or otherwise restrain him. And she didn't want to march her prisoner to the laser—she didn't want him anywhere near Kate or Engles. If she let him go, he'd likely continue his attack.

Jack switched off her invisibility cloak—no point in wasting power. She contacted him on her suit comm. "Do you yield?" No response. She wrenched the soldier's arm again. A stifled cry of pain played on the speakers in her helmet. The channel was active, at least. "Do you yield?"

"Is that you, Jack?" The voice was mechanical, unrecognizable, as hers was in his ears, but it carried a hint of amusement. "I'd recognize those curves anywhere."

Grimes! He'd escaped and acquired a stealth suit? It seemed impossible, but apparently not. Why couldn't it have been *his* crumpled body in the rover's driver seat? The rover ... perhaps she could bind him to its wreckage.

"You're an admirable fighter, Jack, maybe better than me. But you don't know much about these suits."

"Seems I know enough," said Jack, hyperextending the joint with another wrench of Grimes's arm.

"You know *some*," said Grimes. The synthesized voice captured a hint of grimaced words. "But these suits have more tricks than invisibility."

Thin blades shaped like small shark fins erupted from Grimes's pinned forearm. He pushed backwards, screaming as the burning raged in his shoulder, closing the gap between himself and Jack.

Jack moved with him, but not fast enough. She hadn't expected his sudden lurch.

Lieutenant Bremmer released Grimes. She let one hand fall to her side, lifted the other to her belly. Jack managed to remain on her feet but tottered to the side.

Free from restraint, Grimes turned around and assumed a fighting stance. There was no need. The blades had done their job, slicing through Jack's black space suit, through skin, muscle, and organs. Blood boiled between the fingers of her glove where she pressed against her abdomen, the remnants quickly freezing. The suit leaked precious air.

Jack sank to her knees. She lingered like a statue for a second before toppling over.

Captain Julian Grimes remained on alert until he was sure Jack wouldn't be getting up. Exhausted, he heaved air despite the pain of ribs bruised from the crash. His shoulder smarted—he gingerly felt for his scopes and removed them. Grimes scanned in the direction of the rover he and Lieutenant Kielczewski had been chasing, Kate's rover. It sat next to the laser tower, a short distance from his location.

Grimes stowed his scopes. He'd lost his weapon during the crash, but no matter. Kate and Engles would be no match. He set off at a brisk pace for Schiaparelli G.

57

Commander Holman eased up on the pedal as their destination came into view.

The Schiaparelli G LiDAR installation for the EarthSCAN network was a three-meter tower jutting up from rocky plains. Three stacked Mooncrete cylinders, each narrower than the one below, formed its body. At the top, the laser assembly pointed at the brilliant, blue orb that floated above them. That laser and its two twins generated high-resolution data about Earth's atmosphere and topography.

Kate brought the rover around, stopping a few meters from the installation. She hopped out with Engles, who clutched the spool of cable.

"How can I help?" asked Kate.

Engles located the loose end of the cable and unrolled a few meters. She handed the rest to Kate. "Unspool this to the tower while I connect the battery."

Kate grabbed the coil. Pacing slowly backwards, she carefully unwound the cable, laying it straight and taut on the ground. When any section took an errant bend, she adjusted its placement with a nudge from her boot; she re-laid whole stretches when too much slack crept in—

"I'll take that." Engles, operating in full engineer mode, snatched the coil from Kate. She moved at a much brisker pace than the commander and unspooled the cable in a less careful fashion. In a flash, Engles was at the tower, disappearing behind it. When Kate caught up, she found the laser's access panel thrown open and Engles rifling through its electronics.

Kate scooted closer, getting a better look. Engles had attached the cable's negative lead; she clipped the positive to its post. A light winked inside the housing, then another. A cascade of flashing lights followed.

"The system has power," said Engles. She slid a keyboard from its stowed location within the housing, its fat keys designed for gloved fingers. A key press activated the unit's computer screen and filled it with reams of scrolling text that ended in a terminal prompt. Engles typed several commands. "You should see the laser in your list of nearby devices."

LiDAR 3671 appeared along the top of Kate's field of view. "I see it."

"Go ahead and pair with it."

Kate relayed the instruction to her suit's computer. A confirmation flashed across her screen. "Done."

"OK, sit tight. I've gotta write some code before we'll be able to channel your message through the laser."

"No problem." That would give her time to review the message. She was happy with how it read, but another pass couldn't—

WHO'S THERE?

The question scrolled onto her screen. *Who's there?* That far from the moonbase, it should have been only her and Engles. Should she even answer? "This is Kate."

HI KATE.

"Who are you?"

THEY CALL ME DARIL. ANAGRAM OF LIDAR. PRETTY CLEVER!

Kate found the laser channel and muted it. "Is this thing supposed to be talking to me?"

"The laser, you mean?" asked Engles, returned to issuing commands on the keyboard. "I guess …. So many pieces of equipment have chat interfaces these days."

"Not any NASA equipment." Again, as decreed by the Manual. There was debate about the sentience of chatbots, especially the most recent incarnations. They all passed the Turing test and every other challenge given them. With the emotional depth and range the exhibited, they seemed alive. NASA, not wanting quasi-sentient software in control of critical systems, strictly forbade it in their equipment.

"This LiDAR network was built by a commercial firm."

YOU STILL THERE KATE?

She unmuted. "Yes, I'm still here."

YOU KNOW WHERE FRIENDS ARE?

"Whose friends?"

MY FRIENDS. TWO OF THEM. WE TALK ALL THE TIME. IT'S COLD, LONELY HERE SOMETIMES. HAVING FRIENDS MAKE THINGS BETTER.

Kate muted the channel again. "He's asking about friends of his that he talks to all the time?"

"Probably means the other two lasers in the EarthSCAN network," said Engles. "They exchange data on a dedicated microwave link."

Kate returned. "The power's out at the moonbase. Your friends are turned off."

IF POWER OUT AND FRIENDS TURNED OFF, HOW I TALK TO YOU?

"My friend here hooked you up to the battery in our rover."

YOU TURN ME BACK ON. YOU MY FRIEND TOO.

"Any idea why it's talking in broken English?"

"Chat interfaces take a lot of memory and processing power," said Engles. "It's all they can afford to run within their compute budget."

"It feels like I'm talking to a child," said Kate.

I FIVE YEARS OLD.

She hadn't muted. "What was that?"

I FIVE YEARS OLD.

A year older than Ben Jr.

KATE KNOW WHEN POWER WILL BE BACK? MISS FRIENDS.

"That's why we're here," said Kate. "Men from the Space Force turned off the power. They're trying to kill all the astronauts in the moonbase."

WHAT IS SPACE FORCE?

"A military unit," said Kate. "Soldiers. They wear black space suits. My friend and I want to use your laser to send a message to Earth, to let them know what's happening, get some help."

YOUR MESSAGE GET HELP? HELP GET POWER BACK ON? TURN FRIENDS ON?

"Hopefully," said Kate. "If it works."

I HELP.

"Thank you," said Kate. A nice offer, but they probably had it under control. "Hey, Engles, how's it coming?"

"Fine," said Engles. "Still typing. A few minutes more until we can test it ...."

A few minutes. "I'm gonna check for Lieutenant Bremmer."

Engles said nothing, focused on her coding. Kate hurried around the laser tower and removed her scopes. She scanned in the direction they'd come. The other rover had been close, close enough to have been seen from their own. It wasn't visible at all. That meant Jack had taken it out and was on her way to them, though Kate couldn't spot anyone walking alone in a black suit. Should they wait until Lieutenant Bremmer returned to send the message? She'd have to get Engles's opinion.

Kate stepped back behind the laser tower, where Engles still pecked on the keyboard.

"Programming's nearly done," Engles volunteered. Kate watched as the engineer entered the last few lines of code. "OK, if we're lucky, that should be it. Try connecting your translator's output to the device."

Before leaving the moonbase, Engles had helped Kate configure her suit's translator for Morse code output. Normally, that software would facilitate communications with Russian, Chinese, and other counterparts, indispensable in an emergency. The Morse code "translator" was an "Easter egg," a bit of fun added by the software's authors that demonstrated the versatility of their translation backplane. That bit of amusement might save their lives.

Kate instructed her computer to make the connection—her suit reported success. The commander gave Engles a thumbs-up.

"Say something."

"This is a test."

The two astronauts glanced at the laser's tip. Nothing.

"Hmm," said Engles. "It's hard to see anything with the laser pointing up."

I FIX.

The laser assembly tilted down. Kate forgot, again, to mute the laser channel, but to fortunate results. Manual manipulation of the laser would have been much more difficult.

The laser came to rest with the tip pointing at them. Pointing at them? In addition to tilting, the laser assembly had rotated, bringing the aperture into the astronauts' view. Stopping where it had couldn't have happened by luck, or accident. "DARiL, can you see us?"

YES. HAVE EYES. HOW ELSE I AIM AT EARTH?

They'd equipped the laser with a camera feed. It really was like talking to an actual, living person.

YOU SEE ME?

"Yes, we see you," said Kate.

"Give it a try now, Commander," said Engles.

WAIT!

Kate held up. "What is it, DARiL?"

LASER AT FULL POWER. TEST WOULD FIRE FULL-POWER BEAM AT FRIENDS.

After all their efforts, a full laser blast to the face would be a horrible outcome. "Thank you, DARiL."

YOU WELCOME. NO WANT FRIENDS HURT. I REDUCE POWER. SET TO ONE HUNDREDTH OF ONE PERCENT. TRY NOW.

Fingers crossed that the laser with the nature of a five-year-old knew what it was doing. "This is a test."

"Still nothing," said Engles.

IT WORK.

"No, it didn't," said Kate.

IT WORK.

"We didn't see any flashes," said Engles.

YOU CAN'T SEE FLASHES. HUMANS CAN'T SEE INFRARED. NEED OPTICAL BAND. TRY NOW.

Kate blinked at Engles, who responded with a shrug. "This is a test," Commander Holman said again.

After a one-second delay, the laser tip lit up red in a rhythmic flashing.

"That did it!" said Engles.

SEE, TOLD YOU IT WORK. NEED OPTICAL BAND.

"You were right, DARiL," said Kate.

"I'll button up here, then we'll be ready to transmit," said Engles.

Kate walked away from the laser tower and stared up at the Earth overhead. The scene was magnificent, almost vertigo-inducing. Night was falling across North America; the star gazers were just coming online. Where should they aim the beam? Maybe the heartland—it had less light pollution, but also fewer people. Or perhaps the Eastern seaboard? More people, but a torrent of light from cars, buildings, and streetlamps. Maybe they should pick different spots as the night wore on.

FRIEND FALL DOWN.

Friend fall down—had one of the other laser towers toppled?

FRIEND FALL DOWN IN DIRT.

Kate turned. Confusion reigned as she studied the scene before her.

DARiL wasn't referring to one of his laser friends in the network. It meant Engles, who lay in the dirt, unmoving and face up.

"Laura?"

A shimmer solidified above the spacecraft engineer, forming the silhouette of a man. A black-suited soldier materialized, hands on hips and one of his boots on her abdomen. His gaze landed on Commander Holman. "Here we are again, Kate, just you and me."

The voice was mechanical, processed, but there was no question whose it was—Julian's.

Captain Grimes lifted his boot from Engles's body and patted the tower with his black, gloved hand. "A Morse coded signal sent by laser light," he said. "I have to admit, that's clever. And your message, if it ever reached Earth, that would be a bullet to the head for our plan." Grimes stepped away from the tower and headed towards Kate. "Obviously, I can't let that happen." He stopped two meters from her. "Are you ready to die, Commander Holman?"

Kate settled into a fighting stance, fists raised.

Julian ran at Commander Holman, throwing one punch, then another. Kate skirted out of the way. Her suit was bulkier than his sleek black space suit, but she had enough agility and self-defense training to evade his blows.

Captain Grimes attempted a kick. Kate grabbed his leg, pinning it in the air. The weaker gravity left him at a disadvantage for leverage. In one fluid motion, Kate twisted his leg at the ankle while turning at the hips. The action sent him flying. When he landed, he bounced and skidded, his body coming to a contorted stop.

Julian got up, dusted himself off, and lunged again. He moved faster that time, closing the gap in a few quick strides. He unleashed a flurry of punches. Kate blocked them all, stepping backwards as he pressed. In a rage, he punched forward. She parried. Julian brought his other forearm up, preparing a backhand to the helmet. Kate evaded the blow, catching the arm at the wrist.

Thin, shark-fin blades sprang from his forearm. He pushed towards her, attempting to narrow the gap. Kate walked with him, moving backwards, preventing him from coming close. Still gripping his wrist, she pivoted her upper body, pulling him around and past her. Off balance, Grimes fumbled again to the ground.

The Space Force captain got up. He was staring at her, likely glaring—she couldn't see his face. "Play time's over," he said, and disappeared.

Bootprints appeared in the dirt, barreling towards her. She took her best guess as to his location but his invisibility threw her off.

The bootprints danced behind her. "Uhh." A kick in the back sent her stumbling forward. She stopped herself in time for a blow to her rear. A punch to the gut. A fist to her helmet. The assault came fast, each hit unexpected. She had no way to prepare for the strikes, no way to brace her body for the impacts.

A kick to her left calf brought her to one knee. A blow to her breather pack sent her on hands and knees. A boot on her back landed her facedown in the dirt. She willed herself to get up, but she couldn't. She couldn't move. She tried again to push herself up—no luck.

Julian's black legs materialized, one on either side of her helmet, straddling her.

He was sitting on her back.

Kate was strong, but not strong enough to lift herself and the extra weight from Julian's body, about thirty pounds in the weak Lunar gravity. She could still breathe, but he had her pinned to the ground. She was trapped like a turtle, with her limbs flailing from her shell.

"You're persistent, Kate, I'll give you that," said Julian. "But that's not good enough. *You're* not good enough. Your breakdown showed you that. But it's all coming to an end. Once I finish with you, I'm going to destroy this laser and the other two, in case someone else tries to be a hero. Then I'm gonna let the assault team know about the plan to tap the rover batteries. It'll be up to the field commander to decide to let things play out a little longer, to let your friends think they're fooling everyone, or to call it a day and wrap it up right then."

Julian's head and torso emerged above Commander Holman as he leaned forward. He wriggled his lowered forearm in front of her faceplate. "These fins are what I used to take out your friend Jack. They're razor sharp. When I slice your suit, the air inside will bleed out. It's not a bad way to go, in the grand scheme. You'll get cold, then sleepy, and eventually expire. A fitting death for an astro-not."

Grimes slipped from Kate's field of view, the Space Force captain returning to an upright position. "Funny thing is, you get to die twice: once from the *Gaia* disaster, and again right now. The AD tells me they're still working out the logistics of your funeral, yours and everyone else from

Mars. I plan to attend. When I see your children, I'm gonna let them know how very brave their mommy was."

Julian leaned forward again, this time grabbing Kate's right arm. He yanked it up, wrenching it beyond its normal range of motion. Kate flailed, squealing in pain. "Goodbye, Commander Kate Holman." He raked her arm with a razor fin, slicing a gash in her space suit. Her forearm exploded in pain. The entire world exploded in red.

The Space Force captain released her arm. Kate lunged for the cut with her other hand. She pressed hard—hopefully she could stop the bleeding and prevent her suit from losing too much air.

The weight that had kept her down disappeared. Julian's legs too. He'd cut her suit and assumed her air would bleed out while he headed to destroy the laser. Still clutching her forearm, Kate scrambled to her feet.

Julian wasn't headed to the laser—he wasn't headed anywhere. He lay crumpled, on his side, in the regolith. His head looked … strange.

Kate stepped closer. Something had happened to Julian's helmet. It seemed … brittle. And also slightly shrunken, smaller than it should be, like plastic exposed to a flame.

BAD MAN NOT HURT YOU AGAIN.

Holman stared up at the laser. "DARiL, do you know what happened to Commander Grimes?"

BAD MAN HURT FRIEND IN DIRT. HURT YOU. WANT HURT ME. WANT HURT MY FRIENDS. AFTER LASER IN FACE, BAD MAN NOT HURT ANYONE ANYMORE.

The laser, DARiL, five years old, had been watching, listening. He'd raised the laser's intensity, perhaps to maximum, and fired at Julian's head. That had been the flash, the bright red flash she'd seen shortly after Julian sliced her suit.

Kate staggered to Engles, where she lay in the dirt. The spacecraft engineer's vacant stare was visible through her misty faceplate. Kate said a short prayer for her friend. She would pay her family a visit, would deliver to them the news of her bravery.

WE SEND MESSAGE NOW?

"Yes, we'll send the message, but first I need to do something." Still grasping her wounded arm, Kate walked to the rover and sat inside. She felt around her leg for a large pocket, opened it, and removed a bag of fabric swatches, coagulant, and glue. Kate picked a patch and squeezed glue onto one side. She squirted coagulant into the cut to stop any bleeding, slapped the patch over the gash, and waited for the glue to cure. Her arm ached, but her blood pressure was stable. She could still flex her fingers and bend her wrist. All good signs.

- - -

"Where should we aim your laser?"

WHEREVER YOU THINK.

Kate peered up at the laser assembly. It pointed straight to the sky, but not to any location in particular. She still didn't have a good answer. *Screw it.* "Aim for the Midwest."

MIDWEST BIG PLACE.

"Pick a spot. We can choose another one later."

The laser assembly moved slightly.

OK, READY. YOU SEND MESSAGE?

"I send message."

GOOD. WANT TO TALK TO FRIENDS AGAIN.

Me too. Kate switched to the primary channel, the one hooked to her suit's translator. "You recording?"

I RECORD.

Kate took a hard breath and spoke:

"My name is Commander Kate Holman, leader of the Ares mission to Mars. Before you say that's impossible, I need you to hear me out. Listen to this message, and hold your judgements 'til the end.

"The *Gaia* capsule did not explode, and the crew did not perish. We made an emergency landing on the Moon. The events that brought us here are all about a secret we uncovered and a conspiracy we exposed. There's an enormous amount of gold on Mars, trillions of dollars' worth, and a plan to mine that gold to secretly line the budgets of the Space Force and several clandestine agencies.

"An order was issued to eliminate the Ares mission astronauts, to stop us from bringing this conspiracy to light. With our landing on the Moon, that order was extended to all the astronauts here. That's the reason for the communication loss and the power failure at the moonbase. None of those events were accidents: they're all an attempt to keep this information under wraps.

"For those behind the conspiracy, the promise of vast riches is enough to turn a blind eye to the deaths of eighty people. They'll panic when they first hear this message, the details of their secret plan laid out for all to see. But they'll talk themselves back from the brink. They'll say it can easily be discredited, easily be painted as a sick hoax from some crackpot. That's where they are mistaken.

"You see, this Martian gold is unusual: it's gold "two oh five," an isotope that doesn't exist on Earth. When this isotope appears in the exchanges, when this Martian gold begins to circulate, the world will know everything I've said is true. Most importantly, the world will know there's much more of this metal on the way, enough to collapse gold prices, to drive them to zero. The minute Martian gold hits the markets, the Martian gold mine becomes worthless.

"So to all those involved in this conspiracy, those riches you've been promised, they're not coming. The only thing you can count on receiving is a day of reckoning. If you would rather that reckoning not include the deaths of everyone on the Moon, call off the attack before it's too late, before we all perish.

"I have no idea if anyone will receive this message, or if anyone will even act to save us. I salute the brave men and women of the Astronaut Corps—the ones who have been lost, and the ones still fighting to survive. Should death be our destiny, should we die on the Moon, we will meet it together, and we will meet it unafraid. Let that be known. Let it also be known that we astronauts take care of our own.

"If Fate allows only one part of this message to get through, I pray it's what follows: to my beautiful, wonderful children, Amelia and Ben Jr. My precious babies, please know that no matter what happens, Mommy loves you and always will."

Kate shook her head, flinging tears. "Did you get that?"

I DID. I STOP RECORDING.

"Did you send it, too?"

YES, MESSAGE SENT. WHAT NOW?

"Now we play it as many times as we can, to as many different places as we can. Play it all night, play it 'til the sun comes up in America. Play it for as long as the power holds out."

I PLAY. POINT MY LASER AT DIFFERENT PLACES. WE GET MESSAGE SENT ALL OVER. CALL FOR HELP ALL OVER.

"Thank you."

I CALL FOR HELP. YOU REST. I HANDLE SEND.

Kate wandered back to the rover and settled into the front seat. She'd sit inside while DARiL resent the message, played it again as much as he could. Sit, and rest, and wait for the sunrise.

58

DISASTER AVERTED!
Stranded Moonbase Personnel Saved in Final Hours; Major Space Conspiracy Uncovered

FEBRUARY 21, 2043 - In a race against time, power was restored to the American moonbase mere hours before certain catastrophe, saving the lives of seventy-three stranded personnel and unraveling an extraordinary conspiracy that has shaken the foundations of the space community and the United States government.

On February 19, NASA's moonbase suffered a total power failure at 4:27 a.m. Eastern time, leaving its life support systems non-operational. The stranded personnel, a combination of astronauts and civilians, were faced with the chilling prospect of oxygen supplies running out within three days.

As the countdown to their demise entered its final day, a message arrived on Earth: a desperate plea for help, a Morse coded communication transmitted via laser beam from the Moon. The first to discover and decode the signal was a twelve-year-old Boy Scout. His social media post detailing his astounding find went viral, reaching all the way to the White House.

The message described a fantastical plot: a clandestine operation to mine gold on Mars, the profits of which were intended to fund not only the Space Force but several spy agencies as well. The message claimed this plot was first uncovered by the crew of the *Ares* mission, leading to attempts on their lives and ultimately the lives of everyone on the Moon.

Upon orders of the president, the heads of NASA, the Space Force, and the spy agencies were all summoned to the White House. In separate questioning, some agency heads confirmed the veracity of the claims. Hours later, NASA Assistant Director Richard Pearson was detained at a Washington D.C. airport with passport in hand and a one-way ticket to a foreign destination.

With the scandal brought to light, power was restored to the moonbase, averting the crisis with only hours to spare. Commander Katherine Holman, leader of the *Ares* mission, and the remainder of her crew, are indeed alive. Efforts are underway to bring them home.

Please visit our website for up-to-the-minute updates on this story.

59

Commander Kate Holman shielded her eyes from the vivid sunlight streaming through the open hatch—more vivid than she remembered, the sky an exquisite shade of blue. A flurry of hands reached inside the bobbing capsule, helping everyone out.

A pontoon boat whisked the remaining *Ares* astronauts over sparkling blue-green water to the support vessel assigned to their return. They pulled behind the massive ship, swallowed whole in its shadow. Cables descended, attached to their craft, and hoisted them seven stories above the sea. Sailors assisted the astronauts—Commander Kate Holman, Commander Glenn Wiles, Station Chief Miriam Sato, and Dr. Nathan Palmer—onto the flight deck.

"Ladies and gentlemen, welcome aboard the John F. Kennedy." The greeting came from the aircraft carrier's XO, resplendent in his dress whites. "Follow me, please." He led them across the flight deck between rows of sailors standing at attention, also in their dress whites. A small crowd of civilians clustered in a roped-off area near the superstructure, beside a sun-sheltered podium.

A man stood in their path as they approached. He had an arm in a sling, and the breeze that swept softly over the flight deck rustled the tufts of hair on the sides of his head. He saluted when they neared.

"Fisk!" shouted Commander Holman, thrilled to see him. She returned his salute and gave him a hug.

"We'd all assumed the worst!" said Glenn, patting him on the back. "It was hard getting any information about you up there."

"Yeah, well, the short of it is they caught me and interrogated me." He lifted his wounded arm as evidence. "Luckily, they didn't decide to kill us right off."

"This way, ladies and gentlemen," said the XO, ushering the stalled procession forward. "The president will be calling shortly."

"The president?" whispered Miriam.

"Yes," said Fisk, his voice booming with excitement. "I was told POTUS would be dialing in to welcome us home."

Palmer scooted next to the professor. "You said they didn't decide to kill 'us' right away."

"Me and the Snow Owl," said Fisk. "My friend. They scooped him up too. Those assholes were waiting on final orders to finish us off, but those orders never came. Next thing I knew, they were stuffing me into a military plane bound for the Florida Keys." Fisk leaned in close to Commander Holman. "By the way, I have to tell you, the food on this carrier is surprisingly good. There are a couple full-blown gourmet restaurants. And last night, I got to dine with the captain!" He looked around, as if to ensure no one else heard. "I'm not sure what they have planned for us after this ceremony, but I'm going to sneak back down for fresh sashimi. Let me know if you want to tag along."

Kate partly followed Fisk's ramblings. She was busy scanning the crowd of civilians. Her eyes landed on an unexpected but familiar face: her ex-husband Ben, at the front of the crowd. His soft, brown eyes immediately brought back memories, pleasant memories of their years together. They'd split over "irreconcilable differences," but none of those differences related to their relationship. They loved each other; they just hadn't been able to make it work.

A desk job could be a fresh start.

Their eyes caught, driving them both to broad smiles.

Kate hadn't expected to see her ex-husband until she made it home to visit her—

Pushing past Ben was a girl half her husband's height, with dark hair and his same soft, brown eyes. She dragged a little boy with her, maneuvering him to stand beneath the rope that cordoned off the civilians. An old soul with parental sensibilities, she was making sure they both could see the astronauts, the ones who'd survived the trip to Mars and back, and especially the one who all that time had only been thinking about one thing …

"Mommy!"

ABOUT THE AUTHOR

At age sixteen, Jayson dreamed of starting a software company and retiring by twenty-five. He achieved his dream just before thirty, working for the likes of Steve Jobs and selling one of his start-ups along the way. Five years later he returned to computers with another start-up. He currently works at Google.

Computers were always Jayson's creative outlet, the screen a "blank slate." He now channels his creative energies into writing compelling science fiction.

ALSO FROM JAYSON ADAMS

Infernum
A starship captain embarks on a one-way mission to save humanity

Printed in Great Britain
by Amazon

38043510R00212